Also by Michelle Quigley

Hush Hush

To The Moon And Back

Michelle Quigley

To Kieran and the kids.

A huge thank you to Margaret Mount and Vonnie Killen for planting the idea for this book in my head. This story has been inspired by the tale of our ancestor Ellen Coyle and her journey from Derry to New York in the early 1900's, although the main characters in this novel are fictional.

Many thanks to all those that contributed to the success of my debut novel, Hush Hush, particularly Martin Corey for all his effort and hard work.

A special thanks to my husband Kieran for his support and encouragement and all my family members.

Finally, last, but certainly not least, a massive thank you to my sister Ciara McAlister, my right arm, sister and best friend!

Chapter 1

The silent street lay hidden under a thick blanket of snow. Erin stepped outside into the frosty air. Wrapping her shawl tighter and clutching an oil lamp, she carefully began to walk on the slippery, cobblestoned path.

A rush of love filled her heart at the sight of Patrick across the street. There he was, leaning against the lamppost, watching her approach. His lips curled into a smile at the sight of the beautiful young girl that had captured his heart for as long as he could remember. The soft glow from the light above him fell on his handsome face, enhancing his chiseled features. It was then a seed of doubt planted itself in her mind, what was she thinking meeting him to break this news to him on tonight above all nights? Suddenly, she had an urge to turn on her heel and run back through the snow-filled street, back home, back where poverty had gripped them so badly lately.

'Oh, God, please help me?' she murmured softly as she made her way towards him. 'Should I follow my heart or should I listen to the thoughts in my head?' Erin whispered under her breath. Pausing, she tilted her head and looked up into the thick clouds that hung dense in the night sky, clouds that threatened to burst with more snow. 'Dear God, help me,' she pleaded again before returning her eyes back on Patrick.

The icy wind started to pick up and blew sharp against her cheeks. The clouds above their heads began to rip apart and, like invisible angels shaking talcum powder on the land, huge feathery snowflakes parachuted from the sky.

Erin scrunched her nose as the soft, cold flakes fell upon her face.

Patrick removed his peak cap as she approached near. 'Good evening, Miss Coyle,' he beamed as the delicate, glittering snowflakes dropped upon his chocolate-brown hair and at once melted. He reached out, took her in his arms, and placed a loving kiss on her cold cheek.

Erin smiled at him sheepishly and blinked the soft flurry away that had tumbled upon her long, curly lashes. 'Good evening to you also, Mr Brogan,' she said, her voice shaking from both her nerves and the chill in the air. She removed the shawl from her shoulders and placed it over her head to keep her raven-black hair from getting damp.

'What about *me*? I don't hear any good evenins' for your aul' *neighbor*!' an unexpected voice startled them.

Franke McGregor, perching on his front doorstep, looked up at them both from a few doors away and waved his bottle of whiskey in the air. He was barely visible in the dimness, but as they drew near, they could see the buttons of his grey shirt undone and his pot belly spilling out over his trousers. The effects of the alcohol had turned his cheeks pink, making him look more like an overgrown garden gnome.

'Frankie, what are you doing out here in the cold?' Patrick asked, bending his knees and lowering himself to eyelevel with his neighbour. 'C'mon, let's get you inside.'

'What the feck are *you* doin' out in the cold?' Frankie

replied. He swung the whiskey bottle to his lips and knocked back a huge mouthful. 'I'm enjoyin' me self, doin' nobody any harm, am I? I love watchin' the snow droppin' from the sky and fallin' on me bake!'

'Fair point, Frankie, but would it not be better to watch it from inside?' Erin suggested. She could feel her body shivering just watching him sitting on the cold step, his flimsy shirt clearly getting damper by the second.

'You'll catch a cold,' Patrick warned. 'I think Erin's right, it would be warmer inside. I'm not leaving you out here like this.'

'Fur feck's sake, can a man not have a drink in peace,' Frankie slurred.

'C'mon now, Frankie, don't be giving none of your aul' nonsense tonight,' Patrick replied, his tone gentle but firm.

'I'm sittin' where I am, now head on about your business!' Frankie waved the bottle in the air.

'No!' Patrick answered. 'We're not leaving you here. You'll get frostbite! Now come on, in you get.' He nodded towards the open door.

'Ah fur feck's sake! If it feckin' keeps ye happy I'll go inside.' Frankie struggled to get up. 'All I wanted was to 'ave a drink in *peace*!'

Patrick slipped his arm under Frankie's, assisted him to his feet and escorted him back to the warmth of his living room.

'Here,' he said, pulling an armchair close to the window and drawing back the curtains a little more. 'There you are, sit yourself down. Now you can watch the snow and have a drink in *peace*. I'll get you a dry shirt,' Patrick said heading upstairs. 'Get that one off you,' he called over his shoulder.

'Aye whatever,' Frankie grumbled as he did what he was told and wriggled out of the damp clothing.

Back in the living room Patrick handed him another shirt.

'What the feck did ye bring that down for?' Frankie asked eyeing up the blanket in Patrick's hand as he fumbled to put his arms in the sleeves of the dry shirt.

'Put it around your shoulders, it'll keep you warm.'

'Will ye wise up! This is all I need to keep me warm.' He laughed waving his bottle in the air.

'You're something else, Frankie.' Patrick grinned. 'Well, tell you what, put it around your legs,' he suggested as he tucked the blanket around Frankie.

'Naw, you're the wan that's something else. Would ye look at the shape of me.' Frankie began to giggle. 'You've me wrapped up like a kipper!'

Smiling, Patrick patted his arm. 'I'm only looking out for you. Now I'll get that fire sorted and I'll be off.'

'Good! I'll 'ave me drink then in *peace*!'

'Can I get you anything else before I go?' Patrick asked as he threw a few lumps of turf on the fire.

4

Frankie, held the half empty bottle of Bushmills and gazed at it lovingly with his bleary, bloodshot eyes. 'I think 'av everythin' I need unless ye want de get me another wee bottle!' he teased. 'Wan more and I'll be sorted fur the night!'

Smiling, Patrick headed to the door. 'Bottle of what? Holy water?'

'Holy water! Get out, ye wee fecker or ye will need doused in it when I'm finished with ye!' Frankie joked.

Back outside, Erin remained shivering like a wet cat and staring up into the looming snow-filled clouds in a daze.

'Right, let's get you into the church before you turn blue with cold,' Patrick said, taking her hand, he affectionately held it in his own as he led her through the dim streets.

The flurry began to fall heavier than before. They both quickened up their steps, not wanting to be exposed to the winter elements for a second longer than necessary.

'You seem quiet tonight, is there something up?' Patrick asked, his voice soft and caring. 'Have you something on your mind?'

Erin thought about his question for a few seconds and decided she would wait until the service was over. 'Oh, I'm just cold, that's all.'

Well it was half truthful after all; she felt frozen to the bone.

Patrick released her hand and placed his arm around her shoulder, huddling her close to him, 'I'll have you indoors in no time.'

'Good, because I can't feel my toes, perhaps I should have sat in with Frankie,' she joked. 'Maybe a drop of whiskey is just what I need also.'

She wasn't joking this time, a drop of whiskey to calm her nerves may just be the answer.

'I don't think you'd get as much as a sniff of his treasured beverage never mind a sip!' Patrick said, tightening his grasp around her.

They turned a corner and entered a cobbled, narrow street. From a distance the clang of the church bells began ringing to alert the parishioners that midnight mass was fast approaching. Like cockroaches creeping out into the darkness, people clothed in heavy coats, scarves and hats, seemed to come from all directions, coming from the warmth of their homes to enter into the cold blizzard. All going in the one route and following the sound of the chimes, eager to attend the Christmas Eve vigil mass.

The pair continued walking for another few minutes until the streets of the Bogside were long behind them and only the familiar sight of the Long Tower church lay before their eyes. Erin fell silent again and dipped her head.

A broad smile formed on Patrick's face at the sight of the church, barely visible through the heavy snowfall. It reminded him of a little chapel in a snow globe and the blanket of snow on the rooftop sat thickly like the head on a pint of Guinness. He smacked his lips, oh what he would do now for a nice pint of stout, a pint or two would certainly give him much needed courage for his mission tonight.

They entered the gate and made their way up the stony pathway of the chapel grounds. Patrick stopped and gently pulled Erin into his arms before they entered the large heavy doors of the building. 'Are you sure you are okay?' he asked, his brow furrowing with concern.

Erin swallowed the lump that had suddenly sprang into her throat and blinked away the tears that had arrived without warning.

Patrick, fumbling in his coat pocket to check it was still there, smiled as his fingers wrapped around the box, the ring safely inside. He could feel his feet turning numb and his body shivered from his damp clothes, or was it caused by the nerves jangling in his stomach? Earlier it had felt like there were a few caterpillars crawling in his tummy, but somehow those annoying things must have quickly transformed into huge butterflies, and right now they felt like they were in full gear, ricocheting off every bit of his insides. But then again, it's not as if he had done anything like this before, asking a beautiful girl like Erin to marry him.

'Erin? There is something wrong, isn't there? Tell me.' He gently placed wisps of her raven-black hair inside her shawl.

A silent tear escaped and rolled down her soft cheek. She knew in her heart she couldn't lie to him any longer and the words tumbled out, words that would surely break his heart. 'I'm leaving Ireland, I'm heading off to America.'

Chapter 2

'America?' Patrick's eyes widened. 'What do you want go there for?' His gaze holding hers, he waited for her to tell him this was some kind of joke.

'Because I need to,' she replied, hoping he wouldn't notice the sorrow in her voice. Turning to conceal her watery eyes, she quickly made her way up the steps. Placing her oil lamp at the corner of the porch, she wiped her eyes and tried to put on a brave face.

He kicked the concrete steps, shaking off the snow encrusted on his boots, before following her, a look of disbelief etched on his face.

Erin, rummaging in her pocket, retrieved the folded piece of paper. 'Here, read this,' she said, handing it to him.

Frowning, Patrick unfolded the paper and stepped further inside the porch. The frown deepened on his forehead as he read the contents.

Dear Erin,

How are you, my dear sister? I trust you are all well. I am writing this letter to inform you of how great my life is since I arrived here in New York. Firstly, I have found myself a job working in Fitzgerald's Printing Company. They are a family-run firm and are doing amazingly well, in fact they have recently expanded and plan to grow further, which means they need more staff.

With a name like Fitzgerald, I'm sure you have guessed that they have Irish roots, and as soon as I opened my mouth to speak, they just fell in love with my accent and welcomed me on board. I'll tell you, they are a great bunch to work for. Now for the good news, the Fitzgerald's have recently hired me as their manager for their new office. The extra cash means I can now afford my very own apartment! I have just moved into a two-bedroom residence on the top floor of a great block in central Manhattan. Things are definitely looking up for me and believe me, moving from the Bogside is the best thing I have ever done in my life!

This place is totally unbelievable and it is so huge compared to Derry – it's like a wee world of its own and right now, I feel like I have the world at my feet! You really need to see this place, which is why I'm writing you this letter. I want you to come over here, my dear sister, make a life for yourself! Trust me, you will not regret it. You can stay with me and I will try to get you a job. I will also sponsor you. Erin, it would be great to have a member of my family here with me, you and I can take on the world together! So, how about it?

I enclose your boat ticket to leave at the end of January. I really do hope to see you soon.

All my love,

William

Patrick began shaking his head, slowly at first and then more rapidly. 'No, Erin, you can't go to America!' he said, his voice trembling as he tried in desperation to hold back his pain. 'Please think about this! Stay, please stay,' he pleaded placing his hands on her shoulders.

Erin gazed into his chestnut-brown eyes, eyes that were glazed with tears. 'I can't, Patrick, I need to go. William is right, there's nothing here in Derry. Take a look around you,' she spread her arms out, 'there's nothing here but hardship and poverty. I've witnessed my parents struggle to get by day after day. My poor father is out of work more times than he's employed. Many days as children we went hungry as some days there wasn't a morsel of food in our cupboards and we had to depend on my grandparents to feed us. Right now I can tell you my parents are looking at one of the bleakest Christmases ever as far as I can remember. My mother had to pawn her wedding ring once again just so she can put a dinner on our plates tomorrow. Patrick, I don't want to live like that forever and I certainly don't want to bring my future children up in such hardships!'

Patrick sank back against the heavy wooden door of the porch as churchgoers pushed their way inside, some throwing them disapproving looks as they passed.

'Lovers tiff?' asked an elderly lady, her blue-veined, wrinkly hand clutching a cane with her bony fingers. 'You should be ashamed of yourselves, the pair of you! Quarrelling in a sacred place! Get into the church now before I give the two of you a good slap on the backsides. Mass is about to start!' she growled.

'Sorry, madam,' Patrick said, 'we're not arguing, we'll

be in now.'

'Well, whatever it is you're at, hurry up and get inside. You should be seated before the priest is on the altar,' she said, narrowing her beady, crow-like eyes. 'I'm warning you, have a bit of respect!' She barged on in leaving them looking sheepishly at one another.

'She's right, we do need to get seated. What are we thinking having this discussion here and tonight above all nights?' Erin turned to follow the old lady inside.

Patrick, catching her arm, pleaded, 'Wait Erin, please wait. I need to tell you something.'

'What?' Erin turned to meet his solemn gaze.

Taking a deep breath he said, 'I…I…the thing is…'

The choir began to sing Holy Night and the sweet sound could be heard bellowing from the church.

'What is it?' Erin asked.

He couldn't bring himself to express his emotions. How could he tell her he loved her now after all these years of hiding his true feelings?

'Patrick, what is it?'

Blinking rapidly, he went on, 'I can't think of life here without you,' he said, his heart sinking to great depths.

'Then come with me, I'm sure if I get a job I can sponsor you,' Erin suggested.

'I can't. Sure I can't leave my da. He's not getting any better, in fact he's deteriorating by the day. Who would look

11

after him? I'm all he has.'

Erin sighed. 'Of course, Jim needs you. Come on, Father Lavery has started. We can discuss this later,' she whispered before pushing open the church door and tiptoeing quietly inside.

Patrick, pausing, allowed the door to close behind her. Watching her through the glass frames, he observed her sit down, remove her damp shawl and shake her long raven locks loose allowing an avalanche of hair to tumble around her shoulders. He knew she was right to want to leave, after all it's not every day a young girl gets an opportunity to make a better life. His love alone would not be enough to keep her here, and besides, the chances are she doesn't even know how he feels about her. How could she when he did his best to conceal it for so long? He had to let her grasp this opportunity, the chances are they would only end up in a similar predicament as the other families in their streets, in fact the truth was the majority of the people in Derry had no work, no cash and no food, any wonder the opportunity of heading to America was so enticing.

Retrieving the box from his pocket, he pulled out the ring and released a defeated sigh – the little gold band, with its three tiny diamonds sparkled. A rush of love filled his heart as he lifted his head and looked on at Erin. There she was kneeling quietly and throwing herself into a deep prayerful moment.

Standing alone in the cold porch, his eyes still fixed on her, he whispered under his breath. 'I love you, Erin. If only you knew how much you mean to me.' He placed the ring back into its slot, closed the box and sighed. 'My dear, Erin, I love you to the moon and back!'

Chapter 3

Erin gazed around the living area, portraits of family members dotted each of the four walls. A smile crept across her face at the sight of the picture of her mother and father, with herself and her four siblings proudly assembled around her parents. Each of them had their father's striking characteristics, raven-black hair, high cheek bones, Spanish-blue eyes and swarthy toned skin, in fact none of them had inherited their mother's fair hair and green eyes.

John Coyle was a hard working father and Catherine a gentle, loving mother. They were the best parents anyone could ask for but the stress, brought about as a result of the lack of employment, meant it was difficult to make ends meet.

Erin sighed and tears developed as her eyes fell on the image of her father, a man willing to work in all sorts of conditions to provide for the family. This hardworking attitude resulted in him having to face grueling, tedious work that was not good for his health. During potato picking season, John would rise at four o'clock each morning, pull on his working clothes and heavy boots before heading off to meet the other men at the end of the street for their lift in a dirty, old pickup truck, covered with muck from the muddy fields they faced working in.

Sometimes Erin would waken and on those mornings she would get up before her father and creep downstairs. There she would heat his socks at the smoldering fire. John's eyes would dance upon seeing his loving daughter. His heart would melt at her kindness and her loving gesture. He would hold her face in his huge weather-beaten hands, with the earthly soil baked deep into his fingernails, and kiss her on the cheek.

Erin worried about him leaving the house at that time to enter into the darkness of the cold, wet early mornings. Her stomach would tighten if the weather was bad, and as there was more rainy days in Ireland than dry ones, John was forced to toil in the wet and windy conditions, slipping and sliding about the muddy fields as they prodded through the soil in search for the favourite Irish vegetable. It was challenging for the men but they were tough, hearty, hard workers, and besides, with large families to feed, they didn't have much of a choice in the matter.

Erin's mother Catherine had a simplicity about her. She managed to go about her tasks as a wife and mother without a word of complaint, keeping herself to herself and bothering nobody. She loved each of her children equally and devoted herself to her husband and family, no one could take that from her. She worked hard maintaining the home and cooking for the family on a daily basis, in fact, if she was not found scrubbing the house clean, she was up to her elbows in flour, baking breads and cakes.

Erin blinked away the tears, oh how she loved being part of this household, loving each of them with all her heart. For this reason, part of her wanted to stay here in the three-bedroom terraced house in the Bogside, with its drafty windows and leaky roof, no luxuries in sight but a home that was filled with the warmth that came from the love they shared for one another. Then there was Patrick, his words had caused her stomach to clench, *"I can't think of life here without you."*

Ever since he had moved into the house across the street, they had been close from their first encounter. A smile formed on her face at the recollection of that meeting. It was on a beautiful summer evening as Erin and her sister Mary ran through the field at the top of the street in search for daisies. During the search Erin had found a ladybird. She placed the insect on her palm and ran to some kids to tell them of her find. Gathering around her the children looked closely at the beautiful bug with its bright red shell and black dots.

Patrick, coming up behind them, and peering over her shoulder, politely said, 'Can I have that please?'

'No way! Not a chance! It's mine!' Erin exclaimed, closing her hand and backing away.

'Ah, please, it's for my collection, you see I have ninety-nine and I only need one more to make one hundred. I've been searching for ages to make my target, so please can I have it? I did manage to get one the other day but it flew off,' he explained innocently. 'I'll take you to see them if you like.'

Erin, having been naively sucked in by his tale, tutted and sighed, 'Oh go on then, here, take it!' she said as she handed over her precious find with great reluctance. 'But I'm warning you,' she pointed, 'I want to see the ninety-nine and I want to count each and every one of them!'

Patrick, holding the ladybird safely in his hand and covering his palm with his other, replied, 'C'mon then, follow me.' He turned and sprinted towards the lane that led to his backyard. 'Hurry up!' he yelled over his shoulder.

Close to his heels, Erin only stopped when they entered the garden. 'Right, where are they? Let me see them.' She glanced around, hands fixed on her hips.

'In here, behind the shed.' He beckoned her to follow him through the long blades of overgrown grass. 'Oh no, they're gone!' he announced, stepping past some nettles and pointing to an empty box amongst the undergrowth.

'They can't be!' Erin looked horrified.

'They've been stolen!' Patrick tried to smother a laugh.

'But? But ...who would have done such a thing? I can't be...' Erin stopped as she witnessed his mouth twitch at the corners. 'You liar! You're a liar! A *liar* and a *cheat*! Give it back to me!' she screamed pushing him, 'Come on, give it back now!' She pushed again.

Patrick stumbled backwards, and in order to prevent himself falling into the nettles, he opened his hand and grabbed the side of the shed. The ladybird, grasping its opportunity for freedom, spread its wings and flew off.

Erin's lip curled as she watched it take flight and disappear before her eyes. A lump formed in her throat and before she knew it, tears began to escape from her eyes, big childish tears that rolled down her cheeks. Once the tears began to fall, there was no stopping them, and soon, immense sobs that normally come with tears, came with such force.

Watching her reaction with horror, Patrick held his

hands up, 'I'm sorry! I'm so sorry. I didn't mean to make you cry, really I didn't. I was just having a bit of fun with you. I just wanted to make new friends.'

'Make new friends?' Erin couldn't believe her ears. 'How do you expect to make *friends* by doing something so … so …so *sneaky*?'

'I didn't think! Honestly! I'll get you another one, I promise,' he said and without giving it a second thought, he placed his arms around her and gave her a sloppy kiss on the cheek.

'Ah, get away!' Erin stepped back and wiped her face. 'You disgusting boy! I do *not* allow boys to *kiss* me!' she fired back before tossing her long raven-black hair. Shaking her head in disgust, she turned on her heel, stomped through the long grass and ran off.

'I'm sorry!' Patrick yelled after her. But it was of no use, clearly not wanting to be in his company a second longer, Erin kept running.

The next day a loud knock came to the door of the Coyle household. John opened it to find a scruffy Patrick standing on his doorstep, hands firmly in his pockets and looking the picture of innocence.

'Hello, sir, I'm looking for the girl with the long black hair, does she live here?' he asked politely, his round puppy dog eyes wide and curious.

John gazed at the young boy and smiled. 'Well all of my girls have long black hair, do you have a name?' He smothered a grin.

'Oh, I'm not sure, do you mean my name or hers? If it's my name you're looking for, I'm Patrick but I don't know hers.' He scratched his head in thought. 'No, she didn't tell me her name, but I'm eight!' he announced in a childlike fashion. 'She's about my age, I think.' He flashed a huge smile, revealing a gap where his two front teeth were missing from the top row.

Grinning at the friendly little boy before his eyes, John replied, 'Oh, that must be Erin you're looking for. C'mon in, she's in the kitchen.' John stepped aside. 'Follow me.'

'Thank you, sir,' he said before stepping into the house.

'There's someone here to see you, Erin,' John said as he stepped into the kitchen followed by the scruffy youngster.

Erin, looking up from her bowl of porridge, rolled her eyes. 'Oh, it's *you*, what are you looking for? I'm not going out to play if that's what you want!' she said hastily.

'I've come to say I'm sorry and to introduce myself properly. My da said that's what I should do.'

'Well I don't care what your da said, so go away!' Erin stuck out her tongue before directing her attention back to her breakfast.

'Now, Erin, don't be cheeky, watch your manners!' John warned.

'He's the cheeky one!' Erin shrugged before spooning a huge mouthful of porridge into her mouth.

19

'Let the boy introduce himself and say his piece. Go on, son.' John nodded.

'My name is Patrick, Patrick Brogan and I felt since we are going to be living in the same street, then we may as well be friends, what do you think?'

Lifting her spoon and pointing it at him, Erin replied, 'Friends? I don't think so!' A dollop of her porridge slid from the spoon and landed on her clean jumper. 'Ah look what you've made me do now!'

'Now, Erin, what have I warned you about your manners? Don't be rude, the boy has come to be nice to you and besides, everyone needs friends,' John replied in his usual softly spoken tone.

After a few moments Erin gave in. Looking to Patrick she shrugged and replied, 'Ok, I'll be your friend, but you better promise never to kiss me again and I mean never, *ever* try!' She pointed her spoon at him again.

'What?' John queried with amusement. 'Kiss?'

'Oh, sorry, sir.' Patrick glanced at him with his huge puppy dog eyes. 'I only gave her a peck to stop her crying and it was only a little one on the cheek.' Turning to Erin he went on, 'I promise I will *never* try to kiss you again.'

'Well you better not, and,' she pointed her spoon at him once more for emphasis, 'You better never *steal* from me either.'

John's eyebrows shot up, this encounter was getting better by the second. 'Stealing?'

'Ah, I'm sorry about that too, sir. I didn't actually nick anything, I just tricked Erin into giving me a ladybird, but look I brought you this, Erin.' He placed his hand into his pocket and retrieved a matchbox. 'This is for you,' he said with an air of triumph.

'If you think I'm going to light a fire, you can think again, I don't *light* fires.' Erin threw him a look of horror.

'No look! Look inside.' He held the box closer and opened it. 'See!' he beamed with pleasure.

Erin peered at the slightly opened box. Inside on blades of grass was a tiny ladybird crawling about. 'You got another one,' she said, mouth agape.

'Aye, I got up really early this morning and I searched everywhere until I found you one,' he replied as proud as Punch. 'And I mean *everywhere*!'

'Oh, thank you so much. I'm so happy, I could *kiss* you!' Erin bounced off her seat. 'Actually,' she paused. 'I won't go that far. You can have a hug instead,' she said, throwing her arms around him.

From that day on the two children became the best of friends, playing for hours in the hail, rain, snow and sunshine. Patrick, in fairness to him, never did try to kiss Erin again, which kept her happy, well that was until they became teenagers.

She wasn't sure how or when the butterflies started buzzing about her tummy as soon as her eyes set on him. Her feelings certainly changed for him as she witnessed him grow from the scruffy happy-go-lucky boy into the handsome, young man that he was today. Growing to six foot tall, his facial features transforming from the round childish face into chiseled cheekbones and a strong masculine jawline, broad shoulders and the most beautiful heart-melting chestnut-brown eyes, what girl wouldn't find him attractive?

Each time their hands accidently touched, zing went the tingling sensation through her and she began to feel that tingly feeling more and more in his presence. His husky voice saying her name sent her heart beating faster. The very sight of him began to make her crumble. Is that what it felt like to be in love? Those feelings remained with her but for some reason Patrick didn't seem to feel the same and it was for this reason Erin decided to pull herself together and control her emotions. It seemed evident they were never going to be anything more than friends and it was as clear as the nose on her face Patrick looked at her more like a sister than a possible wife. It was for this very reason that Erin got up one day and thought that's it, no more dreaming of love with Patrick Brogan for it was never going to happen. From that day on, she pushed the idea of them becoming a couple out of her mind, well out of her mind until Christmas Eve, the unexpected kiss on her cheek and his words *"I can't think of life here without you"*. Did he feel the same way after all? Surely she was reading too much into it.

Erin sat down on the sofa and buried her head in her hands. She could feel her eyes sting with tears, one escaped and rolled down her cheek.

'I've brought you in a cuppa, love.' John sat down next to her. 'Here get this in you.'

'Thanks, Da.' Erin accepted the warm mug of tea.

Observing her red-rimmed eyes, John frowned. 'Why are you crying? I thought you couldn't wait to go to New York. You should be happy, love.' He placed his arm around her shoulder and gave her a little squeeze.

'I am happy. It's a great opportunity but part of me wants to stay.' Erin sighed as she took a sip of the warm comforting tea.

'Then stay, you don't have to go. You can live in this house with us for as long as you want, nothing would make me happier.' He tucked wisps of her raven-black hair behind her ear. 'No one has asked you to leave.'

'Oh I know that but there's no work here. I should be bringing in a wage instead of depending on you and my ma to feed me and put a roof over my head. It's not fair on you both.' Erin exhaled.

'Erin, don't be silly, we don't mind!' He coughed and a chesty, mucous noise sounded from his lungs. 'You know we don't mind, Erin,' he said, his voice hoarse.

The thoughts of her dear father ploughing the potato fields with his bare hands in all sorts of weather, repulsed her again. She knew he wasn't getting any younger and his health was becoming affected by it.

'No, I need to go. I want to get a good job and I'll promise I'll send you over money so you don't have to work.'

'You don't need to, Erin. You really don't, please don't go for that reason only,' John pleaded before coughing again.

The tears welled up again against her will. As she looked into his blue eyes, her heart twisted with emotion. She knew she would miss Patrick terribly, but only God would know how much she would miss her dear father. The thoughts tumbled around her mind, should she stay and witness his health deteriorate or should she leave, head off with her heart broken and help him have a better life? She didn't need to think twice, her father's health was more important to her. 'No,' she said with a heavy heart. 'I'm going, Da, I must!'

Chapter 4

'You look after yourself, do you hear me, love?' Catherine cupped her daughter's face in her hands. 'Tell that son of mine I send all my love and to behave himself,' she joked.

Erin grinned, she knew exactly what her mother meant, for William could be a bit of a loose cannon at times. 'I will, I promise you, Ma.'

'And listen to me now,' Catherine warned, 'don't be fretting about home, we'll all be fine. I will admit it does surprise me that you are departing, I would have put you down as being too much of a home-bird to be leaving Derry.' She smiled softly at her daughter.

John nodded in agreement. He was unusually quiet, obviously having trouble saying goodbye to his eldest daughter. The tears were evident in his blue eyes and for a man that didn't cry much, it was clear he was struggling to hold back now.

Erin thought about her mother's words and a knot twisted in the pit of her stomach, she was right, she was too much of a home-bird. She had never dreamt of leaving her beloved hometown but what choice had she got? Her father's work had bothered her, but then there was Patrick, he hadn't said much since Christmas Eve. In fact she had barely set eyes on him since that night. The occasional glimpse of him in the street was about all she had seen of him and the odd wave was the only attention he had given her. This gesture he more than likely did only because he felt he had to when their eyes met as she watched him from her bedroom window. Why hadn't he discussed things with her, why hadn't he even bothered to say goodbye? Her heart felt like it was going to explode with pain because the reality was, if he had have expressed any feelings for her, she knew deep down she may not be leaving. The truth of the matter was, she was only going as she felt there was nothing keeping her here in the Bogside and how could she bare to watch her father suffer before her eyes? Then there was the risk of Patrick falling in love with another girl, how could she ever live with that? What a gut-wrenching thought.

'What are you thinking?' Catherine asked as soft flakes of snow fell gently on her face. 'You've gone very quiet, darling.'

'I'm thinking you're probably right about me being a home-bird but I know I need to do this.'

'Erin,' her father said, as he struggled to swallow the boulder that had leapt from his chest and now lodged in his throat, 'I've told you before, you don't have to go.' Smiling gently he went on, 'It's not too late you know.'

'Aye, I know.' She wiped her eyes. 'Would you look at me, I'm being silly, I'll more than likely go to New York and love it so much I may never want to come back here.' She forced a smile.

The thought of Erin never returning sent a shudder of despair along John's spine. 'Oh, Erin, don't say that, love. You will come back to visit us. One day you will return, won't you?'

Reading his worried mind, Erin smiled. 'Ah, Da, of course I'll be back one day, don't you think you're getting rid of me forever.' She patted his arm.

The clouds looming overhead grew thicker, as if they were about to give birth to a huge snowstorm. Erin pulled her shawl closer as the icy Atlantic breeze swept around them, and watched as other passengers began to step on to the ship. All preparing to sail away to the unknown, a mystery of adventures lying ahead of each them. A jangle of both nerves and excitement wavered through her. She shivered against the cold as the snowflakes fell quicker, huge flakes landing from the heavens above, coating everything white and fluffy.

A whistle blew and a loud voice echoed, 'Ten minutes to final boarding. I repeat, ten minutes to boarding!'

'Well, this is it, then.' A warm tear rolled down Erin's cold cheek as she reached out and placed her arms around both her parents. 'I love you two, you both know that, don't you? I love the pair of you with all my heart.' She began to weep.

John, the big strong man that he was, could not hold back the tears any longer, no matter how hard he tried. 'Oh, Erin, my beautiful girl, you have no idea how much we love you, and you have no idea how much we will miss you.'

He held her tight and his tears fell, fast and furious, just like the huge snowflakes, before disappearing into her hair.

'Your father's right, Erin, but we want what's best for you, so you go to America and enjoy every minute of it and we'll be looking forward until the day we meet again. I'll write to you often, I promise.' Catherine smiled softly.

Erin released her grasp and nodded before wiping her tear-stained cheeks. 'I need you to do me a favour, please tell Patrick I said goodbye.'

'I will,' Catherine nodded. 'I know he's breaking his heart, he doesn't want you to go. The poor lad's devastated.'

'He has a funny way of showing it. He hasn't contacted me. He hasn't even made any effort to see me. I called round to his house last night but there was no answer. I had a feeling he was in but didn't want to see me. I just can't understand him.' Erin shook her head.

'Perhaps he can't handle it. Believe me us men act like big machos but the truth is, we're really big softies underneath. I don't think he could cope with watching you leave,' John said.

'No, I don't think I mean that much to him.' Erin sighed with a heavy heart. 'After all we have been through, I expected a goodbye at the very least. We lived and breathed each other's company ever since we were eight years old, how could he not speak to me over the last few weeks? I just don't understand how he could shut me out like he has done.'

Another blow of the whistle rattled through the frosty air. 'Five minutes to boarding! I repeat, five minutes to boarding!'

'Right, I better be off, I'll be in touch.' Erin lifted her bags and gave them both a final kiss on the cheek. 'Love you.'

'Love you too.' John and Catherine chirped together.

'Goodbye,' she said before turning and walking towards the ship.

'Bye, Erin,' John yelled after her.

Erin gave one final glance over her shoulder, 'Bye.' She choked as both of them waved frantically. Not wanting her parents to see the river of tears streaming down her face, she turned away and kept walking.

'Erin! Erin wait!' A memorable voice from behind stopped her from taking another step.

Turning around she watched in disbelief as Patrick came running through the crowds towards her.

'Patrick!' she gasped as the usual butterflies at the sight of him took off at a great speed in her tummy.

'I'm so glad I got here before you left!' He panted. 'I'm sorry I'm late.'

'I didn't think you were coming.' She felt her legs wobble.

'Well, if I'm being honest, at first I couldn't bring myself to see you leave but then the more I thought about it, the more I knew I could never live with myself if I didn't say goodbye.'

'Oh, I'm so glad you did,' she said. The tears were still falling.

'Listen,' he said, wiping her cheeks and holding her face in his hands, 'You take care of yourself, Erin Coyle! Keep in touch.' He forced a smile.

'I will, I promise I will,' she said dropping her cases and throwing her arms around him.

He closed his arms around her waist and held her tight. Oh how good it felt to be in his arms, and oh, how good he smelt. She wanted to freeze the moment and stay here in his embrace forever. Oh how she longed to be his wife, have his children, continue their adventures as they had done so in the past, grow old together… but never mind the daydreaming, imagining a life that was never going to be, she was his friend, his best friend that's all. If he'd wanted to marry her, surely he would have asked by now.

The whistle blew again, so close it caused her to jump as the vibrations rang in her ears.

'Goodbye, Patrick.' She released her grip and picked up her luggage.

'There is no *good* in goodbye.' He choked. 'And certainly nothing *fair* about farewell either.' He tried to stifle a smile again.

She forced a grin. 'That my dear friend is so true.'

'Take care, Erin.' He planted a soft lingering kiss on her cheek. 'And I'm warning you, don't be going running off horrified and wiping your cheek like the first time I kissed you.' He joked before kissing her other cheek.

No chance of that, she thought as the sensation of his soft lips stayed against her skin causing a warm tingling sensation to charge through her. She said, 'We can't have that, perhaps I overreacted a bit back then.' She kissed his cheek and smiled softly. 'I'll be in touch.'

'Okay, look after yourself.' He nodded. 'Bye.'

He placed his hands in his pockets, his broad shoulders slumped and with a heavy heart, he watched her board the huge ship. The journey of her new life about to begin, he thought. A strange sensation gnawed at his insides, a feeling of not knowing how he was going to cope without her. One thing was for sure, it would not be easy.

'I love you, Erin Coyle,' he whispered to himself as she waved her final goodbye and disappeared into the mighty vessel.

A tear rolled down his cheek. As he reached inside his pocket for a hankie, he felt the box containing the ring that his beloved Erin would never wear. He retrieved the box and opened it. An urge to pull it from its case and fire it into the water jumped into his mind, but he also knew that would be pointless. Closing the lid, he placed it back in his pocket with disgust.

Smoke filled the frosty air as it escaped the ship's mighty funnels and the engines began to roar. Huge frothy waves foamed around the sides of the vessel as the ship slowly started to float away. Patrick stood glued to the spot as the enormity of his loss gripped him.

'Life is so cruel,' he whispered as he turned away, not wanting to watch the ship sail off into the distance carrying away the woman he loved. He dipped his head and began walking towards her parents.

'Sorry, son. I only wish we could have persuaded her to stay,' John croaked as Patrick approached.

'Aye me too.' Patrick blew out his cheeks, 'If only I had tried.'

Back in the depressing snow-filled streets of the Bogside, Patrick gathered a handful of snow. Rolling it into a ball, he lobbed it at Erin's bedroom window and yelled, 'There certainly is nothing *good* about goodbyes!'

Chapter 5

Erin, smiling, drank in the view of New York as the ship
crawled closer through the calm waters. The Statue of Liberty
stood proud in the near distance. The robed female figure,
representing freedom, a gift to the United States from the
people of France, offered a welcoming sight for immigrants.
White puffs of fluffy clouds, like candy floss, scudded across a
duck-egg blue Manhattan skyline. The bright day caused an
exciting feeling to develop in the pit of her stomach.

The heavy sensation she had since leaving Derry on that
cold, dull day had dispersed a little. The thought of seeing
William again had caused her heart to race. This place
definitely appears exciting, she thought. As the vessel drew
nearer to the port, the waves of excitement engulfed her even
more. She lowered her lids briefly, fatigue evident in their tiny
folds and wiped away a silent tear. It was difficult, part of her
felt happy to be starting a new life but she was also grieving
over the one she had left behind, but deep down she knew these
feelings had to be natural.

Stepping off the boat on New York Harbor, she sucked
in the fresh crisp air and headed off in search for her beloved
brother. It wasn't too difficult to find him in the huge crowds
of bustling people, there he was, the six-foot-two handsome
man that he always was. His black hair slicked to the side, his
tailored suit fitted perfect to his toned frame.

William's blue eyes danced at the sight of his young
sister, a broad smile developed on his face. A beam so big it lit

up his face.

Erin's heart skipped a beat as she eagerly made her way through the crowds of people, dropping her luggage at her feet, she gave him a huge hug. 'William!' she cried feeling more emotional now than ever.

'Oh, Erin,' William squeezed her in a bear-like fashion, 'you have no idea how good it is to see you!' He planted an affectionate kiss on her cheek. 'I'm not joking, I've missed you all so much! There have been many days I've felt so homesick.'

'Would you take a look at you!' Erin gave him a look of approval. 'You look more like an American film star! What happened to the down and out poverty-stricken young man from the Bogside? Where'd he go?' she laughed.

Smirking, William replied, 'I'll admit, sis, I scrub up well. Do you like the new me?'

'You're looking great,' she admitted. 'It's fantastic to see you. Everyone back in Derry sends their love.'

'That's good to hear, how are they?' William released his grip and picked up her luggage. 'I hope they're all okay.'

'Aye, they're all grand, just the usual.'

'Right, you can tell me all the craic over dinner. I've a car waiting for us and some food prepared back at the apartment. I'm sure you could be doing with a nice bite to eat.'

'Food prepared? *You* have prepared food? Are my ears hearing right? You couldn't be trusted to boil an egg back in

Derry!' She playfully nudged him in the ribs.

'Oh, sis, it's amazing what you can do when you let go of your ma's apron strings. I've had to do a lot of growing up since I moved out here, and without my ma's fine cooking to feed me, I'd have faded away to nothing.' He winked playfully before continuing, 'So I had to take the plunge and book myself some cookery lessons,' he announced with an air of triumph.

'Aye right!' Erin laughed. 'Somehow, brother dearest, I can't imagine you in a pinny up to your elbows in flour.'

'Now, hold your horses, I wouldn't go that far, but trust me, I'm now one of the finest cooks in Manhattan,' William declared proudly. 'You'll see!'

'Aye, dead on, I'll be the judge of that,' Erin said.

With another wink, William replied, 'Just you wait, you'll be proud of me, sis, I'm telling you. The lady that helped me out is called Leonarda. I'll introduce you to her, she's a great woman, you'll like her, she's the Fitzgerald's cook. Speaking of Fitzgeralds, there's Theo.' He nodded toward a parked car. 'He's kindly agreed to give us a lift.' With another wink of the eye and a mischievous grin, he went on, 'And you'll like him too, believe me, all the ladies *like* Theo.'

Erin, feeling her cheeks blush, pulled a face. 'I'm not interested in any matchmaking if that's what you have in mind and I don't care if *all* the ladies like him! So whatever you have in mind you can for...' Her voice trailed at the sight of the drop-dead-gorgeous man emerging from the driver's door.

35

On seeing them both he made his way round the car and opened the door.

'Hi there.' He flashed a pearly smile. 'You must be Erin. I've heard so much about you,' he drawled in his strong irresistible American accent. 'I'm Theodore but please call me Theo, everyone else does,' he said holding out his hand.

Erin shyly accepted his friendly handshake. 'Nice to meet you Theodore, sorry… I mean Theo.' If she had felt her cheeks blush earlier, they now felt like they were on fire. She breathed small measured breaths in an attempt to desperately curb the wild thrashing of her heart.

'Take a seat.' He gestured her inside.

Inside the car felt comfy. Erin rested her head as William sat in the front chatting to the amazingly handsome Theo. Goodness, she thought, how could someone be so good looking, so *perfect*! He had to be just over six-foot tall, he appeared to be the same height as William, and with his thick, dark hair swept back accompanied by pronounced cheek bones, a nose and mouth that suited his face and those eyes! My goodness how could any girl not fall victim to staring into those large, blue, lustrous eyes? It at once became clear why *all* the girls liked Theo.

Lost in her daydream, Erin didn't notice that she hadn't spoken one single word during the journey through the busy streets of Manhattan, until the heart-melting Theo pulled up outside a huge building and turned round to catch her looking at him.

'I said you're in a world of your own.' He grinned with amusement.

'Oh sorry, don't mind me, I'm just tired. I feel a bit strange since coming off the ship. I suppose all that time crossing the Atlantic has left me feeling a bit weird, a bit *floaty!*'

'I was the same,' William said, 'it took me a few days to come round to myself. I remember feeling as if I was still bopping up and down at sea for a few days after I arrived here.'

'Let's get you inside, then, get you some rest.' Theo smiled softly.

Suddenly, without warning, Erin's tummy released a loud embarrassing rumble, like a ravenous, growling caged animal. 'Oh.' Erin grabbed her stomach. 'The thought of William's fine cooking is making me hungry,' she joked, trying to make light of the situation.

Theo nodded, 'Yeah me too. You will not be disappointed,' he said, stepping out of the car. 'He's a great cook.'

The two men hauled Erin's luggage up two flights of stairs until they came to William's apartment. Inside, the accommodation was at once welcoming. The aroma of something good coming from the oven caused Erin's tummy to go into spasms again, only this time she managed to tighten her muscles and cough loudly to disguise the embarrassing noise.

'Right, get yourself a seat in the living room and I'll get the dinner served in no time.' William gestured towards an open door to the left of the kitchen area.

'Actually, William, do you mind if I just get freshened up before we eat?' Erin reached for one of her bags.

'No worries, the bathroom is in there,' he pointed.

Erin ran herself a warm bath whilst she dug out some clean clothes. As she sank into the warm soapy water it dawned on her she hadn't thanked Theo for the lift. How rude of her, she thought. She quickly lathered the soap over her body, hastily washed her hair and decided to get dried and dressed before he left.

Minutes later, dressed in a long, navy, high-waisted skirt and cream blouse, she combed her long, damp raven-black hair and emerged from the bathroom.

'Goodness, that was quick.' Theo beamed eyeing her with approval. 'Come on, we'll get seated.'

Erin felt a kick of adrenalin as she followed him into the dining room and an even bigger kick when she saw the table set for three.

Sitting down facing him, she said, 'I apologise, I should have thanked you earlier for the lift, I'm so grateful.'

'You're very welcome, it's the least I could do. William and I are great friends and he is such a hard worker, he works his fingers to the bone for my family.'

Erin nodded, this much she could imagine, one thing was certain, William was never idle. 'So, tell me, do you both work together? I know he's employed with your father's printing firm.'

'We did and I have to admit we had such fun together but my father expanded the business and offered William a job managing the new office. I still manage the old one. We don't see much of each other now and with the new office a few blocks away, William now sets off earlier for work.'

'Right you two, get tucked into this!' William emerged from the kitchen with two plates.

Erin smiled as he sat the plate in front of her. 'Chicken pie? Creamed potatoes, peas and carrots, one of my favourite meals!'

'It is indeed, sis,' he replied feeling as proud as a peacock.

Erin wasted no time in cutting into the thick pastry and popping a huge portion into her mouth. 'Emmm, this is sooooo good.'

'Well, I did tell you.' He flashed her a grin as he headed back to the kitchen to retrieve his plate.

'Do you know I'm going to have to meet this cook, get some tips off her,' Erin called after him as she ate the tasty creamed potatoes and vegetables.

'I'll take you to meet her,' Theo offered. 'You'll get on well with her. She's a friendly woman, Leonarda is one of the best.'

Erin glanced up from her plate. The thought of Theo accompanying her caused her skin to tingle with excitement.

'Great,' she replied. 'I'd like that.' I like that idea very much indeed, she thought.

Back from the kitchen, William, joining them at the table, started tucking into his dinner. 'So, tell me what's happening back home, anything mad or exciting? How's all the neighbours?' William asked as he forked the creamy chicken pie into his mouth.

'Oh just the usual banter. Frankie's still knocking back the liquor and anything else with alcohol that he can get his hands on. Anne Quigley's still knitting for all the wains in Derry at a rate of knots. Suzy Ferguson's up to her eyes in it doing her bit for the community. I suppose everyone is just carrying on the same as it always was, oh, and wee Nellie McDowell is still queen bee and the oldest woman in the Bog!' Erin's eyes danced.

'Good aul Nellie, no one will take that crown from her just yet!' William smiled.

'Aye you're right there, she's some character,' Erin replied. Reaching for the jug of water she poured herself a glass and took a sip.

'They all sound like characters to me.' Theo grinned.

'Oh they are all a great bunch. There's one thing for sure, in the Bogside, everyone looks out for one another, don't they, William?'

'They do indeed, they're all like one huge family that pull together in times of need. That's the one thing I have to admit that I miss about home.'

All three finished their food in contentment. Erin scraped the last from her plate and licked her fork. 'Right, never mind speaking about missing home or you will make me homesick already, so let's change the subject, get the second course out instead,' she teased. 'I hope you have made dessert or I'll just have to eat the pattern of this plate,' she joked.

William said, 'Your host for the evening will not let you down. I'll be back in a minute.'

'You are so fortunate, boy,' she yelled after him, 'I didn't come all the way from Derry to have no dessert and it better be as good as the first course.'

He returned minutes later with a thick slice of apple pie and custard, much to Erin's delight. In no time the three plates were empty.

The overload of food was enough to make Erin sleepy, together with the long journey she now felt so exhausted she could lie her head down on the table and nod off. 'I have to give credit where credit is due, that meal was delicious,' she said through a yawn.

William, sensing her tiredness, replied, 'Go you in and have a wee nap, I'm sure you're tired.'

'Yeah, William's right, go and have a sleep and we'll clear these dishes,' Theo urged.

'Oh, you boys are such gents,' she teased. 'I don't want to be rude but if you both don't mind I would love to excuse myself, I feel shattered.'

'Of course we don't mind,' Theo chirped, 'Get yourself

rested.'

'Thanks, besides, when men offer to do the dishes, it's best not to refuse!' Erin's eyes danced with mischief.

'Don't get too used to getting your dinner handed into your hand and the dishes cleared up after you. Tomorrow my dear sister, I shall gladly hand the reins over to oneself,' William teased.

'Can't wait, brother dearest!' Erin tossed him a cheeky grin.

'Come on, I'll show you to your room,' William offered.

Erin, following him like a puppy obeying its master, paused and looked over her shoulder before leaving the room. 'Thank you again for the lift, Theo. It's been lovely meeting you.'

Theo threw her a heart-melting smile. 'You're very welcome, it's been nice meeting you, too. I'll pick you up tomorrow around lunchtime to take you to meet Leonarda, and perhaps if we have time, we can squeeze in an ice-cream on the way back.' He flashed her a pearly grin and those dimples deepened again.

'Great, that sounds good. I absolutely love ice-cream so we'll just have to make the time.' She returned the grin.

He lifted his eyebrows. 'Fantastic! You have yourself a date, then.'

Erin felt her heart flip over like a pancake on a pan and

she could feel her cheeks burn, like they were being fried on the same pan! 'A date? I like the sound of that.' She turned, tossed her hair and left.

Theo smiled as he watched her leave. 'I like the sound of that too,' he whispered under his breath.

Chapter 6

Erin drew back the curtains and peered at the quiet, empty street below, not a person in sight, all still tucked up in their beds no doubt and fast asleep.

Earlier, as soon as her head hit the pillows, she had nodded off and had such a peaceful night until the images of Patrick's face had woken her. Her dream had seen them running hand-in-hand through a daisy field, laughing and joking until he lifted her, swirled her around, and like a bolt out of the blue, he kissed her on the lips. Then making their way under the cherry blossom tree, that they used to climb as children, he kissed her again. She closed her eyes and dissolved in his arms, relishing the moment, allowing him to sweep her away by this long awaited embrace.

Moments later she opened her eyes again and reached out to stroke his face. Feeling confused and disappointed, Erin felt herself wakening in a strange room and reaching her hand out to emptiness. It had taken her a few seconds to customize herself. The smell of William's familiar aftershave, mixed with methanol, reminded her that she was no longer in Ireland. Feeling gutted, she soon realized she had certainly not been in Patrick's arms, no, here she was thousands of miles away in an unfamiliar country. Her encounter with Patrick had felt so real. She touched her mouth remembering how true his soft lips had felt brushing against her own only a few minutes ago in her wonderful dream.

Her stomach tied itself in knots, tears sprang to her eyes as a gripping feeling of despair gnawed at her insides. Sitting upright and hugging her knees close to her chest, she wiped her eyes and lowered her head until the sad moment passed.

'Oh look at me,' she whispered in the dark. 'Only gone a short while and I feel homesick already.' She sniffed and lay back down. Resting her head on the comfy pillows, she tried to get back to sleep. She tossed and turned for almost an hour but it was no good, no matter how hard she tried, she just couldn't nod off again. The truth was, no matter how homesick she felt, she knew deep down in her heart she loved Patrick and true love never dies, or so she had been told. Then there was Theo, she had never in her life felt attracted to another man other than Patrick but there was no doubt there were sparks between Theo and herself and these new feelings caused a stir of uncertainness in the pit of her stomach.

Her brain felt like a merry-go-round with thoughts of both men going round and round and round, something she was not accustomed to.

Erin released a long sigh, how stupid she felt, after all Patrick was back in Ireland with thousands of miles between them and had never shown her any feelings other than friendship, so she may as well put him to the back of her mind. Then there was Theo, whom she had just met, and as William had said earlier, "all the girls like Theo" so she may as well put him to the back of her mind also. For goodness sake she had only known him a few hours, how could she obsess over someone she'd only just met? She knew very little about him.

For all she knew he could have a string of annoying habits and an even bigger string of females pursuing the eligible bachelor, surely he could take his pick of ladies.

Feeling as daft as a brush, she exhaled, flung the blankets aside and jumped out of bed. Making her way to the living room window she drew back the curtains and perched herself on the windowsill. She looked up into the inky sky, alive with millions of twinkling glittering stars. The moon shone brightly, lighting up the streets below like a huge torch shinning from above. Gazing up into the moonlit sky she couldn't help but wonder what Patrick was doing right now.

Patrick propped the pillows and helped ease his father to rest his head against them.

'Are you okay, Da?' he asked with concern.

Jim's eyes fixed on his son as he nodded to indicate he was fine. As his ribcage heaved up and down, with every fall of his chest he released a breathless 'Ah.'

Patrick swallowed hard, he knew his father was certainly not okay but there was nothing he could do about it. Clearly the man he loved was deteriorating at an alarming rate, disintegrating like a snowman in sunlight before his eyes.

Patrick's heart twisted with pain. He knew the slightest exertion caused his father so much stress, particularly dressing him. It was a duty he despised doing, the aftermath was just so difficult to watch, but a task that had to be done all the same.

After a few minutes Jim's breathing settled slightly.

Patrick sat down on the wooden chair beside the bed for his usual daily routine. Picking up his father's old, battered bible, he flicked open a page at random and began to read aloud a passage while Jim lay there, as snug as a bug in a rug and listening quietly. Patrick then blessed himself and made the sign of the cross on his father's forehead before beginning to recite the rosary aloud. Again, Jim remained still, answering the devotion would take too much out of him, so he therefore recounted the prayers in his heart.

Patrick finished the rosary, shut the bible and placed it together with the rosary beads on their usual spot next to the oil lamp on the bedside locker.

'What do you fancy for breakfast, Da?' Patrick asked over his shoulder as he made his way over to the window. 'What about a wee boiled egg and toast?' He drew back the curtains to allow God's heavenly light to fill the room. Outside the sun's warm rays flared the birds in the nearby trees into a chorus of melodies. A sound that Jim welcomed every morning.

'Just tea and toast,' Jim replied.

From the window Patrick gazed out into the quiet, lonely street, not a soul about and, apart from the singing birds, not another sound except the faint bark from the Coyle's Labrador dog. Poor Sandy is obviously missing Erin, Patrick thought as his eyes fell on house number 30 across the street. The home that once was occupied by the beautiful Erin. A lump sprang to his throat as he recalled on many a day as he went to draw the curtains, Erin would be waiting from her bedroom window to greet him with a wave, and that heart-melting smile of hers that could light up his heart in an instant.

'Morning, my beautiful Erin. God only knows what your tomorrows will bring,' he whispered under his breath. 'I love you, Erin.'

From the living room window Erin could see Manhattan lit up before her eyes. It was a good height from which to observe her new surroundings.

Soft, amber glows shone from the many lampposts. There were a few dotted lights on in the buildings, but most were in darkness. The only sound to be heard was a chime from the clock on the wall behind her and the faint bark of a dog yelping in the distance.

The moon was slowly closing its eyes, its nightshift now completed, and the early sun, partially cloaked with thick clouds, was now rising in the dull sky and slowly turning the darkness into light as it began spreading its kindling flames of gold through the horizon. The first slither of the sun peeped up behind the rooftops and the delicate glow slowly caressed the land.

The dog continued to bark. Its yelps reminded her of their friendly family pet, Sandy, back home. Her heart ached at the thought of her beloved dog, who, no doubt was missing her too. Sandy, named after the colour of his soft coat, a faithful Labrador that tried to sneak out to join Patrick and herself every time they left the house. On many occasions, Sandy even managed to wangle his way into church unnoticed. He would crawl under the seat and sit with his head on his paws as quiet as a mouse. After a while, Sandy would peep his head out and gaze up at them with those round, innocent chocolate-brown eyes of his. Catching sight of him, Erin always gave him a look of disapproval, but Patrick on the other hand, would smile and tickle him behind the ears.

The memory pulled on her heartstrings. Blowing out her cheeks, she leaned her head against the cool pane of glass and sighed, 'I love you, Patrick,' she whispered under her breath.

'Really? I had no idea!' A soft voice from behind broke the stillness.

Swinging round, Erin clutched at her chest, 'William! You scared the wits out of me! What the heck are you doing up so early?' she said. Glancing over his shoulder at the clock she could see it was almost five o'clock.

'Actually, I could ask you the same,' he said sounding amused.

'I couldn't sleep,' she replied.

'Tell me, did my ears hear correct, are you really in love with Patrick?' he asked.

Dipping her head, Erin released a defeated sigh. 'Aye, there's no point in denying it. I have to confess I've felt this way for a long time.' She raised her head and watched his expression.

'I don't know what to say, I have to admit I'm a bit

49

baffled. How come none of us realised?'

'I guess I'm a good actress,' she said. 'Actually, pay no attention to me, just ignore what I said. I'm going to get a grip of myself and forget about my feelings for him.' She waved dismissively. 'My mind is in turmoil, I'm all over the place, and if I'm being honest, I'm not really sure if coming here is the right move for me after all. I miss the family already.'

William, placing a hand on her shoulder, smiled. 'I can understand how you feel, I felt the same. Trust me, you'll be fine after a while, anyway you've only just arrived. Erin, you need to give yourself time. Besides, if you don't settle here, don't worry, it's not the end of the world. Plus the fact you can always return to Derry if you really wanted to, but believe me, Erin, there's more opportunities here than you'll ever find in the Bogside. I can honestly say, once you're here for a bit, I can't ever see you wanting to return.'

Erin nodded. 'Aye, I suppose you're right. What have I got to lose? I'm going to give it a go and see how things work out.'

'Do you know what, Erin, I have a feeling coming here will prove an experience you will certainly never forget. In fact,' William raised his eyebrows, 'I also have a feeling things just might go well here for you, in fact *very* well indeed.' He grinned mischievously. 'I'll get you a cuppa.'

Erin watched him walk across the room towards the kitchen. 'What do you mean by that?' she called after him.

Her question fell on deaf ears.

Minutes later a smiling face peeped around the door. 'Porridge or scrambled eggs?'

'Oh it definitely has to be scrambled eggs, back at home you used to burn them to the arse of the pot, let's see if this cook has taught you how to make them any better here,' she joked.

William smiled. 'I don't think you made them any better yourself. Even the rats wouldn't eat *your* scrambled eggs,' he teased before disappearing again.

William cracked a few eggs into a pan and whisked in a little milk. He then heated some soda bread in the oven and fried some sausages and mushrooms in the pan, and in no time the aroma travelled from the kitchen to fill Erin's nostrils with the yummy smell.

'Right, get yourself seated, dear, I've made you a brekkie fit for a queen.' William placed the two plates on the dining table. 'I'll just grab the tea.'

Erin, gazing lovingly at the food, realized that she was now so ravenous she could not only eat it all but the plate as well.

'So,' she said through a mouthful of bread, 'what did you mean earlier by your statement about things going well here for me? You had a mischievous grin on your face.' She narrowed her eyes. 'Come on, tell me what that was all about.'

William sipped on his tea and grinned again, 'I mean Theo, he may have only just met you, but trust me also on this one, the man's mad about you!'

51

Jim watched his son with curiosity glinting in his sunken eyes. 'What's up, man?' he asked.

Patrick fixed the curtains into place and made his way back to the bedside. He sat down on the old wooden chair again. 'Do you know something, Da? I let her go! I let her go without telling her how I felt. Call me a man? I'm a failure that's what I am.' He hung his head in despair.

'A failure, eh?' Jim replied.

'Da, I love Erin and I hadn't even the courage to tell her. Now she's in some posh place surrounded by all sorts, no doubt she'll be swept away by someone else and I'll just have to grin and bear it, take my oil as the saying goes. I'll tell you something else, Da, I'm going to end up a sad and lonely man because I will never meet anyone like her. I know I will certainly never love another like I love Erin Coyle. I love that girl and I wasn't even *manly* enough to tell her.' Releasing a long disgusted sigh he continued, 'The truth is, there's not a *manly* bone in my body!'

Jim, exhaling slowly, placed a gnarled, thin hand on his son's shoulder. 'Listen my boy, I know why you didn't stop her.' He paused to gather his breath. 'You let her go because you love her so much... you didn't follow her... you stayed... you remained here to look after me in my final days.' Jim breathed slowly and gave his son's shoulder a gentle squeeze. 'Now... if that's not the actions of a man... then... I don't know what is!'

Patrick's eyes filled with tears but he was adamant he was not going to cry like a baby in front of his father. He swallowed the lump in his throat and sniffed.

Jim continued, 'You're more than a man in my eyes... a man of *steel*...a precious *gem*...a courageous chap. Your mother,... God rest her soul,...will be looking down and proud of the *man* you have grown up to be.' Jim smiled softly with admiration, his sunken blood-shot eyes filled with tears and the wrinkles around his eyes deepened. He gave Patrick's shoulder another gentle squeeze, 'But... not as proud as I am...no one could be as proud of you as me... I love you, son.'

Patrick chewed on the inside of his cheek and allowed the tears to fall. Placing his hand around Jim's and looking into his eyes, he sniffed. 'Love you too, Da.'

The pain of losing his mother at such a young age gripped him to this day and losing Erin was equally as painful. It was just him and his father now. God only knew how he would cope when the day came to say goodbye to his old man. 'I really love you, Da.'

'I know you do, son. I'm not going to be here much longer...my days are numbered my boy. I want you to tell her... tell that girl how you feel. If it's in God's plan...it will not pass you.'

Chapter 7

Erin rested her body further down into the soapy suds. This time she could relax and enjoy the warm water easing her tired muscles.

As she washed her hair, she reflected on the conversation she had with William over breakfast. She could feel herself blushing at the prospect of Theo telling him he believed she was the most beautiful girl he had ever set eyes on. Surely not, she thought as she rinsed her hair. It was the conversation she had with her brother afterwards that ran rampant in her mind. After she spilled out her feelings again for Patrick, William listened carefully and advised his young sister that if Patrick had felt the same, he would have told her by now, after all he'd had more opportunities than enough.

'Put the notion of love for Patrick to the back of your mind and move on with your life,' William had warned. His advice may be as welcome as sour milk in her tea but she knew deep down that her brother was right. A collection of fishermen's knots were developing in the pit of her stomach. Erin knew she had to listen to William, after all he had known Patrick for as long as she had, she therefore had to take into account his advice.

Out of the bath, she towel dried her long hair and got dressed. Her hair now smelled beautifully fresh. Erin finished braiding her hair and spritzed her skin with a delicate spray of eau de roses, which smelt much better than eau de fried sausages from earlier. The sound of a gentle rap on the front door sent a tingle along her spine and she could feel her cheeks blush again.

Theo, dressed in casual black trousers and a blue shirt, smiled as Erin opened the door. There was absolutely no denying it, this man was drop-dead gorgeous and any girl that had his attention would be mad in the head to ignore it. Standing there looking so irresistible, hair slicked back, the colour of his shirt setting off the blue of his irises, his pearly smile shone against his swarthy skin and he smelled so good it was evident he too was just freshly washed. Erin felt her knees wobble.

'You look lovely, Erin. Are you ready to go?' he asked as he flashed her one of his finest heart-melting smiles.

'Yes,' she replied and reached for her cream woollen cardigan.

Watching her place her arm into the sleeve and fumbling about in search of the other one, he offered, 'Here, let me help you.' He gently guided her other arm into the sleeve. His soft fingers brushing against her caused goosebumps to form on her skin.

They reached the bottom of the stairwell when Theo stopped. 'Wait, I forgot my coat. I'll not be a minute,' he said, pulling his key from his pocket and slipping it into the keyhole.

'What are you doing?' Erin questioned as she paused at the doorway.

'Just getting my coat.' Theo looked amused. 'Why?'

'But…' Erin's eyes widened as she looked at the door of the apartment and then up the flight of stairs to their flat directly above. 'I don't understand, why is your coat in there?'

Theo smiled. 'I left it behind, after all I *live* here. Just a second,' he said over his shoulder.

'You what?' Erin looked startled. 'What, directly below us?' she asked after him.

'Yes,' he stepped back into the hallway and closed the door behind him. Smiling at the surprised look etched on her pretty face, he continued, 'Yes, directly below you and I can hear every little footstep you make, not to mention every little word also,' he teased and those dimples appeared again.

Looking from startled to horrified, Erin's eyes widened a fraction more, but the grin on his face indicated that he was joking, surely he was only kidding. Cringing within she hoped he hadn't heard her babble to William earlier about how attractive he was. The very thought of it resulted in her blood curdling and the little drummer boys began banging on her heart once again, only this time just a little bit stronger.

She could feel her legs beneath her buckle with a mixture of the thought of Theo hearing their conversations, together with the fact they lived so close, which meant she would be seeing much more of him than she had initially anticipated. Then there was the question of whether or not she snored, did she snore? She wasn't sure, she would have to ask William later. The image of her lying in her bed snoring and grunting like a pig whilst the perfect Theo listened below was a harrowing picture. Well, if she did, she would just have to sort it out. Perhaps she could stick a clothes peg on her nose, but then again, surely she would wake up next morning with a big, pink swollen snout and never mind sounding like a pig but looking like one! Help! Her head was spinning.

Theo placed a gentle hand on her shoulder. 'I'm only kidding you know, no need to look so bewildered.'

'Oh good.' She breathed slowly. 'So you wouldn't have heard me say all those horrible things about you as soon as you were out the door,' she teased.

'Nah, and besides, when I left last night you were already tucked up in your bed fast asleep and snoring like a pig,' he laughed.

Erin could feel the blood draining from her. 'What?'

Theo, reading the expression on her face laughed again. 'I'm kidding.'

'Oh stop it you!' Erin playfully slapped him on the arm. 'Or you'll be shaking like bacon when I'm finished with you! Come on, get that coat on and let's get going.'

'Okay, I'm coming.' He slipped on his jacket. 'I'm sure you'll be as happy as a pig in mud later after spending the day with me, and you'll fall into your bed exhausted and in no time you'll be snoring ...ouch.' He ducked to avoid another playful slap, this time around the earlobe. 'I mean you'll be dreaming away to your heart's content.'

'Yeah well as long as you don't enter my dreams or it will be more of a nightmare, Mr Fitzgerald!'

Clutching his chest he replied, 'Oh, Erin, I'm wounded.'

They climbed into the spotlessly clean car and Theo pulled away from the parking area to begin the five-minute drive to his parents' home.

'So, Erin, tell me all about yourself, I want to hear everything.' Theo sounded cheery.

Erin shrugged. 'There isn't much to tell, nothing exciting.'

'Well,' he glanced at her with a look of interest in his eyes, 'I'm sure that's not true.'

'I'm pretty sure your life is much more interesting than mine.' She grinned. 'Really.'

'I'll tell you all about me but I want to hear about you, go on, ladies first.'

'I'm twenty-three.'

'Yeah, I know that much.' His eyes danced. 'William told me.'

'Oh did he indeed. Did he also tell you I like nice food, walks in the park, picnics, hate bad manners, and my hobbies are…ladybirds…collecting ladybirds.'

'Ladybirds?' He threw her a puzzled look as he steered the car through the huge metal gates and up the long, winding drive. 'I don't recall him mentioning that one.'

'Only joking.' She tried to surpass the childhood hobby. Taking a deep breath and attempting to put Patrick out of her mind, she continued, 'My hobbies are reading and walking. I just love strolling in the outdoors and feeling the fresh air on my face, nothing beats it for clearing your head. Wow… I wouldn't mind a dander around this place,' she said as she drank in the sight of the grand gardens.

The winding driveway, lined with many rose bushes, Erin imagined would be a pretty sight in full bloom. To her right, fine expensive statues surrounded a huge pond. The sun glistened on its calm surface, making it appear like a fine sheet of glass.

Theo brought the car to a halt outside the huge mansion. Their feet crunched on the gravel as they both stepped from the car. Erin found herself mesmerized as she gazed at the mighty building before her eyes. The house itself was by far the biggest she had ever seen, no chance of anything like this back where she came from.

Never had she imagined Theo coming from such riches. He seemed so full of humour and so grounded, not to mention the fact he was living below her in a two-bedroom apartment. Why on earth he would want to leave a place like this was beyond her.

The large, black, double doors were opened by a smart looking gentleman dressed in a perfect tailored suit, spit-polished shoes and wearing a more than serious look on his stern face.

'Ah, Benson.' Theo held out his hand. 'It's good to see you my friend.'

Benson nodded. 'Theodore, it's good to see you too.' He accepted his handshake before stepping aside and looking at Erin from top to toe.

Erin, dressed in her high-waisted skirt, that she had worn to dinner the previous night, floral blouse and woolly cardigan, was thankful that she had dressed in her Sunday best, however she now regretted not wearing her jacket that matched the skirt. It had crossed her mind earlier, but thinking it might be a bit too formal, she cast it aside and opted for her old cardigan that had seen better days, much better days!

'And this young lady is?' Benson lowered his hazel eyes.

'This is Erin, Erin Coyle, William's sister,' Theo replied with an air of triumph.

'Good afternoon, Miss Coyle, and welcome to the Fitzgerald household,' he said in a friendly tone. Smiling he stepped aside. 'Do come in.'

Never judge a book by its cover, Erin thought as she returned the smile. Benson definitely sounded much nicer than the stern appearance that first greeted them.

Inside the grand hallway, Erin's shoes click-clacked against the porcelain tiles. She drank in the sight of the magnificent sweeping staircase, glistening chandeliers hanging from the high ceiling, expensive ornaments and the shiny mahogany doors. Feeling like she was walking through a palace, her attention was drawn to a room to her left. As she walked past the room, she caught a glimpse of a grand piano which appeared to be situated in a corner of what seemed to be a library. 'A library! A real library!' she whispered aloud.

Erin couldn't contain herself from backtracking. She couldn't imagine anything better than spending hour after hour in this room, delving into the world of books, characters, stories, taking her to a million miles away. Then again, being here in this very house was a far cry from the poverty-stricken streets of the Bogside, sure she may as well be a million miles away. And then there was the piano, oh how she longed to learn to play the piano.

Theo clicked his fingers next to her ear, causing Erin to almost jump out of her skin.

'I said you're in a world of your own.' He smiled, amazed by how taken aback she was.

Erin pulled her gaze away from the library and turned to face him. She was so caught up in her thoughts, she hadn't realised she had been standing still in a daydream. 'Oh Theo.' Erin looked at him and then back at the piano. 'I'm so sorry. I was just thinking how I would *love* to play that,' she said dreamily.

'Feel free, go on give us a sample,' he urged.

Erin stepped aside, a look of horror spread on her face. 'No, Theo, I can't. I would like to *learn* to play but I don't know how.'

'Oh well, I'll just have to teach you, then. We'll make arrangements for when suits us both and I'll give you a few lessons. I'll have you playing like a professional in no time!'

Theo beamed.

Benson lifted an eyebrow and from the look on his face it was clear he didn't think this was a good idea. Obviously with Theo running the printing office, he had enough on his plate without the added job of offering piano lessons to a girl that clearly would need more than a *few*.

Erin, deciphering the look, replied, 'Oh no. It's okay, I honestly wouldn't want to put you to any trouble.'

'Absolutely not! It is no trouble at all, and besides, if it is your dream to play the piano, then you must fulfil that dream. And I really don't mind teaching you,' he said. Placing a gentle hand around her shoulder he continued, 'Now, let's go and meet the others.'

Erin followed him into the dining room where his family were already seated at the luxury oval table, a table fit for a king.

Theo's father was the first to speak. 'Theodore, good to see you, son! We've been waiting for you,' he announced with a smile, and rising to his feet, he walked towards them, 'This must be Erin.' Holding out his hand, he said, 'You are very welcome to our household. We've heard so much about you from William. It's great to meet you at last!'

Erin accepted his warm handshake. 'Nice to meet you too, Mr Fitzgerald.'

'Never mind calling me Mr Fitzgerald.' He waved his hand dismissively. 'Feel free to call me Malcolm. Come on take a seat, we're just about to have lunch.' Malcolm returned to his place at the table.

Erin followed Theo and sat next to him.

Turning to Erin, Theo announced, 'This is my mother, Lilian.'

'Hi Lilian.' Erin looked over at the beautiful well-groomed lady who suppressed a smile and nodded.

'Hello Erin, pleased to meet you.'

'And this is my sister, Maxine,' Theo went on.

'Hi Maxine.' Erin greeted her with a shy smile and observed how she looked so much like Theo, in fact both of them looked very much like their mother.

Maxine smiled just like Theo. 'Lovely to meet you.'

'And this is my brother, Samuel, he's a priest,' Theo announced proudly.

A priest! Erin thought.

Theo's brother leaned across the table and held out his hand. His face lit up with a friendly smile. 'Hello Erin, how nice to meet you.'

Erin accepted his handshake. 'And you too, Father Fitzgerald.' She smiled, thinking how much of a striking resemblance he had to his father, both had the same oval faces, grey eyes and wisps of grey hair.

'Erin, do you think you'll like it here in New York?' Father Fitzgerald asked as he began to butter a bread roll.

'Yes I think so, I certainly hope I do. If the longing for

home doesn't bother me too much, I'm sure I will enjoy life here.'

'Sure, I can understand that. I've had my fair share of homesickness. I've spent the last ten years away from home. During that time I was surrounded by great people but there were always periods when I felt so lonely and all I wanted so much in the world was to return to my roots.' Father Fitzgerald popped some bread into his mouth followed by a sip of water.

'Where have you been?' Erin sounded interested.

'Rome. I've spent quite some time in the Vatican. I've just recently moved back to America. I'm now serving in a cathedral about fifteen miles from here.'

'Oh, that's good, at least you're close to your family now. Did you like Rome?' Erin asked politely.

'I did indeed. Rome is a wonderful place and it felt like I had lived there all my life. The Italians are a great bunch but I'm glad to be back, after all, there's no place like home.'

Erin felt her heart sink, she may have only been here a short time but deep down she knew he was right, there certainly is no place like home. In an attempt to redirect her thoughts she smiled and went on, 'I would love to visit Italy, I believe it is such a beautiful country.'

'Oh, you must, and if you ever do get the chance, you must see Rome, you will not be disappointed,' Father Fitzgerald said.

I wish, thought Erin. The truth was she would never be able to afford such a luxury. She'd have more chance of taking a trip to the moon than Italy!

The conversation ended as a round chubby lady entered the dining room with two huge trays of food.

'Thank you, Leonarda.' Malcolm flashed her a cheery, grateful smile as Leonarda placed the silver bowls on the table. A delicious mouthwatering aroma drifted from the dishes as she lifted the lid off each of them. The smell of chicken casserole, beef bourguignon, rice and potatoes, filled the air.

Theo, placing a napkin on his lap, turned to Leonarda. 'This is Erin Coyle, William's sister, do you mind if we call with you after lunch?'

Leonarda flashed Erin a sunshine smile. 'Hello, Miss Coyle. William has been telling me all about you,' she said in a strong Caribbean accent.

'Hello, Leonarda,' Erin replied.

'William has been so excited the last few weeks, he couldn't wait to have you join him out here. I'll look forward to chatting with you after lunch.' Leonarda lifted her trays and walked towards the door. 'I'll leave you all to eat. Enjoy your meal.' She beamed.

'Thank you.' Erin smiled back.

Lunch had finished and Erin had to admit the food had been sublime and the atmosphere warm and welcoming. Just like Theo, they were all friendly and down to earth. The conversation steered towards Ireland and Erin soon learned that the Fitzgerald family had perhaps more relations in Ireland than she had. Most of them lived in and around Galway, a place Erin never had the privilege of visiting, and from Malcolm's description of the West of Ireland, it sounded like a destination worth viewing.

After lunch she thanked them for their hospitality before following Theo to the kitchen.

Inside the kitchen, Leonarda was up to her elbows in flour, working so hard and singing out loud, she hadn't even noticed their presence until she turned round to reach for her rolling pin. 'Oh my!' She clutched her chest leaving floury patches on her apron and shirt. 'You gave me a fright there.' She looked stunned. 'I'm so used to being down here on my own, I never expect to see anyone and when I do, I'm always taken by surprise.' She chuckled.

'Sorry, Leonarda, we didn't mean to creep up on you like that,' Theo said, taking a seat.

'Never worry, my boy. Sit down, Miss Coyle. Would you like something to drink? Tea? Coffee? Or perhaps a brandy, or is it too early for that?' She laughed.

'I'd love a cup of tea,' Erin said, taking a seat on the high stool next to Theo. 'Us Irish love our tea, we can't live without it.'

'I was going to say coffee, but I don't want to put you to too much trouble, so I'll opt for tea as well,' Theo said.

Leonarda pinched his cheeks. 'Nothing's too much bother for my favourite boy. If you want coffee, you'll have coffee!'

In no time she had placed a lovely cup of tea in front of

Erin and a coffee for Theo, accompanied by a plate full of homemade butter shortbread.

'So, Leonarda, how do you fancy giving Erin here some cookery lessons?' Theo asked before biting into a biscuit.

'No,' Erin said, 'I can see you're up to your eyes with work here, you're busy enough, you don't need me looking over your shoulder. I really don't want to trouble you...'

'Trouble?' Leonarda interrupted. Waving a dismissive hand, she said, 'It will be a pleasure. I would love to teach you to cook, and besides, you and I can get to know one another a bit better.'

'Are you sure?' Erin sipped her tea.

'Of course! You can keep me company down here because my girl I can tell you this much, it sure can get pretty lonely in this kitchen every day.'

'That's great, thank you. I'm looking forward to it.' Erin bit into the delicious shortbread. 'This is good, mmm, so good.'

'You're very welcome, Miss Coyle.' Leonarda observed Erin with satisfaction as she began eating another biscuit.

'Oh, please...' Erin caught some crumbs in her hand, 'Call me Erin.'

'Hey, ladies,' Theo slugged back the remainder of his coffee. 'I'll be back in a few minutes, I just want to have a word with my father.'

'Yes sure, take your time and I'll just show Erin how I make my favourite dessert of all, cheesecake!'

After Theo had spoken to his father, Erin had had her first cookery lesson, and Theo had shown her the horses and stables, introduced her to their chauffer and gardener, it was time to go and get that ice-cream he had promised her.

They had popped back into the house to say their goodbyes. Leonarda, following them to the front hall, placed a gentle hand on Erin's shoulder. 'So, my dear, when would you like to call again?'

'Monday,' Theo answered. 'I've arranged with my father for you to start work here on Monday if you fancy it.'

'Fancy it?' Erin couldn't believe her ears. 'What? You mean your dad has given *me* a *job? Here?*'

'Yes.' Theo grinned. 'The housekeeper left two weeks ago due to ill health and her position hasn't been filled yet. My dad's happy for you to fill her boots if you agree to it, so what do you think?'

I think I want to kiss you Theo Fitzgerald, she thought but then again as Erin gazed around the mansion she began to wonder if she could look after all of this.

Theo, reading her thoughts, laughed. 'I know what's going through your mind, you're thinking this house is much too big, right?'

'Well...' Erin replied, 'It is, but, ...it's fine, I'll work hard.'

Theo, placing an arm around her shoulders continued. 'There's no need, we have two housekeepers, one for upstairs and one for downstairs. You'll be glad to know you will be working down here.'

Erin's eyes darted from left to right, the glistening chandeliers, fine artwork, the piano and the *library*! Then there was the warm and friendly Leonarda. My goodness, she felt as if she had landed on her feet big time. Things were definitely looking on the bright side. 'Yes! Yes, I'll take the job!' she cried.

Chapter 8

Patrick, his heart in his throat, bounded down the stairs two at a time. Opening the front door with a flourish, he ran out into the street.

'Help! Help! Somebody *help* me!' he roared frantically as he searched up and down the street looking for someone, anyone.

From the Coyle house across the road Catherine Coyle had just retrieved the envelopes from their postman Matt and was about to bid him goodbye when Patrick's outburst startled them both.

'Patrick, what's the matter?' Catherine called, running down her garden path.

She dashed across the road, with Matt quick on his heels behind her.

'What's wrong, son?' she asked as she arrived next to him.

'My da, my da,' he replied out of breath. 'It's my poor da!'

'What's happened to him?' Matt asked knowing too well he was not going to hear good news.

'My da! Gees my poor da, he's dying!' Patrick cried. 'Can one of you go and get Father Lavery for him, please. I want him to have his last rites!' he cried. 'He's not going to last much longer.'

'Leave it to me, I'll get him for you, I'll just grab my bike.' Matt, without hesitation, retrieved his bicycle from outside the Coyle house and cycled at great speed out of the street.

Patrick stood glued to the pavement in a daze, and shivered like a stray dog.

'Come on, let's get you inside.' Catherine placed a gentle hand on his shoulders. 'Come on, Patrick.'

Inside the bedroom, Catherine found Doctor Brennan packing his stethoscope into his case.

'I'm sorry, Patrick, I wish there was more I could do.' Doctor Brennan's eyes filled with sympathy. 'This is the part of my job that I don't like.' He patted Patrick's back.

'Thank you, Doctor,' Patrick replied in a low voice that was barely audible.

Doctor Brennan shook his head and pressed his lips together. 'I'll leave you now, take care of yourself, Patrick,' he said, his voice soft and caring. 'Goodbye.' He lifted his case and left.

Patrick's eyes filled with tears as he looked upon his father lying there in the bed motionless. Apart from his chest heaving up and down as he took slow breaths, his eyes shut tight and he remained still.

The tears, like boulders, ran down Patrick's cheeks and the shivers now developing into trembles. He looked upon his loving father, the man that had taught him the value of life, the man that had lived a good life, one of always putting others first. A man whose laugh could light up a room and make others smile was now making him want to weep from the very depths of his soul.

All the memories of the past years came flooding back. The visions of riding on his back as a child as they galloped around the living room, pretending they were in the Wild West chasing cowboys. The fishing trips to the River Faughan, one of the most prolific salmon rivers in Ireland, where they watched the fish dance down the river, where a salmon catch was always inevitable and a place where the pair got up to many an adventure. On many an occasion they would throw the fish back into the river, not wanting to end the creature's life.

The tears continued to roll as Patrick knelt down at his father's bedside and took his hand in his.

'I'm not sure if you can hear me, Da, but I'll speak to you as if you can.' He sniffed. 'First of all, I want to say thanks, Da. Thanks for all you have done for me. I know you will be thinking that I'm a sentimental aul fool, but what odds is it?' He tried to joke. 'I'm not just saying this but I couldn't ask for a better aul man than you.'

The tears were by now rapidly beginning to develop into mighty sobs. Patrick tried his best to compose himself. The tears that he fought back lately set themselves free, and like prisoners escaping from jail, they wasted no time in getting away, rolling at such speed down his cheeks until the tears turned again into sobs, huge manly sobs.

Catherine swallowed hard and placed her hands on

Patrick's shoulders, 'That's it, let it out, son. It's good to have a cry,' she said rubbing his shoulders. 'Go on, let it all go, you're allowed to.'

Father Lavery, who had just entered the room, pulled his little bottle of oil from his pocket and opened his prayer book. Placing one hand on Jim's forehead, he began to administer the last rites of the Catholic Church.

Patrick couldn't lift his head. He tried to control himself to listen to the priest's soft, soothing voice as he prayed with such reverence.

Father Lavery placed the oil of Chrism on Jim's forehead and making the sign of the cross, he whispered the necessary prayers under his breath.

Patrick looked up, his bloodshot eyes met the friendly eyes of their devoted parish priest. 'Thank you, Father,' he whispered. 'Thank you so much.'

Father Lavery smiled sympathetically, 'Not at all, you're welcome, Patrick. I'm glad I was called. Jim is a strong faithful man. He deserves to have a priest available for his final time. He has always been a devoted man of God. He never let Him down and it is only right that God should allow him this privilege. The man above is probably preparing your father's banquet as we speak, getting ready for all his earthly treasures that Jim gained here whilst he walked this earth.'

'Oh, in that case those up above will need a big treasure chest! Are you sure heaven has one big enough?' Patrick forced a smile.

Father Lavery nodded. 'Now you're talking,' he agreed.

'He was so good to me. This man has taught me so much. His knowledge and his example has enlightened the eyes of my mind. He used to say, "If you have no morals, you have nothing" and "Treat others like you would like them treat you".' He sighed at the memory. 'Didn't you, Da?' Patrick stroked his father's head. '"Always do your best" that was another of your favourite sayings.' Patrick patted the bony hand of his father's and swallowed. Trying not to cry again, he continued, 'But my favourite of all was, "Listen to your conscience, if that voice in your head tells you it's wrong, then it's wrong".'

'True words,' Catherine remarked. 'He was a great neighbour and friend, anything we needed, he was always the first to help.'

'He used to take me everywhere with him. If I wasn't found to be out playing with your Erin, I was found tagging along with the aul man here. Do you remember, Da?' Patrick paused again to stroke his father's head while the room fell silent.

'Would you like to join me in praying the rosary?' Father Lavery reached into his pocket and pulled out a pair of brown wooden beads. 'Jim was very fond of this special prayer and I know he would be happy for us to say it now.'

As the three gathered closer around Jim's bedside to recite the rosary, Patrick held his father's hand and watched with a heavy heart as his father's breathing developed into shallow, laboured breaths.

By the time they reached the third decade, Jim was barely breathing at all, and in fact, Patrick had thought his father was gone until suddenly he seemed to come back to life again as a shudder of a breath erupted from his chest, evidently not wanting to leave and clinging on to this world for as long as possible.

They finished the prayers, Patrick made the sign of the cross on his father's forehead and gently kissed his cheek.

'Da, I know you're holding on for me but I'll be okay,' Patrick whispered, 'It's okay, Da, go to your place of rest, you can go, I allow you,' he said, stroking his father's cheek. A burning sensation gripped his chest. 'You don't have to keep fighting it. Remember what you said only weeks ago, I'm a man of steel.' Patrick tried to force a smile. But the smile faded again as he witnessed his father taking another pause and secretly he wanted to scream at him not to go.

This time the pause went on and on, showing no signs of exhaling. Jim's head lowered, his final breath just taken.

Patrick's own head dropped as a waterfall of tears came flowing down his cheeks.

'A man of steel, eh? What an awful year. What a terribly awful year, losing the two people I love more than anything else in the world. What am I going to do without Erin and my da?' he wept bitterly.

In the silent moments, the past came flooding back again. The swing Jim made from an old rope and piece of wood that he tied to their two cherry blossom trees, remained to this day at the bottom of the garden. Erin and Patrick had spent hour after hour taking turns on this plaything.

The many hours he had spent with his father playing marbles against the shed, and then there was the draughts board, his father's favourite game of all. Patrick tried desperately to beat him but his father was just too good, in fact Patrick could not remember anyone ever winning draughts against his old man. "You'll never beat the master!" Jim would sing as they played their game for hour after hour. Jim was right about that, he certainly was the master of this sport.

'Who's going to be the master now, Da? You'll never beat the master! You'll never beat the mast...er,' Patrick sang aloud and, choking on the boulder that had suddenly sprang into his throat, he continued. 'There... will ... be no mast...er, Da, I...I don't think anyone in Derry will be as g..good as a player as you, Da! The best draughts player in Derry, that's what you were!'

The death of his mother flashed into his thoughts causing his heart to twist a little tighter if that was at all possible. Whilst Patrick and Erin played hide-and-seek and his father chopped some firewood, his mother collapsed. His father returned to find her dead on the kitchen floor. Patrick barged through the back door to tell his mother that he had just caught his fifth bumble bee in a jar. He stood in confusion for a few minutes as he gazed down at his beautiful mother, tumbling curls of blonde hair draped around her face, blue lips, grey skin and lying there lifeless. Looking to his father for an explanation he witnessed a sombre expression on his face and knew instantly in his young mind that this was not good.

'Wake up, Mammy!' Patrick dropped the jar to the floor with a crash. The captured creatures made a bee-line for the open door. 'WAKE UP!' he knelt beside her and shouted, but her eyes were already open and she was still not moving. Patrick nudged her a little. 'Mammy! Mammy! Get up! WAKE UP, MAMMY!'

His father's strong arms folded around his waist, lifted him and carried him out of the kitchen. Patrick remembered kicking his legs to and fro to free himself from his grip, 'I want my mammy! I want my mammy!' he sobbed.

Jim carried the child out of sight over the road and into Catherine Coyle's arms. He whispered something in her ear and told Patrick to be good before promising to pick him up soon.

For months Patrick cried his heart out each night, sobbing himself to sleep night after night. He missed his precious mother and life didn't seem fair. What was fair about an eight year old child being left without a mother? She was gone from his life in a flash, gone so cruelly and so sudden. Jim would hold his son each night and rock him to sleep. He put on a brave face for the sake of his child, as he faced the world rearing a young boy on his own and the challenges that came with that. Patrick was wise enough to know that behind that smile, there was a heartbroken widower and nothing in the world could mend a shattered heart.

Patrick wiped his flushed cheeks and sniffed. 'I love you, Da. If you can hear me wherever you are, I love you with all my heart.' Stroking Jim's hand, he went on, 'I didn't get the opportunity to hold my mother's hand and tell her how I felt, I'm glad I can sit here with you because I owe it to you big time. Thank you, Da. Thank you, Da, for everything, but most of all, thank you for being there for me when I needed you. I love you more than you could ever know. Rest in peace, my father, my friend.'

Chapter 9

The two nights of waking his father had taken its toll on Patrick. The endless stream of people coming to say their final farewells to his father or coming to show their support to him, was overwhelming and exhausting. The countless cups of tea and triangle sandwiches were enough to put him off them for life.

The neighbours had been great, everyone in the street had pulled together, helping to get the house prepared for the wake, making pots of stew, beef casserole and of course *triangle* sandwiches. Their hugs, handshakes and sympathetic words were comforting but right now as he prepared to close the lid of the coffin containing his wonderful father, right now, he needed and missed Erin more than ever. Holding back the tears, Patrick leaned over the coffin and gave his father a final kiss on the cheek before the undertaker lifted the heavy lid and placed it down firmly on the casket.

'Let me secure it,' Patrick suggested. 'After all, it is the final thing I will do for him.'

Once the lid was locked, Patrick tapped gently on the polished pine. 'Farewell, Da. I'll miss ye my aul man.'

Outside, a huge group of neighbours, friends and relatives gathered to walk the short distance from the Bogside to the Long Tower Church, with Father Lavery leading the procession, many clutching their rosary beads and bundled up against the elements.

The light drizzle that had fallen on and off all morning was quickly developing into a downpour, drenching the mourners and soaking their clothes and hair. Patrick felt thankful for the rain, at least it would disguise his tears.

No matter how many people accompanied him to pay their respects for his father, he still felt like the loneliest man in Derry. Patrick, simmering with grief, blinked both the rain and tears from his eyes as he followed the cortege into the church grounds with the others close behind.

Inside the church, mourners shook the rain from their hair and quickly removed their wet coats and jackets before taking their seats on the long wooden benches.

Father Lavery began the service, the congregation sat quietly and listened to the priest. Outside the rain continued to pelt against the stained glass windows.

Patrick's stomach did a quick lurch. There was a nasty feeling generating in the pit of his tummy, like blue mould on bread, but regardless of how he felt, he aimed to focus on every detail of the mass. The holy sacrifice of the mass was particularly important to his father and he therefore wanted to show God his respect on today above all days. In his heart he felt like he wanted to cry out but he promised himself he would keep it together during the service for his father. His old man wouldn't have wanted him to be upset, after all he was going home, home to heaven to be joined once again with his beautiful wife. Therefore Patrick had decided he would remain as strong as possible on the outside whilst inside he felt as if his soul was crumbling like a dried up autumn leaf.

When the door of his home was closed later on, and all the friends and family were gone, he could let it all out, cry and sob in secret. Yes, he would let it all out later, but for now there would be no tears in the church, no dramas. He would hold himself together and carry on as best he could.

After the service concluded they made their way to the burial place. Row upon row of tombstones protruded from the earthly soil like teeth. Some shining as the rain washed the dust from their surface, many crumbling from years of harsh weather, others overgrown and unkempt. There amongst them was a freshly excavated opening, waiting patiently for its new resident. The grave was dug in preparation to lay Jim to rest with his beloved wife. Patrick's gaze fell on the modest weather-beaten headstone, *Sarah Brogan, beloved wife and mother, died 28 July 1897*, it read. Patrick remembered that fateful day well, a day that caused a piece of his own heart to die also.

The cemetery was steeped in its usual eerie stillness and the smell of mud and moss filled the air. Patrick stood, under billowing clouds about to give birth to another serious downpour, and watched quietly as the casket was lowered into the ground. With a deep sadness and a heavy heart he observed his devoted father being lowered further and further into the muddy opening.

A damp wind stirred, ripping through the silence and shaking the ancient trees lining the graveyard, causing the ravens nesting in the gnarled branches to screech in dispute. A lonely rabbit, like a sculptured statue, sat perched in the shelter of the trees and watched wide-eyed.

Father Lavery began sprinkling holy water into the grave before reciting the rosary.

Overhead the heavily pregnant clouds grew darker and Patrick figured the downpour was only minutes away from pelting down from the heavens. More hugs, handshakes and kisses from each mourner with their sympathetic words as one by one the gathering came forward to say their goodbyes to him before leaving.

The air became heavier and everyone knew only too well the rain that had washed the streets earlier was about to return imminently. As expected, it came back with a vengeance, falling fast and furious as the clouds above ripped apart. Everyone was aware that the hilly cemetery was exposed to the tough elements; when the wind blew here, there was no escaping its harsh howl. The wind whistled with anger through the trees and the rain ricocheted off the exposed casket and caused the ground below their feet to become muddy and slippery. Without hesitation, the little rabbit hurried for shelter, as did the mourners.

Catherine and John Coyle were the last to step forward. They both embraced Patrick together, getting soaked to the bone but neither of them minded.

'You're always welcome in our house,' John whispered. 'You have forever been like a son to us and you know if there is anything you need, or anything we can do for you, please let us know.'

Patrick wanted to scream out from the depths of his heart that he wanted their daughter back. He longed more than ever to have Erin's arms around him, holding him and comforting him right now. God only knew how much he needed her today more than ever.

The brave face and strong front that Patrick had put on and maintained during the wake and funeral, now dissolved before them as he trembled and released a mighty sob.

'I…I…I've lost them. I…I've lost them both,' he sobbed before looking into the open grave, his tears fused with the rain. 'They're gone, they're gone now, for…for…forever.'

Catherine nodded, she filled with grief at the sight of this young pitiful man. Oh how she longed to make everything better for him. If anyone had had their fair share of heartache, it had been Patrick. Such a good young man doesn't deserve this pain.

'And…' he swallowed hard. 'do you want to know something, John? I…I've lost the only girl I've ever loved. I'll never love another like…like I love your Erin. I've lost her, John. How could I have let her go? I wanted to marry her! God knows I wanted to marry her,' he cried, opening his heart. 'My da said I need to tell her, but what good is it if I tell her now? She's gone, for crying out loud! She's gone, our beautiful Erin's gone,' he wept bitterly, his sobs echoing around the headstones.

'Listen to me, boy, your father was right, you must tell her how you feel regardless of whether she's here or over there. You have my blessing if you want to propose to my daughter.

Tell her, Patrick. It's not too late you know.' John patted him on the back. 'Nothing would make me happier than to have you as part of our family.'

'No,' Patrick nodded and wiped his tearstained cheeks. 'It *is* too late.'

Catherine looked deep into his eyes. 'It is not! It is never too late, trust me, I know my daughter and I have a feeling she feels the same way about you. Believe me now when I say this, I would be over the moon to have you as a son-in-law in our family! We love you, Patrick, and I'm sure our Erin does too.'

Patrick felt his heart ready to burst for love for Catherine and John, right now they were the closest he had to a family, oh how much he desired to be part of the Coyle clan. Patrick smiled and wiped his eyes. 'I guess I've lost everything else in my life, what else have I got to lose? You're right! I'll tell her and I'll ask her to be my wife! If I have to go to the moon and back, I promise, I'll marry Erin Coyle!'

Chapter 10

Despite the porridge being a bit too sweet, as a result of Erin pouring just a little more honey in than usual, she continued to eat it. For as long as she could remember, her mother always taught her not to waste food, she detested this, explaining that so many people all over the world were going to bed hungry and waking up even hungrier. Recalling her mother's words now as she looked into the unappetising bowl, she sighed and forced another spoonful of the horrible substance into her mouth.

'Erin!' William came bounding into the room. 'You're not going to believe this!' he gasped.

Erin, gazing up from her breakfast, knew instantly from the pale look on William's face that he was not going to announce good news. 'What is it? What's wrong, William?' she asked pushing the revolting porridge to the side.

William, hair dishevelled and now looking paler than the whitewashed walls, waved the morning newspaper in one hand and a telegram in the other. Collapsing into a chair at the table he took a deep breath. 'It's…it's…' he stared down at the newspaper.

'Oh for goodness' sake, what is it? Just tell me, you're scaring me, William, what the heck is going on?' She struggled to hide her impatience.

Looking up he replied slowly, 'Erin, I've got some….some …bad news.' His face soured.

'I've figured that much!' Erin could feel her heart ready to explode within her chest. 'What is going on?' she leaned across the table.

'First of all, Patrick's father, Jim, has died, I just got this today.' He waved the telegram in the air.

'Jim?' she asked, shaking her head and sinking back into her chair. 'Jim's dead?' She cast him a nervous glance.

'I'm afraid so,' William replied, drawing in a ragged breath.

'Poor Jim, my goodness he didn't last too long. I knew he was ill but I never thought for a moment he was that ill! And poor Patrick. He'll be devastated. He loved his father so much, they were so close.'

Erin dipped her head, made the sign of the cross and began to recite a silent prayer for Jim's soul and a few for Patrick, for God knew he'd need all the help from heaven as possible. Her heart filled with sadness at the thought of him back home in Derry all alone, no parents, no job and his best friend here in New York. Right now she desperately longed to be able to run across the street to him, put her arms around him and tell him everything would be okay. Most of all she wanted to tell him that she was there for him, except the bitter truth was she was nowhere near him, she was miles away when he needed her the most.

She felt the tears well up in her eyes and before she knew it they began to roll down her cheeks. She missed him terribly and right now she longed for him more than anything.

It was hard to imagine how quickly the last few months had flown by, gone in a flash. Her days had been filled with working at the Fitzgerald's family home, learning to cook with Leonarda, playing the piano and spending any free time walking in the park with Theo. She barely had time to get homesick lately and the harsh truth was even less time to think about Patrick. An uncomfortable feeling tugged at her heart, how could she have pushed him to the back of her mind? Thoughts of him would briefly enter her mind, but with each day here in New York filled with all sorts of new adventures, these thoughts didn't last long. She felt ashamed to admit they didn't linger as they had done during the early days of arriving here. This made her feel selfish. A powerful guilty feeling overwhelmed her and she let out a small sob.

Observing the effect Jim's death had on his sister, William's blood ran cold, the worst news was yet to come. How he was going to break it to her, he wasn't sure.

Wiping her eyes, Erin asked, 'How did he die, William? Was it his lungs? Please don't tell me he died suddenly.' She remembered the grief poor Patrick had to endure after the sudden departing of his dear mother. For him to suffer the sudden death of his father also just didn't bear thinking about.

'No,' William said, his voice a mere whisper. 'No, it wasn't sudden. Mother says in the telegram that she and Father Lavery stayed with Patrick until his father slipped away peacefully shortly after they had prayed the rosary.'

'Oh thank God for that! Thank God they were with him.' Erin sniffed. 'Oh would you look at me, you're probably wondering why I'm crying like this.'

'No, don't be silly, I know how much Jim meant to you,' William said, his tone soft and soothing.

Erin nodded, 'Aye, he meant a lot to me. The thing is Jim was such a good man, he treated me like I was his own daughter.' Erin gazed out the window in a daydream as the many years spent in the Brogan household came flashing back.

'He did indeed,' William said.

Staring out at the glittering wet pavements below, Erin sighed. 'He was the best at playing draughts. He taught me how to play, but I could never beat him. Actually, coming to think of it, I can't remember anyone winning against him for that matter.' Erin smiled at the fond memory. 'He would always make us jam sandwiches and pour us a glass of milk as we played at their kitchen table. Patrick would use the leftover crumbs, smeared in a little jam, to entice bees and wasps into his old jam jar. Oh he loved capturing those insects but I hated him collecting them. I was too afraid of getting stung, but nothing feared Patrick. He enjoyed watching the furry creatures climb about and buzz around in a frantic attempt to escape. Up close you could see the hairy legs of the bees or the ugly shell of a wasp. After a while, his mother would make him take the jar outside and free the captives. Off they flew, not wasting a single second, to their freedom again, out around the fresh air or to dance about the flowerbeds where they belonged.

'Jim loved playing the guitar. It was a real treat to the ear. He was great playing the strings, a fine guitarist. After his wife died, he spent many a lonely hour, playing on the strings to pass the time.'

Turning to William she asked, 'Do you know Patrick is very good…on…the…guit..ar.' She stopped. She had been that lost looking out the window and chatting about the past, she hadn't realised William was crying. 'William?'

William wiped his eyes and sniffed, 'Oh, Erin, there's more bad news,' he said. Unfolding the New York Times, he pointed at the headlines. 'Read this.' He handed her the newspaper.

'Belfast's Mighty Titanic Sunk!' Erin read aloud the headline screaming from the cover. Shaking her head she continued to scan the paper, 'The Titanic, the great ship that the world was waiting for has met a fateful end on its first voyage. The doomed ship hit an iceberg, killing an estimated fifteen hundred as they plunged to their deaths in the icy cold water of the North Atlantic ocean.' Erin couldn't believe her eyes. Glancing up at William, she said, 'What an awful tragedy! An estimated fifteen hundred people are dead, maybe more!' she repeated in disbelief.

'It's shocking!' William replied.

'Oh, may God have mercy on their souls!' Erin cried out. Covering her mouth with her hand, she went on, 'Oh William, what an awful way to die.' A chill ran up her spine. 'Those poor people, freezing to their death like that in the icy, cold darkness, oh how horrible, William. This is just awful news.'

William fell silent as the words he knew would break

her heart caught in his throat.

Watching his reaction Erin knew only too well that her brother wasn't quite finished with the bad news. Getting up of her chair she made her way round the table to him. 'Tell me, William.' She grabbed him by the shoulders. 'Why are you looking at me like that? We don't know someone on that ship, do we?' she asked, her eyes wide with horror. 'Please don't tell me we know someone!' she cried.

'No, no... at least I don't ... think so. I'm sorry I have to be the one to deliver so much bad reports today.'

'What else do you have to tell me?' she asked feeling lightheaded, her flawless complexion paling.

He raised his head to look at her. 'It's our da. I'm sorry to have to tell you, he's critically ill.'

Chapter 11

The screech and squawking from the hungry birds on the rooftop had woken Patrick from his sleep.

'It's only six o'clock,' he grumbled. Turning in his bed and wrapping the blankets around him, he shut his eyes tight.

Two hours later he was still awake. The last few hours he had spent tossing and turning and pulling the blanket over his head but it was no good, he just could not get back to sleep. He tried covering his ears and even shouting aloud for them to 'Piss off!' Again, not surprising, this didn't work either.

'Darn crows!' he yelled, 'I'm going to sort you out today once and for all!' He buried his head back under the blankets. 'The cheek of them nesting in my chimney,' he groaned as he shut his eyes tight and desperately tried to nod off again. His body was crying out for some rest. Three weeks had now passed since he buried his father and he still woke up regularly in the middle of the night, just like he had done when Jim was here, waking up to check on him to make sure he was okay. Patrick would wander into his father's room in his groggy half-awake state and find the bed empty. The sight of the unoccupied room would at once bring him back to earth with a bang as he realised that his gentle father was gone, gone forever. A vacant bed that would never again be filled. He would rub his tired eyes and make his way back to his own bed. Sometimes he would cry in the stillness of the night, other times he would fall asleep and enter into a land of dreams, a land where both his father and Erin were a part of everyday life. Those beautiful peaceful dreams were always interrupted by the rowdy crows and their gang.

Patrick had dozed over again only to be woken once more. A glance at the alarm clock revealed that it was only twenty past eight. He felt his chest swell with anger as he realised he had been sleeping for less than twenty minutes.

'Right that's it!' He fired back the blankets and swung his legs from the bed. 'I mean it, today will be the last day those noisy birds wake me!' he said as he wriggled into his robe and retrieved his house slippers from under the bed. 'Today is eviction day!'

Downstairs he poured himself a steaming hot mug of conker-brown tea and stirred two sugars into it. As he moved the spoon around the mug his father's voice sprang into his mind. His dad loved a good cup of tea and would often look over to Patrick, and with a twinkle in his eyes, he would say "A wee cup of tea, go, go, go, two sugars, stir one to the left and one to the right, go, go, go".

Patrick would at once head for the kitchen. Calling over his shoulder, he would joke, "I'll stir you to the left and to the right!".

He continued to rattle the spoon around the cup and gazed out the window into the backyard. 'Gee, Da, how much I wish you were here now having me make you a cup of tea. I would gladly stir one to the left and one to the right,' he whispered to himself.

A big, slick, black crow landed on the washing line. It

turned its head towards the kitchen window and fixed its beady eyes on Patrick.

Patrick stuck out his tongue at the annoying creature. 'Can't a man get a decent night's sleep without you lot battering my rooftops?' he barged. 'Shoo.' He waved his hand. 'Go on, shove off.'

The cheeky crow sat there unfazed and continued staring in at him as it lazily ruffled its glossy feathers.

Another memory of his father entered his mind. Jim detested wasting food. He often fed the birds their leftovers and scraps of old bread.

Patrick smiled to himself. He knew if his father was here right now he would be mooching through the cupboards in search of something to feed it. He would also have a good old laugh at him for barging a defenseless creature and a bigger laugh at him for talking to himself. He could just picture him saying, "The poor wee thing can't hear you! It's no good you yelling at it unless you can master the skill of crow language!".

'Well, Mr Crow,' Patrick removed the spoon and pointed it at the bird, 'as soon as I finish my brekkie, I'm going to find myself a good chimney sweep and have some wire mesh fixed to it so that you can take your family and your mates off to some tree to nest in like birds are supposed to do! Or if you like, you can always find yourself some posh house on the Culmore Road. That sounds good, and while you're at it, get yourself fixed up with a *posh* bird. Now shoo!' He waved his spoon. This time the bird, ruffled its feathers, spread its wings and flew off, not too far mind you, just back on the rooftop where it came from.

Patrick poured himself a top up of tea from the teapot, cut himself a thick slice of bread and smeared a dollop of strawberry jam on it. Sitting himself down at the kitchen table, he lifted the notebook and pencil and read over what he had scribbled down the night before. Unhappy with the content, he ripped the page out, scrunched it up and tossed it with the others into the waste bin by the kitchen door.

Taking a bite of his bread and a gulp of tea, he started a new page and began to write. This time strongminded to get it right, after all he hadn't much choice in the matter, he was running out of paper.

'How can this be so difficult?' he said puffing out his cheeks and dropping his pencil. Running his hand through his thick hair he took a deep breath and lifted up his pencil again, determined to get on with the job at hand.

Gulping back the remainder of his tea, he sat back minutes later, happy to have finished the letter at last. He folded it, placed it in an envelope and licked the seal. 'That's it, no going back now,' he whispered, placing the envelope into his pocket and feeling his heart thrash against his ribcage. He hoped he was doing the right thing.

After the trip to the post office, he found Marty, the local chimney sweep. Marty was up to his eyes in soot cleaning the chimneys at Tillies factory.

'I need a favour, my aul mate,' Patrick yelled up at him.

'What's up, Pat?' Marty called down.

After explaining his current situation as best he could, he watched as Marty smirked and began descending his ladder.

'If I'd a shilling for every time I heard that yarn, I'd be a rich man.' He grinned as he stepped off the ladder, revealing a dazzling set of teeth that glowed a brilliant white against his blackened, sooty face. 'I wish I could help you out but ye see I've a schedule, I'm really, really busy today, mate. It'll have to do for a day a two.'

'A day or two! Oh please, surely my job is more urgent. C'mon, abandon your agenda. I'll pay you well and I'll fix you a few pints of Guinness later tonight. How does that sound?'

Marty, fond of a nice pint of stout, didn't need much more persuasion. 'Well in that case, you're on. I'll be down to your gaff as soon as I finish here.'

'Thanks, mate. I owe you one!' Patrick threw him an encouraging wink.

'No, I think you owe me at least two!' Marty waggled his finger, 'Or if ye like, ye can always make it three or four.'

Entertained he raised an eyebrow, 'Of course, two it is. Don't push your luck, mate. I'll look forward to it, believe me I could be doing with a few myself. Thanks again, see you soon!' Patrick waved.

'No worries. It won't take me long to sort out your problem, after all sorting out birds is my specialty!' he called after him. Grinning he wiped his dirty hands on his even dirtier trousers and whispered under his breath, 'oh, how easy it is to earn a few pints!'

It took Marty no time to get cleared up, and within an hour, he had set up for business to sort out Patrick's unwanted intruders.

'Eviction time.' Patrick smiled as he watched Marty carefully carry a nest down from the roof.

'It's a good job there's no young ones in this or else I would have had no choice but to leave it,' Marty warned as he descended down the steps. 'I wouldn't have disturbed a nest with little ones in it, it wouldn't be right,' he said, stepping off the ladder.

'Aye of course, I didn't think of that,' Patrick gazed into the hollow nest, 'Thankfully it's empty because I'm not joking you, I don't think I'd have lasted another night with those squatters.' He grinned.

'I'll tell you, there'll be some disappointed birds here tonight, they had some view of the Bogside from up there.' Marty chuckled.

'Well they can find somewhere else!' Patrick replied, his arms folded across his chest. 'My da used to feed the birds every morning. He'd throw out all sorts of scraps of food. Is it any wonder they took up residence up there.'

'Aye well that will explain why they nested here.' Marty replied gazing over Patrick's shoulder, he continued, 'I'm just looking at that cherry blossom.' He pointed to the huge tree rooted at the far end of the garden. 'Did you cut the branches on that lately? It looks a bit bare to me.'

'Actually I did. After my da passed away, I needed

something to keep me busy, and as the limbs were getting a bit out of control, I thought I'd tidy it up a bit.'

Marty nodded, 'Aye I would guess you tidied up their home too. The chances are they had been nesting in that and you disturbed them.'

'Gee, you could be right,' Patrick agreed, 'I never thought about that.'

'You say your da had been feeding them?' Marty asked raising his eyebrows.

'Aye, all the time,' Patrick replied squinting his eyes against the sunlight.

'Crows are considered the most intelligent of all birds. They'll nest close to where they can find food so my guess would be that is the reason why they set up in your chimney,' Marty suggested as he ascended back up the ladder and onto the roof.

'So it's my da's fault, then,' Patrick called up after him. 'He really will be having a good laugh at me from the heavens above.' He smiled at the thought of it.

'Aye and just think, he'll have a *birds-eye-view* from up there.' Marty smirked. 'Right, I'll get this swept now and a wire mesh fixed over the chimney top and that should be your problem sorted.'

'Good on you, thanks a million.' Patrick beamed up as he watched Marty get back to business. The next second, without warning, a great big gooey lump landed in his eye.

'What the heck? Uuurgh!'

'What's wrong?' Marty yelled.

'Bird shit!' Patrick winced as he flicked the goo away.

Marty beamed down, 'Looks like they've left you a wee leaving present!' he burst into a fit of laughing.

'Aye, darn crows. I'll be glad to see the back of them. Make sure that wire mesh is well secured!'

Chapter 12

'Oh, that smells good.' Leonarda, peering over Erin's shoulder, sniffed the strong aroma of garlic and onions sizzling in the pan.

Erin, stirring the contents, grinned, 'I hope it tastes as good.'

'It will, it will, Erin, never worry. All will be fine. Don't forget you're under my watchful eye.' Leonarda gave her a playful tap on the shoulder.

'I must admit, I'm really enjoying these cookery lessons,' Erin said.

'Me too,' Leonarda replied.

'I want you to know I appreciate your time.' Erin looked over her shoulder and beamed.

'You are very welcome, my dear. It's a delight to spend time with you!' Leonarda smiled, her coffee-coloured skin glowed as she grinned.

Erin couldn't help but notice how white her teeth looked against her skin tone.

'Now, add the cumin, cayenne and some paprika, then cook for a further minute,' Leonarda advised.

Erin, reaching for the jars, did as instructed and tossed the onions and garlic around the pan until they were coated with the spices.

'Perfect! Next I want you to stir in the tomato puree and

sprinkle a little oregano.' Peering over Erin's shoulder, Leonarda smiled with satisfaction. 'That's it, now fill your nostrils with that! Mmmm, it sure does smell good if I may say so myself.'

'It does indeed,' Erin replied, a smile of satisfaction spread on her face.

'Finally, add the chopped tomatoes, kidney beans and add it all to the water, bring it to the boil and then simmer for twenty minutes.'

Leonarda's conker-brown eyes sparkled in her round chubby face as she watched with approval how Erin transferred the contents from the pan into a pot of water.

Soon the kitchen filled with the delightful smells emanating from the pot.

Erin, grateful to rest her feet, sat down at the table whist the soup simmered. A tempting bowl of red apples sat in the centre of the huge table. Erin, feeling a bit hungry, reached across and took one. 'Thank you again, Leonarda,' she said as she bit into the juicy fruit. 'Sometimes I feel it's unfair taking up all your time, I know how busy you are.'

'Nonsense, nonsense, my dear.' Leonarda waved her hand dismissively. 'Besides, you've just made me a pot of American red bean soup for today's lunch!' She pulled out a chair opposite Erin and sat down. 'All I have to do is prepare a chicken pie for tonight's dinner, which I'll do in no time. I already have the vegetables peeled and prepared and I have the breads made for today, so I was thinking I'll give you a hand for a few hours.'

Erin took another bite from her apple. The thought of her list of tasks for the day ahead felt exhausting just thinking about them. She knew she could really be doing with the hand today. 'Okay, but only if you're sure you can spare the time, I don't want to keep you back.'

'A bit of housework will do me a world of good. I need something to get rid of this belly.' She held rolls of her stomach between her hands and wobbled it about. 'Too much of the good food and not enough housework.' She released a hearty laugh. 'Perhaps I should have applied for the housekeeper job, then I could have a skinny frame like yours.' She laughed again and the lines around her eyes deepened.

'I know, as soon as I become the greatest cook in New York … actually,' Erin held up a finger, 'I'll make that the second best cook.'

'That sounds better.' Leonarda smiled.

'Yes, once I'm the second best cook, we can then switch places. You can do the cleaning and I'll sort out the dinners. How does that sound?' she teased as she took another crunching bite from her apple.

'What? Are you mad, and risk having an expanded waistline like mine? Then again, you could be doing with a bit of meat on those bones of yours, perhaps it's not a bad idea after all.' Leonarda chuckled.

Erin finished her apple and dumped her core into the rubbish bin before checking on how her soup was cooking. 'I know how to get some meat on my bones,' she replied as she stirred the soup, 'you can always ask me to sample your cakes before serving, especially those chocolatey, creamy ones, do you know those ones I don't like but just eat to keep you happy,' she joked, her mouth watering at the thought of them.

Leonarda's face brightened. 'I know exactly the ones you're talking about!' She laughed again. 'Okay that's a deal,' she teased. 'You know, Erin, it's great to witness you happy again. You've been so down in the dumps the last few weeks. It was breaking my heart to see such pain on that pretty face of yours.'

'Aye,' Erin sighed, replacing the lid securely on the pot. She stood, folded her arms and leaned against the counter. 'It was an awful shock when William told me my dad was unwell. My heart felt like it was going to explode with pain. God only knows how much I love my father, I love all my family but my dad and I have a special bond. If anything had have happened to him, I'd jump on the first boat out of here! Imagine if my dad had have *died*? When I heard he had pneumonia, I felt sick to the pit of my stomach. Honestly I thought he was a goner for sure.'

'Yeah, I can imagine. I will never forget the heartache I felt as a child when I lost both my parents within the space of six months. Losing a parent is the most hardest and biggest loss of all.'

Erin nodded. Thoughts of Patrick entered her mind. Poor Patrick losing his mother so young and now his father too must be so hard for him. Sitting back down at the table she took a deep breath and sniffed as her eyes brimmed with tears.

'You know, Leonarda, I just wanted to crawl into my bed, hide under the blankets and cry myself to death, if that is at all possible. Actually, that is exactly what I did for the first two days. I stayed in bed crying like a baby and not eating a morsel of food until William came bounding in with the telegram with the news from home to say that he was alive and well. I thanked God from the bottom of my heart that my father had pulled through. I couldn't believe it, I really did imagine that he would have succumbed to the infection, honestly, Leonarda, I don't know many folk back home that survived that awful illness. I can tell you this, my father may have been alive and well but at that moment I certainly wasn't.'

'I'm sure you weren't, you poor girl, put to all that trauma.' Leonarda nodded vigorously.

'Yes, I can tell you. I jumped off the bed and threw my arms around William. I gave him the biggest hug for bringing me the great news that my father was alive. At the same time, I felt so guilty, there was Patrick, back home without his father and there were so many other families out there affected by the Titanic tragedy. So many of those would not receive such good news regarding their own loved ones and perhaps never receive a body. I cried from the depths of my soul for them all.'

'Indeed, you are right, so many poor families were not so fortunate. What an awful fate for those on board that tragically lost their lives. It's the biggest death rate on a ship that I have ever heard of in my life and I hope to God and pray I will never hear of anything like it again,' Leonarda said, her face portraying a deep sorrowful expression.

'I hate to think about it. It sends shivers up my spine,' Erin said before jumping off her chair. 'Right, let's change the subject before I start bawling my eyes out. I'm going to make myself a cup of tea before I begin my work, would you like a coffee?'

Leonarda nodded, 'Yes, I would love a nice strong cup.'

For the next few minutes Erin made herself a cup of tea and a coffee for Leonarda. She carried the cups and a plate of shortbread over to the table and sat back down.

'So, Leonarda, how long have you worked here?' she asked as she sipped her tea.

'I'm here just over thirty years. I should be retiring soon but I really don't know what I'd do with my day if I did give up my job.'

Erin smiled, 'You like it here don't you?' She eyed her with interest.

'I do indeed, don't you?' she asked, peering over her cup of coffee.

'Yes. Yes, I do but I don't think I can see myself working here as long as you. I must admit I do still think about home.' Erin felt her heart flip.

'And there's that guy Patrick you had told me about, do you still think about him?' Leonarda questioned before taking a bite of the delicious shortbread.

Erin nodded, a sad expression took over her face.

Taking a slow sip of her tea, she replied, 'I will admit I do. If I'm being honest I do still miss him from time to time.'

'I guess that is only natural,' Leonarda agreed.

'I felt so bad, when I learned of his father's death. I sent him a short telegram; I was too troubled at the time to write him a proper letter. I've been meaning to, but the truth is, I just don't know what to say to him, my heart breaks for him every time I think of him.' She blew out her cheeks and shrugged. 'Imagine not knowing what to say to someone that has been part of my life for so long. Oh it's so hard, Leonarda.' Erin reached for a biscuit.

'No it's not, it's easy, just write from the heart. No lie or weak words will ever come from here.' Leonarda pointed to her chest. 'Only the truth comes from within.'

Erin let out a small laugh, 'Yes, you're right but that's the problem, if I write from the heart then I should be telling him how much I...' Sighing she continued, 'how much I love him.'

Leonarda narrowed her eyes, 'What's so wrong with that? What are you afraid of?'

Blowing out her cheeks again, Erin gazed into the distance. 'It's not as easy as that.'

'You're in a bit of a stew, I can tell. I know what you're scared of, it's clear you also have feelings for our young Theo. Could I be correct?'

Erin's eyes widened. 'What?'

'Oh, come on, my dear, you cannot hide your feelings from me, I might not be a spring chicken anymore but I'm a wise old bird; I can recognise love when I see it!'

Erin could feel the heat rising from her neck and whoosh over her cheeks. Was it really that obvious? Was Theo aware of it also? 'I…am..' she stammered. Leonarda had taken her by surprise. She just couldn't string the words together to answer her.

'Listen to me, Erin.' Leonarda reached across the table and stroked her hand. 'Don't look so horrified, there is nothing wrong with having such emotions for Theo. I see the sparkle in your eyes when you are near him and I know he makes you happy. You two have grown very close, you seem to spend so much time together. If I'm being honest, you're perfect for each other.'

Erin, knowing fine well there was no point in denying it to Leonarda, replied, 'Actually, we practically spend every spare moment we have together. He is perfect and you're right, I am attracted to him, what girl wouldn't be? He's terrific. He's handsome and...'

'I sense a but. Is there a but?' Leonarda pressed her plump lips together and waited for an answer.

Erin met Leonarda's gaze, '*But* he's too perfect. Theo could have his pick of girls and the biggest but of all is…' Erin dipped her head. 'The truth is Patrick also shares a piece of my heart and I can't change how I feel! I have tried! God only knows I have *tried* but it's not that easy.'

106

Leonarda, tapping Erin's hand gently, advised. 'My child, you cannot allow two men to own a piece of your heart, only one will triumph in the end. Patrick is back in Ireland and Theo is here. You have to decide if you really want to return home or if you want to make a life in New York, but either way, you must make that decision for you and only for you.'

Erin nodded. 'Oh Leonarda, you're right. I'm being silly, I've already came to my senses about Patrick, I know deep down if anything was to have come out of our relationship then it would have happened by now. Surely at the very least it would have developed before I came here.' She shrugged. 'I presume I'm just that used to holding him close to my thoughts, it's not so easy to cast him out of my mind.'

'I agree. I guess this may sound hard and I apologise in advance for saying this, but I believe he wouldn't have let you leave if he had thought your friendship was going to develop into a romance.'

Erin swallowed back the lump that had suddenly sprang into her throat. The truth was hard to face but let's face it, Leonarda and William had both said the same. Suddenly she felt as daft as a brush, it was time to face reality, they were both right!

Observing the solemn expression developing on Erin's pretty face, Leonarda gave her hand a light squeeze. 'You mean a lot to me, Erin, I don't want you to be unhappy, I'm just being honest.'

Erin lifted her eyes and tilted her chin in determination. 'There's no need to feel bad, I know you're right and you mean well, I just need to catch myself on.' She tried to suppress a smile. 'It really is about time I got myself together and I'm going to do it from this moment on.'

'Look on the bright side, my dear, Theo is in love with you and it's as clear as the nose on that pretty face of yours.'

'He is not!' Erin blushed again. 'He's just friendly, that's all.'

'My dear, I do not often get things wrong and trust me I've known Theo all his life, I can tell when he's smitten. I can also tell you now he has never spent so much time in the company of a lady as he does with you and I'm sure you will agree Theo is not short of female admirers. I'm telling you he is in love! You watch, he'll make his move soon.' Leonarda chuckled, 'And if you ask me, he better hurry up before some other New Yorker snaps you up!'

Her words had stirred a warmth within her, like smooth hot chocolate on a winter's day. Erin felt her stomach flutter like a heard of wildebeest stampeding through her. Could Leonarda be right? Could he possibly have feelings for her? The idea left her feeling as if she was about to drift off the floorboards. If he did, then Leonarda was right, he better *hurry* up!

The large rest room, with its expensive ornaments and furniture, looked immaculate. Erin gazed around it wondering why she had to wipe down everything today, there wasn't a fleck of dust in sight! However, then again, that is probably why it is so clean. It was maintained on a daily basis, not a speck of dust was allowed to settle in this household.

Erin decided she would get to work with lighting the fire first. Mrs Fitzgerald had a thing about the fire being lit by mid-morning. This was a chore that Erin helped with back at home so she was well used to this task. As she piled on the firewood, Leonarda got the feather duster out and got down to business, humming as she went along.

'Do you know, Erin,' Leonarda stepped up on a stool and waving the duster around the crystal chandelier, she looked over her shoulder, 'I really enjoy your company. I've spent the last thirty years in that kitchen, hour after hour, day after day on my own. I don't know how I did it!' she chuckled.

'What about the last housekeeper, didn't you spend much time with her?' Erin looked up.

'No, not much at all, she preferred to keep herself to herself and we barely saw each other never mind speak to one another.'

'What about Silvia from upstairs? I haven't seen much of her since I arrived here, in fact sometimes I forget we have a second housekeeper working here.'

'Oh you won't see her much at all, I'm surprised if you have seen her at all. Silvia also keeps herself to herself. She's very quiet and prefers to carry out her chores upstairs and leaves as soon as she's finished. The poor girl looks after her mother as well so she has her hands full.'

'Oh well that's understandable why she doesn't hang

about here for any longer than necessary,' Erin replied as she tossed a few lumps of coal on the fire. In no time at all she had created a mighty glowing inferno roaring up the chimney.

Stepping away from the fireplace, Erin dusted her hands on her apron and walked over to the window. 'I'll be back in a few minutes. I'm just going to get some fresh water for these flowers,' she said, removing two porcelain vases from the windowsill.

'Okay my de…' Leonarda turned to reply and only then she spotted the intruder.

Waiting until Erin was safely out of the room, she quickly dragged her stool over in front of the fireplace. She knew only too well how spiders frightened the life out of Erin, the poor girl would run a mile at the sight of one.

'Right, let's get you out of here before our Erin returns.' Leonarda peered up at the creature as she stepped back up on the stool. 'Gosh, look at the size of you! You're so big we ought to be charging you rent!' She chuckled as she carefully leaned closer and tried to capture the imposter. The furry-legged spider, sensing danger, scampered further up the wall.

'Oh, you're playing hard to get are you, you little squatter.' Leonarda stretched upwards but the spider only crawled a little further up the wall. 'C'mon, I haven't time to be playing chase. C'mon, I'm not going to hurt you, I just need to get you out the window, set you free before our Erin comes back and catches sight of you.' Leonarda stood on her tiptoes and stretched a little further, using her feather duster she caught the creature and swiped it gently down on to the rug. As the intruder gently fell on the mat, a glow caught her eye, and before she knew it, the flames were roaring with ferocious speed up her apron. 'HELP! HELP!' Leonarda wailed swatting at the flames with the duster.

Erin dropped the vases at the sight before her eyes sending them to crash to the ground and crumble like a cookie all over the polished parquet floor.

Leonarda leaped off the stool and began hopping around the room like a cat on a hot tin roof, desperately trying to extinguish the flames.

With all her strength Erin pulled her friend's arm and managed to get her on the mat. Rolling the heavy rug around Leonarda's, body she soon put an end to the dangerous flames.

'Th…th…thank you.' Leonarda trembled, 'Er…, Er…in you… you sa… saved my…my life,' she stuttered.

'Let's get you out of these clothes. Is your skin burnt?' Erin asked, fear gripping her at the thought of it.

'I …I don't know,' Leonarda replied.

Erin unravelled the rug and helped Leonarda to her feet, her heart sank at the sight of Leonarda's red scorched hands but thankfully the rest of her skin was not burnt. She sent a silent prayer of thanks to God, knowing only too well the outcome could have been much worse.

'I'll get you some ointment, come on,' Erin urged.

As they crossed the room to leave, a huge tarantula-like spider crawled into the base of the broken vase. Normally Erin would have screeched at the sight of such a creature, but now she gazed at it and sighed, after today's drama, a few broken vases and a huge spider were the last of her worries!

Chapter 13

Needing time to take in the contents of the letter, Erin made herself a cup of tea and a coffee for Theo. She cut a few slices of bread and slathered on some homemade blackberry jam. Back in the living room she found Theo standing gazing at the street below. Since bringing the letter to her earlier, he had fallen quiet, his thoughts clearly a million miles away.

'Here's your coffee. Would you like a slice of bread?' she asked, holding the plate in front of him.

'No, I'm not hungry,' he replied, taking the coffee and sitting down.

Helping herself to a thick slice of bread, Erin sat down opposite him, picked up the letter again and began reading it to herself.

Dear Erin,

I hope this letter finds you well, my dear friend. Thank you for your kind words after my father passed away. Your telegram helped to lift my mood. My heart has been broken, Erin, in more ways than one!

I'm sorry it has taken me so long to write to you, but it hasn't been easy. After you left I found myself experiencing so many emotions, new emotions and an awful sense of emptiness. Not long after you were gone my father's health took a dramatic turn for the worse, and before I knew it, I found myself having to take care of him around the clock.

Nursing my father and nursing my broken heart over losing you, sent my mind into thoughts of wanting to scream out in anguish!

Before my father died he advised me to tell you how I feel, part of me didn't want to, I thought it would be of little benefit, after all you are over there and I'm back here with an ocean between us. Since my father's death, I've pondered his advice but one of the things that I've learned over the years is that I can honestly never remember my old man letting me down. I'm sure you will agree with me, his guidance has always proved correct. It is for this reason I've finally plucked up the courage, so here goes, Erin, I love you (there I've said it!). I LOVE YOU! I've loved you for as long as I can remember. You probably won't believe this but I had planned to propose to you on Christmas Eve, but when you announced you were leaving, I changed my mind. I couldn't stop you and felt it best to let you go.

Now that I have got my feelings off my chest, I really don't know what else to do! I don't expect you to come running back, so perhaps if I can get things sorted, then I could come out to you, that is, if you feel the same way. Maybe you will want to run a mile from me (actually coming to think of it, you've run more than a mile already!). So what do you think, could you possibly see a future with us? I do hope so for I love you, Erin Coyle, I love you to the moon and back!

All my love always,

Patrick

P.S. I'll wait till I hear from you.

Theo swallowed the lukewarm coffee. His mouth had suddenly felt as dry as sawdust. It was clear from the sparkle on Erin's face, as she sat opposite him reading the letter, that something was in it, something had sent her heart ablaze. As he observed her face beam, he secretly prayed it wasn't from that Patrick boy William had mentioned weeks ago. He couldn't help but feel a pang of jealousy as he handed her the envelope earlier. On retrieving it initially from the postman, he had noticed the Irish stamp on it and there was something about the bold scrawled handwriting, it didn't seem like it was written by a girl.

'Do you still feel up to our walk in the park? We can always leave it until another day if you want.' Theo watched as Erin folded the piece of paper and placed it back in the envelope.

'No,' she looked up and smiled, 'We'll still go, I've been looking forward to it.'

Sprinkles of warm sunshine cascaded through the leafy oak trees that lined Central Park and shone a dandelion yellow in the sky above. Erin and Theo sat down on the wooden bench and watched in silence as a couple of children kicked a ball on the grassy area beside them.

The contents of the letter was gnawing at Theo's insides. Should he just ask her outright or would that be too invasive? Then again, he had only known her a few months, it really was none of his business, he thought, but on the other hand, he may have only known her a short while, but he knew her long enough to have fallen head over heels for the beautiful Irish girl sitting next to him. One thing he was sure of, he certainly wasn't prepared to lose her. The very thought of not being with Erin sent a shudder up his spine. An overwhelming urge came over him to kiss her, oh how he badly wanted to take her in his arms and press his lips against hers.

'Do you fancy a sandwich?' Erin, reaching into her bag, retrieved two roast beef sandwiches that she had made earlier.

I fancy you, fancy you rotten, he wanted to reply but instead he accepted the sandwich, smiled and said, 'Thanks.' Taking a bite of the tender roast beef and mustard snack, he asked, 'So, anything exciting happening back in Derry?' There, he had said it. He knew he shouldn't be nosey but to heck with it the not knowing was killing him.

Erin swallowed her food and shrugged, her eyes focusing on the ducks in the nearby pond. She watched how they waddled about carefully close to their mother. Now and again they would dip their heads into the water in search of something to eat. She broke up the crusts of her bread and tossed them into the pond and at once the gathering began munching on the offerings.

'The letter was from a friend of mine,' she said in a mere whisper. 'My friend Patrick,' she added.

Theo took another bite of his food and nodded, 'Yeah, I thought so.' Trying not to choke on his grub, he asked, 'How is he?'

'He seems better,' Erin replied. She tossed another few crusts into the water and pondered over what to say next. Should she just be honest with him? Life was so unfair at times. How can it be possible to be in love with two men? Surely these situations didn't arise often, she'd certainly never heard of it before, but then again, this type of scenario would just happen to her, nothing was ever straightforward when it came to Erin Coyle! She decided against telling him. No, she mustn't inform him of the contents of the letter and besides she needed more time to think about her situation and discuss things with William and Leonarda, well definitely Leonarda, knowing William he would just advise her to forget about Patrick. Then there was Leonarda's predictions, if Theo did have feelings for her, she didn't want to hurt him. 'Actually,' she broke the silence, 'Patrick seems good. I was worried how he would cope on his own now that his dad is no longer here but he seems to be keeping things together.'

'I'm sure he's missing you,' Theo said, his gaze drifting up at the soft puffy clouds scudding across the pastel blue sky.

Erin shrugged, 'He'll be fine, the neighbours are like one big family, there's plenty of them to care about him and my parents will no doubt look out for him. He'll have that many people fussing over him, he'll not have time to pine for me!' she joked.

Theo smiled. Good, that sounds positive enough, he thought. He wanted to jump for joy. So there must not have been any mention of him missing Erin and wanting her to come running back to him to soothe his aching heart. Nothing stating

117

that he couldn't live without her, and better still, not a mention of him declaring feelings of love. Thank God, he silently prayed. That was good news, no actually that was excellent news! William was right after all, this Patrick boy saw Erin as a friend and nothing else.

Theo finished his sandwich in satisfaction and he too lobbed the crusts of his bread into the water and watched the hungry ducks dive in a frenzy towards the food. A cheeky seagull whooshed in overhead, and before the other birds knew it, the gull had the bread in its greedy beak and flew away as fast as it had arrived.

Theo turned and gazed at Erin. He found he couldn't take his eyes of her. The warm sun glowed on her olive skin turning her cheeks a peachy-pink shade. Wisps of her long raven-black hair blew against her face as the gentle breeze swirled around them and he wanted so badly to run his fingers through her gorgeous hair and touch her soft cheek. My goodness he had never imagined loving someone as much as he loved Erin right now. There had been many girls that had come into his life and had gone and a few that had got close to his heart but none as close as Erin. His mind was made up, Erin Coyle was the girl he wanted to spend the rest of his life with, the one he would have loads of children with, the one he would grow old with. He had certainly never imagined a girl having such an impact on him. Normally he would have taken the plunge and kissed her, when it came to women he had certainly plenty of confidence but right now he felt shy. Shy! For goodness' sake this was new, he had never been *shy* in his entire life! What was this girl doing to him? An idea suddenly struck him, was this the same effect she had on Patrick? Could this possibly be the reason he hadn't made that move she had longed for? Well, he certainly was not going to end up losing her like the young Irish boy had done, no, he was going to pluck up all his courage and take that plunge!

Leaning closer, his heart thumping hard against his rib cage, he placed his hand casually over her shoulder and drew her nearer. Moving his head a fraction closer to hers, he could feel her soft breaths on the verge of his own lips and then it happened… just as his lips were about to close in on hers, the long awaited kiss was interrupted by the hot liquid soaking through his trousers. Theo jumped up as the golden Labrador continued urinating on his leg.

'Stupid dog!' Theo leapt away from the bench shaking his trousers in fury. 'Shouldn't dogs do that against a tree?' he said, his tone clearly revealing his irritation. 'Perfect bloody timing!' he said under his breath.

'I'm so sorry.' An elderly lady chuckled, 'Old age it is. Poor Doris. Her eyesight is a bit like my own,' she cackled.

Poor Doris? What about poor me? Theo thought.

Clutching a cane in one hand and patting Doris with the other, the pensioner smiled with affection at her beloved pet, 'You naughty girl. Say sorry to the young man. Show him how sorry you are. Go on.' Nodding from Doris to Theo, she continued 'Don't be shy, say sorry!'

Theo looked at Erin and rolled his eyes, the old lady had clearly lost her marbles.

Doris, understanding what her owner meant, barked with delight and leapt towards Theo. Suddenly she began jumping and leaping around him in frantic circles. Doris was getting more excited by the second.

'Okay, it's fine now.' Theo waved his hands about, 'You can calm down now.'

Doris was only getting started. Dashing in and out of his legs, tail swishing back and forth at a rate of knots, she was as happy as any dog could be and enjoying every second of it.

Erin looked on amused at the expression on *poor* Theo's face, he certainly was not enjoying this attention.

Then to add to his misery, Doris jumped up on him and placed her muddy paws on his trousers, on his best, favourite trousers! Typical!

'Okay, down, down now boy!' Theo shooed the dog away. 'Down boy!'

'She's a girl!' the old lady, clearly insulted, fired back. 'Don't call her a boy! You silly young man!' she growled, her face twisting with the insult.

'Nothing wrong with your hearing,' Theo mumbled under his breath. 'Okay, I'm sorry, down girl, down, down NOW!'

Erin, trying hard not to burst into a fit of laughter, replied, 'I think with a name like Doris, you can safely say she *is* a girl, Theo.'

'Come here, Doris, come to Mommy!' The old lady

patted her leg, 'Come on now and leave the silly young man alone. He knows now how sorry you are,' she cooed.

The faithful dog sprang to her owner and was soon bounding around her feet.

'We'll leave you to enjoy the rest of your evening, sorry to interrupt.' The old lady turned and hobbled away, Doris yapping faithfully beside her.

Theo, clearly reading the amused look on Erin's face, smiled. 'You loved every second of that, didn't you?' He gave her a playful nudge and reached for his jacket.

'Poor, poor, *poor* Doris!' she teased.

Theo grinned. 'Don't you start too! Come on, let's go.'

'Aye I think you're right,' she beamed back and released a little giggle. I would have preferred the kiss, she secretly told herself as they walked through the park, but never mind, at least she knew now he wanted to. Erin couldn't help herself smirking again.

'What are you laughing at now?' he gave her another playful nudge.

'Nothing,' she replied linking her arm with his, 'I was just wondering who said a dog was a man's best friend?'

Chapter 14

Erin lay in the bath, circling her toes in and out of the warm
soapy water, pondering over her situation. This time last year,
life may have been a struggle from one day to the next, but
how much things had changed. She was now eating roast beef
sandwiches on a Saturday trip to the park, for goodness'
sake... roast beef sandwiches! Back home she was lucky if
they had a bit of beef as a treat on a Sunday or at Christmas.
Not to mention back in Derry she had one man to occupy her
thoughts, which was bad enough and certainly a lot easier than
having two men running rampant through her mind.

Closing her eyes, allowing the soft bubbles to swirl
around her thin shoulders, Erin recalled the moment in the park
the day before. A surge of butterflies took flight in her stomach
as the memory of how close Theo had been to kissing her. At
that moment she had tingled in anticipation, she had so badly
wanted him to, but right now her mind was tortured by guilt.
She kept asking herself over and over again how it was
possible to be in love with two men? She knew it wasn't fair
but also had no idea how to solve the matter.

Suddenly, she sat upright, like a lightbulb moment she
realised with a pang of anxiety that Patrick needed her more!
There was no way she could turn him down after everything he
had been through and after all the years they had spent
together. He had been her first love; she knew deep down she
had to choose him. The thought of breaking Theo's heart was
like a knife had been plunged into her own, but then again

maybe Theo was only going through a phase. Surely he could meet other girls, he would get over her. Somehow she couldn't imagine Patrick meeting anyone else but she definitely could see Theo with another.

An hour later, dried and dressed, and after discussing the decision with William, Erin, going against her brother's advice, curled up on her bed, pulled out her notebook and began to write.

Dear Patrick,

It was so good to hear from you. I want you to know that I do feel the same way! I LOVE YOU (There, I've said it too!). I only wish you'd have told me before I left, it would have certainly been much easier for us both.

I don't feel ready to return to Derry. Now that I'm here, I think I may as well stay in New York. There are certainly more opportunities in America than we will ever both find back in Ireland. As I have secured a job and you are still not working, perhaps it's best if you come to me and find work. It will be a new start for you, you can leave all the doom and gloom back in the Bogside. We'll be sooooo happy together. We can get things sorted here and plan our marriage.

I have arranged with William for you to stay with us but you'll have to sleep on the sofa. It won't be for long, we'll get married soon, find a place of our own and live happily ever after.

Love you also to the moon and back!

123

Erin xx

P.S. I'll look forward to hearing from you.

'You're mad, Erin. I can't see it working out like that. I'm not so sure about agreeing to let him stay here either.' William, finishing reading the letter, waved it about in disgust. An overwhelming urge to rip it into shreds came over him. 'If I were you I'd bin this rubbish!' he said as he handed it back to his sister, looking like he had just swallowed a mouthful of maggots. 'I'm telling you, you're wasting your time!'

Erin looked at him gobsmacked. 'Oh don't be so negative! You are always sooooo *negative*!'

'Erin, you're always so bloody well naïve! Seriously, do you believe bringing Patrick here will solve all your problems? Because if you think so then you can think again!' Throwing his hands in the air, he continued. 'It's a stupid idea! It's just downright ridiculous! You need to grow up, Erin, and you need to do it sooner rather than later!'

Hurt by his tone, Erin fired back, 'What exactly do you mean by that?'

'Well think about it, you're planning on bringing him over here and suggesting marriage!'

'Hold on.' Erin pointed, 'I didn't suggest marriage! He did!'

'Whatever!' William shrugged. 'But for goodness' sake, it may not be as easy to just get married here, neither of you are citizens. I don't deem it's as easy as you're contemplating and I certainly wouldn't be dreaming about living *happily* ever after! You're not thinking straight, sis, and if you ask me, you're being selfish!'

'Selfish! Selfish? You cheeky …'

'Stop!' William held up a hand. 'I'm being realistic. The man has just buried his father, he doesn't need to be rushing into upping sticks and travelling across the ocean. *He's* not thinking straight right now either. You're making a fool of yourself!'

'Wha…what! He's the one that wrote to me first, how can I be making a fool of myself? Do you know what I think? I believe you're just jealous! You're jealous because you've been out here all this time and you haven't found someone to care for you and you certainly have no one special wanting to travel across an ocean because they love you!' she fired back, her face ablaze with anger.

'Oh really? That goes to show you how much you know.' William pointed a finger again. 'For your information, I *have* a special lady in my life!'

'No way!' She shook her head with disbelief. 'You're telling me a lie!'

'It's true, but it's early days yet, she's had her heart broken once and she wants us to take things slowly.' William lowered his tone.

'Who is she?' Erin asked, the curiosity getting the better of her.

125

'Never you mind.' William shrugged.

'I want to know! You can't just tell me something like that and not tell me who she is. You can tell me, I'm your *sister* and you're my *brother*!' Erin shot back.

William couldn't help grinning at her. 'What were you going to call me before I stopped you earlier, a cheeky what?'

Sensing he was teasing her, Erin flicked back her hair and stuck out her chin, 'Never mind, it doesn't matter now.'

'Oh but it does, remember, you can tell me! You're my *sister* and I'm your *brother*!' William pretended to mimic her.

'Pig! I was going to call you a cheeky pig! By the way, why are we discussing this? We're supposed to be talking about your love life. Who is she and do you love her?'

'Oink, oink! No.'

Erin, trying her best not to laugh replied, 'What, you don't love her?'

'No, we're supposed to be talking about *your* love life, not *mine* and yes, I do love her. I love her very much indeed.'

Erin's eyes danced with excitement and for a moment she forgot that just minutes ago they were embroiled in a heated argument. Curling herself up on the sofa, she flashed him a smile. 'Go on, tell me all the juicy details and start by telling me who she is.'

'Listen, sis, never mind about me and my girl, you'll meet her when the time is right, I'm more concerned about your dilemma. Let's stop wandering off the subject and let's get this matter resolved somehow.'

'There's nothing to resolve, I'm sending Patrick this letter.' She waved it in the air. 'We can sort things out when he arrives, and if you don't want him living here, then we'll have to sort that out too.' She shrugged.

'You make it all sound so easy.' William released a long sigh.

'What's wrong with you, William? You've known Patrick for as long as I have. I thought you liked him.'

'I do! Of course I like him! Patrick is a great bloke, I've nothing against him, I'm just worried that he's declaring this love for you now because he's not thinking straight. His heart has been broken, he's grieving.' William sighed again. Lowering his tone once more, he continued, 'Erin, it looks to me as if he's just trying to fill the emptiness in his heart.'

Erin opened her mouth to speak but shut it again, her mother always taught her if she hadn't anything good to say then say nothing at all. Right now she wanted to call William more than a cheeky pig! How he could imply Patrick wasn't thinking straight was just so unfair, but then again maybe he was right and she was wrong. Awash with emotion, she struggled to fight back the tears.

William, sensing he had upset her, stepped towards her and placed his arms around his sister. 'I'm sorry for arguing with you, sis. I care about you, that's all. I don't want you ending up hurt.'

'I...I... wo...won't get hurt,' Erin cried, 'He loves me

and… and I love him.'

'Okay fine, but you must realise that if you bring Patrick here, you'll cause Theo a lot of pain.'

'Theo will be okay.' She sniffed and dried her eyes. 'He can have his pick of any girl, believe me, everywhere we go, Theo is eyed up. He is constantly getting eyelids batted at him whilst they throw me imaginary daggers!'

'Maybe he doesn't want any other eyes on him, have you thought about that? It'll be awkward for him having to witness you and Patrick here together. It's for this reason I think it may not be a great idea him staying here.'

'Theo will understand and besides it's not as if he's serious about me, we're not even a proper couple. Actually, we're not even a couple at all! I'm not exactly his girlfriend! Theo will meet someone else in no time and he'll forget about me.'

'What? Are you joking? He'll certainly not forget about you and he will certainly find it hard to cope when Patrick comes here. Erin, the man is crazy about you! Theo's in *love* with you for crying out loud! If you ask me he's not interested in you just being his *girlfriend*, from where I'm standing, it appears Theo would prefer you to be his wife!'

Chapter 15

Frankie McGregor mumbled under his breath, 'Feckin' door! Bangin' on my door at this time of tha mornin', who'd ye think ye are! Keep it up and I'll kick your arse!' he yelled.

Slugging back a huge gulp of Guinness, he slammed the bottle of stout on the table and shouted, 'I'm comin'. I'm bloody well comin', ye annoyin' wee fecker!'

Wiping the frothy moustache from around his mouth and drying it on his dirty, smelly shirt, he opened the door with a flourish.

'What ye want?' he released a huge mighty burp. 'What tha feck de ye want?' he growled at the unfamiliar male before his eyes and tried to steady himself by leaning against the doorframe.

'I'm your new postman,' the young lad replied, trying to smother a laugh at the expression on Frankie's face.

'So? What tha feck has that got de do wi' me? Just throw the letthers' in de tha box like the other wan did,' Frankie said, fixing the new postman a bewildered drunken stare.

'I just wanted to introduce myself. I'm Kieran O'Hara and I'll be delivering your mail for the next few months.' Kieran smiled, revealing a set of clean, straight, pearly white teeth and held out his hand for a polite introductory handshake.

Frankie wiped his snotty nose with the back of his hand, rubbed the contents on his shirt and held out the same hand to accept the gesture.

Kieran cringed as he felt the sweaty, snotty palm of Frankie's hand close firmly around his own.

'Pleashed de meet ye,' Frankie slurred, still holding on tight to Kieran's hand. 'Francis McGregor, but ye can call me Frankie, tha's what everyone else calls me. Ye can actually call me whatever tha feck ye like, I don't give a feck, just don't call me too early in the feckin' mornin'! Now, tell me wha' happened de tha other wan?'

Pulling his hand away as gently as he could, after all he didn't want Frankie to topple over, Kieran replied, 'Matt broke his leg. It looks like he's going to be off for a bit, well at least a few months, I would guess. I'm sure you will agree with me a one-legged postman is as helpful as an elephant in a ceramic shop.' He laughed.

Frankie's breakfast of eight bottles of stout and six cigarettes left his brain function a little slower. Once he caught the joke he began to titter at first, seconds later the titter developed into a hearty laugh, so loud his chuckles could be heard by Patrick down in number seven, just a few doors away.

Patrick locked his front door, removed the key and made his way down the street. 'Someone's in good form today,' he said, stopping outside Frankie's house and placing his peak cap on his head as a light drizzle began to fall.

'Our wee postman here ish tellin' me a wee joke,' Frankie slurred again. 'Gone tell him wan, tell him a wee wan too.' Frankie nudged Kieran, causing himself to stumble forwards and almost knock Kieran over.

Patrick, quick to react, grabbed hold of Frankie's arm and steadied him back on his feet.

'Hurry up, tell him a joke,' Frankie went on, swaying in the doorway.

Kieran thought for a minute, 'Okay, a husband and wife were out walking the country roads. They had an argument before they left the house so they continued their journey in silence, all picture and no sound if you know what I mean. They walked past a field of pigs and the husband nudged the wife, relatives of yours? he asked sarcastically. Yes, she replied... INLAWS!'

Patrick laughed. 'Ha, very good.'

Frankie, still swaying in the doorway, one eye closed in deep thought, replied, 'What tha *feck* are ye talkin' about, ye feckin' eejit? I don't get it!'

Kieran and Patrick looked at one another before bursting into a fit of laughter.

'It's okay, we'll tell you some other time. Listen lads, I'd really like to stand here and chat but I'm heading to morning mass, I must go,' Patrick said, 'Watch yourself, Frankie,' he added before jogging away.

Kieran, looking at the number one on the door above Frankie's head, said, 'I must go too. If I stop this long with everyone in the street, I'll be here all day.'

'Aye you're right there!' Frankie agreed. 'Head on your

way an' give me peace de finish my brekkie.'

Kieran, placing two envelopes into Frankie's hand, said, 'Goodbye, it's been nice meeting you, Frankie. Must dash now, bye.'

Back in the kitchen Frankie gulped down the remainder of the bottle of stout and sat down to open the letters.

'Ah, the stupid wee fecker,' he steadied himself, squinted his eyes and read the envelope again. Yes, the neat handwritten envelope, stamped from the United States of America, was definitely addressed to Patrick Brogan.

'Stupid wee fecker!' Frankie shrugged, stuffed the envelope into his trouser pocket and opened another bottle of stout.

Chapter 16

Erin gazed upwards. The late afternoon sun streamed through the trees as little sprinkles of light cascaded between the swaying branches in the warm light breeze. The sun's rays glittered on the calm lake. The only sound to be heard was tiny ripples as some swans floated elegantly on the smooth glass-like water, several had gathered around the banks, nesting in the shade of the tall reeds, others drifted further ahead.

A single blackbird hovered idly overhead. Erin watched as the bird circled the lake before landing close to one of the tall chestnut trees and began to nibble on some crumbs of bread. She sensed a nasty feeling developing in the pit of her stomach at the memory of how Patrick and herself would feed the birds in the street with leftover stale bread, in fact they would both feed the birds anything they could get their hands on.

A weak smile formed on her face as she recalled how one day they came running out with some tomatoes. They placed the food on the pavement before crossing the road to Erin's home to wait for the birds to come in large numbers, as usual, to eat this new treat. They waited and waited but nothing came, not a single bird landed.

Frankie McGregor appeared at the bottom of the street, swaying to and fro in his usual drunken state. He began singing Amazing Grace at the top of his voice, 'Amazthin' Grace!' he sang before stumbling against a lamppost. Holding on to the lamppost, like a koala on a branch, he continued in his own made up words, 'Shhaved a bloody wretch, aye a bloody wan lick meeeeeeeeeeeeeeeee.'

The two kids began to snigger until Frankie let go and began to dance up the street. To their horror Frankie stepped on a tomato and slid flat on his face. Worse still, they observed how he lay there spread-eagled on the pavement and not moving a single muscle.

'He's dead!' Patrick whispered, 'We've killed him!' His eyes widened with fright. 'Gee, Erin, what are we going to do?' he asked as panic started to grip him.

Erin froze to the spot, her mouth gaped open like a goldfish's and her heart pacing like a racehorse's, she hadn't a clue what they should do. Feeling a crushing guilt take over her, so bad she couldn't bring herself to say anything, she just stood there like a statue and stared at poor Frankie.

Suddenly Frankie's hand shot up into the air and fell back down on the road. 'Amazthin' Gr...' he slurred unable to string the words together.

'Oh thank God, he's alive!' Patrick looked to the heavens and blessed himself before running across the road, Erin close behind him.

The two kids tried their best to pick up the drunk but it was proving a difficult task to move their burly pink-cheeked neighbour. Each time they lifted an arm, it just fell helplessly to the ground again.

'Come on get up, Frankie!' Erin yelled.

'You can't lie there!' Patrick said, pulling Frankie's

arms with all his strength. 'Get up, Frankie!'

Suddenly, Frankie getting a new lease of life, lifted his head, and crawling along the ground like a snail, he made his way to the lamppost. With great difficulty he managed to pull himself up using the streetlight for assistance. Soon he was back on his unsteady feet. Looking at the two kids, his eyes glassy and his gaze unfocused, he tried to balance himself to concentrate on the children.

'Wha... wha... the feck's goin' on?' he slurred as his head bopped about like a puppet without a puppeteer. 'Wha's' goin' on, wains?'

'You slipped,' Patrick replied in a polite tone of voice. 'We're very, very sorry.'

'Wha... wha... ye mean slithpped? What the feck?' Frankie, bleary-eyed, asked as he lifted his head and gazed at them both.

'You slipped on the tomatoes. We left them out for the birds.' Erin spread out her arms, 'Look they haven't eaten any of them yet.'

'Birds? Tomatoes?'

'Aye and they haven't eaten a single one,' Patrick said.

'Ha, ha! Ye feckin' daft bats! Birds don't eat tomatoes!' Frankie let out a mighty over-exaggerated roar of laughter. 'Birds eatin' tomatoes!' he cackled. 'Gee I've heard it all! Ha, ha...ha, feckin eejits!' Frankie, pointing a grubby finger at them, went on, 'You two are gone way tha fairies! Birds eatin' tomatoes!' he repeated before bursting into another fit of

135

giggles.

'You're in a world of your own.' Leonarda broke the silence. 'Come on, let's stretch our legs, go for a walk.'

'Oh, Leonarda, I'm just thinking how Patrick and I had some great times together,' Erin said as she reluctantly got up from the bench.

Leonarda linked her arm through Erin's and nodded, 'Yeah, I know from the many stories you've told me over the last few months, it sure did sound as if you had many good times and many adventures in the past.' Leonarda smiled and her conker-brown eyes sparkled.

'I can't understand him, I really can't figure him out. The worst about it is, I thought I knew him better than anyone else,' Erin said. 'We spent practically most of our lives together. I thought if anyone knew him best it was me!' she lowered her tone and continued, 'I guess I was wrong. It seems William was right after all. He said Patrick wasn't thinking straight when he had written to me and I know now William hit the nail on the head with that prediction.'

Erin sighed, her gaze followed a butterfly as it joined another one just like it. Their velvet wings, a beautiful vibrant mixture of red and orange, fluttered delicately. The two insects danced about, with not a care in the world, around the rose bushes that lined the twisty path. Many a summer's evening Patrick and herself would chase after butterflies.

'To heck with this!' Erin patted her forehead. 'I need to

stop thinking about Patrick Brogan! Seriously, that boy is going to drive me insane!' she said, blowing out her cheeks. 'This is so *hard*!'

Leonarda nodded and smiled, 'Yeah, you're right, my dear. It is hard for you. When you allow someone a piece of your heart it's very difficult to take it back.' She stroked Erin's arm as they strolled under the afternoon's warm rays.

'I have only myself to blame. I recall you saying in the past something about two men having a piece of my heart and only one will triumph in the end. I should have listened to you. I should have listened to William also. I'm stupid!' she cried. 'I'm *so* stupid!'

'No you're not, don't say that!'

'I certainly *feel* stupid right now.'

'Everything will work out for you, I'm sure of that. I truly believe that God has our lives planned out for each of us. Life is a journey we all must follow. None of us know where that destination we must travel will end, and as we don't have a map to guide us, we must follow our heart.'

'I thought that was what I was doing. I'm never following *my* heart again.' Erin tried her best to smile, but the smile was weak, and soon it vanished like morning dew in the sun's rays. Against her wishes she could feel her eyes fill with tears and before she knew it, they were fighting for freedom. Soon they escaped and came tumbling down her cheeks.

'Oh, Erin. My dear Erin, don't cry.' Leonarda paused under an elm tree.

Erin's lips started to twitch. 'I…I…I ju…st do…n't kn…ow wh…at to do.' She sobbed, collapsing on the soft grass under the thick branches.

Sitting down next to her, Leonarda stroked Erin's hair. 'A good cry is as good as a good laugh. Did you know that? Let it all out, you'll feel much better.' Pulling a clean hankie from her pocket, she passed it to Erin. 'Here, take this, love.'

Erin blew noisily into the hankie and released a huge sigh. Wiping her tears, she smiled and attempted to put on a brave face. 'You're right. That's it, Leonarda, I've cried bucketsful over the past few weeks and I am adamant I am not going to waste another tear! I came here with the high hopes that my life would get better, my goodness, God only knows I've never felt worse in my entire life!' She released a little laugh at the irony of it.

'Things will get better, I promise.'

'I'm not so sure they will! I can't believe he didn't answer my letter. I even put the boat ticket in it for him! William was so right, Patrick's initial letter was obviously written when he was at his lowest, then as soon as I agree to marriage in my reply, it scares him away! That's it, I mean it, Leonarda, I will never contact him again! He will never hear from me or see me again!' Erin felt her heart sink to great depths at the realisation that Patrick obviously loved her as a friend, not a wife.

'Erin, you're just saying that now because you're angry. I guess you've a right to feel annoyed at him but you two were such great friends, it would be a pity to throw all that away.

Maybe your friendship with one another is part of the problem with both of you.'

'What do you mean?' Erin asked.

'Well, sometimes people can misinterpret friendship with love, perhaps that is how it has been for you both. Maybe this possibility will explain why you feel you love Patrick and at the same time are attracted to Theo.'

Erin felt her cheeks turn red at the mention of Theo and her heart did that little leap that she had come so accustomed to on hearing his name. 'Is it that obvious I care for Theo also?'

Leonarda smiled. 'It is, my dear. I know you like him a lot. Could it be that you and Patrick are not in love at all but just miss the relationship you both had?'

'You could be right,' Erin nodded. 'Oh, Leonarda you must be right! I've been beating myself up about this, questioning over and over in my mind how it was possible to be in love with the two of them.'

'So, Erin, are you admitting that you *are* in love with Theo? I mean real love?' Leonarda asked with a twinkle in her eye.

Erin's eyes widened, her heart began thumping at an alarming rate. 'Yes, yes I suppose I am!'

Chapter 17

Leaving the noise and chaos of the city behind, Erin and Theo strolled through Grand Central Park. The park was busy with the usual Saturday visitors chilling out, reading their newspapers, eating picnics, and playing recreational games.

Erin wasn't sure how her hand managed to join with Theo's but one thing she was sure of; she didn't mind in the slightest. His hand clasping hers felt perfect. She just hoped he wouldn't sense the wild beating of her heart as it banged away relentlessly in her chest. Then again the area was buzzing with activity, much too busy for him to notice the sparks between them, she hoped.

A male voice yelled out from his horse-driven carriage, 'Do you want to get in? I'll take you through the rambler.'

'Sounds good, thanks,' Theo called and led them both to the carriage.

The lush woodland, composed of acres of winding pathways, home to an abundance of wildlife and pretty plants was something Erin had never witnessed before in her life. The place was amazing. They had visited the park on many occasions but hadn't ventured this far. Erin drank in the alluring sights around her as the carriage passed many birdwatchers, dotted around the woodland, in search for the opportunity to get a glimpse of the numerous species settled in the area.

'This is certainly the best way of taking in the beauty of

the park. It allows you to get a real taste and experience of nature,' Theo said as they were transported deeper into the park.

'Oh, Theo, I love this place,' Erin said as she watched a starling pick at the berries of a nearby bush. The noisy bird nibbled away before ruffling its lustrous feathers and taking flight to its next venture.

'Yeah, it's like a huge wild garden. Some New Yorkers like to call it their backyard. It's a great place, where many can find peace away from the hustle and bustle of their hectic lifestyles.'

'It is indeed,' Erin exclaimed.

'We used to come here regularly as kids. My father had a great interest in the wildlife. See that tree there.' Theo pointed, 'That one is a hackberry. It's a bit like an elm but it's not used much as the wood is soft and inclined to rot. The next ones further along are cucumber magnolias. They're native to North America. Their yellow-green flowers and fruit is similar in appearance to cucumbers, which I guess inspired the name.'

'They're beautiful.' Erin gasped.

'That one's a black cherry.' Theo pointed again. 'It's widespread and common in both North and South America.'

The warm afternoon breeze, laden with a mixture of various fragrances, filled their nostrils. 'I love the smell,' Erin said, tilting her head and breathing in the delightful woodland aroma.

'Yeah there's all sorts of lovely odours coming from the

trees and plants,' Theo agreed.

The carriage continued until they reached Bow Bridge, the cast-iron crossing linking the woodland area with Cherry Hill and shaped and designed similar to that of a bow of an archer or violinist.

'Do you mind if we stop here for a few minutes, sir?' Theo yelled.

'Not a problem,' the driver called over his shoulder and at once brought the horses to a standstill. 'Take your time, I'll wait for you.' He turned around and smiled.

Taking Erin's hand, Theo helped her step out of the wagon and led her onto the crossing. Pausing as they reached the centre, they both leaned over and gazed at the lake beneath them and watched the sun's rays dancing on the shiny surface.

Towards the end of the span, an elderly lady sat at an easel, painting the spectacular view ahead of her. Looking up from her task she saw the young couple and smiled. 'Hello there,' she called.

Theo and Erin both glanced at her.

'Hi, how are you?' Theo waved.

'I'm great. Would you two like a portrait? Come on over, I would love to paint you.' She flashed a wide grin.

Theo, looking to Erin, raised his eyebrows. 'Shall we?' he asked.

'Okay, fine, I've never had my portrait done before,' Erin said as the pair made their way over to the artist.

'I love to draw young lovers,' she said with a bright smile. 'Stand over there and I'll have this finished in no time.' Pointing to the opposite side of the bridge she continued 'Just there, the scenery is better and the sunlight is just perfect.'

Erin could feel her cheeks burn as Theo took her by the hand and led her to the position indicated. At once the artist got to work. Erin marvelled at how the lady's eyes danced as she allowed the brush to sweep in all directions, adding a little colour here and a little there, she smiled with satisfaction as she went about her task at hand. Now and again she would lean forward at times to concentrate on the finer details, then the next minute she would lean back to survey the results. It was clear the elderly lady did this on a regular basis, the pleasure she gained from this work was evident on her face.

'Not much longer, nearly done!' the artist called from over her easel.

The afternoon sun was warm and Erin could feel the rays toasting her as they filtered through the lush, green leafy trees. She had to admit she would be glad when the portrait was finished, the temperature was rising at an alarming rate and Theo's hand resting on her shoulder was sending her blood to pump through her veins.

A smile of satisfaction lit up the artist's face. 'All done!' she said turning the easel at an angle for them to see the finished result.

Erin gasped as they both made their way over to take a closer look. 'It's wonderful! I love it!' she proclaimed, astonished at how the old lady had managed to paint them both to perfection.

'I agree!' Theo said, lifting the painting from the stand and holding it up. He realised now why the lady had mistaken them to be in love. It was easy to think that they were indeed a couple. He couldn't help but notice how perfect they looked together. 'How much should I pay you for this?'

'Nothing at all.' The lady waved her hand dismissively. 'I don't do this for money, I love painting, it's my hobby.'

'No, no I insist, I must give you something for your work,' Theo argued. 'I can't take this without paying you.'

'Tell you what, make a donation to the homeless. There's no shortage of such unfortunate people about this place.' She smiled softly.

'Okay, I will indeed,' Theo promised. 'Thank you so much.'

'Right, that's me finished for the day.' The lady began to clear away her bits and pieces. 'I'll be off. I must say, you two make a beautiful pair! It was such a pleasure to paint your pretty faces.' She beamed as she placed the remainder of her brushes away.

Theo bent down to help her place her paints in her bag whilst Erin could feel her cheeks burning now more than ever before, but the peculiar thing was, neither herself nor Theo corrected the old lady's assumption that they were a couple, not once but twice! Well, if he wasn't going to say anything, then neither was she.

'I'll be off, goodbye,' she said lifting her easel and

tucking it under her arm.

'Thank you again,' Theo said as he watched her turn and head away.

'Goodbye, thank you,' Erin yelled after her.

'You're welcome,' she called over her shoulder before disappearing behind a clump of trees and out of sight.

Back on the bridge, Theo came to a halt at the centre once again. His earlier plans slightly interrupted, but he didn't care, it was worth having this treasured painting.

Erin, stopping next to him, smiled, 'I really enjoyed our trip today. I have to say this place is so romantic.' The phrase she had been secretly thinking had slipped out and here she was, blushing again like an idiot.

'I know, I agree.' Theo nodded as he leaned the portrait against the bridge. 'That's why I brought you here.'

Across the bridge the carriage driver was sitting on the grass verge allowing the sun's rays to warm his face, his attention a million miles away. In the distance, the sweet tune of birds chirping and a saxophone echoed in the air. Below, the soft ripples of the water gently licking the embankment, were the only other sounds to be heard.

'Listen, even the music is perfect.' He flashed her a grin and took a step near. 'Erin, I'm not going to beat about the bush, I'm sure you've sensed that there's an attraction between you and I, even that lady recognised it.' He looked deep into her eyes.

Feeling herself tremble from her head to her foot, Erin swallowed and nodded, 'I guess there is.'

Cupping her face in his hands, Theo titled her head towards his and expertly kissed her on her warm, velvety and welcoming lips.

Erin, found herself putting her arms around his neck and allowed herself to melt in his embrace.

They both kissed with so much passion and love, there was no doubt they belonged together.

'I've never felt this way about any other girl, Erin,' he murmured through his kisses. 'I've fallen head over heels in love with you! Erin Coyle, I love you!'

Erin, couldn't believe her ears. Clinging on to him to steady her trembling legs, 'I... I love you too,' she heard herself echo.

Releasing his embrace and falling on his knee, Theo, taking her by the hand, retrieved the box from his trouser pocket and smiling said, 'I promise you, Erin, I will love you all the days of my life, I want you to be my wife!' Opening the box and producing a glittering diamond ring, Theo continued, 'Marry me!'

Needless to say she almost toppled over.

Chapter 18

The heavy rain subsided to a light drizzle, falling barely detectable on Patrick's face. Over his head shards of sunlight streamed through the murky clouds. Pulling a handkerchief from his coat pocket, he mopped up droplets of the shower from the granite kneeler. Retrieving his rosary beads from the same pocket, he knelt down in front of the statue of the Blessed Virgin and blessed himself.

As much as he tried to concentrate on reciting the rosary, it was useless. His mind was in too much turmoil. He had found it difficult to concentrate earlier during morning mass and thought perhaps he could find some peace now at the statue in the church grounds. Patrick appreciated the stillness at the beautiful stone grotto, but then again, the moments of quietness caused him to think too much, think of how things were and more importantly how things should be.

Most of the mass-goers were now gone. Having lit more than enough candles to light up the planet, said their prayers and their nattering now done and dusted, they were off for their Sunday lunch with their families. He would be gone too if he had a family to share a Sunday roast with, but no, his Sundays and every other day were faced alone. He hated cooking for himself and above all he hated eating alone. Catherine and John Coyle were forever inviting him to join them. He had refused on many an occasion for he didn't want to impose on them but above all there was an awful sense of awkwardness at the Coyle household, he knew they were as every bit annoyed with Erin as he was for not replying to his letter.

As he began the first joyful mystery, his shoulders sagged in defeat. There was no joy in his life right now and at this very moment he could not foresee any happiness for the future. With a pang of anxiety and a deep sadness, a realisation hit him, his dreams were well and truly over.

He observed how the sun glittered on the raindrops on Our Lady's cheek, looking as if she had just cried tears of diamonds from her cobalt-blue eyes. A single robin redbreast hovered lazily overhead and rested on the shoulder of the statue. It was unusual to see such a bird in July, thought Patrick, with them more accustomed to being spotted in winter. Seeing the bird now reminded him of Christmas and of course Christmas also reminded him of his lack of courage last Christmas Eve when he should have gone ahead and proposed to Erin. He wanted to kick himself and while he was at it perhaps a good kick for the fancy American that swept Erin off her feet! Yes, a good kick, that's what they both needed!

Bumping into Mary Coyle earlier, had proved a meeting he would certainly never forget, an encounter that would change his life forever. Linking her arm with his and walking with him to the Long Tower church, she tried as best as she could to subtly break the news to him of Erin's forthcoming marriage. An announcement that almost knocked him off his feet. It was just as difficult for Mary; he could tell by the tremor in her voice.

At first it felt like someone had plunged a knife into his heart, then privately he thought Mary must be away with the fairies, surely Erin would not get engaged so soon, in fact *surely* Erin wouldn't get engaged at all! For goodness' sake she barely knew this swanky Yank! Some rich American named Theo, how dare he ask Erin to marry him! *His* Erin for crying out loud!

Mary's words had developed into a tornado in his brain. Suddenly it felt as if he had been whisked off the face of the earth and plunged down on the moon. He must be dreaming, Erin wouldn't marry another man, she just wouldn't!

Then reality struck him. As the rain began to pelt down on them both, Mary ran for cover in the church porch and he was forced to come back to earth with a bang. Of course this Theo had fallen in love with Erin, *his* Erin, the beautiful Erin that *he* let go! What man wouldn't fall for her?

Inside the church he couldn't bring himself to sit next to Mary, she reminded him too much of the girl he lost. Instead, he made his way upstairs, where he sat on the wooden bench shivering in his damp clothes. With the blood pumping through his veins, he watched, where he had a full view of the congregation below and wanted to cry out from the depths of his soul. He didn't listen to the mass, he just couldn't take in a single word Father Lavery was saying. With each passing second, his brain felt like a volcano lurking ominously below the surface, threatening to explode at any moment.

Shoving his rosary beads back into his pocket and running a hand through his damp hair, he gazed up into the porcelain eyes of the statue. 'I'm fed up! Do you hear me? I'm seriously *fed up* with it all. I've had enough!' His chestnut-brown eyes flooded with emotion. 'Enough is *enough*, don't you think?'

'I think you're mad!'

'What?' Patrick swung around, mouth agape. After a few seconds he continued, 'Chris, you scared the wits out of me! I didn't know you were behind me!'

'Ha, of course you didn't, mate.' Chris took a long drag from his cigarette. 'Who'd you think answered you, the robin? Or Our Lady?' Holding the cigarette between his nicotine stained fingers he waggled it in front of Patrick, 'You know, mate, neither that bird nor the Blessed Virgin can answer your question.'

Chris took another puff before stubbing his cigarette out against the stone grotto. 'So what's up with you? Talking to yourself is a sign of madness, so tell me, Pat, are you losing your marbles or what?'

Rising to his feet Patrick smiled weakly and decided to ignore Chris' question. 'What are you doing here?' he asked blinking away the tears. One thing was for sure, he had no intentions of crying in front of Chris Ferguson.

'After mass I wandered around the graves. My grandfather is buried here in the church grounds. I had spotted you earlier kneeling at the alter waiting for communion but when I looked again you were gone. I want to have a chat with you about something but first you haven't told me what's up with you. Do you want to come back to my ma's for a drink and you can tell me what's wrong? I've brought a bottle of whiskey back from Dublin.'

The thought of a few shots of whiskey turned Patrick's empty stomach. 'Actually, come back to mine, I'll make us a bit of a fry, I rushed out this morning without breakfast and I'm feeling peckish now.'

The drizzle had passed, the rain clouds moved on to their next destination whilst the sun now bounced its warm rays down over the Bogside. Chris lit a cigarette and leaned against the back door and gazed lovingly at his mother next door as she went about hanging his wet shirts on the washing line. Suzy Ferguson loved to dance and sing. Chris felt his heart fill with love as he watched her doing a little dance as she went about her chore and singing a tune he wasn't familiar with. He loved the fact that his mother always danced like no one was watching and she sang like no one was listening.

It pained him that he had to leave his hometown just over one year ago, but then again he had no choice in the matter. With very little work in the Maiden City, Dublin had lured him away. With no shortage of work in the Irish capital, many men found they had to make that move, after all, a man cannot lie about idle. Suzy understood, but still he knew she missed him terribly. With both his brothers working in London, they rarely were able to come back to visit, and it was for this reason Chris deliberately took the route to Dublin in search of employment. At least this meant he could visit his widowed mother once a month. He loved the monthly visits, coming home to be greeted with his mother's welcoming arms, delicious cooking and his own cozy bed, but he hated leaving her again, knowing she was here all alone in her humble abode and missing her three sons terribly.

Oh how he wished she would meet someone else and perhaps marry again. She was still a young woman, and a beautiful woman at that, but he knew there was more chance finding a hen with teeth than his mother ever finding love again. She had never as much as looked at another man in that way since his father died.

'C'mon, Chris, the fry is ready.' Patrick placed two plates on the table, plates filled high with sausages, bacon rashers, scrambled eggs and mushrooms.

'I'll be in now,' Chris called over his shoulder before taking a drag of his cigarette. The smoke filled his lungs with satisfaction, although he knew he needed so badly to kick this addiction out of his life, but not just now, he told himself, maybe by the end of the summer he would try to quit. He exhaled the last puff in a cloud of contentment and watched as it whirled and danced towards the summer skyline, actually, he thought, maybe he'd leave it until next Lent then he could finally give them up for good but for now he'd enjoy his habit.

'Are you going to stand there smoking all day or what? C'mon, your food will get cold,' Patrick said taking his seat at the table.

'You sound like my ma!' Chris joked as he stumped out his cigarette on the window ledge. 'No, in fact, you're worse!'

Back in the kitchen, Chris munched on the delicious

food. 'Gee, Pat, I'm telling you, mate, you must come to Dublin with me. We seriously could be doing with an extra pair of hands at the minute.'

'I don't know, Chris.' Patrick bit into a sausage. 'I'm not sure if it's for me.'

Waving his fork in the air, Chris continued, 'You'll love it, Pat. I'm not joking, you'll *love* it!'

'Do you think so?' Patrick questioned. Taking a slow sip of his strong tea, he pondered over the idea.

'There's plenty of work.' Chris popped some egg into his mouth. 'I'm telling you, Pat, you'll not want to return here! On the way back from the church you admitted there's nothing in Derry for you anymore. Pat, you need to accept what you've told me and move on. I was looking at my ma out there, she might be on her own but I know she has so much to fill her day, baking for the parish hall, helping out at the charity shop, and perhaps her biggest challenge of all, cooking and cleaning for Frankie McGregor. So you see what I'm trying to explain to you, mate, her day is filled but yours is not! I know you were looking after your da before he passed away and that passed your time but what have you got now? Your da's gone, Erin's gone and I'm gone. All you have most days is your morning mass and then back here to look at these four dreary walls.' Leaning across the table Chris raised his eyebrows in concern and continued, 'I'm telling you, mate, that's enough to drive any man mad!'

Patrick, remaining silent, just nodded and took in everything his friend had just said.

153

'So what do you think? Will you come with me and help us build this department store? Put your stamp on it and be proud to be part of the establishment of one of Ireland's biggest stores! And, just think, you can nag me into stopping smoking too!'

Patrick, entertained by the idea of a new adventure, raised an eyebrow and with a hint of a sparkle in his eyes, replied. 'Do you know what, you're right, Chris! I'll go, sure, what have I got to lose?'

'Take care, son.' Suzy planted a loving kiss on each of Chris' cheeks. 'Love you.'

'Love you too, Ma.' Chris returned the kiss before making his way to the car and climbing in.

'C'mon, c'mon, Pat, what's keeping you, man?' Chris yelled from the open window.

After locking the door and placing his peak cap on his head, Patrick took a final glance up and down the street. Catching his eye at the bottom of the path was Frankie McGregor. He watched in amusement as Frankie attempted to teach Anne Quigley's grandchildren the tango, which looked more like *tangled,* Patrick thought with a grin. Anne, being one of the best dancers in the town, would have a good laugh at this scenario.

The children let out a mighty roar as Frankie tumbled to the ground and rolled on to his back. With his legs and arms in the air, Frankie looked more like a dog waiting to be tickled and Conor, the mischievous one of the bunch, jumped upon him and did just that, tickling him under the chin and arms. Frankie howled with laughter.

'Thath's enuf'! Enuf' of thath now,' Frankie slurred. 'Help me up, wains.'

Andrew, the oldest of the group, grabbed him by the arms, and with all his strength, he helped Frankie to his feet.

'C'mon you! C'mon daydreamer!' Chris, with his arm hanging out over the window, tapped impatiently on the car door. 'Will you c'mon, Pat.' Chris peered up at the gun-metal, heavy clouds that were rolling towards them. 'It looks like it's going to rain.'

Back on his feet, Frankie spotted Patrick and waved. 'Hi you, Paddy boy, I've somethin' fur ye.' He swayed and the kids began to giggle again, their laughter filling the street. 'I've a letther from tha States.' Making his way towards the house, he mumbled over his shoulder, 'I'll be back in a wee minute.' He waved his hand dismissively and disappeared inside.

'What's he hammering on about?' Chris sighed as he watched the kids scatter on further down the street to play hide and seek.

Patrick threw his cases into the dusty back seat of the car and shrugged, 'I haven't a clue, couldn't make out a word he said, sure he doesn't make much sense when he's on the drink.' He grinned. 'Oh wait, sorry, I forgot something. Give me a minute.'

Patrick dashed back inside the house and bounded up

the stairs taking two at a time.

'Here it is.' Frankie stumbled out of his front door. 'I've got it!' He waved the letter in the air as his bloodshot eyes scanned the street. 'Where the feck is he? The stupid wee fecker!' he grumbled, dancing from one foot to the other as a desperate urge to use the toilet sprang upon him.

'Are you looking for Pat? He'll be out in a minute,' Chris yelled.

'Aye I've a letther fur him, fink it's from that …Coyle…wan,' Frankie yelled hopping from one foot to the other.

Barely able to make out what Frankie was blabbering about, Chris yelled back, 'Aye you're right, Frankie, it is indeed a cold wan.'

Picking up the black and white photograph in its carved wooden frame and wiping the dust from it, Patrick smiled, 'How could I forget you two?' He kissed the frame, placed it in his pocket and made his way back outside.

On spotting Patrick emerge from the house fumbling for his keys, Frankie waved with excitement. 'Paddy, 'ere it is.' He waved the letter in the air and swayed from side to side. 'And will ye hurry up de feck before I piss meself!'

The thick, burly clouds were by now hanging directly above their heads and the howling wind blew with an angry rage. The change in the weather today had been a bolt out of the blue, after weeks of glorious sunshine, except for a brief downpour the day before, a storm appeared to be brewing overhead, threatening to ravish the city at any minute.

Patrick locked the door and dashed towards the car. Before climbing back into the seat, a gusty wind ambushed his cap, sending it flying across the street. Patrick chased after it as a spectacular flash of lightning lit up the sky, followed by a mighty crackle of thunder. Moments later the heavens opened and the thick clouds hanging over Derry burst with enthusiasm, giving way to a serious downpour.

Suzy, waving from the open front door, shivered as the rain pelted towards her and the billowing wind swept through her auburn hair. 'See you, boys,' she said stepping into her hall.

'Aye, Ma, get in before you get soaked to the bone,' Chris called.

'Fur feck's sake!' Frankie watched with regret as Patrick ran for cover in the car. 'The stupid wee fecker didn't hear me!' Frankie barged and staggered back inside to avoid getting drenched and also to make an urgent dash to the toilet. Well, the eight bottles of stout he had drunk earlier were now about to run down his legs!

'See you, Ma.' Chris waved as he steered the car away from the kerb.

'Suzy closed her door and made her way into the front room. Observing from her open window, she watched the car speed down the street and waved until they were out of sight.

'Cheer up, mate!' Chris gave Patrick a friendly slap on the knee. 'Just think, a new and exciting chapter is about to start in your life! Dublin here we come!'

Chapter 19

Suzy poured herself a strong cup of tea and stirred in an extra spoonful of sugar to cheer herself up. She hated it when Chris had to leave, the loneliness gripped her. God only knows how she hated being alone. Never in her wildest dreams did she think she would feel like this, and on no account did she ever imagine herself in this position.

Sitting down at the kitchen table she sipped her tea slowly and wallowing in self-pity, she felt the tears welling up in her eyes. It hadn't seemed that long ago the house had been buzzing with activity and each of them getting in each other's way. The Brogan family to the right of them understood the Ferguson's busy household but the elderly couple on their other side used to bang on the walls telling them to "shut their gobs!" Back in those days, Suzy used to cry out for a bit of peace and quiet. With three young boys running rampant around the small compact house, there were days Suzy felt like pulling her hair out. Most days were filled with the constant fighting, bickering, yelling, crying and let's not forget the mud! Many a day they would come home mucked to their eyeballs, much like their father. But with the trials of rearing a young family came the triumph. There were many hugs, kisses, and laughter that echoed from one room to the other and when a child wraps their tiny arms around your neck and whispers "*I love you, Mammy!*" any parent's heart should explode with affection and joy, for there is no other love like it between a parent and a child. God knows, Suzy would go hungry many days for the sake of her kids, she would die for each of them.

A silent tear rolled down her soft cheek. Chris had wrapped his big strong arms around her neck earlier and whispered, "*I love you, Ma.*" He may be the youngest of the family, her baby, but he was now a huge strapping young man that never left home without giving her a cuddle and telling her he loved her. His affection always brought back that memory of how she felt when her kids hugged her all those years ago.

Oh how proud she was of all her sons, like any Irish mother should be. Life in Derry was not easy with so much lack of employment but each of her boys had taken it upon themselves to find work. Just like their father, they would never sit about idle. She knew one day they would have to make their own way in life but she never expected it to come so fast. Here she was now like a sombre mother bird with an empty nest and no one to look after her. She wouldn't mind so much if she had Jack to keep her company, but her darling husband was gone, gone before she knew it with not even a chance to say goodbye, surely this was the bitterest thing to happen to anyone.

The morning of Jack's death would trouble her until she takes her final breath. Her last words over the breakfast table will haunt her forever. The morning of 6 April 1904 will be a date she will always regret. Having overslept that particular morning, they both bounced out of bed. Normally Suzy would have made him a bowl of porridge or boiled him a few eggs for breakfast, but as he was dashing about getting himself ready for work, Jack had opted for some scone bread with blackberry jam and a mug of tea. He'd slugged back the tea in two gulps and lashed the scone bread into him.

160

'You've jam stuck all over your beard, man! Get it cleaned you dirty git!' Suzy had barged.

'A buckin' bit of jam won't do me any harm!' Reaching for his peak cap and coat, he wiped the jam off with the back of his hand and called over his shoulder, 'There, are ye happy now? Ye aul crier. Did you get out of the wrong side of the bed or what?' he mumbled under his breath as he opened the door with a flourish.

Before Suzy could reply or say goodbye, Jack was gone, the door shut behind him and that was the last she saw of him.

Minutes after he had gone, she had made herself some porridge and smiled at the silly row they had just engaged in. Normally they were a happy couple and very rarely argued. She ate her porridge slowly and decided she would make his favourite dinner for him to come home to. He would eat the dinner and they would have a good laugh at how childish they had behaved. Everything would be okay again, except Suzy would soon learn that everything would certainly not be okay.

Only a few hours after he had left, an urgent knock on the door almost caused Suzy to jump out of her skin. The loud banging was not the only scare she would have that day. The visitor brought with him the news that would break Suzy's heart forever. Apparently Jack had been helping the farmer he worked for to mend the roof of his barn instead of his usual task of potato picking. Jack, not accustomed to using ladders, had fallen to his death, dying instantly from what appeared to be a head injury. As Suzy sat on the living room sofa holding this stranger's hand she recalled the silly row she and Jack had earlier. Those stupid few words had put them both in bad mood and neither of them had meant it. Suzy learned a hard lesson that morning, be careful what you say to others for you don't know, it may just be your last. Never in her life had Suzy felt pain like it and she truly believed a part of her died with her gentle, loving husband.

Suzy swirled the contents of the tea in the cup and drank it back. She decided enough of the reminiscing in the past. She made up her mind, she'd dry her eyes and make Frankie something to eat instead of sitting here feeling sorry for herself.

Making her way out the back door and down the alleyway, Suzy jumped as the sound of metal hitting the ground echoed in her ears. The gusty wind took up speed and howled through the lane. The ferocious storm had now arrived.

Suzy pulled her woollen cardigan closer around her as the rain came pelting down heavier than it had earlier. Quickening up her steps, she struggled against the fierce gale and entered Frankie's backyard.

To her horror, there on the ground was the dustbin tumbled over, the contents spilled out over the garden, a newspaper flying about in the wind, and there was Frankie, lying on the soaking wet ground, blood spilling from his nose and looking as dead as a doornail.

Chapter 20

'Frankie, you need to wise up! You're going to end up killing yourself,' Suzy warned, dabbing the cold sponge on the egg-sized bump on her friend's forehead.

Frankie closed his eyes and his shoulders slumped in defeat. He didn't have the energy to argue back and besides what was the use of that. He knew deep down Suzy was right, Suzy, his best friend was *always* right.

The alcohol he had drank earlier was beginning to wear off. He could feel himself sobering up and he didn't like that feeling. Oh how he longed for another drink, just one bottle of stout would do the trick and would surely quench this awful thirst. Surely only a drink of Guinness would take away the sawdust feeling gathering at the back of his throat.

'I want to help you,' Suzy whispered.

'You help me every day, Suze. I don't know what I would do without you,' he said, opening his eyes and sitting upright. 'Gee my mouth feels like a fur boot.'

'Here drink this.' She handed him a glass of water.

'Thanks,' he said, taking the glass from her, his hands trembling like leaves in the wind. He gulped back the water in one go and reached for her hand. 'God knows I'd probably be dead now if it wasn't for you cooking, cleaning and looking out for me.' He smiled and stroked her fingers. 'I'm a pain you could be doing without!'

Suzy shrugged dismissively. 'Ah listen to you! Hold

your tongue, we're neighbours, it's the very least I can do! Besides, making a pot of stew for one is no fun at all. Tell me what bother is there in putting on an extra few spuds for a friend.'

'It's the thought, Suze, you're always so thoughtful. I don't deserve it! I'm a feckin' mess, that's what I am!'

'Frankie, I don't mind helping you!'

Letting go of her hand he pointed a grubby finger in her direction. 'I'll tell you what you are, you're an angel! And you're a feckin' good angel at that! One of the best,' he said, taking her hand again and giving it a light squeeze.

Blushing, Suzy shrugged again. 'I'm only doing the human thing, I'm certainly no angel.'

Tears filled Frankie's bloodshot eyes, 'It's not fair on you, I depend on you too much, Suze.'

'It's okay,' Suzy said, patting him on the back of his hand. 'Really, I don't mind, Frankie, and that's the truth.'

'It's not *okay*. I'm fifty years of age this year and look at me. Look at the shape of me. I've wasted my entire life, no wife, no kids and no job. Why is that? I'll tell you why, it's easy, alcohol! It's as clear to me as it is to the rest of you, alcohol is ruining me. The bloody demon drink has taken over my life and I couldn't do anything to stop it in the past and I still can't. I have no control over my addiction, Suze. I've put drink before everything and what have I got in return? Nothin'! Absolutely nothin'! Feck all!'

Suzy dipped her head, she had no idea how to answer

Frankie because there was no pussy-footing about it, he was certainly right and everyone could see that.

'I want to help myself, Suze. I really want to set myself free. I have tried you know, God only knows I have tried but I keep falling and every time I get back up I fall again, back into the world of drink, drink, DRINK!' he said through gritted teeth. 'I'm pissed off with my life!'

There was something in his eye and a tone in his voice, Suzy knew he meant it. Determination, that's what it was.

'You know, Suze, I pray, I pray to Jesus every day. Did you know that, Suze?' he asked, his eyes wide and serious.

'No, no I didn't, Frankie,' Suzy replied, praying now that Frankie wouldn't see the pity for him on her face.

'Aye, I pray away every day. I get on my knees and I look up at the picture of the Sacred Heart of Jesus, hanging on my wall. He looks down on me all mercifully and I look deep into his eyes. I say the same thing over and over day after day. I hold my bottle of wine up in front of him and I say…' Tears fell down his flushed red face and he released a shaky sob. 'I… I… I say…' Frankie stopped and using the sleeve of his jumper, wiped his eyes.

'Don't upset yourself, Frankie.' Suzy placed a hand on his shoulder, 'C'mon now don't annoy yourself.'

Sniffing and taking a deep breath, Frankie continued. 'I say to him, Jesus, you performed a miracle of changing water into wine now please take this wine and change it into water!' Placing a hand on his heart and looking deep into Suzy's eyes,

165

he continued, 'Because, Suze, Jesus knows how much I don't want to drink but as long as there is alcohol in the bottle, then I'll knock it back whether I want to or not. To an alcoholic, alcohol becomes their friend, their life, their everything! Think about it, Suze, I'm your friend, would you say no to me?'

'Of course I wouldn't, Frankie.'

'Of course you wouldn't and the same applies to me for my bottles of stout and whiskey, they're my comfort I can't live without.' He dipped his head and continued. 'I long to but I can't, I just can't beat this soul-destroying addiction.'

Suzy turned her gaze away, unable to look at the pitiful man in front of her. She had known him for many years but had no idea how hard life was for him. She couldn't even begin to imagine the fight an alcoholic must face every minute of their day. 'That's it, Frankie, I want you to move in here with me! You can stay in Chris' bed, he won't mind. I'm going to look after you properly and I promise you, Frankie, I'm going to help you with this battle!'

'No, Suze, no, I'm not going to put you through that. It just wouldn't be fair on you.' Frankie shook his head.

Suzy just smiled back. 'Frankie, you must know me better than that, I do *not* take no for an answer. Now,' she patted his hand again, 'you sit there and I'll go make us a nice cup of tea and then I'll head back to yours and get you a few of your belongings and bring them here.'

Alone in the living room, Frankie drank in the sight of the bright airy room and smiled. He felt safe. For once in a long time he felt good. What better hands to be in than Suzy Ferguson's? A thumper of a headache came on him so quickly, he closed his eyes and rested his head against the soft cushion.

Frankie blinked. The dazzling light penetrated him. The figure in front of him was a stranger to him but at the same time, intriguingly familiar. Unable to pull his gaze away, Frankie continued to stare at the gentleman.

Then, Frankie realising who the man was, reached out to touch him. 'Is it really you?' he asked, feeling a warm glow arise within him.

'It is I,' the male whispered softly, taking Frankie's hand.

Frankie felt the love tingle through him from his head to his feet, the glow now becoming stronger. His heart felt like it was going to explode into a million pieces and he sensed as if his body was beginning to float off the floorboards.

'It really is you! You've came at last!' Frankie said, mesmerized by the reality that his dreams had finally came true. Still holding on tight to the man's hand, he looked at him from head to feet and tried to make sense of it all.

Frankie felt a gentle hand rest on his shoulder and for the first time he realised they were not alone.

Unable to draw his gaze away from the man, to check who was behind him, he kept his attention on the gentle face before him, Frankie's eyes glued to his soothing stare.

'The Lord has heard your prayer. You will feel lost and overwhelmed but you must know I will assist you. I will help you find your way. Take shelter under the angel's wings that I have sent for you and follow me for I am the way.'

Frankie felt the person behind him squeeze his shoulders, 'I am your angel,' the voice replied in soft, velvety tones.

Frankie, still unable to pull his stare away from the man in front of him, could not turn to see the angel behind him with a hand firmly on his shoulder. Frankie's eyes were still glued on the soft eyes that held his. 'Thank you,' he heard himself reply. 'Thank you, Jesus!'

Suzy's hand remained on Frankie's shoulder, 'I said your tea is ready, Frankie.' She gave him another squeeze.

Opening his eyes and sitting up, Frankie turned and smiled at Suzy.

'You must have dozed over.' She smiled softly.

'Aye I did indeed,' he said. Taking the cup from her he replied, 'Thanks, Suze, you truly are my *angel*!'

Chapter 21

The poignant aroma of the Liffey River was overwhelmingly strong. Patrick leaned further out the window and drank in the magnificent sight of Dublin.

The storm that ravished the north of Ireland earlier had clearly missed the south. Dublin appeared bright, the pavements dry and a hazy sunshine reflected on the Liffey. The grey-blue water looked smooth and appeared calm apart from frothy waves gently licking the stone canal.

Anticipation tingled through him. He had two aims in mind, firstly to get the thought of Erin Coyle out of his mind once and for all and secondly to get on with his life once and for all.

'In Dubin's fair citeee!' Chris began to sing as he drove through the streets of the hustling Irish capital mimicking the strong Dublin accent.

Feeling groggy and tired from the long journey, Patrick stretched and yawned and hoped they would be stopping soon, enduring the lengthy drive was one thing but having to listen to Chris' awful singing was quite simply torture.

Finally, Chris came to a halt at a fine three-storey Georgian building. 'Right, Pat, out you get, we've arrived!'

Patrick didn't need to be asked twice, he jumped out of the car with a shot of eagerness and stretched his legs. From the corner of his eye, he noticed a pretty blonde girl glancing out at them from behind the curtain in the front room of the house. As their gaze met she flashed him a warm smile and waved. Patrick, not sure if she was signalling at him, decided not to be rude and waved back anyway, just in case.

'C'mon,' Chris urged as he opened the door and stepped into the hall. Uneven cracked tiling floored the narrow hallway leading to the kitchen. Suddenly Patrick felt quite hungry as he breathed in the delicious smell of cooking emanating from the kitchen.

An overweight pink-cheeked man in his forties appeared at the door. 'Chris, good to see you, boy!' His squirrel-bright brown eyes looked over Chris' shoulder and his gaze fell on Patrick. 'So, have you done what I asked, found me another hard worker like yourself?' he beamed.

Chris nodded, 'I have indeed, Gerry, and I promise you Pat here will work his socks off for you.'

'Nice to meet you, Pat.' Gerry held out a huge hand and gave Patrick a warm handshake. 'Come in, boy, you're welcome here! I'm so glad for the extra pair of hands, we're snowed under with work. C'mon in and we'll get you both a bite to eat.'

Inside the kitchen, a short, plump lady dressed in a pink floral dress the colour of her cheeks, and a white apron, glanced over her shoulder.

'Patrick, this is Netta,' Gerry announced proudly, 'The missus and the best cook in Dublin!' He winked.

Netta stirred the pot on the stove with a huge wooden spoon and turned round. 'Hello, Patrick,' she said, and flashed him a welcoming smile. 'I've a pot of stew ready, enough to feed the whole of Dublin! Do ya' fancy a plate? Or if you prefer, I'll throw on a few sausages and bacon. What will ye be havin'?'

Patrick, feeling his tummy growling nosily, replied, 'Stew is *perfect* and it's actually one of my favourite meals.'

'Glad to hear, stew it is then!' Netta chirped.

The stew was in fact perfect, nice and thick, just as he liked it and it reminded him of how his mother had made it for him as a youngster. Dessert was just as scrumptious, warm rhubarb crumble with a dollop of hot custard, went down a treat. Patrick now felt his stomach was about to explode and if that wasn't bad enough, the sight of the blonde girl he had spotted at the window earlier, was now walking across the kitchen towards the seat next to him.

'Hi there, my name's Charlotte.' She flashed him a pearly smile and sat down.

Patrick felt himself blush, he was sure his cheeks had turned the same colour as Netta's dress. Other than Erin, he had never felt attracted to another girl, but right now, as his heart was banging somewhere in his chest and feeling more like mush than muscle, he knew instantly that he was drawn to this pretty girl next to him and there was nothing he could do about it.

'Hello, Charlotte, I'm Patrick,' he managed to say, trying to control the nerves jangling in the pit of his stomach.

Charlotte was undeniably a very beautiful girl. Her long

171

blonde hair was pulled back from her face in a braid, emphasising her high cheekbones. Her skin was peachy and flawless, her lips and nose just perfect for her oval face, and her green blouse set off the colour of her emerald eyes.

Here she was right beside him, looking stunning and smelling delightful and he could do nothing about it apart from feel himself blush a little more.

'So, Patrick, have you been to Dublin before?' Charlotte asked, reaching for the carafe of water from the middle of the table and causing her silky blouse to brush against his bare arm.

'No, no, never here before,' Patrick replied, every nerve in his body jumping.

'Good, I'll just have to show you about the place then,' Charlotte purred.

Patrick, feeling his palms going sweaty, took a deep steadying breath and replied, 'Okay, that sounds good, thanks.'

Charlotte sipped on her ice water, her eyes glittering with mischief. 'We can start with the Voltra on Friday night. I'll allow you to take me there to celebrate your first wage packet.' She winked. 'I'll check out which movie is being shown this week.'

Gerry cleared his throat, 'Charlotte, for goodness' sake, where's your manners? Wouldn't it be better to show Patrick the landmarks in Dublin. The Voltra isn't exactly a tourist attraction!'

'Father dearest, the Voltra cinema is Ireland's first ever

cinema, of course it's a tourist attraction. I'm sure he can't wait to see it. Isn't that right, Patrick?' she said as she placed a hand on his arm.

Patrick prayed she couldn't feel the goose bumps forming under her palm.

From across the table Chris smirked, clearly he was struggling not to laugh.

Patrick cast him a wait-till-I-get-my-hands-on-you look and wished so badly that Chris had warned him how pushy Charlotte was.

'Well, has the cat got your tongue?' Charlotte smirked and gave him a kick in the shins from under the table. 'Tell my father you want to go to the cinema too! Go on!'

Patrick shrugged and replied, 'Aye, whatever, I... ah... I don't care.' In a valiant effort to change the subject, he got up from his seat and continued, 'If you'll excuse me, I wouldn't mind taking my bags to the room now, if that's okay?'

'Of course! C'mon, I'll show you.' Charlotte beamed, jumping up at once from her seat.

'No!' Gerry stepped in. 'Your mother will fix you up your dinner, I'll show him. C'mon, Pat, follow me,' he said, getting up and straightening his back. Placing his burly hands on his daughter's shoulders he gently forced her to sit back down.

The bedroom, a spacious airy room situated on the top floor, had a magnificent view of Dublin from the huge Georgian-style windows. Two single beds sat against opposite sides of the walls between the window.

'Chris sleeps over there,' Gerry pointed to the bed on the left, 'and that's your one.'

'Great, thanks,' Patrick said, placing his case at the foot of his bed.

'Listen, Patrick, I'm sorry about that daughter of mine. She can be a bit over the top at times, if you know what I mean.' He raised a brow and sighed. 'No matter what blarney she comes up with, pay no attention to her. She can be a right wee attention seeker.'

'It's fine,' Patrick shrugged. 'I don't mind.'

Gerry narrowed his eyes, 'Well, I can tell ye this much, *I* mind and it's not *fine*! I don't like the idea of my daughter throwing herself at young men and especially one that is staying under the same bleedin' roof! For crying out loud, I need eyes in the back of my head to watch her as it is! I'll need another pair fixed to me arse at this rate!'

Patrick could feel his cheeks burning but at the same time he tried not to laugh at Gerry's use of words.

Gerry, pointing a grubby finger in Patrick's direction, went on, 'I'm warning ye, boy, I don't want any funny business going on between the pair of ye! Do ye understand what I mean?'

The urge to laugh had vanished like mist meeting the sun's warm rays, the tone of Gerry's words signalled loud and clear that this man was not to be messed with. Patrick could feel his cheeks on fire now more than ever. How dare Gerry imply that he would consider taking advantage of Charlotte? 'I can assure you, there will not be any funny business. I understand perfectly where you are coming from but you must also understand that I do not jump at the advances of every girl I meet!' he said, his voice raised a fraction and he didn't care what Gerry thought of it.

'Good, I'm glad we're clear on that issue, and now since the matter is done and dusted, we'll leave it at that.' Gerry held out his hand. 'Stay away from my daughter and I'm sure we will have a good working relationship,' he warned with a wink of his eye.

'Fine, I've got the message,' Patrick replied with caution. Taking Gerry's offer of a handshake, he registered how firm the grip was and thought he certainly didn't want to be on the receiving end of a punch from this man's fist.

'Right, I'll leave you to unpack your bits and pieces,' Gerry said, making his way to the door. Looking over his shoulder he narrowed his eyes again, 'I saw the way ye looked at her by the way, so if ye have any sense, you'll keep them eyes of yours to yourself from now on!'

Like a flash of lightning, Patrick fired back, 'I didn't!'

Reading his worried mind, Gerry grinned with mischief. 'Aye, ye did! I'm not stupid and I don't blame any man for eyeing her up but she's too young to get involved in any relationship. The perfect man will come along at the correct time but now is not the right time, my daughter has a lot of growing up to do. So, as I said, do yourself a favour, keep your eyes to yourself or I'll be shining my boots up your backside!'

He laughed.

Patrick laughed back, 'I'll just have to wear horse blinkers then,' he said, watching Gerry leave and thinking to himself he would be avoiding Charlotte like the plague. 'There's no chance I'm getting involved with her,' he whispered under his breath.

'Well, he is single and should be ready to mingle,' Chris said with a hint of mischief. 'Then again, Charlotte, I wouldn't exactly advise it, the look on your da's face was enough to put any man off, poor Pat, your aul man will not be long in scaring him away. That was one heck of a sharp look he threw him!'

'Oh I know, ye would have thought he swallowed a bleedin' wasp but the truth is, me da wouldn't be happy if I dated the richest bleedin' man in Ireland! Do ye know what his problem is, having an only child! He's too protective and always has been. It's a wonder he hasn't me wrapped in cotton wool. Chris, I'm telling ye, I'm eighteen, I'm not a baby anymore and I'll do what I want to do and he'll just have to like it or lump it!'

Chris tried not to laugh, he wanted to tell Charlotte that she certainly acted like a baby at times and a spoilt baby at that. He decided to remain quiet, after all he didn't want the jug of ice water poured over his head.

'I tink Patrick Brogan is just simply gorgeous,' Charlotte drawled, 'And I don't care what me da has to say, if he tinks he's going to keep us apart, he can bleedin' piss off!'

'I tink you're mad!' Chris mimicked her strong Dublin accent, 'Don't even tink about it,' he went on mockingly, waggling his finger in the air.

'Listen to me, Chris,' Charlotte raised her perfectly arched eyebrows, 'I'm going to get Patrick one way or another. You watch this space, and in no time at all he'll be mine!'

Chapter 22

The Volta cinema, situated on Mary Street, appeared quiet with not much activity going on.

'What's on tonight?' Charlotte quizzed an elderly man before he approached the doors of the cinema.

'It's an Italian movie,' he replied. 'I hear it's a goodun',' he beamed.

'Oh for goodness' sake.' Charlotte frowned in disgust. 'I knew I should have checked first!'

'It's okay,' Patrick tried to reassure her.

'No it's *not* okay! Why are they bleedin' well showing Italian films all the time to us Dubliners! It's not as if many of us can speak Italian! Well, Patrick, I tink we'll say *ciao* to that one!'

Patrick couldn't help but smile at her, she certainly was unique.

'C'mon, we'll dander to West Moreland Street and grab a coffee in Bewley's.' She linked her arm in his and steered him away from the cinema. 'Do ye like coffee?'

'I prefer tea actually.' Patrick smiled, examining her glittering emerald eyes.

'Aye well you've no choice in the matter, you're getting coffee!' She grinned. 'And besides you'll prefer coffee after tonight because believe me you cannot actually order a cup of tea in a place like Bewley's. They sell the finest roasted coffee beans in Ireland and their cakes are not bad either, and if you're good,' she gave him a cheeky wink. 'I'll allow you to buy me one!'

'Okay,' Patrick grinned at her, 'you win.'

As they approached Bewley's the strong waft of the fine beverage filled the street and Patrick had to admit the smell of coffee was actually so appealing that he would indeed be mad to order tea.

Bewley's was bustling but they managed to find a table in a corner close to the window. After ordering two coffees and sponge cream cakes, they sat down.

As Charlotte peered at him across the table over her coffee cup, Patrick couldn't help those sparks igniting again. There was no doubt the girl in front of him was beautiful with those thickly lashed green eyes, magnificent cheekbones and an incredible quirky smile. How could he not be affected by her presence? She was perfect, almost too perfect. Her pleated hair had been set free and it now sat tousled around her shoulders. Charlotte O'Flaherty exuded attraction without even trying. There was no denying it, she was pretty eye-catching but he had to remind himself that he was here for work, not pleasure and certainly no funny business as her father had so bluntly put it.

After completing his first week of work he figured Gerry had begun to trust him. It had taken Charlotte a bit of persuading to get her father to agree to them going to the cinema tonight but Patrick had quickly learned that Gerry was a big softie when it came to his daughter. He gave in to her in the end but had made sure to throw Patrick that stern look before they left. The look that said more than a million words. The look that came with a warning that if Patrick dared to cross the line, he would more than certainly be sent packing back home to Derry. And as he'd just arrived here, and was actually enjoying working for the company, Patrick felt he certainly didn't want to return so soon.

Frankie crept out of Chris' bed and tiptoed across the landing. 'Feckin' floorboards,' he whispered under his breath as the old wood creaked beneath his feet. Like a burglar on a mission, he carefully made his way down the stairs, through the living room and out to the kitchen. He paused to listen, directly above him was Suzy's bedroom, he prayed he hadn't woken her when he heard her bed creak as she tossed about. Satisfied that she hadn't got up, Frankie went about his task.

It had been a long, tiring and extremely difficult fortnight. Coming off the effects of alcohol was the hardest task Frankie had ever had to face. The thumping headaches brought about extreme mood swings and he cringed at the memory of snapping at Suzy earlier in the week after she had made him a *nice cup of tea* as she had put it.

His reply now made him cringe further. "I don't want a *nice* cup of tea!" he had shouted back. "I want a *nice* bottle of whiskey or an amazing pint of stout or perhaps a nicer bottle of wine!" he yelled.

Poor Suzy visibly trembled in her shoes and Frankie had at once felt instantly ashamed of himself. Suzy being the angel that she was, quietly nodded and mumbled that it was okay and explained that she understood how he must be craving badly for alcohol. She then smiled gently at him before leaving the room, tears glistening in her beautiful, kind eyes and Frankie hated himself for hurting his friend.

Later that night Frankie lay in bed cursing himself and cursing God, after it all it was all God's fault wasn't it? All his life he had blamed God for his downfalls and it was for this reason he had fallen away from Him. He stopped going to mass, stopped praying the rosary and as for confession, he hadn't stepped into a confessional box in as long as he could remember. How the heck can anyone benefit from telling a priest their sins? This had been his outlook for many years but for some reason, he still needed to fall to his knees in his drunken state every night and pray in front of the picture of the Sacred Heart of Jesus, begging for help, because he felt the need to do so.

Unable to bear the torture in his mind for a second longer, Frankie fired back the blankets and climbed out of bed. Falling to his knees below the crucifix hanging above the bedroom door, Frankie stared up at Jesus on the cross. 'Right,' he whispered in the dim room, 'I've told you before and I'm telling you again, you gotta help me! How many times have I asked you for your assistance? Are you even listening to *me*?' he asked as tears flooded his tired eyes. 'I can't do this anymore on my own, Lord. I can't, I just can't,' he sniffed. 'I'm not strong enough.' He dipped his head and allowed the tears to trickle down his cheeks.

181

Suddenly, like a bolt out of the blue, a thought entered his mind, he wasn't on his own, he had Suzy and at once he remembered his dream. Was that God's way of letting him know he had heard his pleas or was it just a coincidence? Either way, Frankie knew there and then in his heart that this was a battle that was not going to be easy but one that he was determined to win.

He released an exhausted sigh. 'Sorry, Jesus, for doubting you,' he whispered. 'I *will* fight this addiction, I promise you.' He blessed himself and made his way back into the comfy bed where he lay, arms folded under his head, and gazed at the ceiling. Outside the sound of rain began to hammer mercilessly against the window. His heart felt like it was going to explode with pain as the many years of turmoil he had suffered as a result of his addiction came flooding into his thoughts, and like the rain outside, this pain hammered severely against his heart. Before he knew it, he was sobbing, crying like a baby and allowing all his sorrow to flow with his tears.

The rest of that week Frankie continued to withdraw from alcoholism and he thirsted, a thirst like never before, not for a glass of water or *a nice cup of tea* but for alcohol. He longed for anything that he could get as pissed as a parrot on. Anything that would do the job and no matter how hard he tried to win the battle he felt he was about to be defeated at any minute. He badly wanted to slip out to get his hands on a bottle or two of wine but Suzy had him here. He felt imprisoned under her watchful eye, like an eagle guarding over its young, Suzy was not going to let him out of her sight, even if that meant she had to miss out on helping out at the charity shop and avoiding doing her weekly duties for the parish. Deep down he was grateful to have Suzy to stand in his way but the fight against his addiction was becoming harder and harder as every second passed.

During the week he had remembered there was a bottle of whiskey stashed in a cupboard in his bedroom. A bottle he had saved for a rainy day. Well on this particular day the rain was thrashing against the windowpane, and as he watched it pelt down angry against the frame, he thought you can't get any rainier than that! Unable to compete against his habit for any longer he decided to give in. Just one drink wouldn't do him any harm and after convincing himself that he would never go back to the past but just have one or two glasses of whiskey a day rather than bottles, he decided to fetch the bottle. As he sneaked out the back door, as quiet as a mouse, he dashed towards the back gate, getting drenched in the short distance. Just as he opened the gate, Suzy grabbed hold of his arm and led him back inside to safety. In his hyper state, with only one goal in mind, he hadn't even noticed her following him.

This morning Frankie had woken up feeling unusually fresh. His mind seemed clearer and the shakes had eased. He lay in bed recalling again the beautiful dream he had weeks ago of Jesus and the angel's hand on his shoulder. His thoughts also filled with Suzy and on how she really was an angel sent to him when he needed her the most. Without her patience and care he surely would not be waking up today feeling much better, and for the first time in many years he wanted to go to mass. He felt the need to go as a thanksgiving to God. Most surprising of all, he had an overwhelming urge to go to confession. He wanted so badly to lift the burdens off his chest, to remove all the hurt he had caused to both himself and others as a result of his addiction. His mind now clearer, he was able to realise that he had over the years cut himself off from family, friends, and society. He had been mean and uncaring at times as the effects of alcohol transformed his personality. Whist under the influence of the addictive substance, he didn't care what way he treated others. It was for this reason this morning he had made up his mind, there would be no more turning himself inward, it was now outward and onwards for him and he was going to start with making Suzy her breakfast and then he would shock her further by offering to attend Sunday mass with her today.

Frankie stirred the porridge in the pan and sighed. It had been so long since he had cooked anything, and looking at the porridge now, turning sticky and appearing like something a cat threw up, he frowned with disgust. 'Ah fur feck's sake, it's sticking to the arse of the pot!' he growled, quickly lifting the pot away. 'I'm making a right pig's ear of this job.' He sighed again in defeat. 'Right, boiled eggs and toast it is then, surely I can't go wrong with that.'

As the eggs were boiling away Frankie had an idea. He dashed outside into the backyard. Suzy adored her garden. It was evident in her beautiful display of flowers that she took great pride in keeping it well-groomed. Frankie stood, hands on hips, and studied the myriad blossoms. Flowers, however, were evidently not his strong point, he had never in his life picked flowers for a woman before and right now he hadn't a clue where to start. He scanned his eyes over the yellow sunflowers, absolutely not them, too big, he thought. His gaze then looked at the blood-red roses, baby-pink carnations, and bluebells. Remembering that Suzy once said her favourite colour was blue, he opted for the bluebells and a single red rose. His attention was then drawn to the golden daffodils dancing to the gentle wind's whistling tune. Just as he was about to pick one, he changed his mind. They looked beautiful and happy as they swayed to and fro in the breeze and much too content to pull from their abode, he therefore left them to enjoy the sun's rays.

Back in the house, he placed his selection into a vase of water and together with the breakfast, he sat it all on the tray. Smiling to himself and feeling as pound as punch, he tiptoed upstairs.

Frankie knocked on the door of Suzy's bedroom and waited. After a few seconds he pushed the door open a fraction and peeped his head in. Suzy lay there in the bed fast asleep, her thick, wavy auburn hair resting around her on the pillow.

Tiptoeing into the room, Frankie whispered, 'Suze, I've a wee surprise for you.'

Suzy, opening her eyes a little, yawned and closed them again.

'Wake up, Suze,' he said gently.

Suzy opened her eyes a little again, 'Wh… what time is it?' She yawned once more and opened her eyes wide this time. 'Frankie? What are you doing here?' she asked smiling sleepily up at him.

'Brought you this,' he replied with a grin.

She sat up and rested her head on the pillows, her gaze falling on the tray in his hands.

'Well, Suze, you've been looking after me for the last few weeks, spoiling me rotten with breakfast in bed and what not, so I thought as I'm feeling much better, I'd treat you for a change.' He beamed and placed the tray on her lap.

'Oh, Frankie! Thanks, you didn't need to go to all this bother.' Flowers and all, Suzy thought, how sweet of him. She took a bite of the cold toast.

'Not at all, you deserve it,' Frankie replied with an air of triumph. 'Now you eat that all up and I'll go and get myself a wee wash for I'm going to chapel with you today.'

Suzy almost choked on her toast. 'What? You're going to mass?' she asked, astonished at the prospect of Frankie wanting to go to church without her nagging at him.

'And confession!' he added with determination. 'I'll be a new man by the day's out, Suze,' he joked. 'My halo will be shining bright!' he chuckled.

By now Suzy's eyes had widened so much she thought they would pop out of her head at any second. 'Well… that's a goodun'! That really is! I feel like I'm still dreaming!' she teased.

Back in his room, Frankie filled his wash bowl with water, scooped the liquid into his hands and splashed it over his face. He then mixed the water with a little shaving cream and rubbed it around his cheeks and under his chin to begin shaving off the unsightly stubble. After he had finished shaving, he filled the bath and scrubbed himself until he was spotless clean.

An hour later, dressed in his Sunday best, he was looking younger, cleaner and as fresh as a daisy. All he needed now was to cleanse his soul.

'Psst, Father,' Frankie whispered, peering into the sacristy.

Father Lavery turned around. 'Oh, hello there, can I help you?'

Frankie stepped into the room, the waft of incense was overwhelming and it felt so good to be breathing in this smell that he had always enjoyed as a child. The aroma took him back to his younger years when he came to church with his grandmother on a weekly basis.

'My goodness, Frankie McGregor, is it really you?' Father Lavery teased and greeted him with a warm welcoming smile. 'What's up with you, is everything okay?'

'No, I need you to hear my confession, and please, I need you to do it before mass, if you don't mind,' Frankie pleaded. His grandmother had always warned him never to receive Holy Communion unless his soul was spotless clean. She had drummed it into his head that one wouldn't go to greet a friend dressed in dirty soiled clothes and therefore the same should be said when welcoming Jesus in Holy Communion. This idea never left Frankie and it was for this very reason he wanted to wipe the slate clean and get rid of all his sins before mass started.

Father Lavery glanced over Frankie's shoulder to the clock hanging on the wall behind him. 'I don't normally hear confession on Sundays before mass but I've got a few minutes, come with me, Frankie.'

'A few minutes? Gee, Father, it's a few hours I need. In fact, I hope you have a packed lunch with you, Father, you'll need it, I'll have you here all day,' Frankie joked as he followed the priest out of the sacristy and into the confessional box.

Fifteen minutes later Frankie walked down the front of the church, where Suzy sat in silent prayer. He felt as if he was floating down the aisle, a weight had truly been lifted off his shoulders, never in his life could he remember feeling so good about himself. Father Lavery's words would remain with him forever. "We are all guilty of sin," Father Lavery had warned, "whether you are an alcoholic or an aristocrat we are all the same in God's eyes, all capable of sinning and all deserving of God's mercy. Each of us are beautiful children of God and when we say sorry to Him, God and his holy angels rejoice. No matter how sinful you are, God will welcome you back home, home, Frankie, with open arms and I have no doubt that Jesus will be smiling down on you right now. The prodigal son has returned! Welcome back to the Catholic faith, Frankie!'

Father Lavery's kind words meant a lot to Frankie and soon he found himself not only opening his mouth to confess all his wrongdoings but also opening his heart and mind.

As Frankie now looked upon the magnificent altar decorated with an arrangement of beautiful baby-pink roses and white carnations, and burning candles, he felt uplifted. The candles flickered and cascaded a soft light upon the marble altar and surrounding statues. For the first time in his life Frankie felt at home just as Father Lavery had said. Right now as he sat in the wonderful chapel of the Long Tower, his heart wanted to burst with love for God and for His son Jesus Christ.

Turning his gaze away from the altar, Frankie's eyes fell upon Suzy. She remained kneeling, her eyes closed tight in prayer, her soft, thick auburn hair falling loosely over her shoulders. His stomach did a little flip as a warm, tingling sensation pulsed through him. He realised his heart was swelling at an alarming rate and skipping a beat now and again. His heart began feeling like it was going to explode at any second, not only for the newfound love for God but the truth was, he was falling head over heels in love... in love with Suzy Ferguson!

Chapter 23

'I now pronounce you husband and wife!' Father Fitzgerald announced proudly. 'My dear brother, you may kiss your beautiful wife!'

Theo's cobalt-blue eyes danced as he placed his hand under Erin's chin, tilted his head and kissed her inviting rosebud lips. Erin's heart melted in the surreal moment, so much so she felt as if she was about to float off the parquet tiled floor, never had she felt so happy.

Turning round to smile at the applauding congregation, Erin's gaze fell on the front row. Erin, still trembling from the shock of seeing them only hours earlier, felt her knees wobble. She still could not take it in that they were here. They were really here in New York and all thanks to Theo, what an amazing surprise.

Her heart skipped a beat as she recalled the shock earlier. Leonarda had just finished pinning Erin's hair when she announced that she was to close her eyes tight as Theo had arranged a surprise for her. Dressed in her bridal gown, Erin had taken Leonarda's hand and allowed her to lead her through to the living area of William's small apartment. Teetering close to Leonarda, Erin could feel a jittery feeling forming in the pit of her tummy, she loved surprises. At first she had thought Theo must have arranged for a bunch of flowers to be sent to her before the wedding ceremony. Erin had never received flowers as a gift before and the thought of receiving them now was as exciting as the wedding itself. When Leonarda asked her to open her eyes and shouted '*Surprise!*' Erin almost fainted with the shock at the sight of her parents, her sisters Mary and Sarah, and brother Aaron.

'Oh my…' Erin screeched, feeling she had to pinch herself to ensure this was truly happening. 'I don't bel…' but before she had a chance to continue, her father threw his arms around her in a huge bear hug.

'We've missed you, Erin!' Kissing her on both cheeks, he continued, 'We have missed you so much, darling!'

Behind him her mother swallowed the lump in her throat and dabbed at the corner of her eyes before both herself and the others joined then in a group hug.

Leonarda's chubby cheeks glowed, she could feel the love this family had for one another. As an orphaned child, Leonarda always yearned for the family she never knew. She had loved Erin like she was her own daughter, ever since Erin had started working in the Fitzgerald household, Leonarda had found the beautiful Irish girl intriguing. Her warm, loving, innocent nature had reminded Leonarda of herself. Erin could be a bit naïve at times and that made Leonarda love her that little bit more. It was due to this simplistic nature of Erin's, she wanted to protect her, especially her heart. She knew how hard the young girl battled over her feelings for Patrick Brogan and for Theo. In the end, Patrick's unresponsiveness had led Erin to choose Theo and she had to admit, that wasn't an easy choice for the young Irish beauty. She was aware Erin's heart had been broken but she knew she loved Theo very much. If anyone could make Erin happy, Theo could.

My goodness, Leonarda thought, as she watched Erin weep into the arms of her family, Theo loved this girl more than anything in the world, they would make each other happy.

As she observed Erin dressed in her beautiful, white lace bodice gown, her hair falling gently over her shoulders, Leonarda not only adored Erin as a daughter but she was proud of her as if she was her own offspring. She could imagine right now how John and Catherine Coyle felt, for at this very moment, Leonarda felt as proud as any parent.

'How did you all get here?' Erin asked, pulling away and reaching for a handkerchief.

'The same as you, on a boat!' Aaron teased.

Erin smiled as she ruffled her little brother's thick hair. 'Cheeky little monkey! I can't believe you are all actually here. I mean, who organised all this?'

'Theo did,' Leonarda replied, removing the hankie from Erin and gently dabbing Erin's cheeks and the corners of her eyes. 'Young Theo knew how much this surprise would mean to you, he wasted no time in sending them the boat tickets.'

'And we've been hiding in the Fitzgerald household for the last few days,' Sarah chuckled. 'What a house! Fit for kings and queens, that house is. I've never seen anything like it in my life.'

'I agree,' John said. 'They've made us so welcome.' Tapping Erin's shoulders, he continued, 'Theo seems like a fine man and I give you both my blessing.' John smiled. He couldn't understand why Erin had rejected Patrick but had decided that he would mind his own business and accept his daughter's decision. He was certainly confused about her reactions but he wasn't going to bring up the subject on her wedding day. 'All I want is for you to be happy, Erin, and I can tell that young man loves you with all of his heart. God bless you both on your marriage journey, may you both we very happy together.'

'That means a lot to me,' she replied before throwing her arms around her dad and giving him another hug. 'You've no idea just how much that means to me!'

The ceremony ended and Father Fitzgerald gave his final blessing for the newlyweds and the congregation.

As Theo and Erin walked arm-in-arm up the aisle, Erin's gaze fell upon her family, all looking happy for her except Mary. Is it really them? Erin thought as she caught sight of Mary staring back at her from under her brimmed hat. She still couldn't believe the events of the day and was sure she must be dreaming but Mary's stern look bothered her.

Outside the church, John hugged his daughter. 'Congratulations, Erin!' Looking to Theo he went on, 'You've got yourself a fantastic girl, look after her.'

'I will, Mr Coyle, don't you worry, I'll ensure Erin is the happiest girl in the world,' he said and planted a kiss on her cheek.

Squeezing his way in between them, William said, 'Father dear, don't you worry about your little girl, sure hasn't she got two fine men here to look after her, don't fret, I'll keep her out of mischief,' he teased. 'Congratulations, sis, you've got yourself a great husband.' Turning to Theo he gave him a playful pat on the back, 'And you, my dear friend have got yourself the best wife ever possible so you better make her the happiest girl in the world or you'll have me to deal with.' He narrowed his eyes. Pulling Maxine closer, William slipped his hand around her waist.

'Oh, now that's a worrying thought.' Theo grinned. 'And speaking of worrying thoughts, is my eyesight deceiving me?' he glanced from William to Maxine.

Erin opened her mouth to speak but the shock froze her tongue.

'No,' William replied before planting a kiss on Maxine's cheek. 'My dear friend, it's time we let you all know, Maxine and I are in love!'

'You rascal!' Erin joked. 'I can't *believe* I hadn't guessed and I can't *believe* you didn't tell me! I begged you to tell me!'

'It was my fault, I asked him to keep it low key.' Maxine beamed. 'I had my heart broken once before and I guess I wanted to ensure William wasn't just going through a phase but I know now it's the real thing.' She smiled up at him and he kissed her again.

'I'm so happy for you both!' Theo announced. Giving William a playful punch, he continued. 'Looks like we'll both have to keep an eye on one another!' he joked. Before he could say another word Leonarda enveloped Theo and Erin in a great big hug.

Kissing Theo on the cheek and then Erin, she beamed, 'I don't know about the rest of you guys but I certainly am the most excited person standing on this earth today.' Looking from one to the other, she went on, 'God bless you both, I couldn't have picked a better partner for each of you. This surely is a match made in heaven.'

Theo, pressing a kiss on Erin's cheek, replied, 'I couldn't agree with you more!'

The huge marquee situated on the neatly trimmed, lush green lawns to the back of the Fitzgerald's household, erupted into a mighty round of applause as the newlyweds emerged through the floral entrance. Standing joyfully under the display of pink and white roses, they smiled for the camera.

'This feels a bit odd,' Erin whispered through closed teeth. 'I've never seen a camera before never mind have one flash at me. 'We had our picture taken once but I was too young to remember it.'

'Just keep showing those pearly whites.' Theo grinned.

Tables had been set up all around the marquee, each with expensive white linen tablecloths trimmed with pink lace and on the centre of each table sat a glass vase, all displaying pink and white roses.

Family, friends, and neighbours occupied the tables. Erin smiled as she drank in the sight of them all, their friendly faces looking back at her, everyone dressed in their expensive tailored suits, fancy dresses and magnificent hats.

Her heart felt like it had suddenly expanded like a hot air balloon as her gaze fell on her own little gathering of the Coyle family.

Next to her Theo gave her hand a reassuring squeeze. Releasing his grasp, he placed his hand around her waist and gently pulled her nearer. 'Look, there's cousin Ralph, I haven't seen him in a long time.'

Erin watched as Ralph set up his tripod and beamed at her. 'Give me a great big smile, Erin,' he drawled in his strong Californian accent.

Before she knew it the flashbulbs had dazzled her eyes.

'One more,' Ralph called as he clicked away. 'That's it, all done and free to go!'

Blushing and smiling Erin followed Theo as he led her from one table to another to introduce her to each of their guests. By the time they finally sat down at their own, Erin felt her cheeks hurt so much from the constant smiling and her head twirling with so many new faces and names tumbling about inside.

Theo, lifting a bottle of Veuve Clicquot and wrestling with the cork, grinned, 'Let's celebrate!' With a mighty pop the cork burst out with a bang. The bubbles and the champagne exploded from the bottle with the enthusiasm of lava erupting from Mount Etna.

Filling two glasses, he looked to Erin with pride and

handed her one. 'To my beautiful wife.' He beamed as he clicked his glass against hers. 'I love you, Erin!'

'I love you too!' Erin replied before taking a sip of the expensive beverage. The liquid tasted so good she found herself wanting to drink the entire glass.

After a few minutes, Erin, not being used to such expensive luxury and not one to normally drink alcohol, now felt a little tipsy. Settling back in her chair she gazed at the guests in front of her, everyone seemed to be having a fantastic time, every face her gaze fell on she witnessed joy and happiness. The day had gone well and thankfully the weather for mid-September was just perfect, not too warm and not a drop of rain in sight. Her thoughts trailed to Ireland. There was no doubt had she gotten married back home, her day would have been quite the opposite. For a start the odds of rain back in Derry would have been high and she certainly would not be sitting in a grand marquee drinking champagne and about to eat her first course of none other than salmon mousse!

Erin had to admit that both Mrs Fitzgerald and Leonarda had done a fantastic job preparing for today. As soon as they had announced their engagement, only weeks ago back in July, the pair had wasted no time in organizing everything. Erin now marvelled at how great a job they had done.

Leonarda had been in touch with some local cooks and they had all got together to prepare the finniest of dining. The first course consisted of a choice of grapefruit or salmon mousse, followed by a choice of either cream butternut squash and sweet potato soup or Erin's favorite American bean soup.

The main course comprised of a choice of fillet mignon, roasted chicken or poached salmon and to finish with, dessert involved a choice of vanilla cheesecake or fruit salad. Erin had to admit the food had been sublime and from the look at the empty plates, everyone else had thought so too, with not a morsel left behind on most plates.

'What are you thinking, Mrs Fitzgerald?' Theo leaned closer, draping one hand over her shoulder and taking her hand in his other.

'I'm just thinking what a wonderful day this has been, from the chapel, the food, the weather, the marquee, my family being here and most of all you, being married to you, Theo!' She gave his hand a squeeze. 'How perfect my life feels right now. I love you, Theo.'

Theo gazed lovingly at her, kissed her lips and replied, 'I'm so glad, you deserve nothing less, Erin. I love you, darling, I love you soooo much.'

As the entertainment began to set up and Theo busied himself ensuring everyone was okay, Erin felt the need to grab a bit of time with her sister Mary.

Mary linked her arm with Erin's as they both walked along the stoned pathway that ran though the neatly trimmed lawn. Making their way to a wooden bench under the patchy shade of some huge elm trees, they sat down. The leaves above their heads rustled in the light, warm afternoon breeze.

'So tell me, how's things back in Derry?' Erin gathered her dress and made herself comfortable on the bench.

'Oh you know, same old, same old.' Mary hugged a glass of champagne and gazed up at the fluffy white clouds scudding across a duck-egg-blue sky. Taking a sip of the bubbly drink, she kicked off her shoes and went on, 'Well, everyone back in Derry is doing fine. Father Lavery sends his blessings.'

'Oh he's such a great priest, tell him I said hello,' Erin replied. 'What else is going on?' she asked with interest.

'You're not going to believe this, Frankie McGregor is now a tea drinker and no longer on the alcohol…'

'You're kidding me?' Erin interrupted. 'You must be joking! Aul Frankie off the liquor? I don't believe that for a second.'

'Well he was the last I heard.' Mary continued, 'Mind you I doubt if he'll stay off it but I do have to admit he seems to be doing a good job so far. I have to give him credit where credit is due and Suzy Ferguson has been helping him. Suzy has been amazing with him.'

'Fair play to him. I'm delighted to hear that news and fair play to Suzy too, I'm sure she has her hands full. Anything else happening?' Erin sipped her champagne.

'Aye well, Patrick… Patrick's gone to Dublin.'

'Dublin?' Erin shooed away a flying insect. 'What has taken him to Dublin?'

'Apparently he was offered work down there but if I'm being honest, I think the reason he went is that he needed to get away from Derry for a bit.'

199

'Why?' Erin's brow furrowed in concern.

Mary, flicking back her black hair, replied, 'Because of you, silly! Don't you realise he's lost everything? Erin there's nothing to keep him in the Bogside any longer. When I told him you were getting married he looked horrified. I'm not joking you, you would have thought I had told him the world was about to end by the look on his face. I'm telling you, Erin, he didn't appear happy but then again, I suppose the news of you getting married to another man was just like the end of his world.' Mary, squinting against the sun's rays, finished off the remainder of her drink and wiggled her toes in the soft grass.

Erin twisted her wedding ring around her finger. 'If that's the case then he should have done something about it!' she replied through gritted teeth.

'What do you mean? He told me he had written to you and you hadn't bothered to reply. He asked you to marry him, Erin!' Mary, remembering her father's warnings earlier not to bring up the subject of Patrick, decided to ignore his advice, after all it was too late, she had mentioned him now and may as well continue.

'Mary, I wrote to *him*! I told him I would marry him but he was the one that didn't bother replying to *me*!' Erin fired back.

Theo, after spotting his wife at the bottom of the garden earlier, decided to join them. He had stopped in his tracks and now he wished he had just stayed put in the marquee.

Clutching a bottle of champagne, his hands trembled and he felt himself glued to the grass verge beneath his feet.

Forcing himself to step back behind the huge rose bush, he took refuge in the shadows beneath the mighty elm trees.

A fiery sensation caught in his chest whilst he tried to control his rapid breathing, as Erin's statement, '*I told him I would marry him.*' rung in his ears.

Chapter 24

'You wanted to marry him? He never said! Erin, I don't understand it!' Mary shook her head.

'Oh I can understand it clearly.' Erin took a gulp of her drink. 'Patrick Brogan thought he wanted me as his wife and as soon as I said yes he changed his mind! William tried to warn me but I didn't listen. William did his best to stop me writing to him, but I went ahead. I waited and waited for his reply but got nothing!' she said, the effects of the alcohol raising her voice a fraction.

'I don't believe he got your letter. Erin, think about it, he couldn't have done!' Mary swallowed, remembering her conversation with him back in July, she was sure he mustn't have received that letter. 'Listen, Erin, you've got to believe me, he didn't get your reply.'

'Really?' Erin shrugged. 'I can't imagine that to be true, he got my letter, I have no doubt about that!'

'No he didn't! I've spoken to him. I know how heartbroken he was. He didn't get your reply, trust me, Erin. He told me how gutted he was that you didn't respond. He also said he was waiting for your answer and if you felt the same about him he would come out to you.'

Erin couldn't believe her ears. The late afternoon sun glistened on the tears welling up in her eyes. 'What a mess, well it's too late now, it's too late.'

'I can't believe you went ahead and married Theo! If

I'm being honest part of me resented you going ahead with this marriage today. Talk about rushing in at the deep end!'

'That's hardly fair,' Erin fired back. 'In fact, Mary, that's a terrible thing to say!'

'No it's not! Think about it, Erin, you and Patrick were made for each other. He loves you for crying out loud and you love him!'

'Why are you telling me all this now?' Erin snapped back, 'Why have this conversation with me on my wedding day? I told you it's too late!' Erin said, feeling her jaw tighten.

'Because I know you, Erin, and I know how much Patrick means to you. I'm your sister for crying out loud, I know you too well.'

'Listen, Mary, he did mean something to me in the past, you're right, but he does not anymore. Please don't get me wrong, I will always care about him and he will always have a piece of my heart, but as I said earlier, it is now too late. Perhaps if he did get the letter then things might have worked out differently, I don't know.' Erin shrugged. 'Either way we can't change things now. Things are meant to happen for a reason.'

In the distance, they could hear the party in full swing carrying on without them, and with the sweet melody of music and whoops of laughter sailing through the warm breeze, it was clear the guests were having a great time.

'Well I certainly know things would have been much different, so much *different*! I truly believe you wouldn't have married Theo for a start. For goodness' sake you hardly even know him.'

Erin's gaze fell on her wedding ring and she recalled how happy she had felt earlier. Today was supposed to continue with joy but Mary had put a damper on that. Perhaps she was right to tell her all this but surely not on her wedding day. She certainly did not want to have this conversation today above all days.

Theo could hear the happy cheers of his guests in the marquee not far away and he prayed silently no one would catch him eavesdropping. What would he look like listening in on his wife's conversation? Bloody Patrick Brogan, he thought, why could he not just let her go and worse still why could Erin not have just let him go. Life was so unfair at times. One thing was sure, his marriage could not continue with the joy he had felt earlier. If Erin didn't love him like he loved her, he wasn't sure how he would cope.

'Did you hear me, Erin? You would *not* have married Theo for a start,' Mary repeated.

Erin lifted her head to look Mary in the eyes, she knew it wasn't like her sister to interfere like this, and part of her wanted to scream at her for bringing up this subject today. 'Look, Mary, I know you're very fond of Patrick. He's been my friend for most of my life and he's also like part of the Coyle family. We all care about him and none of us want to see him hurting, but as I said before, it is too late and I am not going to say that again so therefore we are going to *end* this topic now. As I said earlier perhaps this is the way things are meant to be. He obviously wasn't meant to receive that letter for some reason. Do you want to know what I think?'

'What?'

'I believe the reason was because I was meant to marry Theo and not Patrick. God has each of our lives planned out for us. I have heard that often enough to believe it. I truly accept that, so I will therefore look upon my letter going astray as a blessing.'

Mary nodded and shrugged her shoulders, 'I suppose you could be right.'

'Mary, regardless of what you might think, or any of the rest of my family, or any of the neighbours and friends back in the Bog for that matter, I didn't marry Theo on some kind of rebound and I certainly did not marry him as a second best. Can I also add, with regards your comments about me hardly knowing Theo, I can assure you I have known that man long enough to have made my decision! I married Theo because I *wanted* to be his wife. You must believe that. I promise you I will be happy with him. I married him as I want to spend the rest of my life with him and I'm attracted to Theo. Each time I set my eyes on him I feel this warm sensation come over me, my heart beats faster and I want to throw my arms around him and cling to him forever. I want to have his children and most of all, Mary, I married him because I truly love Theo Fitzgerald. So no more talk about any love or what ifs or what should have been with Patrick, I'm a Fitzgerald now and I'm proud to be Theo's wife!'

Theo's heart warmed at this. He raised his gaze to the

heavens above, 'Thank you God, thank you my Lord,' he whispered under his breath.

Mary, taking Erin's hand in hers, lowered her tone and replied, 'I'm sorry, of course you love Theo and I don't know what came over me, after all I'm the one that hardly knows your husband. He seems nice and I should trust your judgment.'

Smiling, Erin replied, 'Thanks, sis, and please don't worry about my life. I've found myself a good man.'

'I'm sure he is indeed and I mustn't forget to mention that he is also drop-dead gorgeous, which is a real bonus.' Mary giggled.

Erin laughed. 'Well it does help and I must agree with you, he is very handsome but I didn't marry him for his beauty alone, as I said earlier, I truly love Theo.' She squeezed Mary's hand and in a more serious tone went on, 'Listen, thank you for coming. I'm so happy that you are all here to share this day with me, it means so much to me, you have no idea.'

Mary, hugging her sister, replied, 'Oh, Erin, thank God we could be here. I wouldn't have wanted to miss this for the world and it's all thanks to Theo.'

'Well, now as this is supposed to be the best day of my life, let's go and have some fun.' Erin stood up and gathered her dress. 'C'mon, we're missing out on all the entertainment.'

Theo's heart skipped a beat. Before he was caught lurking in the bushes he stepped out from his hiding place and turning the corner so he was now visible, he exclaimed. 'There you are, Mrs Fitzgerald! I've been wondering where you got to.' Holding up two empty glasses and a bottle of champagne he said, 'I thought you and I could have another celebratory drink or two together.'

'You two lovebirds sit here, I'll head back to the party,' Mary chirped in. Rising to her feet she smiled. 'You never know I may just get a dance with one of Theo's handsome cousins!' She winked.

Spotting her empty glass in her hand, Theo replied, 'No, stay here and have a drink with us,' he insisted.

'No honestly, it's fine and besides you two need a little time to yourselves.' Mary, replacing her shoes, continued, 'My mother and father are probably wondering where I got to and then there's those cousins of yours, I'm sure one or two will be looking for a wee dance,' she teased.

Grinning, Theo replied, 'Well, my cousin Ralph is in there dancing about like his arms are made from spaghetti, maybe you could show him a few moves.'

'Hey, now you're talking, what am I waiting for!' Mary beamed.

'Although, mind you, I think he's had a fair bit of champagne in him, maybe he's no longer king of the dance floor.'

Shrugging, Mary replied, 'Ah well that will be his loss, I'll just have to find myself another one of your handsome cousins, then.' With a wink of an eye and a grin, she continued. 'I'll leave you alone now in peace, bye.'

Theo sat down on the bench and watched until Mary was out of sight. Sitting back down next to him Erin held out her glass and allowed him to top it up.

'I'm sorry I left the party for a while, I just needed to catch up with Mary, you know, find out how things are back in Derry,' Erin said as she sipped on the bubbly drink.

'Of course, I can understand that. I'm sure you two have so much to discuss.' He smiled lovingly at his beautiful bride.

The brilliant tangerine sun was slowly sinking bit by bit until it slid from sight on the western horizon, painting the sky with a majesty of beautiful vibrant red and orange threads of lingering glows. Up ahead, surrounding the marquee, the candles, encased in lanterns, danced in the delicate warm breeze and the white fairy lights decorating the trees dazzled like little stars as evening began to creep in.

'I'm so happy I married you, Theo.' Erin placed a hand on his knee.

'Me too!' he kissed the tip of her nose and each cheek in turn before finally brushing against her soft lips. 'I love you,' he murmured. 'Now, let's have a toast.' He tapped her glass with his. 'To us!'

'I'll toast to that, to us and our future children!' Erin giggled.

Theo's eyes widened, 'Future children? Well in that case what are we doing sitting here? Let's go! C'mon it's about time there was a little Fitzgerald in the family!'

Chapter 25

The moon shimmered over the Liffey and lit up the cloudless inky sky above their heads. Patrick, feeling a slight chill in the October air, buttoned up his coat. The delicate wind stirred the crisp autumn leaves to twirl like ballet dancers at their feet and some tumbled into the curling waters below. The breeze brushed against the water's surface, causing the ripples to tousle a little more and shatter their reflection. Leaning over O'Connell Bridge, he watched the silver rippling stream carry the fallen autumn leaves of red and gold on their journey as the river twisted and curled through the city.

Charlotte popped a boiled sweet into her mouth and gazed at him fondly. Like a moth attracted to a flame, she couldn't help but feel drawn to him, even if that did mean she was likely to get burned in the end. She also could not prevent feeling a pang of jealousy for this Erin one that had captured his heart. Patrick had told her all about this girl over the coffee they shared on their first trip to Bewley's and it was clear she had broken his heart. At first, Charlotte didn't think much of it, surely she would persuade his thoughts away from her, but as the weeks turned into months and she had clearly shown him how much she liked him, he hadn't as much as kissed her on the cheek. However, she wasn't stupid, there was a spark between them, she had seen it in his eyes. Whether he liked it or not, or chose to admit it, he was attracted to her and if he wasn't going to make the first move then she was going to simply have to do it for him!

'What are you thinking?' Charlotte asked as she slipped her hand over his.

Patrick, turning to face her, replied, 'Nothing,' he lied. 'Nothing much.'

'I know what's going through that head of yours, you're thinking it's your birthday today and you haven't received a birthday kiss yet!' Charlotte teased. Edging closer to him she whispered, 'Will I do?' she asked moving her lips nearer.

Patrick, taking a step back, smiled, 'No, Charlotte, your dad wouldn't be happy.'

'Oh for crying out loud, don't you give me that excuse again! I'm bleedin' sick and tired of hearing it. Let me tell you something, Patrick, my father is not going to rule my bleedin' life and he certainly cannot rule yours! And by the way,' she pointed her finger at him for emphasis, 'stop bleedin' well looking into that water daydreaming of Erin Boyle or … or Coyle … or whatever her flippin' name is. She's now married! She's with someone else! You silly aul fool! She's now a married woman, so you can grow up and catch yourself on! Shame on you! Get over her, you loser!' she yelled, the veins on her neck protruding with rage.

'Have you finished?' he asked raising an eyebrow.

Charlotte flicked back her long, silver-blonde hair, shrugged her shoulders and looked away.

'If you must know I have *not* been daydreaming about Erin Coyle. I haven't even been *thinking* about her today, if I'm being honest.'

Fixing her gaze back on him, Charlotte stuck out her chin and threw him a sarcastic stare. 'Well that's a first! Hip, hip hooray!'

'You're right, Charlotte, Erin is now married and I have accepted that. I've decided to put her out of my mind. If you really want to know what I've been thinking about all day, I will tell you.'

'No, it doesn't matter, I don't care,' she lied.

'You obviously care enough to mention it so I'll tell you.'

'No, don't bother cause I don't give a hoot!' she fired back.

'My thoughts have been plagued with memories of my parents. I miss their birthday greetings, especially my da's.' Patrick fixed his attention back to the water. 'He always made a huge fuss over my birthday, bouncing into my room early in the morning before I could barely open my eyes, singing happy birthday, and do you know what the worst is?' he asked and swallowed the lump in his throat before continuing, 'The worst is I used to get so annoyed at him for waking me from my sleep. I'd bury my head under the blanket hoping he would just go away so I could get back to sleep again.' He watched the leaves float further down the stream with an ache in his heart. 'You see back then I never imagined that one day he wouldn't be here to do that and now that he is no longer alive, I'd give anything to have him spring into the room this morning singing happy birthday at the top of his voice.' The lump in his throat mushroomed. Awash with emotion, he struggled to fight back

211

the tears knowing as he observed the leaves drift out of sight, he would never see them again, just like his parents, gone from sight forever. Taking a deep breath, he continued, 'And then there was my mother, she used to bake me the most mouth-watering cake on my birthday, filled with thick cream for my sweet tooth, just how I liked it.'

Charlotte, feeling instantly ashamed for her outburst, dipped her head. 'I'm sorry,' she mumbled. Her heart went out to him.

'I know it might seem stupid but it's days like these that bring it all back to me that my parents are gone. They're truly gone and I have to face it. I'm never going to see them on this earth again, never will I hear that annoying happy birthday from my dad, or taste my mother's cooking and believe me at this very moment God only knows how I long to be able to step back in time right now.' The tears swimming in his eyes escaped, and like captives set free, they wasted no time in rolling down his cheeks at a great speed.

Patrick wiped his face and sniffed. 'I'm sorry, you probably think I'm a sentimental aul fool.'

'No I don't.' Charlotte shook her head and fixed him a loving stare. 'I'm the fool, not you.'

'It's hard that's all, it's just so hard.' Patrick swallowed as he tried to pull himself together.

Charlotte felt her heart swell. It wasn't easy watching a grown man cry. The tears glistened in her own emerald eyes. 'No, I'm sorry, I'm so sorry, I've been stupid. Come here. Let me give you a hug.' She held out her arms as a token of sympathy.

He didn't need to be asked twice, he needed a hug now more than anything. As her gentle arms enveloped around his neck, he locked his own arms around her waist and felt himself wanting to cry over again.

'I should have known, Patrick, that today would have been difficult for you. I suppose I didn't tink. I've no idea what you're going through, I can only imagine. I guess I'm fortunate to have both my parents, even if my da can be a right pain at times.'

'Never worry. Thank God you have your parents, treasure them now while you have that chance. Trust me, the loss is hard. It's so difficult to lose a parent. I believe part of me died also the day they died.' His voice cracked.

'Let it out, Patrick. Let all your grief flow out,' she said softly as she stroked the back of his neck.

'When I think back to my mother's death, I think I coped better. It was hard at the time but I guess children are more resilient than adults. I don't know what I'm saying, Charlotte, but what I mean is, I'm finding my dad's death much, much more difficult. I guess the reason being is because it was just me and him for so long together, we were a team, the best of buddies.'

'I can understand what you're saying, and when your mum passed away you had your dad to lean on,' she replied gently.

Gazing off into the distance, Patrick nodded, he wanted to tell her he also had Erin. 'Aye you're right. Gee I miss him so badly.' Patrick sighed and rubbed his hand over his chin. 'I never thought I would see the day that I'd have to say goodbye to him, honestly, you think you have them forever but the reality is that is not the case. I'm not joking you, Charlotte, my aul man was more than a father, he was my mucker and I'll tell you now, he may be gone but his memory will always live on in my heart.' The tears blinded him again, so much so they blurred his vision.

'It'll get easier, I'm sure it will,' Charlotte reassured.

'Aye of course it will. Right, that's enough.' He pulled away, 'Look at the state of me. I'm supposed to be meeting Chris and the lads from work for a game of cards and a pint of Guinness. I think they might have a good laugh if I turned up with swollen eyes looking like a frog!' He sighed and tried to execute a grin. 'Imagine what Chris would say if he knew I was standing here crying like a big wain.'

Charlotte smiled with an understanding look. 'Never mind what Chris would say. Take a look up there.' She pointed to the inky night sky, now alive with millions of twinkling stars. 'Your parents will be looking down at you from the heavens above and they'll be saying wow look at our boy standing with the finest girl in Dublin's fair city!'

Patrick couldn't help but smile at her.

'Only joking.' She continued in a more serious tone. 'They'll be saying we'll always be with you in spirit, we'll walk along the journey of your life each step of the way, you

214

may not see or hear us but remember we'll never leave your side.'

Patrick, running his fingers through her silky hair, smiled again, 'For such young shoulders you sure have a sensible head on you. You're right.'

'I'm always right,' Charlotte purred.

His eyes locked on hers for a few seconds before his gaze moved to her inviting lips. The urge to kiss her was so overwhelming but he knew it was best not to. 'C'mon, let's go.' He released his hold and casually threw his arm over her shoulder. As they walked under the blanket of twinkling stars and the moonlight illuminated their pathway, a warm glow developed within him. 'Thanks Charlotte, I feel better already.' He gave her shoulder an affectionate squeeze.

You'd feel even more better if you could just *feel* my lips on yours, she was dying to reply but decided against it, after all the night was still young, who knows what might happen later, she thought with a mischievous grin. Instead she replied, 'You're welcome.'

'And, by the way, if you don't mind me saying, you certainly *are* the *finest* girl in Dublin's fair City!'

Foley's pub was buzzing with activity, the drunken revellers packed in like sardines. The flow of conversations and tobacco smoke escaped through the open door as they approached. Patrick stood in the doorway and scanned the rowdy bunch in search of Chris as wisps of smoke curled and danced towards him catching in the back of his throat and causing his eyes to water.

'Over here, Pat.' Chris waved through the murky air.

Patrick, making his way over to the far corner of the bar, where a large group of men were engaging in a serious game of poker, grinned and waved through the opaque air.

'Oi, Paul, a pint of Guinness here for Pat!' Chris yelled to the sweaty barman.

Paul, clearly run off his feet, didn't hear a word he said.

'PAUL!' Chris yelled louder, 'A drink here for the birthday boy!'

'Feck off! Birthday boy or no birthday boy, he'll wait his feckin' turn,' Paul growled, wiping the sweat off his forehead with the palm of his hand. 'Can't you see I'm feckin' busy! Get off your arse and get it yourself.'

The rowdy gamblers cheered and whistled, 'Somebody's in a bad mood!' one shouted.

'Here, Pat, sit here, I'll get you a pint,' Chris indicated a seat next to him and rose to his feet.

Patrick did what he was told and sat down. Across the table sat a bulky fierce-looking giant who introduced himself as Chuckie Maguire. Chuckie, a man in his forties with thick arms, muscles bulging under his shirt, broad shoulders, stubbly chin and a glass eye that reflected the light from the candles on the centre of the table, withdrew his cigarette from his mouth and grinned a toothless smile as he held out his sweaty, grubby palm.

Patrick accepted the strong handshake with caution.

'Hope ye 'av' a load of dosh in them pockets of yours cause I'm gonna enjoy takin' the money of ye tonight.' Chuckie cackled as he stubbed out his cigarette. 'Nothin' feels as good as takin' money off a new boy!' he said as he gathered the cards up and began shuffling them.

Less than an hour later Chuckie's predictions were correct, the new boy was losing at an alarming rate and his head was now feeling fuzzy from the shots of whiskey produced by Chuckie from a bottle hidden under the table.

Patrick fumbled around his pocket in search for his last few coins, determined this time to focus on the next round of poker.

The game commenced and much to Patrick's dismay, it was not going according to his anticipations, but more alarmingly, what he witnessed from the corner of his eye, gave him further concern than the hand of cards he had been dealt.

Chuckie, fixing him a blood-shot stare from his good eye, his face glowing with perspiration, raised his bushy eyebrows and smirked, 'All in!'

Patrick shook his head, 'You're having a laugh! I've just saw what your mate did!' Firing his cards down hard on the table, he shouted, 'I don't play with cheats!'

Chuckie, his face twisting with fury, snarled, 'What did ye just say?' he leaned across the table, clenching his fists and exhaling heavy whiskey fumes. 'What the feck did ye just

217

say?' he spat, a fire of fury smouldering in his good eye.

Chris, sensing this was about to turn nasty, intervened, 'Leave it, Pat,' he said, taking Patrick by the arm. 'Just leave it, mate.' Chris swallowed hard.

'No! He's cheating! I saw him!' Shaking off Chris' grasp, he continued, 'And he's in on it too!' He pointed at the bulky accomplice by Chuckie's side. 'I saw you passing the cards under the table! Seriously, what the heck do you lot think we are? You're taking the piss out of us all!'

'I said leave it, c'mon let's go,' Chris said. 'Sorry, Chuckie, he's had a bit too much to drink.'

Chuckie swigged back the remainder of his whiskey and banged the empty glass on the table. Turning to Chris, he gritted his teeth. 'No feckin' excuses. No one accuses us of cheating and gets away with it,' he hissed, spittle firing from his mouth, and before anyone had a chance to intervene he grabbed Patrick by the collar and head-butted him full on the nose.

Patrick, losing his balance, tumbled backwards, crashing to the floor as the rowdy revellers came to a shuddering standstill.

'And here's one for the road for you!' Chuckie cracked Chris, catching him with a mighty blow on the jaw.

Chris, falling over Patrick's chair, plunged to the ground in shock on top of his mate.

'Get up! C'mon ya feckin' losers!' Chuckie banged on his chest. 'C'mon give me your shots!'

Both men staggered to their feet in a daze.

Patrick, warm blood oozing from his nose, reached out for a wooden post to steady himself, swayed instead towards the table, lost his balance and came plummeting on the table knocking over the candles and, worse still, spilling the remainder of the drinks.

'You stupid Derry fecker! Look what you did!' Chuckie growled reaching for Patrick and firing blow after blow on his face as the crowd cheered and encouraged him for more. 'Ye spilled my feckin' drink!' he shouted, the saliva foaming through his clenched teeth.

With all his strength Patrick caught Chuckie with a mighty punch in his good eye sending the bully stumbling to the ground in a bewildered state, the effects of alcohol slowing his reactions. He fell flat on his rear and, like a turtle on its back, couldn't manage to get back on his feet.

Within seconds the entire pub erupted into chaos, chairs flying, tables turned and drinks spilling.

Minutes later, and countless punches, Patrick and Chris found themselves being grabbed by the collars of their shirts and dragged towards the door.

'Piss off and don't come back!' two angry drinkers growled as they bundled the pair out the door and, like two stray cats hoisted from a dinner party, threw them both on the pavement.

'Ouch.' Patrick winced as the cold sponge pressed against his cheek.

'That'll teach ye for messing with Chuckie and the gang,' Charlotte warned.

'Messing with him?' He's the one that was messing, he's a cheating bast... ouch! Just leave me, please.' Patrick, catching Charlotte's wrist, groaned, 'I'm too sore, honestly, I'll be okay, please leave it now.'

'Nearly finished, I just need to clean you up a bit, I'm telling ye, ye look a right mess.'

'Believe me, you don't need to tell me how I look, I feel it! My body is aching all over,' he grumbled, pushing her hand away again and wishing he had just gone on to bed like Chris had done.

The soft flicker from the oil lamp caught in Charlotte's emerald eyes and Patrick sensed her hurt. Still holding her wrist, he said softly, 'Sorry, I don't mean to be so grumpy, my head feels like it has been thrashed about between two tin lids. I'm sorry, I should never have snapped at you.'

'It's okay, I understand.' She blinked away the tears swimming in her eyes. 'I just hate to see your pretty face all swollen and bruised.'

Placing his other hand around her neck, he pulled her closer. 'It's okay. I'll be fine in a few days,' he whispered before taking them both my surprise, he closed his lips over hers and almost knocked the air from her lungs as he gave her a sloppy, whiskey-fumed kiss.

The swollen eyes, lips and battered cheeks were soon

forgotten about as they melted into each other's arms in a tingling passionate embrace.

Chapter 26

Opening his eyelids slowly, like a newborn seeing the world for the first time, Patrick gradually stirred from his sleep and gazed at the unfamiliar surroundings before him. A soft glow from the lamppost outside filtered through a small gap in the flimsy curtains. At once he sensed he was in unknown territory but hadn't the faintest idea where he was, or worse still how he got here.

His head hurt badly, so bad it felt like it had been cracked open like a nut. He groaned as the flashbacks from the night before came into his thoughts and he cringed as he realised he had been in a bust up at the local pub. The effects of over indulging in alcohol had left him with a stinking hangover. Glugging back pints of Guinness and knocking back shots of whiskey had seemed great at the time, but right now he felt as if he had been kicked up and down Grafton street, then again he may as well have been, being knocked about the pub, it was as good as being kicked up and down Grafton street!

Lying still, facing the window, he was afraid to move, his insides felt as if they were about to come shooting out his throat at any minute and the time bomb in his head was ready to explode.

A warm hand slid around his waist, almost causing him to jump out of his skin. He slowly turned around, mouth agape and came face to face with Charlotte, barely visible in the darkened room.

'Wh... what the heck are you doing here?' Patrick

croaked, his mouth feeling like he had just chewed a handful of sawdust. He began to feel more sick now than ever as he watched in horror as Charlotte pulled the blanket closer to cover her semi naked body.

'Ha, well it is *my* bed!' Charlotte replied in a casual tone. 'I should ask you what the heck are *you* doing here?' Raising herself up on one elbow, she continued, 'But then again, I wasn't the one that was as drunk as a skunk last night, I know what you're doing here,' she murmured in a teasing throaty voice. 'I can remember everything and I mean *everything*!' she giggled and turned to reach for a cigarette from the bedside locker.

Cringing at the very thought at what she was implying, Patrick closed his heavy eyelids and asked, 'What do you mean, Charlotte?' He spoke in an edgy whisper, his heart jackhammering away inside his ribcage at an alarming rate. He knew only too well Gerry would go off his head if he found out he had spent the night in his daughter's bed! Last night's boxing match in the pub would only be a taster of what was to come from Gerry, surely he would make mincemeat out of him!

Patrick felt his blood run cold. Beads of sweat formed on his brow, why could his life not be straight forward like everyone else's? No, his always had to have a drama!

Charlotte, lighting her cigarette, took a slow drag. Smoke billowed from her mouth like a blocked chimney.

How could I have been so stupid? Patrick thought, feeling the urge to slap himself. Instead he pulled the blankets around his bare shoulders, released another disgusted groan and began sliding down under the blankets. Silently he hated himself for letting his guard down and above all for losing his mind to the effects of alcohol. His father had always warned him never to get drunk, for once the mind is saturated with alcohol, all sorts of trouble can happen. Patrick knew if he had been sober last night he would never have struck up the argument with Chuckie Maguire.

'Cat got your tongue?' Charlotte asked. 'Oh, come on, don't be acting like a sulking baby.'

Unable to string two words together, Patrick just released a deep sigh and kept his eyes closed tight; by this time he had disappeared from view.

Charlotte stubbed out her cigarette in a nearby ashtray and turned around on her side to face him. 'Was it really that bad?' she purred. 'Surely you must have enjoyed it as much as I did?'

Turning to lie on his back, Patrick looked at her and asked, 'What?'

'Oh, you don't remember?' she goaded as she ran a slow finger across his collarbone and began to plant teasing kisses on his cheek until her lips got nearer to his.

Before she got a chance to come any closer with her smoky breath, he pushed her gently away. 'Don't. I'm sorry, I can't. I just can't.'

Leaning back, she gaped at him in shock. 'What do you mean by sorry?' she asked sounding wounded.

'I'm sorry about last night,' he whispered. 'You know about… us.' He could feel himself blush. 'Sorry about all this, us in bed together! It's shameful. My father, God rest his soul, would be disappointed with me, and your father will go nuts if he finds out!'

Charlotte released a little snort of laughter. 'He's not going to find out, you egit! Plus, if it makes you feel any better, we didn't actually do anything wrong!'

'We didn't?' he sat upright and immediately felt a wave of nausea sweep over him once more.

Charlotte began to laugh again. 'No, you silly clown! Besides, if we did do anything, surely you would have remembered that much! Well I certainly would like to tink so,' she replied, her tone playful. 'Patrick Brogan, it seems you had a little more to drink than I initially anticipated.' She tut-tutted.

Thank God, Patrick silently prayed.

'We actually did do something inappropriate, no matter what way we look at this. I should not be here in your bed and I am sorry for that, Charlotte.'

'There's nothing to be sorry about. It's okay.' She shrugged.

'It certainly is not okay and I can assure you this will not happen again!'

Charlotte began stroking his collarbone once more in that erotic, suggestive fashion that made him cringe again. 'Oh, don't say that, Patrick,' she cooed, allowing her silver-blonde hair to fall over his bare skin and brush against his chest. 'You certainly know how to lead a girl on, though, don't you? Taking me by the hand and directing me here.'

Patrick, his head feeling fuzzy, couldn't imagine such a thing, 'I did not! Surely I did no such thing!' he replied, rubbing his throbbing head and sighing, as he desperately tried to recall the events of last night. It was no good, very little was coming back to him and the likelihood was she was telling him the truth.

'Oh yes, surely you did and you seemed up for a bit of fun, that was, until you crashed out on my bed. Before I knew it, you were fast asleep and snoring like an aul hog! So don't you worry, the drink took over and didn't allow you to do anything else!' she laughed.

Thank you, Guinness, Patrick thought. At least now he didn't feel so bad for drinking so much.

Running a fingernail seductively down his bare chest, Charlotte whispered, 'But now that you're awake we could always...'

Grabbing hold of her hand, before she went any further, Patrick shook his head, 'No! Absolutely not! I'm sorry but last night was a drunken... *mistake*, or should I say it *could* have been a drunken mistake.'

'How dare you!' Charlotte glared at him.

'Look, I'm sorry. I'll admit, I lost control of my senses in a moment of lust and I'm sorry. I promise you, Charlotte, it won't happen again.'

'What? You're right it won't happen again! You will

certainly not be leading me up the garden path for a second time! What's wrong with me, don't you find me attractive?'

'Charlotte, that's the problem, aye, I do find you attractive, but can't you see, this is not right? You're young and naive and I should not try to take advantage of that, and besides should you not be saving yourself for marriage?'

Rolling her eyes, Charlotte replied, 'Shut up, you're starting to sound like my aul man!'

Stepping out of the bed, Patrick threw on his bloodstained shirt and searched around for the remainder of his clothes. He quickly got dressed and headed towards the door. Stopping to look over his shoulder, he said in a mere whisper, 'Sorry, Charlotte. I'm really sorry. I was drunk and I shouldn't have got myself into that state.'

'Get out!' she fired back. 'Just go!'

Sensing her displeasure at him, he murmured, 'I care about you, I don't want to hurt you.'

'Oh of course ye do, although you've a funny way of showing it!' she replied, her tone clearly portraying sarcasm.

'Honestly, I do care about you, much more than you actually think.'

'If that's the case then please don't end things,' she pleaded, her voice softening.

'There's nothing to end. Charlotte, we didn't exactly start anything to end it.' He rubbed his tired forehead.

'But, I thought you... Listen, you and I could be great

together! We get on well, don't we? You can't deny you're not attracted to me; I *know* that you are.'

He *was* attracted to her! For goodness' sake she was such a gorgeous girl, what man wouldn't? Then again, what man would be walking out of this room right now?

'You can't let my father rule our lives for us. If we get together and become a proper couple, then he's just going to have to deal with it!'

'He would be so mad.'

'No, he wouldn't! The ironic thing is he likes you! So stop making excuses because I know you want me as much as I want you! If it makes you feel better we can wait for… you know… for… ' she sighed before continuing, 'what I mean to say is we don't have to get intimate until we're married. Oh, listen to me, I don't mean I'm looking to rush you to the altar but I'm sure you know what I'm going on about.'

Smiling, Patrick nodded, 'I know what you mean.'

'So be truthful, if you are attracted to me then tell me, and if you're not then just head on out the door and we'll forget about it once and for all.'

Patrick slumped against the door in defeat, she was right and there was no denying it, drunk or not drunk last night, his heart was being pulled towards her but his brain was telling him to stay clear.

A smile swept across Charlotte's face as she watched him tiptoe back over to the bed. Taking her in his arms he kissed her warm, welcoming lips. 'You're right, your father can't rule our lives and if you want to know, I *am* attracted to you, you're beautiful,' he whispered softly.

'So, we're going to give it a go, then?' she asked, her face bright with joy.

Stroking wisps of her hair back from her face, he kissed her again.

'I take it that's a yes?' She ran her fingers through his thick hair.

'It's a definite yes,' he replied breathlessly as he smothered her with more kisses. His heart thrashed against his ribcage as he held her close and managed with all his self-control from getting back into the bed next to her. 'I better go now,' he rasped, pulling himself away and tiptoeing towards the door again.

Glancing over his shoulder, he smiled, 'Aye, I would like to give it a go, after all, what have I got to lose?'

'Only your job, if my da finds out,' she teased as she wriggled back under the blankets.

Patrick shrugged, 'Ah well, who cares, it won't be the end of the world.'

'Wait, one more thing,' she said, before he turned the handle.

'What?'

'Just thought you'd like to know, you kiss better when you're sober!'

With a wink of an eye and a cheeky grin, he blew her a

kiss and slipped quietly out of the room.

Chapter 27

'Here, get this into you, you'll feel better after a while.' Chris grinned, shoving a mug of tea into Patrick's unsteady hand.

Staring at the conker-brown liquid, Patrick suddenly felt quite sick. 'I'm never drinking again! I mean it!' He took a gulp of the strong tea and felt his stomach turn more than ever. 'Yuck! Gee, man, this is far too sweet.' Patrick pulled a face. 'What have you put in it, the entire sugar bowl?'

'It'll bring you round a bit. An extra lump of sugar or two won't do you any harm. Hurry up and drink it up, you'll feel better soon and then you can tell me where the heck you got to last night.' Chris sat down on his own bed opposite and grinned over at him with a look of amusement in his eyes.

'What time of the day is it?' Patrick yawned and rubbed his tired eyes.

'Don't bother trying to change the subject. It's almost time for dinner; I think it's about four thirty.'

'Four thirty! I've slept in for Sunday mass! Why didn't you wake me?' Patrick sounded annoyed.

'Are you having a laugh or what? Sunday mass? You must be joking, have you seen the state of your face? You'd scare the priest off the altar looking like that!'

Patrick glugged back another mouthful of the disgusting tea and immediately felt ashamed with himself for getting into such a state last night. If only he hadn't gotten so drunk, he would never have been involved in the fight and he certainly would never have missed mass. Then there was Charlotte, he could feel his face redden as the flashbacks of him sneaking shamefully into her room the night before came back bit by bit like a jigsaw puzzle. My goodness, he had done all of the opposite from what his father had taught him, surely his old man would be turning in his grave right now!

'So, Pat, tell me,' Chris fixed him a stare, 'do you plan to continue seeing Charlotte or was spending the night in her bed last night just a one off?' he raised an eyebrow.

'Sssh! Keep your voice down!' Patrick warned, looking mortified. 'Who told you?'

Chris folded his arms, a look of enjoyment plastered over his face.

'How the heck did you know that?' Patrick asked.

'I didn't, but you just confirmed my suspicions. There I was, thinking Patrick Brogan was an angel. Butter wouldn't melt in that mouth of yours, sure it wouldn't, Pat?' Chris grinned. 'Shame on you.' He tut-tutted.

'Ah sssh, would you!' Patrick groaned.

'Oh dear, oh dear, oh dear, taking advantage of a young lady, I never put you down for that type.' Chris, still smirking, shook his head and tutted again.

'I am *not* that *type* and you know it!' Patrick fired back.

'Exactly! That's what I find so amusing!'

Disgust and self-loathing was beginning to eat away at Patrick's insides, but then again, he hadn't actually done anything wrong to feel such guilt, but right now, he felt like a vegetarian caught eyeing up a sirloin steak!

Placing his cup on the bedside locker, Patrick glared at his mate. 'Listen, Chris, nothing happened and you must believe me.'

'Aye right, pull the other one.' Chris smirked.

'I'm telling you, nothing happened, you've got to *believe* me. Trust me, I'm telling you the truth.'

'Aye, I believe you, thousands wouldn't.'

'Well, I don't care if you do or not. I'll be honest with you, I did make my way to her room and I feel so ashamed of myself for that but I was so drunk, I just passed out. Can you imagine how bad I felt this morning? I cringed with embarrassment! In fact, I'm still *cringing*! I couldn't believe it when I woke up next to her this morning, I still can't believe it!'

Chris' mouth began to twitch, 'Aye, okay, I do believe you. You were in some state last night, boy!'

'I know, I know! Don't remind me.'

'Ha, if you think you were bad last night, you want to see the shape of you today, you look like you were kicked around Dublin!'

Recalling the chaos last night in the bar again, Patrick winced, 'I may as well have.'

'*We* may as well have, you mean!'

Through his swollen eyes, he glared at Chris, 'Actually you're right and by the way, you don't look so good yourself!'

'I know, I've already seen my face but I'm telling you, mate, you got the worst of it! Then again you did start it,' Chris teased.

'I did not! Didn't you see him cheat?'

Chris shrugged, 'No, I did hear a rumour in the past that he was a trickster but I have to admit I've never detected it. I suppose I've always enjoyed the game of cards too much to notice, then again perhaps Chuckie and the gang are so good at conning money from everyone else, they had us all fooled.'

'Aye, and I'd say you enjoyed the drink too much also to notice!'

'You've a cheek!' Chris let out a hearty laugh, 'You were knocking back the shots like it was no one's business.'

'Aye, true enough. I'm never drinking again! I mean it! Never again!'

'I wish I had a penny for every time I heard that line!' Chris smirked.

'One thing is for sure, I'll never be back in the company of those two swindlers. It makes me so mad that they're getting away with it! I wouldn't be surprised if there's others in on it too.'

'Aye, well let them be, I'm sure they'll meet their match one of these days, dishonesty always comes back to bite you in the arse.'

Patrick lay back against the pillows, folding his hands under his head, he stared at the ceiling. His father detested gambling and in particular poker, in fact he hated anything to do with cards and went so far as never letting a pack into their home.

He once told him of a story involving Frankie McGregor. Apparently Frankie's mother Nancy had sent him to his father's place of work one Friday afternoon to ask for his dad's wages so that she could feed her hungry children. On the way home, with the wages tucked safely in his trouser pocket, the young teenager stopped off at a neighbour's house to ask for a cigarette. Unfortunately for Frankie there was a card school in full swing in the garden shed. Following the sound of laughter and banter, Frankie made his way to the smoke-filled hut. Amazed by the amount of cash in the middle of the table, Frankie found himself sitting down, and enticed with the prospect of doubling his father's wages, he asked if he could join them. With a pat on the back from a stranger in the group and a bottle of Guinness put into his hand, Frankie took his first sip of alcohol and learned how to play poker. In no time the youngster had tripled his father's hard-earned cash. Thinking this was the best game ever and the luckiest day of his life, Frankie knocked back the free drink; he was on a roll and soon he would be making his parents the richest couple in the Bogside.

Things were going great for Frankie until another neighbour joined them. Frankie's young head, obviously in a fuzzy state with the Guinness, could not focus any longer on the game and soon his dazzling winnings were dwindling away at the same rate as his concentration. In his drunken state, Frankie watched helplessly as his winnings diminished and his father's wages decreased as he lost game after game to the man that just joined them. With perspiration trickling down his face, Frankie began to panic and chased after his lost cash. Finally, he was down to his last, he looked to the heavens above and whispered a prayer before pushing the remainder of the money into the centre of the table and saying, '*All in.*' His voice shaking and the sweat now running down his cheeks, it was clear he was crying out to the Lord from his heart to allow him to win this hand.

Jim explained there was terror in the young man's eyes, a fear he had never witnessed before in a game of cards. The cards were revealed and Frankie almost collapsed in front of them, he had lost! Every penny of his father's hard-earned wages were to be transferred into another man's pocket.

Frankie, pushing his chair back, stood up and staggered out. Trembling like a leaf in a hurricane, he made his way home to face the music. Home to his starving siblings, home to explain his shame to his poverty-stricken parents.

Later that night, Nancy McGregor, crying like a banshee, could be heard wailing all over the street.

Jim Brogan, not being able to stand it any longer, threw on his coat and knocked at the door of the McGregor's home. 'Can I come in?' he asked.

Frankie's father Charlie nodded and held the door open.

Inside the house, the family gathered round the smouldering hearth, each of them looking gloomily into the dying fire.

'A game is supposed to be fun,' Jim said to the solemn group, 'But I can tell you, making a man rich and witness a family go hungry, there's no fun in that.' He reached inside his pocket and counted out some money. 'I want you to have this.'

'No.' Charlie shook his head, too proud to accept help from his neighbour.

Nancy could have slapped her husband. Never mind taking the money, she wanted to take his hand and all; they were hungry and needed help badly!

'You're taking it,' Jim urged. 'I was the one that was dealt the winning hands. Me, I'm the so-called winner! I'm ashamed to tell you I'm responsible for taking all your son had to offer and I sure as God am not going to take a man's wages! In fact, I promise you right now, I will never play another game of cards again! I have learned my lesson, it's a fool's game! Making one man rich and another man poor is no fun in my eyes. From this day on, I'm done with gambling!'

Charlie found himself nodding in agreement, after all, everything Jim had just said was true. 'Most folks don't look at it like that, but you're right,' Charlie said. Holding out his hand he shook Jim's and continued, 'But you won the money fair and square. You keep it.'

Nancy's eyes almost fell out of her head, never mind slapping her husband, she was going to give him a good punch!

237

'No.' Jim placed the money on the mantelpiece and made his way towards the door. Pausing to look over his shoulder, he said, 'There's nothing fair and square about poker! I'm sorry, I'm sorry from the bottom of my heart for the pain I have caused this family. God bless you all, I'll see myself out.'

'Thank you, God bless! You're a gentleman, Jim Brogan! A true gent!' Charlie called after him.

Outside, Jim found young Frankie slumped against a lamppost clutching a bottle of stout and looking as if his whole world was about to crumble. Jim shook his hand and explained how sorry he was and that the money had been returned to his father, however, the impact this event had on poor Frankie had been life-changing. From that day on, Frankie never stopped drinking, his whole world had certainly started to crumble.

Jim, true to his word, never did gamble again. Over the years he watched with regret as young Frankie gradually turned into an alcoholic, a tragedy that Jim couldn't help but feel partly responsible for. Each night he prayed from the depths of his heart for the Lord to forgive him but more importantly he prayed that one day Frankie McGregor, chained to his addiction, would one day be set free. Jim told Patrick this story on many occasions and warned him about the dangers of associating himself with both gambling and drunkenness.

As he lay nursing his stinking whiskey hangover, Patrick felt more and more disgusted with himself. If only he'd remembered his father's tale, goodness knows he had heard it often enough! And if only he'd listened to his dad, he would not be lying here battered and bruised, not to mention one of the hardest men in Dublin possibly looking for him to make mincemeat out of him!

'What are you thinking, Pat, you've gone all quiet on me?' Chris asked as he lit a cigarette.

'I'm thinking you're gonna kill yourself with all that smoking!' Patrick waved away the annoying fumes.

'Ah, dry your eyes! You non-smokers are hard to listen to!' Chris blew out rings of smoke from his mouth. 'Tell me what you're really thinking about?'

'I'm thinking I'm done with drink and I'm done with gambling also. I'm never playing another hand of cards again. If I hadn't gone there last night I wouldn't be lying here with a busting headache and a black eye!'

'Ha,' Chris grinned. 'Never mind that, mate. If Gerry Flanagan finds out you're messing around with his daughter, trust me, you'll have more than a black eye to worry about!'

Chapter 28

Suzy, up to her elbows in flour, kneaded the dough and blew a loose tendril of hair out of her eyes. 'Frankie,' she smiled over her shoulder, 'I should have asked earlier, have you a decent suit for tonight?'

Frankie, busy setting the fairy cakes neatly on the tray, looked up, 'Why? Don't tell me this is a fancy do we're for? Gees, Suze, ye know me, I'm not into any posh craic.'

Suzy grinned, 'Oh I know that, you're certainly no *swanky Frankie*. That's why I love... you... so much,' she replied, dipping her head and closing her eyes in embarrassment, at once regretting her choice of words. My goodness, she couldn't believe she had just said the *love* word. Where the heck had that come from? A certain slip of the tongue could reveal her inner thoughts.

Suzy, usually more guarded, was disappointed with herself. At least she had her back to him, thankfully he couldn't see her cheeks blushing like ripe tomatoes. Surely he would want to run a mile away if he thought the lady that was helping him was secretly in love with him! Heaven forbid he might think she just brought him into her home to get her womanly claws into him! Which of course was so untrue. Offering to help Frankie was her way of supporting a neighbour in need. She had a soft spot for him, this much was true, but she wasn't in love with him back then. She certainly hadn't offered her help with romance on her mind but he would undoubtedly think that now! More than likely he would grab his things and likely run a mile!

Oh, but the past few months have been so bliss. She had not been as happy as this in a long time. His company had been so wonderful, knowing that he was there in the morning, greeting her with a smile and a cup of tea, and welcoming her home in the evening and offering to assist with the cooking and cleaning, felt perfect. His presence in the home was such a breath of fresh air. She loved his companionship and adored nothing more than the two of them curl up in their separate armchairs and snuggle up with a cup of tea as they watched the crackling fire dance in the hearth and the mighty inferno roar up the chimney. Winter was creeping in at an alarming rate, but regardless what the elements of December were throwing about outdoors, inside the modest house in the Bogside, Suzy felt warmth and safety in the company of Frankie.

Each night, as they sat by the turf-filled fire, Frankie would tell her his stories of times gone by, well, the ones that he could remember. He had admitted that the neighbours could probably remember more of the exciting, juicy tales of his life than he could. Most of it had not embedded in his memory during his more drunken states. Each night Suzy looked forward to their routine. She enjoyed listening to Frankie's stories and seeing the corners of his eyes crinkle when he laughed. She also observed how handsome Frankie McGregor was looking lately. His face was no longer puffy, a positive result of his drink-free months, his blue eyes brighter and his skin much healthier looking… and where had those cheek bones been hiding all these years? My goodness, she had never noticed that he had such amazing facial structure, high cheek bones and a strong masculine jawline. The beer belly had faded away and Frankie McGregor was beginning to look quite… well, simply quite attractive, she had to admit!

The thought of Frankie leaving her had been playing on her mind lately. Suzy didn't want him to go but she knew he was well on his feet again and it would just be a matter of time before he upped sticks and left. In no time, she would be back to the lonely widow with her life filled with boring nights and depressing silence. With Chris so busy working hard in Dublin, to meet the deadline for the department store to be opened by Christmas, he wasn't able to visit since he left back in the summer with Patrick Brogan. He had written a few times explaining his hectic schedule and she understood they were under pressure. Thankfully she had Frankie, for her life would have been so dull without him.

The very thought of Frankie caused her toes to curl and her heart to tick at an alarming rate like a love-struck teenager. Part of her felt so stupid for having these feelings, part of her felt so guilty; was she being unfaithful to her dear departed husband? Regardless of these feelings she couldn't possibly deny that she was truly falling head over heels in love with Frankie McGregor, whether she liked it or not, he had captured her heart.

Frankie's own heart did a little leap. She said she loved him! She LOVED him, he thought. Surely he was reading too much into it. Susy couldn't possibly feel the same way for him as he did for her. My word, she was much too good for him.

Why would a beautiful woman like Suzy Ferguson fall in love with a former alcoholic? No, he was, by far, reading too much into it, she loved him as a friend and a neighbour, nothing else and he would just have to accept that but her words had caused a warmth and that tingling sensation he had become so accustomed to lately.

Breaking the awkward silence between the two of them, Frankie said, 'Not sure if I do have a suit, Suze. To be honest, it's a long time since I wore one, in fact I don't think I've ever worn one in my life!' he joked. 'I'll have a look in that wardrobe of mine in the back room, the one I never use. I'll brush away the cobwebs, you never know what I might find in there. Perhaps if I'm lucky I might find some ancient treasure! Or there might even be a cure for TB in there!'

Suzy laughed at his innocent humour, 'Never mind a cure for tuberculosis or a suit, you might have a better chance of finding last year's snow! Anyway, don't worry, it's only the pensioners Christmas dance, they do all dress in their Sunday best but if you don't find a suit it's no big deal.'

'Are ye joking or what? Those aul biddies will be barging through their false teeth if I'm not dressed to impress!' Frankie pulled a face. 'No, I'll get it sorted. I promise you I'll sort something out.'

'You're probably right.' Suzy grinned again. 'I can just picture them. Okay, you take a look in that wardrobe of yours and meanwhile, I'll pop down to Masie's charity shop, she might have something nice.'

243

Frankie's heartbeat suddenly started hammering against his ribcage. After rummaging through the dusty wardrobe and finding nothing but junk, and certainly nothing to wear to the Christmas dance, his eyes fell upon the old trunk containing his parents' keepsakes. After they had died, as the eldest of the family, he was given the battered leather case. Inside he found documents relating to the births of his siblings, candlesticks, an old tie belonging to his father, love letters from his parents, and a wedding ring belonging to his mother. But there was something else in there, the item that made his heart thrash frantically – a bottle of Bushmills whiskey.

Lifting it carefully from the box, Frankie could feel himself breathing faster. Oh the temptation to take a sip was so overwhelming. Just one sip wouldn't do him any harm, one tiny little drop wouldn't hurt anyone, after all he was an adult, a man that could easily handle one glass or perhaps even two!

After pondering over it for a few seconds, he made up his mind.

Clutching the bottle of whiskey and holding it with care, like cradling a newborn in his arms, Frankie carefully tiptoed downstairs with caution.

In a daze he walked through the living room and entered the kitchen, his heart racing like never before as he opened the backdoor with a flourish. After making his way to the far end of the back garden, Frankie knelt down on his honkers, unscrewed the top of the bottle and breathed in the fine overwhelming fumes of Ireland's finest beverage.

Chapter 29

Frankie eyed the empty bottle of whiskey with satisfaction. Never had he felt so good in his entire life and never had he felt so powerful. It was all finished with, every last drop of it was gone and it felt blissful. The first soft snowflakes of winter were tumbling from the thick, puffy clouds above, melting into his hair and sliding down the back of his neck but he didn't care. He remained there fixed to the spot clutching the empty bottle, feeling a warmness in the pit of his stomach and smiling from one ear to the next like a Cheshire cat. This is what it felt like to be in control of his life again.

Lifting his head, Frankie gazed at the heavens above. 'Thank you, Lord!' he yelled aloud, a smile of satisfaction etched on his face.

'Frankie!' Suzy called as she entered the back yard. 'Oh there you... are. What's up?' she asked, her gaze falling on first Frankie and then on the empty bottle in his hands. 'Wha... what are you doing, Frankie?' Her heart plunged to the pit of her stomach as she secretly prayed under her breath, 'Please God, no, please don't let him have started drinking again.' Tears welled up in her eyes. All the months of hard work of helping him to overcome his addiction was wasted. Feeling like she had just been kicked in the teeth, her body began to tremble.

Frankie, getting to his feet, walked over to her and placed his arms around her shoulders. Surprisingly he didn't stagger, nor did he look drunk, Suzy thought. Still, surely a reformed alcoholic would need more than a bottle of whiskey before it takes effect. Not like her, she thought, one glass and she would be as pissed as a parrot.

'Oh ye of little faith.' He grinned before planting a soft kiss on her cool cheek. 'I know what it looks like but I didn't drink it. I didn't touch a drop.' He smiled at her, his eyes full of love for the woman that had captured his heart.

'You didn't?' she asked, her voice shaking.

'No, and if you don't believe me, go over there and smell that drain, that's where it all went. I poured every last drop down there.' He pointed with an air of fulfilment. 'And it felt amazing,' he added with joy.

'Oh, Frankie.' Suzy hugged him, 'Thank God! I'm so proud of you! I'm sure that wasn't easy!'

'No, I'll admit it wasn't. Believe me for a second I was about to give in to a moment of weakness. I thought perhaps a sip wouldn't do me any harm until suddenly I was toying with the idea of first one glass, then two! Then I thought about you, I thought about how hard you worked to help me and I couldn't do it to you.' He also thought about how much he loved her but obviously didn't add this last important bit.

Walking over to the dustbin, he lifted the lid, shook off the snow and dumped the bottle inside. 'I promise ye, Suze, I will never have another bottle of that stuff in my hand and you can take my word for that.'

'I knew you could do it!' Suzy beamed back. 'I take it

246

you didn't find a suit, then?'

'No, nothing but junk in there.'

'Well it's a good job I found you one. Masie had it displayed in the window, just had it up there five minutes when I arrived,' she replied with a tone of excitement.

'Brilliant!' Frankie exclaimed.

'It's perfect, you'll look great in it.' There you go again! Stop it Suzy Ferguson! her mind screamed at her, stop cooing over him like an inexperienced teenager!

Placing his arms back around her shoulders, he said, 'C'mon, Suze, what are we waiting for, then?'

No sooner had he came in contact with her when the zing she had been feeling lately shot through her. Pull yourself together, she thought.

'Let's go get ready, after all I have an aul doll or two to chat up! You never know I might just get myself a woman tonight.' He winked and flashed her a wicked smile.

Suzy smiled back, her heavy heart sinking. That's it then, he's made it as clear as the nose on her face, he certainly doesn't see any romance between the two of them. Talk about coming back to earth with a bang.

Each year for the Christmas dance, John Coyle helpfully got a loan of the transport truck from the farmer he worked for. He used the old battered wagon to help transfer the baking to the parish hall.

Catherine, just like Suzy, had spent hours, up from the crack of dawn to bake for the special occasion. They were responsible for creating cakes and buns whilst their neighbour Anne Quigley arranged the scone bread and pancakes, and all the other neighbours in the street made soup and sandwiches and anything else they fancied.

Anne, with the help of her grandson Andrew, was busy placing the trays in the truck. She looked up and smiled as Frankie approached.

Frankie, with a hint of pride etched on his face, placed his tray of fairy cakes next to the rows of all the delicious iced buns and cream cakes. 'Anne Quigley, what are you giving me those eyes for?' he joked.

'What are you going on about, Frankie?' Anne asked, doing her best to smother a laugh.

'You're dying to have a good aul laugh! I can tell by that smirk on your face. I know you're thinking, what's he not like, making fairy buns?' Frankie beamed.

'Well…' Anne smiled, 'I didn't realise that was your specialty.'

'Fairy buns?' Andrew asked as he headed back into the house. 'We always thought you were away with the fairies.' He looked over his shoulder and his face broke into a huge grin.

'I'd agree with you on that, Andrew,' Frankie teased. Turning back to Anne he grinned, 'Did you ever think ye'd see the day aul Frankie McGregor cooking? Never mind me making wee fairy buns!'

Anne chuckled and nodded. 'Well, if I'm being honest, Frankie, there was many a day I thought you were in cloud cuckoo land, I do admit.' On a more serious note she added, 'Frankie it's great to see you looking so well *and* so happy! I haven't seen you this happy in a long, long time, it's well overdue.'

'Do you know, Anne, you're right. I haven't felt like this since you and I used to dance as teenagers. We had some great times back then.'

'We did in deed, Frankie,' Anne agreed.

'I was happy back then, that was until everything went pear-shaped.' Frankie paused as a deep sorrow filled his heart. The reality of how much enjoyment he had missed out on due to his addiction suddenly hit him like a ton of bricks. Filled with emotion, he fought to hold back the tears.

Anne, reading the signs, placed a gentle hand on Frankie's shoulder and gave him a light squeeze. 'Don't beat yourself up about it, Frankie. That was then but this is now. Leave the past in the past where it belongs and grasp the future.'

'Aye you're right, Anne.' Frankie brightened.

'I hope to see you out strutting your dance moves on the floor tonight,' Anne joked.

'I'm a bit rusty but I'm sure it won't take me long in getting the hang of it again, after all how could I forget to dance when I had you teaching me all those years ago, and what a great teacher you were!'

'What can I say, Frankie, it's in my blood to dance!' Anne replied as she witnessed Frankie's eyes light up as he glanced over her shoulder. Turning around she followed his gaze and they watched Suzy and Catherine cross the street, carrying more trays from the other neighbours.

'Now, Catherine,' Frankie pointed as Catherine and Suzy approached. 'Don't you be eyeing up my wee fairy buns because you're not getting any!' he joked.

'Actually, if you must know, I wasn't eyeing up your wee buns I was eyeing up you! You look so handsome with your fancy suit and your slick combed back hair, not to mention those shiny shoes!' Catherine beamed.

Suzy could feel her cheeks burn, Catherine was not the only one to notice how well Frankie looked today.

'Ah well, them toothless grannies better watch out!' he winked. 'I might just sweep one or two off their feet! I believe they are the ones to watch out for,' Frankie joked, taking a tray from Suzy and placing it in the cart; he noted Suzy looked sombre. 'Ye okay, Suze? What's up?'

Suzy, wishing he would dream of sweeping her off her feet instead of all this talk of the older women, felt a pang of jealousy. Pulling herself together, she brushed her stupid thoughts out of her mind and brightened, 'I'm fine, but I'm just thinking while you're busy looking for a woman, can you check out if there's any aul boys for me?' she teased, 'But one thing, make sure they've all their own teeth!'

Father Lavery surveyed the parish hall with a look of satisfaction. He was amazed at how much hard work and creative effort had taken place here over the last few days. His parishioners never failed to impress him. They had worked tirelessly to transform the dull hall into an impressive function room for their annual Christmas dance, filled with colour and festivity to enhance the Christmas atmosphere. Out went the ancient brown curtains, that were hideously too short. In their place hung beautiful crimson velvet ones that fitted perfectly. Each round table was draped with cream linen tablecloths trimmed with a red velvet ribbon to match the curtains. Even the scruffy floorboards were polished to perfection.

To the back of the room, many rectangular tables had been pushed together and covered also with tablecloths. Trays of food from the endless baking lined each table. There were mouth-watering cream cakes, mince pies, sandwiches, buns and scones. Without a shadow of a doubt, a great deal of time went into this evening's preparations.

Nellie McDowell, known to concoct a good yarn and possibly the oldest woman in the Bogside, caught sight of Father Lavery. Nellie liked to believe she was younger than she actually was and never admitted her age to anyone, although everyone that knew her guessed she was not a day younger than ninety. The stiffness that had started settling into her joints many years ago were now more evident. Hooked over and walking with her stick, she slowly made her way to the back of the hall at a tortoise's pace. Her legs may be slow, but her mind was as sharp as a blade, nothing passed by good old Nellie.

251

'Father Lavery, me aul friend, how are ye?' Nellie flashed him a toothless smile.

'Hello Nellie. I'm very well thank you, but more to the point, how are you?' he asked politely, knowing that poor Nellie may be crippled with joint pain but her mind had her fooled to think she was as fit as a flea.

'Ah, ye know me, Father, I'm grand! I can't complain.'

'Good for you, Nellie.' Father Lavery smiled. 'I'm glad to hear that.'

'And I'll be glad to hear ye asking me out for a dance. I'll be expecting a wee waltz of ye the night. But,' she pointed a bony finger at him, 'Ye better watch out because I intend to dance the feet of ye! I'll show ye how *well* I am! After all I might as well enjoy my time while I have it, we're long enough dead!' she cackled. 'Isn't that right, Father?'

Father Lavery threw his head back and laughed, 'True enough, true enough, Nellie.'

'Aye, Father, I know my days are numbered but I can tell ye as much as I'm looking forward to meeting the man above, I'm just not ready to go yet,' she laughed, clutching her cane with her wrinkly hand and swinging her handbag in the other. 'I hope He has no plans to close my eyes just yet!'

'It amazes me, Nellie, we're all dying to get to heaven but none of us wants to die!' he teased, 'And I'm certainly not ready to go yet either so I hope He doesn't have those plans for me either,' the friendly priest joked.

'Speaking of death, how many do ye think is dead in

our cemetery, Father?' Nellie squinted her beady crow-like eyes and waited for his reply.

'Oh gosh, Nellie, you've got me there. Let me think, a few thousand, I'd say. Why how many do you think is dead in there?' he asked.

Nellie released a hearty laugh, 'Hopefully for their sakes them all!'

'Oh Nellie, you're one to watch!' Father Lavery grinned, linking his arm in hers he gently led her to the food, 'You've caught me there. C'mon let's get something to eat.'

'Aye good idea and then we'll get this show on the road!' she flashed him a gummy smile.

Fifteen minutes later, after getting Nellie a plate piled high with sausage rolls, sandwiches and cakes, Father Lavery helped her to a seat at one of the tables from where they had a full view of the surrounding tables and dancefloor.

'Lean closer, Father, my hearing's not the best, I want to tell ye something.' Nellie beckoned.

'Hope you're not going to tell me your confession in public,' Father Lavery kidded as he watched the hall quickly fill up and indicated to John and Catherine Coyle to take a seat next to him. 'Or we'll be here all night and we'll end up missing the dancing.'

'Not at all! Me a sinner? Sure, Father, I've no sins,' she joked. 'Sure I should be called Saint Nellie of the Bogside!'

'Aye, you're right there, Nellie, Saint Nellie, patron

saint of mischief!' Father Lavery replied with a grin.

Giggling, she patted him on the arm, 'Now I'm being serious, come here to I tell ye this. Look over there to the left. Do ye see Suzy Ferguson and what's his name Frankie... Frankie McGregor.' Nellie's voice went up a notch like a Punch and Judy puppet show.

Suzy, on hearing Frankie's name, looked across and waved. Catherine, sitting down next to Father Lavery, raised her eyebrows.

'My goodness, is that Frankie McGregor? I didn't even recognise him all spruced up!' Father Lavery smiled with approval. 'Fair play to him, he's doing well off the drink, it's great to see it!'

'Aye, I bet ye didn't recognise something else.' Nellie nodded with a look on her face that revealed she had discovered something interesting.

Father Lavery shrugged. 'What else, Nellie?'

'Love! Love is in the air! I'm telling ye, them two have a notion for one another.' She waved her bony finger in their direction.

Catherine Coyle's eyebrows shot up a little further.

Father Lavery gently patted Nellie's arm, 'Now, Nellie, don't you be going around spreading a rumour or I'm going to have to march you over to the confessional box after all!' he smirked.

Catherine, turning to John, whispered, 'Did you hear

that? She could be right you know. Nellie's no dozer, she seldom gets things wrong.'

John, not one to get himself concerned in other people's business, sipped his tea, bit into a turkey sandwich and shrugged, 'Not the worst thing to happen.'

'Exactly! I agree.' Catherine's eyes twinkled.

Nellie, nothing much wrong with her hearing after all, picked up John's statement, roared with laughter and clasped her hands together, 'I think it's brilliant, John! The problem is, I think they need a little help, a little nudge to get that spark ignited. What do ye say, Father?' She pursed her thin lips together and waited for his reply.

Eyeing up a mince pie on the plate, Father Lavery lifted it and took a bite. 'If I'm being honest, I think we should mind our own business. The pair of them are good friends that's all. Suzy has been helping him get off the drink, you could be reading the signals wrong, Nellie.'

'Reading the signals wrong?' Nellie looked horrified. 'Father, I've been married and widowed twice and I was almost up the aisle a third time, only a few years ago, until he decided to keel over with a heart attack just before the wedding. I know love when I see it. I'm an expert and it's written all over their faces!'

'Well, true, Nellie, you certainly are more experienced in marriage than I ever will be,' Father Lavery joked, polishing off the last mouthful of the tasty mince pie, he added, 'But we really shouldn't meddle in other people's affairs. If they are meant to be together then God will sort it out, let Him let it all happen.'

Catherine Coyle sipped her tea slowly from her china cup and watched Suzy and Frankie at the far end of the room talking causally to Suzy's elderly neighbours. Every time Suzy said something Frankie's face appeared to light up. There was a look on his face that Catherine had never saw before, was it sheer happiness, or perhaps Nellie wasn't losing her marbles just yet, could it possibly be that Frankie McGregor's expression portrayed love? As she watched him moving closer to Suzy and placing his arm gently around her shoulders, Catherine caught the look on Suzy's face as she glanced up at him, smiled and held his gaze. Bingo! Nosy Nellie was right after all!

Nellie blew out her cheeks and puffed, 'Father, we will not be meddling, we will just simply be truthful with them. Young one's nowadays, they don't know love if it hit them up their bakes, look at the pair of them, I know what's happening here. He's out of practice, he's been a slave to the drink for too long, and as for Suzy, she's been on her own for too many years. Leave it to me. I'll not be long in sorting the shenanigans out, before ye know it, I'll have them up the aisle! Now be a good priest,' she patted him on the hand, 'reach into that handbag of mine and open that bottle of sherry for me.'

Father Lavery, like a puppy obeying his master, did what he was told. 'And there I was thinking this was a tea dance,' he joked.

Nellie, holding out her empty china cup, winked, 'Don't

look at me like that, I'm not a batty aul fool. I know what I'm at. How else do ye think I'm still alive at ninety…' she paused, not one to tell her age, but now that she started, she may as well continue, unable to lie to a priest, she lowered her voice, 'Three? Now fill it to the brim.' She waggled her bony finger. 'I call it my medicine! It keeps my aul ticker ticking.'

After downing her first cup of sherry, Nellie was well and truly on her way to finishing a second. The band had begun and the dancefloor was just warming up for an old time waltz. Slugging back the final mouthfuls, she wiped her mouth with the hem of the tablecloth and pushed back her chair. 'Now, Father, that dance ye promised me, my feet are calling out for it. C'mon, let's show them how it's done.'

On the dancefloor, Father Lavery danced with caution as he led Nellie in time to the music, surprisingly enough, with him holding her and supporting her steps, her timing was near perfect. 'I told ye I could dance,' she cackled. 'There's life in the aul biddy yet.' She flashed her toothless smile.

'Let's dance,' Frankie whispered in Suzy's ear. Jovially, he led her by the hand out to the dancefloor next to Nellie and Father Lavery.

As Frankie slipped one hand around her waist and the other hand clasping hers, Suzy's body tingled. She hadn't danced in public in years and now as they moved along to the music, it felt wonderful. Oh how it felt so good to be in his arms. In fact, not only did it feel good, it felt perfect!

'Excuse me.' Nellie tapped Suzy on the shoulder, 'Do ye mind if I steel your partner for the next dance? I promise ye

257

I'll give him back.' Nellie smiled and the lines around her face deepened.

'Not at all.' Suzy put on a bright face. Secretly she felt raging at the old woman for spoiling her blissful moment, but as Nellie was a well-respected member of the community, she couldn't refuse her.

Suzy and Father Lavery returned to their seats and left Nellie and Frankie to strut their moves on the dancefloor.

'Now that I have ye to myself, I want a wee word with ye,' Nellie said, her voice a fraction above everyone else's.

'What is it, Nellie? What have I done?' Frankie smiled down at the old woman.

Peering up at him, she narrowed her crow-like eyes, 'It's what ye haven't done, ye silly egit!'

With a puzzled look, Frankie asked, 'And what's that?'

'And what's that, ye ask?' Nellie shouted over the music, 'I might be an aul bird but I'm a wise aul bird and ye need to take my advice before it's too late!' Nellie's voice was loud enough, anyone eavesdropping close by would have no problem hearing her.

Mystified, Frankie shook his head, 'I haven't a clue what you're talking about, Nellie. You've lost me.' He grinned.

'You'll have lost *her* if ye don't catch herself on!' Nellie warned.

'Lost who?' Frankie asked, clearly confused, his grin vanishing.

Nellie began shaking her head with impatience. So wrapped up in her conversation she hadn't noticed the band coming to a standstill. 'Suzy!' she yelled in his ear for the entire hall to hear, 'You need to tell Suzy Ferguson you love her! Do it before I do!'

Chapter 30

Frankie, still holding on to Nellie, wanted the ground to open up and swallow him in. Blushing with embarrassment he helped Nellie walk slowly back to her table. Why did her seat have to be at the very back of the room? he thought as he steered her through a sea of curious heads, all looking at them, peering at them both like they had two heads on their shoulders.

This was not the way he wanted Suzy to find out. He couldn't bring himself to look in her direction, silently he had prayed she had nipped out to use the toilet but no such luck, from the corner of his eye he caught sight of her emerald dress. She had been sitting on her seat, and like the entire gathering, heard every word from Nosy Nellie's big blabbering mouth! Honestly, why couldn't the old biddy have stayed at home and sat crocheting or knitting or whatever it is old ladies do in their spare time? Anything rather than butt her thin, pokey snout in his affairs. After tonight, Suzy would be sure to pack his things and send him back home. Home to look at four depressing walls, where the loneliness would surely grip him so much it would be enough to put him back on the drink!

As they reached her table, Frankie met Father Lavery's gaze, eyes that bore a look of sympathy.

'Catherine, my dear, all that tea has gone straight to my bladder! Be a good wee pet and help me out to the ladies before you find a puddle under my table.' Nellie smiled across at Catherine, totally oblivious to the embarrassment she'd caused minutes earlier. 'And you, John boy.' She waggled her bony finger at him, 'Fill my cup up! Doctor's orders! My doc advises me to finish at least half a bottle a day.' Pointing around the table, she continued, 'Now don't any of you lot drink it on me! I need my sherry, it keeps me merry!' she cackled. 'And more to the point, it keeps my joints loose.'

'It keeps her tongue loose too.' Frankie mumbled under his breath, still writhing with embarrassment.

John shot him a look of amusement.

Frankie couldn't help but grin. How could he be angry with an old neighbour like Nellie McDowell? She was a character to say the very least and everyone loved her. This time last year he had been just as bad. Goodness only knows what outbursts he had come out with over the years whilst on the liquor. During his own drinking sessions in the past, the alcohol likely had the ability to loosen his own tongue more times than enough. Thankfully he couldn't remember most of it.

Giving her a hug, he looked at her and smiled, 'Head you on to the loo and don't worry about your sherry, we'll look after it,' Frankie assured her.

'Good boy.' Nellie nodded before hobbling away.

'Frankie, take a seat here.' Father Lavery indicated to the empty chair next to him. 'I did try to tell her to mind her own business,' he whispered, as they watched Nellie linking her arm around Catherine's and shuffling slowly towards the

261

toilet. 'But you know Nellie, she's normally a wise old owl at the best of times, she didn't mean any harm. She honestly just wanted to help you.'

Frankie ran his fingers through his thick, silvery-black hair. 'Oh I know, Father. I know she means well. I'm not mad at her, after all, if I was, it would be like the pot calling the kettle black. God only knows what has come out of this mouth of mine over the years.' He laughed, trying to make light of the situation. 'This time last year I wouldn't have cared what others thought of me, or said about me for that matter, but right now in my sober state, I do worry. After tonight, I'll be the talk of the Bogside!'

'Never fret about that.' Father Lavery waved a hand dismissively. 'It will be you today and someone else tomorrow, before you know it, it will be yesterday's news.'

'Aye, you're right, Father. I shouldn't care, I'm used to being the talk of the street. I should be well used to it by now. I dare say this time last year I was hanging on to some lamppost singing my heart out, slipping and sliding all over the place, acting the egit and giving everyone a chance of a good laugh. Some change this Christmas,' he said. Lifting his gaze, he looked over to Suzy. Catching his eye, she quickly looked away and began sipping on her cold tea. 'Look at me, did you ever think you would see the day Frankie McGregor would be clean-shaven, washed and dressed in a fancy three-piece suit?'

'Well I must admit, Frankie, no, I never imagined you coming on so well and looking such a picture of health,' Father Lavery agreed with a smile.

'Nor me neither, Father, and it's all thanks to that woman over there.' He nodded in the direction of Suzy. Suzy, getting caught for a second time staring over at him, dipped her head and blushed.

Father Lavery smiled. 'Good on you both! I must give the pair of you credit! You have overcome a terrible addiction and you should be so proud of yourself! I always hoped one day you would turn your life around and you've certainly done a great job!'

The music started up again and soon the dancefloor was filled with a sea of dancers obscuring Frankie's view of Suzy.

'I'm not an expert on marriage and relationships but I must say, Frankie, I do believe Nellie hit the nail on the head tonight. You are in love with her, aren't you?' Father Lavery quizzed. 'You haven't taken your eyes off her since you sat down!'

Turning to look at their friendly priest, Frankie smiled. 'My mother always taught me to tell the truth, Father, and I would never lie to a priest.' Frankie sighed. 'Aye, I'm in love with her. I love every bone in that woman's body, every hair on her head, each and every freckle on her arms!'

Sitting back in his chair, Father Lavery grinned, 'Well what are you doing telling me all this? Go over there, Frankie, and tell Suzy *it*.'

Frankie shrugged. 'Nellie just did.'

'She needs to hear it from you. What are you frightened off, Frankie? What is the worst thing that can happen? Are you afraid that perhaps she doesn't feel the same? And if that's the case, which I suspect it's not, so what? It will not be the end of the world.'

'What would a beautiful woman like Suzy Ferguson see in a fool like me? She's too good for me, Father!'

'Nonsense! Never say that. There is no such thing as someone being too good for another. We are all equal in God's eyes and you, Frankie, are no different. I'm sure Suzy feels the same but you will never know if you sit about doing nothing. So what are you waiting for? Are you going to tell her or are you going to look back one day, raging with yourself for letting an opportunity pass?'

Courage suddenly taking over him, Frankie jumped to his feet. 'You're right, Father, you are *so* right! What am *I* waiting for? I'm going to tell her. I'll chat to you later, Father.'

'Before you go, Frankie, I'm free the next two Saturdays if you want to pencil me in for a wedding.' Father Lavery flashed him a grin.

'Put it in your diary just in case.' Frankie winked. 'Excuse me, excuse me, sorry,' Frankie said as he edged his way across the dancefloor like a man on a mission.

Stopping at Suzy's table he took hold of her hand. 'Come with me.' He helped her up and led her back to the dancefloor.

'Excuse me again,' Frankie said, as he weaved in amongst the crowd once more until they came to the middle of the floor. Waving at the band, Frankie shouted up, 'Stop the music for a minute, just one minute please.'

The band came to a standstill and the dancers came to a halt.

Holding on to Suzy's hand, Frankie cleared his voice. 'Ladies and gentlemen, can I have your attention please.' He raised his voice loud so all at the back of the room could hear him.

All eyes were firmly glued to the pair.

'I'm sure you all heard Nellie McDowell's words earlier, well now it's my turn for a speech.' He glanced around the room before fixing his sight on Suzy, who by now was quivering like a candle flame in a breeze and blushing as red as the velvet curtains. 'I want everyone to know, but especially Suzy, that I, Frankie McGregor, am so grateful to this wonderful lady here. Suzy Ferguson has helped me become the man that I am today and if it wasn't for her, I would more than likely be six foot under and kicking up the daises! Over the past few months Suzy has shown me kindness, support and courage.'

'It was really no bother,' Suzy dismissed the compliments.

'Exactly! Did you all hear her? It was *no* bother, *no* bother to her because she is such a wonderful person and I want everyone to hear this.' Frankie let go of her hand. Closing the distance between them, he slipped his hands around her waist and drew her nearer. Looking deeply into her eyes he said, 'I love you, Suzy Ferguson!'

'Wh... what?' Suzy heard herself answer.

'I said I love you! I love you so much and I want you to marry me!'

Needless to say Suzy almost fainted, good job Frankie was holding her up.

'Ye... yes, YES! I'LL MARRY YOU!' Suzy heard herself reply.

Lifting her up into his arms, Frankie swirled her round the dancefloor as the hall filled with rip-roaring applause and cheers.

From the back of the room Nellie let out a shriek and waved her walking stick in the air. 'Yee ha! Told ye so!' she cackled, 'The aul bird's not doting yet!'

Without giving it a second thought, Frankie lifted Suzy's chin and raising her mouth to his he kissed her, and kissed her, and kissed her a little more.

Suzy felt her fingers run through his hair as she melted in his arms.

Feeling dizzy, Suzy pulled away, 'Should we be doing this here?' she asked, feeling flustered and feeling more like a teenager now than ever before. Embarrassingly, her fingers were still entwined in his thick, silky hair.

'Darling, Suze, you are my future wife, who cares?' He kissed her again. 'Okay, let's go, I think we've given the pensioners enough entertainment for one night.' He took her by the hand, grabbed their coats and headed for the door.

As they passed, Father Lavery waved at them. 'Let me know the date, I can't wait to marry you two!' he beamed.

'And make sure I'm a bridesmaid!' Nellie crowed before glugging back another cupful of sherry.

The full moon lit up the sky like a giant oil lamp. The snow from earlier was beginning to turn to slush. Stopping under a street lamp on the way home, Frankie took Suzy in his arms again. 'I can't believe we've lived next to each other all our lives and all that time I wasted getting myself drunk when I could have been with you!'

'Me neither,' she replied.

'Oh Suze, you make me so happy. I love you so much!'

'Life is full of surprises. I never imagined that one day I would have fallen in love with you.' Suzy's eyes twinkled from the dim amber glow from the light overhead. 'Frankie McGregor, you make my heart smile, I love you, Frankie!'

Before she knew it his mouth had closed over hers again and Suzy felt herself dissolving on the spot, just like the snow under her feet.

'Are you free next week?' Frankie murmured, running his fingers through her tumbling auburn hair.

'Why?'

'Just wondered if you would like to walk down the aisle and tie the knot, that's all.' He shrugged, a cheeky grin on his face but a with a hint of determination glinting in his eye. 'We've wasted enough time; I can't wait any longer!'

'Sounds good to me.' She smiled up at him. 'And there I was thinking earlier that you were on the hunt for an older woman tonight.'

'Aye, I was, but then I changed my mind and thought I'd take a leaf out of your book, so I decided you would do, after all you do have all your own teeth. I hope!'

Chapter 31

'It's Charlotte.' Patrick, plucked up the courage to begin. 'The thing is…'

'I knew it.' Gerry flapped his hands in the air. 'I wondered why you invited me to the pub today.' Taking a gulp of his pint, giving himself a frothy Guinness moustache in the process, he continued, 'With you not being one to drink much, coming to tink of it, ye haven't had a drink since your birthday! After sufferin' from that stinkin' hangover that knocked ye off your feet for a few days, any wonder ye've become a teetotaler the last few months.' He chuckled and playfully punched him, 'Never mind a good hangover, it will harden ye up, boy! Now tell me what's she gone and done? I knew that girl of mine would do your bleedin' head in.'

Patrick knocked back the remainder of his pint, a little extra Dutch courage needed. Pulling a face as the bitter taste coated his tongue, he cleared his throat and began again, 'No, you've got it wrong. She hasn't done anything and she certainly hasn't done my head in.'

'Charlotte does everyone's head in, especially mine!' Gerry shrugged, 'Daughters! They certainly know how to keep their aul da's on their toes. There was one time, a few years back, I tink she had just turned sixteen, she started dating a wee one across the road. A scruffy wee shit he was, never liked him!' Gerry glugged back another huge mouthful of stout. Wiping the froth from his mouth with the back of his hand he continued. 'Well anyway as I was saying, this fella, he was about eighteen, maybe nineteen, can't remember now, but what I do recall, as far as I was concerned, he was much too old for my daughter. Her mother said let them go, they're in love. In love! Imagine a sixteen-year-old in love! What the feck does a child at that age know about love? Back then our Charlotte fell head-over-heels with any man that batted their bleedin' lashes at her! Can you honestly say, Pat, did you experience love at that young age?'

Patrick could feel his heart quicken, was he in love with Erin back then? If he was being honest, it certainly felt like it. If what he felt for Erin Coyle wasn't love, then he wasn't sure what was. Before he had a chance to answer, Gerry burst into a fit of giggles.

In his tipsy state Gerry couldn't stop laughing, 'Pat, look at that expression on your feckin' face! I'm not joking ye, I wish I could freeze it and frame it! You silly egit! You were about to tell me you had been in love! You're a bleedin silly fool! Ye weren't! Ye might 'ave thought ye were but believe me ye were only a bit of a wain back then! So as I was saying, there's no such thing as falling in love at that age. Now back to my story, our Charlotte thought the world of this boy. It was all Trevor this and Trevor that until the chat turned to marriage. She wanted to be with him forever but in my eyes it was Trevor feckin' NEVER! I knew if I had anything to do with this I was going to get rid of the Trevor boy before he had a chance to say *I do!*'

Horrified, Patrick's eyes widened, 'You didn't kill him,

270

did you?' he asked. Alarm bells ringing in his ears, he suddenly felt sick.

'Ha, ha, ye feckin' egit! Ha! Do ye really tink I would murder a man? For feck's sake, Pat, ye certainly don't know me as well as ye thought! I'm not that bleedin' mad!'

Patrick took a long slow swallow and tried hard to keep the nerves from his voice. 'No, of course not. It was just the way you said it, you caught me off guard there. So what did you do then, how did you get rid of him from Charlotte's life?'

'It was simple, I did nothing! Not a ting. The egit did it himself. As I was planning to tell him what I thought of him, he came to me one day and said he didn't feel welcome in the family and was fed up with Charlotte and her childish behaviour and had decided not to marry her after all.'

Raising his eyebrows Patrick replied, 'Oh. What did you say to that?'

Gerry grinned at the memory, 'I went right up close to his face one morning at work. Trevor, the wee arse, was in the building trade so I told him in the politest of voice that I knew he couldn't *marry* two bricks together never mind *marry* my daughter and if he didn't piss off out of my sight my fist would *marry* his feckin' jaw!'

Patrick couldn't help but laugh at this statement, he knew Gerry was telling the truth, it was something only Gerry would come out with. Intrigued by this story and intrigued even more as to why Charlotte had never mentioned this before, Patrick felt he needed to know the full tale. 'So what happened next?'

'Next ting was picking up the pieces of my daughter's broken heart. She was devastated, traumatised, heartbroken like none other. We did our best to cheer her but the poor girl was so low, she found it hard to pick herself up. We did everything we could to try to ensure her confidence again. We told her there was plenty more fish in the sea and that next time she would find herself a salmon and she would forget about that slimy eel! This heartbreak went on for month after month. So now can ye see why I'm so over protective of her! I can guarantee ye this, the next man that asks my daughter for his hand in marriage better mean it from the heart because I'm tellin' ye, I will not stand back and witness her heart broken for a second time!'

Nodding, Patrick replied, 'Of course, I can understand that.'

'Aye I'm sure ye can. So tell me now, boy, what was it that you wanted to talk to me about regarding Charlotte?' Gerry, narrowing his eyes, watched intensely from across the table.

The very mention of Charlotte's name caused a tingly sensation to run through Patrick. Since October the pair of them had been sneaking off together, eloping in the darkness to catch a passionate kiss or two.

Each encounter had been filled with excitement and longing for one another, every embrace felt like they belonged in each other's arms. Never in his life had Patrick felt such a buzz that came with the thrill of knowing they held a secret that no one else knew about. However, Patrick was wise enough to know that they could not keep up this double life, sooner or later they would be caught out. Chris had warned him on many occasions that it would be better if Gerry heard it from the horse's mouth than hear such news from another. Listening to Gerry's story, it had crossed Patrick's mind not to tell him tonight after all about his relationship with his daughter, but at the same time, he knew it was bound to come out soon enough.

'Well, what is it?' Gerry asked as he started drumming his fingers on the table. 'C'mon spit it out, boy!'

Finishing off his pint and clearing his throat again, Patrick, trying his best to steady his voice said, 'Well it's, it's just...'

A smirk crawled across Gerry's stubbled face. 'It's just that you're seeing my daughter and creeping off together each night? Slipping your hand in hers and skipping off under the moonlight to smooch under the stars?'

Patrick's face froze. 'What?' he asked, dumbfounded.

Tut-tutting, Gerry went on. 'Ah don't *what* me, Paddy boy! I know! I've been watching ye!' he raised his voice slightly.

'Have you been spying on us?' Patrick asked, horrified at the prospect, surely this couldn't be right, they had always been so careful to ensure no one saw them.

Gerry's bloodshot eyes danced as he smirked again.

'You *have*, haven't you?' Patrick fired back.

273

'No, I wouldn't call it spying, more like I was keeping an eye on my girl!' Gerry winked before taking another gulp of his drink.

'You *were* spying on us! Why didn't you just say?' Outraged, Patrick could feel a burning sensation develop on his neck.

'I was havin' fun! It was feckin' hilarious watching ye two act like ye didn't have a care for one another back in the house and then once alone, the pair of ye couldn't pull yourselves away from one another!' Leaning across the table, Gerry's eyes softened. 'I'm going to let ye into a little secret. Normally I would have come down on ye like a ton of bricks and halted this relationship before now but I didn't and I'll tell ye why. I followed the pair of ye for the first couple of weeks. I'm not stupid, I saw how genuinely happy ye both were, ye looked perfect together for feck's sake! I couldn't break that bond up, for I knew if I had have done, I would have lost my daughter completely, and besides you're a goodun. I like ye and if I'm being honest, I couldn't have handpicked a better man for my girl. I therefore stopped spying and let ye both carry on.'

'Oh, I see. Well that's a relief.'

'Aye for me too. I can honestly say I tink Charlotte may have found herself that salmon we had told her about. But I'm warning ye, there better not be anyting *fishy* about ye,' Gerry joked. 'Only *codding.* I'm sure ye two will have a *whale* of a time!'

Patrick grinned and joined in on the joke, 'Well, if you

hadn't been so kind enough to allow me to stay at your *plaice,* we'd never have met each other!'

'So true.' Gerry nodded. 'I'm sure ye deserve as much happiness in your life as Charlotte does, I'm happy for ye both.'

On a more serious note Patrick continued, 'I'm glad you are and I promise you, I won't break her heart.'

'Good because believe me, you'll get a good kick up the arse to begin with.' Leaning back on his chair, Gerry folded his arms and said, 'So, Pat, if ye have brought me here tonight to ask me for my daughter's hand in marriage, I give ye my blessing, but I am warning ye, don't ask her unless ye really mean, until death do us part!'

Chapter 32

Why did time always go so slowly when you wanted it to speed up? Erin thought as she gazed out the window, waiting patiently for Theo and William to return from work. She couldn't wait a second longer for her husband to arrive. After her discovery earlier, she wondered if she was going to burst with excitement. Feeling that an extra special treat was called for, Erin had popped out to the local butchers and picked up a fresh chicken. She had marinated the chicken with garlic and olive oil, tossed some broad beans in a little butter and seasoned the roast potatoes with thyme, just as Theo liked it. She had even went the extra mile and made pudding, a delicious mouth-watering cream cheesecake.

All the preparations were done; all she needed now was her husband. Collapsing into a chair, she pulled her legs up and gazed around her. Her gaze lingered on the pine conifer adorned with its glistening festive decorations. They had so much fun the night before decorating it and it looked beautiful with its swathes of crimson and gold satin bows. After the wedding, she had moved her belongings into Theo's apartment. He had suggested on many occasions that as they were now married they could look for a place of their own. The tiny apartment was practical but small, much too small if they were ever blessed with children but Erin refused to go anywhere else. She loved Theo's dwelling. It was plain and simple just as she liked it. Perhaps it needed a woman's touch here and there, but it was cosy and in no time they had made it their marital home, and besides she liked the apartment block, and loved the idea of having her brother live up above her. She knew that Theo was right, the place wasn't exactly suitable for children but she didn't feel the need to rush out and look for another property, not just yet anyway, they could worry about that when the time came.

Outside, the sky had grown murky and big fluffy snowflakes drifted past the window. Erin, wrapping her cardigan tighter around her, watched the blizzard as it coated the street. A squirmy feeling developed in the pit of her stomach, no matter how hard she tried, she was still unable to stop Patrick entering her thoughts but was glad however that the feelings were more due to the fact that she cared for him, nothing else, and she told herself this every time she thought of him. She was married now to Theo and he deserved all her love and attention, but right now as the heavens opened and sprinkled the angel dust over the land, she couldn't help remember last Christmas Eve back in Derry with Patrick. That memory of them slipping and sliding on their way to church, with the snow up to their ankles, and his face when she broke the news to him inside the church, would always remain with her. The last day she had saw him, as he waved goodbye from the docks, it had snowed then, oh how handsome he looked as the flakes melted into his dark hair. Tears sprang into her eyes.

'Stop!' she yelled aloud. No more thinking of the past, she thought to herself.

'Stop what?' Theo called out as he stepped into the warm hallway. Running his hand through his damp hair, he made his way into the living room. Lumps of snow trailed behind him falling from his snow-encrusted shoes and creating slush on the tiled flooring.

'Ah… nothing. It's just, I… I… am… I have a surprise for you in the kitchen! I didn't want you to see it,' she lied. Oh she hated fibs but she couldn't tell him she was talking to herself, then again she did have a cheesecake waiting for him in the kitchen, so it wasn't exactly a lie.

'It's soooo cold out there.' Theo, pink-cheeked, rubbed his hands together. 'It looks like we're going to have a white Christmas. If this weather keeps up, we may even get snowed in, actually what a lovely thought.' He sat down next to her. Lifting his hands to his mouth, he blew his warm breath on them in an attempt to defrost his frozen fingertips. 'Actually I've a better idea.' Before she realised, Theo drew her closer, and taking her by surprise, plunged his cold hands down her back.

'Ahhhh, you rotten rascal!' Erin screeched with laughter as his cold hands began tickling her warm back. 'Get off!'

'Not until you say Theo is the greatest, most wonderful person you have *ever* met!'

'Ahhhh! No chance! Theo is a bloody sh… it!'

'Oh dear, Mrs Fitzgerald, that is certainly not true! C'mon, say it, Theo is the *greatest*.' he began tickling her a little more. 'And the most *wonderful*… oh and let's add *handsome* too for good measure.'

'Ahhhh! Theo you're dead! Your hands are soooo

COLD!' she shivered.

'C'mon now let's hear it.' He grinned, his eyes dancing with mischief.

'Ahhh! Theo is the... bloody ... GREATEST! Ahhhh... WONDERFUL! Now get away!'

'And handsome! Don't forget *handsome!*'

'Ha... nd... some!' she cried. 'Now get away!'

Lifting his hands out, he placed them around her waist and pulled her nearer. 'I love you,' he murmured and kissed her lovingly on the cheek.

'Love you too.' She smiled to herself. Reaching behind her back she pulled out a cushion and before he knew it she fired playful blows at him.

'Ouch.'

'Say Erin is *greater*, most *wonderful* and by far much better looking than her *handsome* husband!' She walloped the cushion around his head. 'C'mon let's hear it!'

'No chance! I would only be telling lies and we can't have that, Mrs Fitzgerald!'

'Oh yes we can! So come on now let me hear it!' Erin began playfully walloping the cushion against his cheeks.

'Never!' he laughed as he effortlessly removed the cushion from her grasp and tossed it over his shoulder. 'Well, well, well, how big are you now without your fierce weapon?' he flashed her a flirtatious smile.

'That's not fair, you're too strong for me.' Erin,

pretending to huff, stuck out her bottom lip like a baby.

Grinning, he scooped her into his arms and whispered, 'My beautiful, precious Erin is the *greater*, most *wonderful* and by far much more *handsome* than her husband! And... what's... what's that smell?'

'I can't smell any... oh no! The CHICKEN!' Erin cried. Wriggling from his grasp, she ran to the kitchen. Smoke billowed out from the oven. 'Oh, I've ruined it!' she yelled pulling on the oven gloves. 'It's charcoaled!' she screeched, tears springing to her eyes as she placed the tray on the counter.

Settling his hands on her shoulders, Theo said in his best reassuring voice, 'It will be fine, we'll just remove the skin, and then we'll strip down the budgie... I mean chicken,' he teased.

Erin turned round and looked up, 'What? Is it too small?' Tears trickled down her cheeks.

Seeing her upset, Theo retracted. 'I was only kidding with you, of course it doesn't look like a budgie! It will be perfect!'

'B... ut, you don't understand, I... I wan... ted th... is to be spec... ial,' she wailed.

'I'm... sorry.' Theo, handing her a handkerchief and taking her in his arms, kissed her tearstained cheek. 'I didn't mean to upset you.'

'No I'm so... rry, I do... n't kn... ow what came over me. It's only a stup... id chicken, no big deal.' She wiped her cheeks. 'I have no... id... ea why I'm cr... ying like this, it's not as if I weep over silly things and here I am act... ing like a baby. You must think I'm a complete idiot.' She sniffed and tried to pull herself together.

'No, not at all.' Theo's eyes softened.

Taking a deep breath, Erin composed herself, 'You know... I cried this morning... with Leo... narda, after I spilled some milk. She just shrugged and laughed it off and told me not to worry, but that was easier said than done, inside I wanted to sob.'

'Well, Leonarda is right, as the saying goes, never cry over spilled milk.' Theo grinned.

'Then just before you arrived home, as I watched the snow fall it reminded me of last Christmas Eve back in Derry and I was just about to start... start bawling again.'

'It's only natural to feel homesick, especially at this time of the year. Christmas is a time for families.' He stroked her glossy, raven hair. 'Perhaps that's the reason you're feeling so fragile, honey.'

'No, I don't think it's because I'm homesick,' she said, breathing slowly and trying her best to stop crying. 'I admit I still miss Derry, but since you have come into my life, it's easier. I feel I belong here, New York is my home now.' Erin blew noisily into the tissue. 'Listen to me honking like a big goose!' she sniffed, 'I wonder if it's due to my condition. You see I haven't been feeling very well and I wanted to make you a special dinner to tell you the news.'

Frowning Theo asked, 'What news?'

'I've been to see a doctor today.' She blew her nose again.

'Erin,' Theo frowned, 'you're scaring me,' he said and wrapped his arms tighter around her. 'Erin, please don't tell me you're ill!'

'Ill? No, you silly fool!' she replied looking into his eyes. A smile crept over her face, 'I'm not *sick*! I'm *pregnant*!'

Chapter 33

'PREGNANT! WHOO HOO!' Theo yelled, lifting her off the ground and spinning her round. 'Sorry.' He stopped. Placing her feet back on the ground, he continued, 'I think I got a bit overexcited! Are you really having our baby?'

'YES!' Erin beamed. 'Really and truly!'

'What a wonderful Christmas present,' he said, his expression emitting a warm glow. 'Oh Erin, this is the best news I've heard in my *life!*'

'I did wonder if I should wait and tell you tomorrow on Christmas morning but there was no way I could have kept it to myself. The excitement was killing me!'

Theo, head spinning and feeling as if he was about to float off the face of the earth, reached for Erin's hand and gently led her back through to the sitting area. 'I'm so happy that you told me tonight. Erin, this really is the best news I have heard in my life! Take a seat,' he urged.

Erin, sitting down on the comfortable settee, smiled, 'You don't have to make a fuss, I told you I'm pregnant, not ill.' She laughed.

Placing a stool next to her, Theo propped both legs up and removed her shoes. 'Right, feet up! You, my dear, need to rest. From now, I'll take care of things.' Ignoring the jabbing sensation in his abdomen that had been troubling him off and on over the past few weeks but more so today, he headed back to the kitchen, 'Although,' he said, looking over his shoulder with a grin, 'If I'm to do the cooking round here, you may as well get used to burnt chicken!'

Wiggling her stockinged toes in front of the crackling fire, Erin called after him, 'In that case, I think I may have to call in Leonarda for help!' she joked.

In the kitchen, Theo salvaged the chicken and served it on the plates together with the potatoes and broad beans. 'Dinner is served, hon… ouch!' Theo yelled as a sharp painful sensation shot through him. Grasping his stomach, he stumbled against a chair.

'What's the matter?' Erin called.

Theo, gripping his tummy replied through clenched teeth, 'Noth… ing!' The pain was excruciating but the last thing he wanted was to worry his pregnant wife. 'Nothing at all, love,' he said as he reached for a chair.

Erin, stepping into the kitchen, witnessed Theo struggling to sit down. 'Theo!' she said with alarm, rushing to his side and aiding him into the seat. 'What's the matter?'

'Ahhhh…' Theo cried, his face twisting with pain.

'Theo, what's wrong?'

'I'm not sure! My insides feel as if they've been tied in knots,' he gasped. Beads of sweat formed on his forehead and trickled down his cheeks. 'I've been having a niggling ache in my abdomen and around my lower back for a few days but… but today… it has been really… really bad… but it will pass. It's really nothing to worry about.'

'Oh Theo, what should I do?' Erin asked with concern.

'Never mind. It's probably nothing. Maybe I ate something earlier that didn't agree with me.'

'Should I call a doctor?' Erin questioned, feeling as useless as a chocolate teapot.

'No! Ahhh… no, no, I'll be fine soon, honestly.'

'You look an awful shade. I'll go and get William. He'll know what to do.'

'Merry Christmas, my darling!' Theo tilted his head up for a kiss.

'Merry Christmas to you also! Although, I must admit, I did *not* plan to spend my first Christmas with my new husband stuck here in hospital.' Erin smiled and planted a loving kiss on his lips. 'How are you feeling now, love?' She stroked her fingers through his thick hair.

'Much better. The doctor has given me some pain relief, but never mind me, more importantly, how are you?'

'I'm okay,' she replied, taking a seat next to his bedside. 'It was strange waking up this morning without you. You gave me a fright last night. I have never witnessed anyone turning such an awful colour. It's crazy how fast things can change. One minute you were twirling me around and the next you were doubled over in pain.'

'Yeah, I agree.' Theo nodded.

'Did the doctor give you a diagnosis?' Erin asked as she

began fixing his blankets around him.

Theo, suppressing a smile, shuffled in the bed and sat upright. Taking hold of her hand he replied, 'No, they're not sure what happened but they're optimistic that I'll be back home in a few days. As I suspected, they think it's just an upset tummy and I'll be back to myself in no time.'

'Great, because I'm telling you, I can't bear the thought of staying on my own, so you better hurry up and get yourself out of that bed and back into ours!' Erin teased.

'Don't you worry, I'll be on my feet in no time.' He kissed her hand.

'You better,' Erin joked, 'There I was thinking I was going to be getting spoilt rotten, putting my feet up and getting my dinner served.'

'Ha, the extent I would go to get out of that task.' Theo grinned. Glancing over her shoulder to the street below, he continued, 'Oh look, it's snowing again.'

Outside the soft flurry tumbled from the sky, glittering flakes coating everything with a fresh coat of white snow. A group of carol singers gathered around the gates of the infirmary. Minutes later the sweet sound of Silent Night drifted through the cool air.

'Listen, that's one of my favourite Christmas carols.' Theo smiled.

'I like that one too but I have to admit my favourite is Holy Night. It reminds me of home, my dad used to sing it every year at Christmas,' Erin's tone lowered, tears welled up in her eyes. 'In fact sometimes he would sing it throughout the year, he loved it that much.' She smiled at the memory.

Squeezing her hand, Theo replied, 'It must be hard for you being so far from the rest of your family at this time of year.'

Nodding, Erin, wiped her eyes. 'I'm okay.' She laughed. 'And besides, *you* are my family and this time next year we'll have a little bundle of joy in our arms.'

'Roll on next Christmas! I can't wait to hold our precious little child.'

Erin could feel herself wanting to cry again. 'Look at me, ready to bawl like a baby at any opportunity! This tearfulness must be something to do with the pregnancy.'

'Yeah, possibly. Still, being away from home at Christmas must be tough, I can't imagine I would be okay if it was me. I'll make you a promise, this time next year I'll have your feet back on Irish soil. If I have my way, you my dear, will spend Christmas next year in Derry!'

'Back on Irish soil? I like the sound of that, although I must warn you, there is nothing glamorous or fancy back where I come from.' Erin laughed.

'Never worry, I'm not fussed as long as we're together, that's all that matters. I'll make arrangements for a trip to Derry, you, me and this little boy here.' He placed a hand on her tummy.'

Erin, raising her eyebrows, asked, 'This little boy?'

'Sorry, I don't know where that came from, this little boy or this little girl.' He stroked her abdomen. 'I can't wait and it doesn't matter whether it's a boy or girl, I will be looking forward to holding our baby in my arms; roll on the birth!'

'If it's a boy, shall we call him Theo? Little Theodore junior, that would be nice.'

'No.' Theo shook his head. 'I would rather we didn't. I know it's nice to call a first son after the father but I would prefer my child to have its own name.'

'Oh, well, I don't mind, I thought you would prefer a son named after you but that's fine,' Erin agreed.

'We'll give him or her their very own name, we'll think of something special.' Theo yawned. 'I feel so exhausted,' he said, struggling to keep his eyes open. 'The name will come to us.' He rubbed his eyes as his lids became heavier.

'Take a sleep, love. I'll sit here and read a bit from this bible.' Erin lifted the bible from the bedside locker.

'No, I'm sure you're tired too.' Theo yawned again. 'I suppose you didn't get much sleep last night, honey.'

Erin, mirroring his infectious yawn, stretched her arms out and said, 'Look, you're making me yawn too. I don't mind staying here, I'll keep you company.'

'If I'm lying here sleeping, I won't be much company for you. Darling, go on and get some rest for yourself and our precious little one.'

'Okay, I think you're right. I'll go and let you get some rest. I'll call back after dinner.' She stroked his head. 'My goodness, Theo, your skin feels so warm, shall I get you...?'

'Never mind, I'll take care of that.' A friendly voice from behind her spoke.

'Father Fitzgerald! I didn't hear you come in! What are you doing here?' Erin beamed. 'I thought you would be busy with the Christmas services.'

Lifting a sponge and soaking it in the bowl of water next to Theo's bedside, Father Fitzgerald rung it out and patted it gently on his brother's forehead. 'I met your brother William at the midnight service last night. He informed me Theo was unwell so I came over today as fast as I could and I am free for the remainder of the day. One of the other priests has kindly offered to celebrate mass in my place.'

'Hope you're not planning on administering my last rites,' Theo joked as he rested his head against the pillows and welcomed the cooling sponge.

Taking a seat next to the bed and placing the sponge back into the water, Father Fitzgerald smiled and pulled out his leather covered bible. 'No, hopefully not, but I thought I would read you a few pages from the main book.' He tapped lightly on the cover. Looking up and smiling from Theo to Erin, he said, 'I hear congratulations are in order, William told me the good news. I'm very much pleased for you both!'

Placing Theo's bible back on the locker, Erin, taking Theo's hand, grinned back. 'Thank you, we can't wait.'

'And I can't wait to get out of this hospital and look after my wife! My goodness I've only been here a short while and it's driving me insane.' Theo glanced around the room, 'These dull, dreary walls are depressing!'

'Offer your suffering up,' Father Fitzgerald replied with a smile. Opening the bible, he began to flick through a few pages. Looking up at Erin, his face full of compassion, he said, 'Erin you must rest, you need to look after yourself and the little gift God has sent you. I'm not needed for anything else today so I plan to stay here and keep Theo company, go and get Christmas dinner, Leonarda is still expecting you. I nipped over this morning and told them the news. I hope you don't mind, I told them about the baby also, William asked me to.'

'No not at all, I told William to pass that message on,' Erin replied. 'Thank you.'

'The rest of the family send their love. They'll be over here to visit you after dinner, Theo. Leonarda is over the moon, she said to tell you, Erin, that there will be an extra portion of plum pudding for your little one and she cannot wait until she hears the pitter-patter of little feet in the house.'

A new wave of excitement washed over Erin. 'Oh, this is going to be the longest pregnancy *ever*. We all can't wait for that sound!'

Theo, unable to keep his eyes open for a second longer, just nodded in agreement.

'Now, as I said earlier, you can go and have your dinner and a rest and I will sit here.' Father Fitzgerald placed a gentle hand on her shoulder.

Feeling her stomach rumble like a volcano, Erin beamed. 'I think I will, that plum pudding is calling me! I'll be back in later,' she said, kissing Theo's forehead.

'Emmm,' he nodded, half dozing, 'Love you.'

'Love you too,' she whispered. 'I love you so much, my darling.'

Erin buttoned up her coat and stepped outside the infirmary into the frosty air, and wrapping her scarf around her neck, she prepared to walk the few blocks back to the apartment.

'Merry Christmas!' William sang, launching a soft snowball in her direction.

Ducking to dodge the missile, Erin yelled, 'I'll merry Christmas you!' Gathering a handful of snow, she fired it back at him. 'Don't you know I should be handled with caution in my present condition?' she joked before collecting more snow as he approached.

Holding up his hands he said, 'Sorry, sis. I forgot.'

'How could you forget something so important?' she teased and before he could move out of the way, Erin launched the handful of snow down his jumper. 'Ha, that will teach you for messing with me.' She giggled.

'Ah you little...' William, wriggling about to free himself from the cold snow laughed as Erin launched more upon him. 'Get away!'

Erin, enjoying every second, gathered more and rubbed it into his damp hair. 'Ha, your beautiful shiny black hair looks like something the cat dragged in!'

'And there I was being a good thoughtful brother and arranging for the chauffer to come all the way over here to give you a lift to the Fitzgerald's house for dinner. I'll tell Carson you can walk now!'

'Aye right.' Erin smiled, walking past him through the wrought iron gates and heading towards the spanking new ruby-red Locomobile. Climbing into the backseat of the gleaming car, she watched as William followed her, shaking off the remaining snow from his hair.

'How is Theo now?' he asked, taking a seat next to her. 'Maxine and I called in earlier, he seemed much more settled than last night.'

Erin, watching passers-by walk carefully along the streets, bundled up against the elements and arms full of presents, replied, 'He's okay. Thankfully he'll be back on his feet in no time.' Releasing a sigh, she continued, 'Although I can't believe our first Christmas together has been ruined with him taking unwell. Still, thankfully it doesn't seem to be anything serious.'

Mr Carson steered the vehicle through the pillared entrance of the long, winding, tree-lined drive and came to a crunching halt outside the magnificent mansion. The extensive lawns looked wonderful with a thick blanket of untouched snow and the abundance of mature plants, shrubs and trees glistened in the frosty air, all coated with thin crystalline fragments.

Mr Benson, on seeing the guests arrive, opened the grand doors with a flourish and greeted the pair with a broad smile.

The tempting aroma of fine cooking and spices filled the air. Stepping inside the warm, welcoming hallway, Erin suddenly felt quite weak. The hunger pains she had experienced earlier were now rumbling like mad though her tummy. 'I'm starving,' she whispered with a grin to William.

'Aye me too,' William replied, cleaning his shoes on the doormat, he followed her into the hallway.

'Come this way, dinner is just about to be served.' Benson led them both to the dining room.

Inside the grand dining room, Erin felt the atmosphere charged with festivity. A huge log fire crackled to her left. To the right of the fireplace, a magnificent Christmas tree had been expertly decorated with swaths of gold and red ribbons. The warm scent of pine and cinnamon filled the air and the vast arrangement of candles flickering throughout the room cast a warm glow all around.

'My dear, Erin. So good to see you.' Mr Fitzgerald, stood up from his chair and enveloped her in a warm, friendly embrace. Kissing both her cheeks, he said, 'William has been telling us all the news, you must have had such a fright,' he said as he led them both to their seats.

'Yes, such a fright indeed, and in your condition.' Mrs Fitzgerald smiled. 'Congratulations on the news of the baby.

We are so pleased for you both.'

'We are indeed!' Mr Fitzgerald piped in, pouring William a large sherry and a glass of alcohol-free punch for Erin, he continued, 'Theo must be over the moon.'

'Thank you.' Erin returned the smile as she accepted the drink. 'Oh, Theo is certainly over the moon. He's so excited, he just can't wait to become a dad.'

Maxine's heart did a little flip, oh how she longed to have a child of her own one day and that day couldn't come quick enough. Giving William a kick under the table, she nodded at him as their eyes met. 'Go on tell them,' she whispered.

Clutching his glass of sherry, William took an extra huge gulp to steady the caterpillars crawling around the pit of his tummy. 'Ladies and gentlemen.' William cleared his throat. 'Can I have your attention for a minute, I have a little announcement to make.'

'Oh, this sounds interesting.' Mrs Fitzgerald's eyebrows shot up.

Looking to Maxine and reaching for her hand, William executed a smile. 'Yes it is very interesting. My darling Maxine here has agreed to become my wife!'

A round of applause and cheers echoed in the huge room.

Throwing her arms around her brother, Erin hugged him tight. 'Oh, congratulations!' Releasing her grip, she teased, 'However, hold on a minute, I'm just thinking, it's bad enough you being my *brother*, I now have to put up with you being my *brother-in-law* also!'

'Cheeky!' William replied, ruffling her hair. 'Oh, I almost forgot, speaking of engagements and in-laws, you're never going to guess what's going on back in Ireland.' William laughed.

'What? What is it?' Erin asked, her face beaming and dying to hear the latest news.

'We received a letter yesterday from Mum, it was addressed to us both so I opened it.'

'Go on,' Erin urged, almost on the edge of her seat, she couldn't wait to hear what the letter had contained. 'Don't tell me our Mary has finally found herself a man!' she teased taking a sip of her punch.

'No, it's better than that! Suzy Ferguson is engaged. Actually they're probably married and all by now, apparently they were to get married before Christmas. Isn't it great news?'

'What? I don't believe it! I never imagined Suzy falling in love again. Who's she engaged to?' Erin asked.

'This is the best bit, Frankie McGregor! Can you imag...?'

'Frankie McGregor? You're pulling my leg.' Erin, interrupting him, released a riotous roar of laughter. 'No, you must have picked it up wrong or you're winding me up.'

'Seriously, I'm not! Apparently, according to Mum's letter, he hasn't touched a drop of alcohol in months! He's turned his life around and he and Suzy are head over heels in love! I think it's brilliant!'

'Well I never!' Erin, still grinning from ear to ear, replied. 'I'm delighted for them both, I still can't believe it, though!'

'Actually, there's something else you're not going to believe.'

Erin, her eyes dancing with excitement, replied, 'This sounds good. What is it?'

William, taking a drink of the tasty sherry, continued, 'It's Patrick. He's only gone and asked some Dublin girl to marry him!'

Chapter 34

Clutching a fork and knife and the plate of food, carefully wrapped for Theo, Erin smiled. 'Thank you, Mr Carson,' she said as the quiet chauffeur assisted her out of the Locomobile. 'It was very kind of you to drop the others off earlier and return for us.'

'You are very welcome, Mrs Fitzgerald.' He smiled. 'I will be back at seven thirty for Mr and Mrs Fitzgerald and William and Maxine. I shall drop them all off and come back and get you and Leonarda, shall we say about eight fifteen?'

'That's fine, thank you.' Erin nodded.

'Give my regards to Theo. Please tell him I hope he gets better soon.' He smiled as he closed the door behind them.

'I will, thank you, Mr Carson.'

Stepping into the frosty air, Erin linked arms with Leonarda and together they carefully walked on the slippery pavement towards the hospital gates.

'I'm sure Theo will be pleased we brought him some Christmas dinner. It was a very thoughtful gesture, Leonarda.'

Leonarda released one of her trademark hearty laughs. 'My dear, Erin, I have cooked for that boy all of his life, there is no way I was going to let him suffer the prospect of missing his dinner on today above all days. I'm sure he's sitting in there now waiting patiently for us to arrive with it.'

The night sky had grown dark earlier in the day and the looming clouds above threatened to explode with more snowfall. On entering the wrought iron gates of the hospital, Erin noticed someone slouched against the pillared entrance. The glow from the street lamp and the light spilling from the hospital windows, streamed over him, illuminating his wrinkled face. Shoulders hunched in defeat and shivering like a wet dog, he looked up at them as they approached. His eyes portrayed a deep sadness, his face one of perfect gloom.

Erin, removing her gloves, bent her knees and looking into his eyes she asked, 'What are you doing lying here on such a cold night, haven't you got no home?' her voice croaked.

'No... no, I'm h-homeless,' he stammered.

Erin, took a deep breath and experienced a horrifying sense of guilt. Her heart cried out to this poor man, slumped outside a hospital on the damp ground and looking chilled to the bone. 'What's your name?' she asked, swallowing back the boulder in her throat and handing him her gloves.

'Ron,' he replied. Gratefully he accepted her gift and gingerly placed the gloves on his icy fingers.

Erin, tears welling in her eyes began unravelling her scarf and wrapped it around Ron's neck. Looking up to Leonarda, she went on, 'Theo will already have had the hospital dinner, I know he would prefer Ron to have this food.'

Leonarda, placing her hand on Erin's shoulder, gave her a light pat and nodded in agreement. 'Yes, you're right my dear, I agree.'

Erin handed him the fork, knife and the plate, still warm from being in the oven. 'Here, please accept this.' She helped remove the wrapping and at once the tantalising aroma of roast beef and turkey, together with seasoned vegetables, filled their nostrils.

'May God bless you both!' Ron's eyes danced with the prospect of filling his empty stomach as he accepted her offering. 'I shall pray the rosary for you later. Thank you.'

Erin felt her heart plummet into the pit of her stomach. Here was this hungry, cold, homeless man, who needed divine help more than she did, promising to pray for her. She felt so fortunate for the blessings in her life. She had to admit more than often she had taken life for granted. Then again she was no different from most folk, but still, sometimes it takes incidents like these to shake you up to face reality and realise that not everyone is fortunate to have a roof over their heads or a stomach about to burst at the seams from the overindulgence of food.

The clouds, as expected, ripped apart and big fluffy snowflakes came parachuting to the earth.

'It looks like the angels are having a pillow fight up there again.' Ron smiled as the cool flakes fell delicately upon his cold face.

A pang of anxiety gripped Erin. She had always loved to watch the snow coat the streets with its glitter but had never imagined how, for someone like Ron, this would be an added suffering to enhance his hardships. Erin watched with regret as Ron licked the gravy off the fork, like a hungry kitten licking a bowl of milk, as the snow fell upon his silver-grey hair and melted.

'Where will you sleep tonight?' she asked, almost afraid of his answer, for she knew he certainly wouldn't be climbing into a clean, warm bed. The thought of this unfortunate man lying on a park bench was too unbearable.

Biting into the tender roast beef with satisfaction, Ron looked up at her. 'I'll let you into a secret, there's a very kind nurse that works in there.' He nodded towards the doors of the hospital. 'Each night, as soon as the matron leaves her ward, she sneaks me in. She allows me to sleep in a cupboard and brings me a warm drink, some food and blankets. She's an angel.'

'She certainly is,' Leonarda said. 'Thank God for humanity.'

'I agree.' Erin smiled before straightening up. 'I shall have to go now, my husband is in there. He'll be waiting for me.'

'I will pray also tonight for your husband, may God return him to full health,' Ron said.

'Thank you, Ron.' Erin smiled.

'No thank you! Thank you so much for the food. Take care, God bless!'

'You too, you're very welcome,' Erin replied and sent a silent pray to the heavens above for someone up there to help this man.

Walking along the winding corridors Erin promised that she would not forget Ron and made a vow to herself that one day she would help turn his life around. A pang of guilt shot through her, earlier when William had broken the news about Patrick's engagement, the shock was overwhelming. Part of her felt bitter, perhaps even jealous, after all how could Patrick ask someone he hardly even knew to marry him? He truly was not the person she had thought he was. Then reality hit her like a ton of bricks, regardless of what she thought, Patrick was entitled to get on with his life, just like she had done with Theo. She loved Theo with all her heart and she hoped Patrick and this new girl in his life felt the same love for one another. As she witnessed Ron's dilemma, she realised that there was more to life than pondering over the past. The truth is, regardless of what problems you think you have in your life, there is always someone else worse off.

'You have gone terribly quiet,' Leonarda remarked.

Releasing a sigh, Erin replied, 'Ron's situation has made me think how fortunate we are.' She sniffed. 'I woke this morning full of self-pity thinking *poor me* with my husband in hospital over Christmas. I feel so bad now because I have nothing really to whine about. That man out there has plenty to moan about, the reality is, that is someone with real problems!'

'It sure does open your mind when you witness another human being suffering like that,' Leonarda agreed.

'I have an idea, but I need to speak to Mr Fitzgerald first. Do you remember him saying that he needs a new groundsman as the work is getting a bit too much for Malcolm?

Malcolm's arthritis is slowing him down.'

'Yes, that is true, he did say at some stage in the New Year he would look to employ someone else to give him a hand.'

'That's right, I'm going to have a word with him, I'm sure between us all we could sort something out for Ron.'

'Erin that's a great idea! Mr Fitzgerald will agree, that I am sure! Yes, speak to him …' Leonarda's voice trailed as her gaze fell upon William and Maxine standing outside Theo's room. 'What is the matter? Maxine why are you crying?' She secretly prayed they were not about to hear bad news.

Maxine, clutching a handkerchief, looked up, her eyes swollen. 'I… I… ca… can't be… lieve it,' she stammered.

William slid his arm from around Maxine's waist and with sorrow and pain in his eyes he threw his arms around Erin. Taking hold of his sister he whispered softly, 'Oh, Erin, I'm so sorry, we are so, so sorry.'

'What are you talking about, William?' she asked, unravelling herself from his grasp.

'It's Theo,' William answered, tears rolling down his cheeks. 'I'm… I'm so sorry.'

Chapter 35

'Theo has Bright's disease. I'm so sorry, Erin,' William said with a tone of pity.

'Bright's disease?' What the heck is *Bright's* disease?' Erin stared at him confused.

Leonarda, her complexion turning greyer by the second, clutched at her chest and cried, 'Oh please, God, no!'

Doctor Harrison, who had been attending Theo since his admission, came rushing up the corridor and stopped at Erin's side. 'I take it, Mrs Fitzgerald, you have heard the news.'

Turning to the doctor, Erin's eyes narrowed. 'I have heard but I haven't got a clue what it is and why they are looking as if my husband is *dead*. Look at him in there.' Erin nodded towards the door of Theo's room. Through the glass frame she could see him propped up on the bed. Turning back to William she lowered her voice and pointed a finger at him, 'You gave me such a fright just now, repeating how sorry you were, what is that all about?' she asked through gritted teeth. 'You had me thinking he was bloody well *dead*!'

Placing a hand lightly on her shoulder, Dr Harrison replied in soothing tones, 'I think what he means is that Theo is very ill. Bright's disease is an ailment of the kidneys. This condition normally causes swelling of the skin, pressure in the back, together with severe vomiting and high fevers. As we speak, we are struggling to control your husband's temperature and he is not even keeping down small amounts of fluids. As I have explained earlier to Theodore's family, I am so sorry to have to break this news to you, I believe the disease is at an advanced stage.'

'Advanced stage?' Erin asked.

'Yes, in all due respect to you, I'm afraid so.'

'Doctor, no disrespect to your better judgement but my husband was only taken ill yesterday! This disease that you are talking about could not possibly be at an *advanced* stage in such a short space of time! He had absolutely no symptoms up until twenty-four hours ago!' Erin wailed, her voice rising a fraction. 'Please excuse me, I want to see my husband now. I have wasted enough time standing here listening to this. So if you will be good enough to move out of my way, I would appreciate it very much.'

William, taking hold of Erin's arm before she had time to reach the door handle, pleaded, 'Wait, Erin, you must listen to the doctor. The thing is Theo has had symptoms, I have seen him unwell at work for several weeks.'

Glancing over her shoulder, Erin replied, 'Don't be ridiculous, if Theo had been unwell, surely I would have known. I am his *wife* after all!' Looking to the doctor, she asked, 'Tell me, doctor, how does one come down with such an ailment in such a short period of time?'

'I don't believe it was that short, he tells me he has indeed felt unwell for some time. He didn't want to worry you

304

as he felt it was nothing to be alarmed about,' Dr Harrison replied.

'I don't believe he is as sick as you are making out. I'm sorry, Doctor Harrison, but I'm only speaking my mind. Yes, he was very unwell last night, and I admit he was the colour of death warmed up, but let me tell you, when I was here only hours ago, Theo was bright and perky and in no pain whatsoever! He's getting better not worse!' Erin's eyes widened.

Releasing a sigh, Doctor Harrison nodded in disagreement. 'I am afraid he may very well have appeared to be looking, and perhaps sounding better to you, but that was because he'd had quite a lot of pain relief at that stage.'

Maxine, drying her eyes and sniffing, croaked, 'Erin, you must realise, our grandfather passed away a few years back with the same problem. This is an illness that has plagued our family for many generations!'

'Theo is not going to pass *away* if that is what you're thinking, Maxine!' Erin, screeched. Feeling more irritated by the second, this conversation was the last thing she needed now, she rubbed her tired forehead and continued, 'Put such thoughts out of your mind!'

Maxine, shrugging, turned away to avoid Erin seeing the tears fill up again.

'Mrs Fitzgerald, you must prepare yourself, Theo is very, very unwell.'

'Well, I'm afraid, doctor, you must prepare yourself to

be proved wrong. Do not lose patience with Theo! He's a strong man, he will pull through!' Erin pointed directly at him. 'You mark my words, my husband will pull through!' Waving her hands in the air and looking at each of the others, Erin continued, 'Do not even waste your time entertaining the idea that my husband is dying because he is not! I'm telling you all now, he's not! I can't believe the rest of you have given up on him!'

'No, Erin, no one has given up on him.' Leonarda stepped in. 'Please do not annoy yourself, you're getting yourself worked up, you must take it easy and calm yourself down.'

'But that's just it, I can't because all of you seem to have accepted that he's not going to make it out of this dreary hospital! I can tell you all right now that you are wrong! WRONG, WRONG, WRONG!' Turning her attention back to Doctor Harrison, Erin, went on, 'Also for your information, doctor, we just got married back in September and we are expecting our first baby in August. If anything will make him want to live, it will be this baby! He can't wait to become a father. I can therefore reassure you he will not depart this world without a fight, and I will be next to him to fight all the way, so you better try everything possible and get him back to good health!'

Doctor Harrison stared back with a blank expression etched on his face.

'Please do not give up on him!' Erin grabbed hold of the doctor's arm. 'Please, I'm begging you!'

Doctor Harrison dipped his head. He had learned over the years that the human way to survive problems was to throw oneself into denial. This behaviour from the gentle girl he had met the night before was no different to how most would react when forced to deal with losing a loved one. His words fell on deaf ears, he may as well have talked to the brick wall next to her. Right now as she glared at him, as if he'd suddenly sprouted horns from his head, he pitied her, little did she know what lay ahead.

'Look at me! Did you hear me?' Erin cried.

Lifting his head to look into her beautiful tear-filled eyes, Doctor Harrison nodded, 'Yes, yes I did hear you,' he replied softy.

'Take a look at Theo in there,' Erin urged as her eyes settled on Theo. 'He is sitting upright and he is talking to his father. Look he is *talking!*'

Doctor Harrison followed Erin's gaze. Yes, she was right, he was talking, but what Erin didn't notice was that his body was trembling as a result of the high fever, an indication that his temperature was through the roof. Erin also was not near enough to witness his breathing change, nor see his skin swelling at an alarming rate.

'Does he look like a man that is dying? It sure doesn't look like it to me,' Erin cried.

Leonarda added, 'Erin, no one has actually said that Theo is going to die, those exact words have not been used. Doctor Harrison has said he is very ill, isn't that correct, doctor? I'm sure you will do everything to have young Theo back on his feet again.'

Doctor Harrison shook his head. 'I appreciate that this news is difficult to take in, Mrs Fitzgerald, but again in all due respect to you, you must accept your husband is a very ill man.'

'Nonsense! Doctor, in all due respect to you, I don't believe you know what you're talking about!' Erin fired back. From over her shoulder she could see Ron being led into a cupboard at the end of the corridor, presumably by the nurse he had told her about earlier. Catching a glimpse of Erin, Ron paused, lifted his rosary beads into the air, made a sign of the cross, pointed his finger at himself then at Erin and mouthed 'I'll pray for you now.'

In a daze Erin answered back aloud as he disappeared out of sight, 'It's a miracle I need!' Reverting her attention back to Doctor Harrison, Erin asked, 'So, doctor, tell me what happens next. What treatment are you proposing for Theo and when should I expect him to be well again? Also when do you expect my husband to get out of here?' Erin, tilting her head and jutting her chin out, waited for his response.

'I will not lie to you, Mrs Fitzgerald. The truth is the disease is far too progressed for us to do anything. Mrs Fitzgerald, I am afraid his organs are failing and in due course he will develop heart failure, you therefore must prepare yourself for the worst. I regret to be so blunt, but I am afraid I predict your husband will be dead within a few weeks.'

Chapter 36

'Nonsense! I am *not* standing here listening to any more of this!' Erin fired back. Pushing past Doctor Harrison, she opened the door with a flourish and made her way to the far end of the room where Theo's bed sat next to the window. William, Maxine and Leonarda followed close behind her.

A draft from the old frames set the flimsy curtains to sway as the howling wind from outside sneaked its way in. Erin, feeling a chilling bite in the air, pulled her cardigan closer around her skinny frame.

On seeing her approach, Theo mustered a smile. 'Hi, my darling,' he said, reaching for her hand.

Erin noted that despite the chilly air, Theo's hand was warm and clammy. Bending down to kiss his cheek, she observed that too was unusually hot.

'I saw you talking with the others, I assume you have heard the news.' Theo, squeezed her hand.

'My dearest Theo, you will get better.' Erin sat down next to him.

On the other side of the door in the corridor, Erin had felt a fight in her, a denial that she had never experienced before, but now as she sat perched on the bed next to him, a fear was beginning to develop. What if the doctor was right? Feeling her insides twist into knots she ran for the window, opened it and stuck her head out. Sensing as if she was about to pass out, she gripped the ledge and gasped in breaths of frosty air. The carol singers from earlier gathered again outside the hospital gates, the sweet sound of Hark! The Herald Angels Sing came drifting in.

Humming aloud to the Christmas carol, Erin found herself gazing out the window in a world of her own. From her position she could see the sludgy dregs of snow below as a new fresh flurry came bounding from the sky above. Across the rooftops of Manhattan, thick blankets of undisturbed snow lay. Directly across the street a nativity crib had been erected to celebrate the birth of Jesus. Inside the crib, lanterns had been placed, each holding a flickering candle, which cast a soft glow around the Christmas scene. Everything looked so full of joy and festivity, so perfect, but the reality was here inside these walls there was a homeless man taking shelter in a cupboard and her husband was dying and God only knows what else was going on! Right now nothing could be further from perfect. Erin wanted to scream from the depths of her heart that life was so unfair! The tears that she had held back earlier unleashed themselves and whether she liked it or not they came rolling down her pink, flushed cheeks.

Wiping her eyes and looking up towards the heavens, Erin prayed a silent prayer to Jesus to help her husband. Please God make everything okay, she silently desired as she made her way back to Theo's bedside. The silence in the room was gripping and the sound of the carol singers now singing Holy Night was welcomed by all present.

William, reading Erin's thoughts, said softly, 'Dad's favourite song.'

Nodding, Erin looked up at him. 'It is indeed. I was telling Theo that earlier. It wouldn't be so bad if he could actually sing,' she replied, trying to stifle a grin. 'He sounds more like a cat on a hot tin roof.'

Theo, taking Erin's hand again in hers, teased, 'He couldn't be any worse than me.'

Although Erin knew this conversation was intended to make light of their situation and Theo was only trying to keep her mood up, he actually did the opposite. Regardless of how poor a singer Theo was, the truth was, if Doctor Harrison's prediction was correct, Erin wouldn't hear her husband singing as he normally did as he arrived back from work or blast out a tuneless melody in the bath or croon about the kitchen. Never would she hear him sing lullabies to their new baby! My God the stark truth was he may never see his child and this baby in her womb would never meet its father! Before she knew it Erin was sobbing and Leonarda was holding her in her arms, rocking her to and fro as she wailed like a baby.

Unable to watch this pain for a second longer, Maxine nodded to her parents to follow her outside. She knew by the look on their faces that they too were about to melt down in front of Theo, and surely if they did, poor Theo's heart would break that little bit more.

'Everything will be okay, Erin, I promise you, it will all work out.' Theo ran his clammy hand through wisps of her raven black hair and glancing from his brother to William he nodded. 'I have come to a decision, I have talked it over with William and my brother and we all think it is for the best.'

Looking up, her cheeks damp and on fire, Erin's eyes met Theo's, 'What decision? What do you mean?'

'We will arrange for you to return to Derry,' Theo replied, his heart breaking at the prospect of it.

'What?' Erin wriggled herself from Leonarda's arms and sat up straight. 'Theo you have got to be joking! I'm not going! There is absolutely no way I'm leaving!' Erin wailed. Her heart began beating so fast, it felt like it was banging against her ribcage at an alarming rate. She was so shocked by Theo's idea that she hadn't noticed Leonarda slipping out the door with William.

Father Fitzgerald, clutching his bible and rosary beads, allowed the tears to flow from his own eyes. A man that very rarely cried, he now felt like he was about to release bucketsful that had been stored up over the years. Quietly and discretely he slipped out past them and closed the door gently behind him leaving Erin and Theo alone.

'Yes, Erin,' Theo answered, his tone soft and soothing. 'William and Maxine are planning to get married. My father is expanding the business and it's likely that William will take up the position of running the new office in New Jersey.'

'That's the first I've heard of New Jersey but I can't see what that has got to do with me moving back to Ireland.'

Taking a deep breath, Theo continued, 'Erin, it has much to do with you. Don't you realise once I am gone you will have nobody apart from my parents and Leonarda. You will have no income coming in to keep up the payments of our current home and you will more than likely have to move in with my mother and father.'

'But you're not going, please, Theo, don't die! Don't let go! Don't give up!' Feeling herself tremble, Erin grasped his night shirt. 'Don't leave me, Theo! You can't! I won't be able to cope without you!'

'Erin, that is why I want you to return to your own family. If you had to face moving into my family dwelling you would only get swallowed up in that big house with boredom. I know you, Erin, you need more than that. You need to be surrounded by your own familiar territory. As I say, you will have no one close at hand here apart from Leonarda and my parents. Erin, you really do need more than that.'

'No, you're wrong! Are you forgetting something? I will have our *baby* and I will have *you*! Listen now to me, Theo, never mind what the doctor has said, doctors are not always right. Doctor Harrison hasn't a clue what he is talking about!'

'Erin, he is a great doctor.'

'Yes but he is wrong! Doctors can get things wrong at times!'

'He has practiced for a long time; I do not question his judgement. If he says my condition is too advanced, then so be it,' Theo replied with regret.

'I can't believe what I'm hearing! I know you well enough to know that you're a fighter and you will win this battle, regardless what he thinks or what anyone else thinks for

313

that matter! In no time you and I will be strolling around the park again, feeding the ducks, sitting on the bench and watching the world go by like we have done in the past. We will go and see the Statue of Liberty, we'll head up and visit William and Maxine! Then, remember what you said to me yesterday? This time next year you promised my feet will be back on Irish soil, well then, you and I can look forward to that! We'll celebrate Christmas in Derry, where the banter and fun will be like nothing you have ever experienced. My family will be delighted to see us all. They will make you so welcome! I'll even get my dad to sing Holy Night! We can then head up to the local parish hall and bring in the New Year with a night filled with dancing. Oh, Theo, you will love Ireland!' Erin babbled on with excitement. 'We don't have much material things back in Derry but we have love, yes, love and friendship! Sure isn't that better than all the materials of the world!'

Theo blinked away the tears and swallowed the lump that had mushroomed in his throat. Never had he felt such a strong urge to lift his wife into his arms and tell her he couldn't wait to enter her land of her dreams and participate in all those things that he normally would have taken for granted. Yes, he would have loved to visit Ireland, New Jersey and sit in the park watching the world go by, but the reality was right before him he was watching his own life going by. He knew he no longer had much of a future, and when something so precious is taken from you in a blink of an eye, there is nothing you can do but surrender to God's will.

'I want you to listen to me now, my sweetheart. You

314

must do as I say,' he said slowly. 'Please, Erin, go back to Derry and…' he paused as he tried to say the unimaginable words of advice, 'I… I want you to find… love again. I give you my blessing to… to remarry.'

'No! Don't be silly!' Erin wailed. 'I can't believe you're saying all this!' Fresh tears began to escape from her eyes.

Again, Theo wanted so badly to scoop her into his arms and tell her everything would be okay but he knew he would only be kidding them both.

'No,' he shook his tired head. 'No, Erin, I'm not being silly, I'm being realistic. You're only a young, beautiful girl.' He lifted wisps of her hair from her wet cheeks. 'You must not be alone; you should not face life by yourself. Go back to Derry and rekindle your relationship with Patrick. I know you both meant a lot to one another so go back and perhaps things will work out for you both.'

'No chance! I don't want *him*! I want *you*! Besides, Patrick is in Dublin and is engaged to be married.'

'Well that's fine. Perhaps you will meet another, therefore if you do, you must not feel guilty. I give you my blessing, and as much as it is tearing me apart inside, it also comforts me to think that someone else will love you again and look after you.' He swallowed, feeling like his heart had just been ripped from him. 'But, Erin, I promise you this, if you do meet someone else, they will never love you like I love you.' A single tear escaped and trickled down his cheek.

Erin, on seeing the tear flow, caught it with her thumb, like a precious diamond. 'I don't want anyone else, I want you!' she croaked. 'Please, Theo, tell yourself you're going to get better! Go on tell yourself! Start believing and it will happen. You'll be back to good health and our baby will be born. We'll be happy! We'll be so *happy*! We can have more children! As many as you want!' Erin began babbling again.

Theo watched her facial expression and witnessed denial written all over it. His heart sunk to great depths as he knew only too well she would have to face the truth one day, and when that day came, he wouldn't be here to scoop her in his arms and tell her everything would be okay.

'Erin, the truth is, our lives our not ours to plan. We can scheme and design our route to our heart's content but God may have a different strategy and He can change things in a flash. His idea for me is not to be part of your journey for much longer, and sadly, I am not to be part of our baby's life at all.' Theo blinked rapidly, determined to keep up his strength and not to break down, for God only knew, if he did, no one on this earth would be able to stop him.

'How can you say that?' Erin said, her voice a mere whisper. Her heart felt it was going to explode. 'I can now imagine how Our Lady's heart felt, pierced with sorrow as she witnessed her son about to be crucified. Theo, my heart can't take this pain any longer. Please don't cause me such pain! You're giving up! I told you don't give up!'

'No, Erin, I am rising above it. Therefore, I want you to return to Derry. This is my dying wish. There is a boat leaving in a few weeks' time, and *you* must get on it.'

Chapter 37

Outside the temperature had fallen and a thick frost had coated the pavements. The Bogside was engulfed in a dense fog that hung heavy in the air and wrapped itself around every object in sight. Inside Suzy McGregor's home was quite the opposite. After pulling the curtains closed, she kicked off her shoes and threw another lump of turf onto the fire. The modest living room was warm and cosy and the blaze from the mighty inferno illuminated the place in a soft orange glow.

Settling into her armchair by the fire, Suzy sat back and watched as the flames danced and roared up the chimney. The last few weeks had been a journey she certainly would never forget, both memorable and delightful and amongst the best moments of her life. Twisting her wedding band around her finger, she still could not believe that Frankie had proposed and within weeks they had tied the knot. He no sooner had the question out of his mouth and they were fast at work preparing the event. Catherine Coyle had taken care of their outfits, ensuring they were washed and pressed for the special occasion. Once the paperwork was completed, Father Lavery had them both standing at the altar, exchanging their vows. Anne Quigley and the rest of the neighbours had got together as usual and decorated the parish hall and prepared the food, cuisine fit for royalty for the after party and what a party that was! They had danced into the small hours of the morning until their feet could take no more. The warmth and generosity of the neighbours was overwhelming, Suzy smiled to herself, her neighbours were not just their friends, they were all like one big close-knit family. With her sons unable to make it home for the event except Chris, Suzy was glad to have her friends by her side.

Christmas Day was one of the best she had experienced in a long time. The last few years it had just been herself and Chris, and once the dinner was over, Chris normally headed off with his mates for a few whiskeys, leaving her alone staring at four walls and with only the aroma of turkey in the air to remind her of the special day. This year had been quite the opposite. Frankie was here to help her prepare the meal as he sang carols at the top of his voice. Chris and Patrick had travelled up from Dublin and had joined in with the banter and fun. The house was thriving just like it should be and just like it had been all those years ago. Suzy too felt a buzz, she felt fantastic. Patrick looked cheery and alive also but there was something missing, she knew heartache when she saw it. It was clear Patrick was finding his first Christmas without his father difficult. No matter how hard he tried to put on a brave face, his young heart was breaking, still, Suzy was delighted that he had found love and the announcement of his plans to marry this girl in February in the New Year was both surprising and exciting. The young man deserved to be happy.

She had to admit it was wonderful having Chris and Patrick with them over the Christmas period. However, unlike previous years, when Suzy had to help Chris pack his belongings and wave him goodbye with a heavy heart, this year she had to acknowledge she was glad to see them off so that she and Frankie could have the house to themselves again. Was she being selfish? Absolutely not! She was a newlywed and spending quality time with her new husband felt perfect.

'Your tea's ready,' Frankie sang, nudging the kitchen door open with his hip, clasping the handles of two mugs of tea in one hand and a plate of digestive biscuits in the other.

'A nice cup of tea, just what the doctor ordered.' Suzy smiled and took one of the cups from him.

'Happy New Year, Mrs McGregor!' he tapped his cup against hers.

'Cheers,' she replied with a grin, 'And a very happy New Year to you also!'

'Cheers to us! Sorry it has to be tea. I've nothing stronger and I wouldn't swap it for a glass of whiskey for all the gold in the world!' Frankie glowed.

'You better not!' she warned taking a sip, 'Or I shall have to swap you!' she teased.

Taking a seat in the armchair next to her, Frankie looked at her, the flames glittering in his eyes. He placed the plate of biscuits on her lap and took her hand in his. 'The last few months have been incredible, I can't believe how blessed I've been to have you in my life, Suze.'

Suzy, gazing at him over the rim of her cup, nodded, 'We're both blessed. This time last year I sat here alone. I remember outside it was blowing a gale. The house was so empty and silent, apart from the sound of the wind howling down the chimney, and I felt so lonely. I went to bed before midnight, said a few prayers and cried for a little but then I pulled myself together and stopped wallowing in self-pity. I told myself this was what I needed to get used to, for my life was never going to change. How wrong was I!' She took another sip of her tea and smiled affectionately at her new husband. 'Little did I know what treasures God had in store for me.'

'I can't tell you what I did this time last year. Sorry, I don't remember much about it, but what I can say, I was most likely curled up in my bed as drunk as a lord!' he laughed.

'I can imagine that to be true. Oh, Frankie, you've done so well staying off the drink, I'm proud of you, love.' She gave his hand a little squeeze.

'No. I'm proud of you! I would never have taken that plunge if it were not for you, Suze. As the last year comes to a close and the new one just begins, I have butterflies squirming around by stomach because I know I'm going to be so happy with you.'

Susy blushed and smiled. 'And I'll be so happy with you also.'

'Look at us, what are we not like, you and me holding hands, drinking tea at one o'clock in the morning, we're like two love-struck teenagers,' he beamed.

Suzy grinned. 'We are indeed and what's wrong with that? We're not too old to be in love.'

'You're right, Suze. Falling in love has no age limits. I love you so much, I can't take my eyes off you.' He leaned across and kissed her cheek. Squeezing her hand, he went on. 'Thank you for being there for me, Suze. I really appreciate all you've done for me.'

'Frankie, you seem to forget, you are also here for me. I know you don't think so but you have no idea how much *you* have changed *my* life. I feel *so* uplifted having you here and I'm *so* happy we're married; I still can't believe it!'

'It is hard for me to grasp how much my life has changed in such a short space of time. As I look at you, I feel I have to pinch myself, sometimes I have to ask myself are you really mine?'

'I do the same.' Suzy, not used to so many compliments felt herself blush a little more. 'I enjoyed the New Year's party tonight,' Suzy said, dunking a biscuit in her tea.

'Me too. My goodness, over the last few weeks I've had more dances than hot dinners! Anne Quigley taught me how to dance when I was a young teenager, I'm sure as she witnessed me falling into the drink over the years she must have thought she'd wasted her time. I'm not joking you, that woman has the patience of a saint! We spent hour after hour in her kitchen learning how to master moving in time to the music.'

'Oh, she was so delighted tonight to see that you remembered the dance steps.'

'Aye I know, she smiled over at me and gave me the thumbs-up,' Frankie replied, taking a sip of his tea.

'Frankie, tonight the dance was good and the atmosphere was so joyous but I feel so sorry for the Coyle family. Catherine read me the telegram she received from William. It's so sad. After I heard the latest update from New York I just wanted to weep for young Erin. It doesn't look as if her new husband will pull through and she's just discovered she's pregnant.'

'Aye, poor Erin. I was chatting to John, he filled me in on the news. My heart goes out to her, leaving Derry for a better life and having to come back here under such heartbreaking circumstances.'

'Catherine and John are heartbroken, but it just goes to show you how good they are, they didn't want to attend the event tonight but they came along and helped out just like they had done every other year. In simple terms, it's fair to say, they wouldn't let others down. In fact, it's fair to say that everyone in this street goes out of their way to help others.'

'Aye, you're right, they sure do, Suze,' Frankie agreed. Sitting upright, he released her hand and, clicking his fingers, he said, 'An idea's just struck me on how we can help young Erin!'

Frowning, Suzy replied, 'How? I'm not sure we can do much in this situation.'

'Of course we can! The Coyle's have been so good to everyone else. Catherine and John would give the shirts off their backs to help others.'

'You're right, I agree,' Suzy nodded.

'Well think about this, soon Erin will be back and in no time she will have her baby. The Coyle's household is packed as it is. They have barely enough room to contain themselves never mind house Erin and her new child.'

'Oh, Frankie, they will welcome them back and fit them in somehow, they won't exactly see them homeless.'

'Exactly and neither will we! Now that I'm living here with you I can give them my house! Sure it's no good to me, it will only lie empty.'

'Fantastic! That's a great idea, we'll get it cleared up and ready for her. I've been that caught up with our new life, and so used to you being here, I almost forgot about your house. Yes, offer it to Erin!'

'Poor Erin, such a beautiful, friendly, young girl, she doesn't deserve such heartache.' Frankie sighed. 'Giving her a home is the least we can do. I suppose it will help her a little, but God only knows, that wee girl is going to have to carry a very, very, heavy heart back to Derry.'

Chapter 38

The atmosphere was choking, Erin felt someone had placed their hands around her throat and ever so slowly the air was being restricted from her lungs more and more. The reality was her airways were perfectly normal; her husband's, on the other hand, were quite the opposite. Theo's breathing had begun to slow down, little by little. Erin watched with horror as he faded away before her. She longed to take him in her arms and shake him until he was full of life again.

Tick, tick, tick… the clock and Theo's small breaths were the only sounds in the deathly silent room.

'New Year's Day. The day of new beginnings,' Erin whispered. Sitting glued to a chair next to his bed, she held Theo's hand and stroked his puffy skin. 'We should be making our plans, our resolutions, setting our goals and planning for our dreams to come true,' she murmured in his ear.

Tears welled up in her bewildered eyes as she observed him, lying still, eyelids closed and his chest rising up and down ever so slowly. Closing her own eyes, the events of the previous year flashed before her. The good times, the bad times, the ups and downs, and finally the last week, discovering the joy of a new life set to begin then being thrown in at the deep end to face the trauma of an existing one about to end. 'It's not fair,' Erin cried, running her fingers through his thick, dark hair, 'life is not fair!'

Father Fitzgerald's hands settled on her shoulders, 'Come, Erin, you need to get some rest. You've been here for hours now.'

Feeling the energy drain from her, Erin kissed Theo's cheek and whispered, 'I'll be back soon my darling.' She sighed and allowed her brother-in-law to help her to her feet, and like a lamb following its master, she trailed behind him.

Outside on the slippery pavement, Father Fitzgerald carefully led her to the waiting car and whispered, 'I want you to get something to eat and some rest. This suffering is awful for you and the baby.'

Looking into his eyes as he climbed into the seat next to her, Erin, her own eyes swollen and bloodshot, replied, 'I have always considered myself to have a strong Christian faith but right now I do wonder if there really is a God.'

'I can understand your doubt, Erin,' he whispered.

As the car pulled away she sighed, her gaze moved to the hospital window on the second floor. Behind the curtain, Theo remained clinging to his life. 'I know it's pointless asking you this because I know what you're going to say but do you really think there is a God? Actually, don't answer that question, I already know that you do.' She sighed again, feeling defeated and as lost as a petal on the wind.

'Erin, I can appreciate your feelings but you must also remember that God's ways are not ours and it is not for us to ask why, we should never question the will of God.'

'That's easy for you to sit there and say! It's not you carrying a child and watching the father of that baby die!' Erin wept.

Looking at her with a compassionate gaze, he replied, 'That is true. I cannot begin to imagine your pain.'

'Look, I'm sorry, that was wrong of me. You're losing your younger brother, after all, and I should never have spoken to you like that, I'm being snappy, I'm sorry.'

'My agony cannot match what you are going through. I can only imagine how difficult this situation is for you. We are all here for you, Erin. You'll manage to cope.'

Erin, shrugging, blinked away her tears and exhaled slowly. 'I'm going to have to, I don't have much of a choice in the matter.'

Falling silent, Erin gazed out the window, her thoughts a million miles away, feeling as if she had entered a world of her own. She knew the others would support her as Father Fitzgerald had just said but right now, as she peered at the silent streets, she felt like the only person on the planet.

Catching sight of the familiar figure walking at a snail's pace along the slippery pavement, Erin cried, 'Oh look! There's Ron!' She pointed out to the glittering street and at once was brought to earth with a bang. The reality was she wasn't the only one suffering a misfortune. 'He's a homeless man,' she said as she witnessed him clutching some railings to prevent himself slipping on the icy surface, his old boots had seen better days and clearly the soles were too worn to provide him any grip. 'He hangs around the hospital,' she continued, her heart going out to him. 'One of the nurses sneaks him in each night and gives him shelter.'

'That's very kind of her.' Father Fitzgerald peered out at the dishevelled man walking slowly towards the hospital. 'I guess that's where he's heading to now.'

'Yes, he's glad to have a roof over his head but he needs somewhere that he can call home. Will you do me a favour?' she asked turning to face him. 'Can you arrange for your father to give him employment? He can help out around the grounds and live in the staff quarters.'

'I will indeed, leave it with me. That's a good idea. I'll take care of it.'

'Thanks, if only you could take care of a few other things.' She sighed. 'It's not fair what's happing to Theo. Why do you think God allows bad things like this to happen to good people?' she asked, returning her attention back to the frost-covered streets.

'Bad? Who says it is bad? We don't know what awaits Theodore in the spiritual world. I can only imagine that there will be great treasures, joy and happiness. Just because you no longer will see, feel or hear him, that doesn't mean he'll not be with you. Theo will watch over you every step of your journey on earth until you meet again.'

'Do you really believe that? I want to, but how do we know all this for sure?'

'That much is true, but we have to cling on to hope, we have to believe in our God. Our bible tells us that there is a heaven waiting for us all if we follow God's will. Theodore has lived a good life in the eyes of God, I'm sure if anyone will get through the pearly gates it will be him! The man in that hospital bed would give the shirt off his back to help another. He would also give his last bite to eat for someone in need.'

A weak smile formed on Erin's face, 'That much is true, however, you have had the privilege of coming from a wealthy background, I cannot imagine Theo ever having to go hungry.' She looked at him.

'Actually you are wrong. When we were kids, Mom and Dad would regularly pack a picnic and take us to Central Park. One Friday afternoon, there was a young boy sitting on a bench under the shade of some elm trees. He looked shabby and dirty and wore an expression that told a story of a hungry, unhappy child. Theodore, on witnessing this boy's dilemma, handed him his share of the picnic. We tried to split ours with Theodore but he insisted that he was not going to eat our sandwiches. The next week he begged our parents to take him to the park to meet the little boy again. They agreed and brought along extra food but he was nowhere in sight. Theodore could not settle. Instead of playing, he roamed the park in search of the hungry boy but never found him.'

'That's so typical of Theo. I can imagine his determination to find that boy.' Erin sniffed.

'Indeed, and it was this determination that drove Theodore to fast each Friday. From that week on, he would abstain from eating food during the day and offer this sacrifice up to God for all the hungry children throughout the world.'

'What? That's amazing!' Erin's face filled with surprise. 'Coming to think of it now, he normally has his

329

dinner around seven o'clock on a Thursday night and doesn't eat again until around seven on a Friday. So... so he has actually been going without food for twenty-four hours and... and I didn't pay much attention to this!'

'No, he's a very humble man. He would never broadcast this from the rooftops and besides as long as God knows the reason why then no one else needs to.'

Mr Carson steered the car through the gates of the Fitzgerald's property and carefully began driving along the snow-covered driveway. The statues surrounding the pond peeped out under their new snow caps and the shrubs and bushes glistened. The skeleton trees, coated with frost, sparkled proudly. The scene before her looked like a perfect winter wonderland, if only everything was as *perfect*!

'Right, let's get you inside, I'm sure Leonarda will have something tasty waiting for you.' Father Fitzgerald smiled weakly as they came to halt.

Erin, following him inside the house, felt her tummy crying out for food but the thought of eating was making her feel ill. How could she possibly enjoy food right now?

'Come in here and get warm.' Father Fitzgerald indicated to the sitting area where a crackling fire was roaring and twirling in a fiery dance up the chimney.

'I'll join you in a few minutes, I just want to say hello to Leonarda.' Erin smiled softly.

Pouring himself a glass of ice water, he glanced up and replied, 'Okay.'

Feeling weary, Erin made her way to the kitchen where Leonarda was busy carving a succulent roast beef joint.

'Hello, Erin.' Leonarda peered up from her task. 'It's good to see you, my dear!'

The familiar aroma of the kitchen was too much. The memorable smells took her right back to the happy days when they worked here together. Those joy-filled days were only weeks ago but felt like a distant memory. Feeling overwhelmed, Erin felt herself tremble.

'Oh, Erin, don't cry, honey.' Leonarda put her knife down and placed her welcoming arms around her.

'Leonarda, I've been fooling myself, Theo's never going to be back here, is he?' she wailed. 'He's never going to stand in this kitchen, smell the usual aromas or taste your delicious food.'

'Leave it all in the hands of God. You never know, you just never know he could pull through. I, for one, am still clinging to hope, my dear. I'm not giving up just yet!'

'There's no point, Leonarda. I'm not giving myself false hope. I've been storming heaven with my prayers. I've been telling myself he's going to get better but he's not. I know now, deep down, he's not going to get better!'

'Erin, Erin, wake up.' Leonarda nudged her gently.

Opening her eyes a fraction, Erin replied in her sleepy state, 'Just another five… five minutes.'

'No, Erin, you must come now, it's urgent!'

'Wh… what's up? Have I been sleeping long?' Erin asked, sitting up straight and now fully awake.

'You dosed over after a few mouthfuls of your dinner. I woke you and brought you here to have a better rest. You've been asleep for about four hours but you must get up now,' Leonarda urged.

'Sleeping for four hours? But I need to get back to the hospital!'

'Exactly, I must warn you, my dear, Theo is very unwell.'

The drive back to the hospital seemed to take forever and the heavy snowfall tumbling from the heavens didn't help matters. After hearing the news that Theo may have had a heart attack, Erin felt her own heart stop beating and right now she didn't want to waste another second, she needed to be with him. Pulling up at the hospital, Erin opened the door of the car with a flourish and rushed towards the heavy hospital doors, Leonarda and Father Fitzgerald following quickly behind. All three sprinted along the narrow corridors, not stopping until they reached Theo's bedside.

Panting and shaking with nerves, Erin squeezed her way through William and Maxine and made her way over to her husband's side. The grave look on Mr and Mrs Fitzgerald's faces said it all, there was certainly no need for words.

Kneeling next to him, Erin took his hand in hers. 'I'm

warning you, Theo, don't leave me!' A storm of emotion brewed up in her eyes. 'Don't let go!' she wailed.

Father Fitzgerald knelt at the opposite side of the bed, placed his hand on Theo's forehead and began to administer the last rites.

'What are you doing?' Erin cried. 'Stop! STOP THIS MINUTE!' she shrieked, pushing his hand away. 'He's not going to die! He's going to pull through! Come on, my darling!' Erin, taking Theo in her arms, began shaking him, 'Don't listen to them all, you're not going to *die!*'

'Don't, Erin,' William said, stepping closer.

'Come on, *Theo! Wake* up! Wake up this minute! Stop this nonsense now! Do you hear me?' Erin yelled frantically. 'Open your eyes!'

'Let him go, Erin.' William, taking hold of her, gently pulled her fingers away and lifted her to her feet. 'He needs his last rites,' he said, holding her tight.

'Let go of me!' she shrugged. 'I'm warning you, William, let go of me!' she wriggled like a fish on a line as William carted her towards the door. 'What are you doing, William? I LOVE YOU, THEO!' she yelled over William's shoulder. 'Don't leave me, please don't leave me!'

William, holding her in his strong arms, carried her outside to the corridor. 'Listen to me, Erin, you have to calm yourself down.'

'Calm myself down! That's my husband lying in that bed and I'm not letting him go without a fight. Theo will not

333

leave me, he just needs to know how much I want him here then he won't go. He'll not enter into the light or whatever it is that happens when someone dies.'

'Theo knows how much you love him, if he could stay he would,' William replied, his voice soft and soothing.

'Don't say that!' Erin wailed. 'He's not going anywhere!' Turning her head to look through the small glass window in the door, she watched as the others began to recite the rosary. 'Look at them all, they're letting him go! They're giving up on him!'

William, a lump mushrooming in his throat, looked over her shoulder and gazed into the room. Theo, his lips blue and his skin grey, was slipping away as they peacefully prayed.

'Jesus if you are really up there then help him!' Erin thumped the door. 'Please God, all the angels and saints help him!' Erin, falling to her knees, cried out from the depths of her soul. On the floor she began to weep bitterly. 'If there really is a God then you won't take him! Leave him here another few years! Let him see his baby born! Let him hold his child in his arms!' Erin banged her fists against the door. 'Let him hold his child in his *arms*!' she repeated, her lungs struggling for breath, her emotional pain flowing from every pore.

William, tears welling up in his eyes, longed to tell his sister that everything would be okay but as he stared into the room he watched as Theo took one final breath. Seconds later Leonarda met his gaze and with a heavy heart nodded. 'He's gone,' she mouthed.

Chapter 39

'Fresh fish for sale! Buy one get one free!' echoed amongst the huge hordes on Grafton Street. 'The finest cod in Dublin's fair city!' a male voice yelled above the shoppers. 'And the best cockles and mussels in Ireland!'

The area was busy with the usual hustle and bustle associated with the Saturday markets, the place alive with traders and punters. Every stall was surrounded by Dubliners, like wasps around a cream cake, all eager to pick up bargains and negotiate the best deals.

Charlotte linked her arm with Patrick's as they made their way through the rowdy crowds haggling over the prices of goods.

'I'm soooo excited,' she purred and gave his arm a gentle squeeze.

'Aye me too.' He smiled as they waited for a horse and cart to pass before they entered the jewellers shop.

A bell above the door tinkled as they walked in, alerting the male behind the counter of a possible sale. The freshly shaved jeweller immediately sat up straight, looked at them both and smiled. 'Hello there, how can I help you?' he asked, adjusting his spectacles.

'We want to buy some wedding rings!' Charlotte, grinning from ear to ear, replied.

'Well you have come to the right shop! There's nothing I like better to hear than two young lovebirds tying the knot!

When's the big day?' he asked, flashing them a huge friendly smile.

'February fourteenth!' Charlotte replied with an air of triumph.

'Saint Valentine's Day! My goodness what a wonderful romantic day to pledge your love for one another. A perfect date to seal your commitment!' he beamed at them both. 'You too must be so in love with one another,' he chuckled as he pulled out a tray of polished wedding bands. 'I can see it in your eyes. The affection the pair of you share is beaming out from you both.'

'Oh, you've hit the nail on the head, you're sooo right!' Charlotte flashed him a pearly smile. 'I love this man so much and I know we will not only be husband and wife, we'll be best friends and we will remain loyal to each other till we die!'

'Love, friendship and loyalty! Now you have given me an idea,' he replied placing the tray back under the glass counter. 'I've just the perfect rings for you!' He eagerly lifted out a second tray with a twinkle in his grey eyes. 'Here we are, the Claddagh ring! These are just in and I must admit, they're becoming more and more popular. Have you heard about the Claddagh ring?' he asked, leaning over the counter.

'I've seen the ring before but I don't know much about it if I'm being honest,' Patrick replied as he gazed at the beautiful display.

Lifting out a solid gold band engraved with the distinctive Claddagh features, the jeweller held it up. 'The

Claddagh dates from Roman times. The gesture of clasped hands is a symbol of pledging vows, making it the ideal choice for engagements or marriages. Richard Joyce, a silversmith from Galway, is said to have designed the ring. It's believed Joyce was seized and held captive by Algerian Corsairs around 1675 while on a journey to the West Indies. Apparently he was sold into slavery to a Moorish goldsmith who taught him his skills.'

'That's interesting,' Patrick replied. 'But, if he was enslaved, then how come his design is so widely used in Ireland?'

'Well that's just it, he was freed after being held for fourteen years. An ambassador of King William III visited Algeria and demanded that all British who were locked up in the country be released and Richard Joyce was also included. Once set free, he returned to Galway with the ring he had created while in captivity. It is believed, he gave it to his sweetheart and married her.'

Charlotte clasped her hands together. 'We'll just have to have them. How romantic.'

'It is indeed. It's well known that Joyce became a successful goldsmith once he was back home on Irish soil.'

'Do you know what the features symbolise?' asked Charlotte with interest.

'I do indeed. As you can see each Claddagh features two hands clasping a heart topped by a crown. These elements represent different qualities. The heart obviously denotes love, the hands signify friendship and the crown is a symbol of loyalty. So you see now why I think this type of ring is just perfect for you two!' He waggled a finger.

'Oh, we must have them!' Charlotte cried with joy.

'Aye, I agree,' Patrick nodded.

'Wonderful! Now I'll just sort out your sizes and I'll have them boxed and ready for your special day in no time. So tell me, what church are you getting married in?'

'Saint Francis Xavier Church in Upper Gardiners Road,' Patrick answered him as he held out his ring finger to be measured.

'Ah, sure I know it well. It's the very chapel I got married in myself! Some lovely paintings in it, most of them originate from Italy and they date back to the Victorian period. Nice altar it has too.' The friendly jeweller chuckled.

'Yes, it's a great church,' Patrick agreed. 'Thank you, sir,' he said as the jeweler finished measuring his finger.

'Not at all, you're very welcome. May God bless the pair of you on your special day and what a great day that will be. You have picked a perfect church, perfect date, perfect rings, ah sure you couldn't make a more perfect couple if you tried. A match made in heaven! All you need now is to say I do and you'll live happy ever after,' he said, his eyes twinkling as he turned and took Charlotte's hand. 'Now my dear, you next.'

'This is sooo exciting,' Charlotte announced as she allowed the friendly attendant to size her thin finger.

338

'I'm sure it is, sure isn't every bride excited about their special day. It will be blissful, I can tell! Now, that's you done and dusted too, miss.'

Charlotte, beaming into Patrick's eyes, said, 'Oh, I can't wait. We now have all the preparations sorted. I won't be able to sleep with excitement. I wish I could forward the next few weeks with a click of the finger!' She tilted her head up and kissed him. 'I love you my darling.'

'Love you too, Charlotte,' Patrick replied.

'Just tink, in only a few weeks we'll be married! My darling, Patrick, Valentine's Day can't come quick enough!'

The weather reflected her mood, cold, and grey, very, very grey. Escorted to the docks with Father Fitzgerald and William, Erin, clutching the portrait of herself and Theo and wearing Theo's scarf around her neck, inhaled his familiar scent and wanted to cry out from the depths of her soul. Had the last few weeks really happened? As the three approached their destination, Erin felt someone was bound to wake her up at any minute from this never-ending nightmare, any second now she would come to her senses and find her head in her porridge! Surely her life had not taken such a dramatic U-turn?

The mighty ship, shining proud as can be, floated on the calm glass-like, silver water. White frothy waves gently whipped against the vessel as it waited for its passengers.

Erin's eyes darted to the groups of people gathered on the dull Saturday morning. What was she doing here? This time last year she was getting off the very same ship, stepping on to the longed-for American soil, greeted by William and... and Theo. 'Theo!' she yelled aloud much to the alarm of others.

Feeling overwhelmed, Erin released herself from their grip and like a child lost she began looking around. 'What am I doing here? I can't leave Theo!'

'Erin...' William reached out and gently grabbed hold of her arm.

'No, William! I'm not going, I can't leave him!'

Holding on to her, William replied, 'But you must, Erin.'

'Get your hands off me!' she yelled through gritted teeth.

'Erin, stop it! You know you have to go back to Derry, it's for the best.'

'Best for me or best for you! Do you think I'd be a burden to you? Because if you do, you can think again! I can look after myself, William!'

'Now you're being silly! You're my sister for crying out loud. Of course you wouldn't be a burden to me but this is Theo's dying request and you know everything he said makes sense,' William pleaded.

'It does *not* make any sense to me! I arrived here last year full of dreams and expectations. My goodness if only I knew what lay ahead! My husband is still here! I need to visit his grave! I'm not going back, William, you can't make me!'

Father Fitzgerald, stepping forward, placed his arms around her shoulders and in soft soothing tones said, 'Erin, we both know this is not easy for you, but you must realise that it is only in your best interests.'

Turning to face him, Erin grasped his vestments. 'My best interests are to stay here in New York with my husband! *You* are a man of God, I therefore plead with you to take pity on me and allow me to stay, I promise you I will be okay!'

'Erin, please, Theodore asked me to promise him that you will get back on that ship, I can't break my pledge to him.'

'Oh, I see, blood certainly is thicker than water. You care more about how Theo feels, even though he's no longer here, than you do for me. I *need* to be with my *husband!*' she wailed, her eyes wide and the whites of them pink from the weeks of crying.

'Erin, that's unfair!' William raised his voice.

'It's not unfair, William. I'll tell you what's unfair, it's *unfair* that God took my husband! It's *unfair* that I should have to journey back to Ireland a widow and carrying a child that will never know its father! How is that for *unfair?*' Turning her head to look at her brother-in-law, Erin gritted her teeth again. 'I'm done with the Catholic Church! There is no God because if there was *He* wouldn't have taken the man I loved!' She pointed a finger at him. 'Do you know what? You've been fooled for years, so if I were you, I would take off those stupid garments that you have to wear! We're being fooled! Fooled!

Fooled!' she hissed. 'We're all being fooled. Do you know I actually used to believe in miracles! Not anymore I can tell you. I'm not just saying this but I truly am done with *Him* up there!' she yelled, bursting into tears. 'Done with *Him*!'

Father Fitzgerald sighed and handed her a hankie. 'Erin, it's normal to be angry with God, I don't blame you. You have had your heart broken but, Erin, trust me, you will look back on this event and you will realise that it was all part of God's plan for some reason or another. It's...'

'Excuse me.' An elderly lady tapped his shoulder. 'I'm sorry to interrupt you but it's just I see you're a man of God. Can you therefore say a wee prayer over me before I travel back to Ireland? I'm so terrified after what happened to the Titanic.' She clutched her chest. 'Can you please give me God's blessing before I board the ship?'

'Of course I will.' Father Fitzgerald turned to the lady, blessed himself and then placing a hand on her head, he closed his eyes and threw himself into prayer.

Above them the dull, grey New York clouds looming overhead, looked down upon them and began to weep bitterly.

Erin, seizing the opportunity, took to her heel and fled. Dashing and diving and clutching the portrait close to her chest, she sprinted through the crowds, not stopping to look behind her. The rain fell heavy, drenching her clothes and running down her cheeks as she frantically pushed past crowds of others, all running in the opposite direction to escape the elements. Coming to a halt at a parked car, she opened the door and attempted to get in.

342

'Stop, Erin!' William, zigzagging through the passengers, followed close behind. 'Stop, Erin!' he said as he reached out and took hold of her arm. Lifting her into his arms he carted her back through the hordes of people. 'You're going on that ship and that is final!'

Kicking and flinging her arms about frantically, Erin wailed, 'I'm not leaving my husband! I told you, I'm not leaving *him*!'

Catching up with them, Father Fitzgerald said, 'Erin, Theo will be with you in spirit, you must believe that. I will keep you in my prayers,' he promised as they headed back towards the vessel.

William, placing her back on the ground, held her tight and turned her face towards him. 'Now listen to me, Erin,' his tone serious, 'this matter is settled. You have to go home, back where you can be looked after properly and that my dear sister *is* final!'

'Erin, before we depart I feel I must remind you of something.' Father Fitzgerald looked at her with compassion. 'Theo was a man of great faith in God. You see how he surrendered his sickness during his final days.'

'He didn't have much *choice* in the matter, did he? It's not as if God listened to our pleading, did *He*?' Erin fired back. 'Surrender to his illness was all poor Theo could do because all our prayers fell on deaf ears!'

'Erin, sometimes we must thank God for unanswered prayers. Now, I want you to carry something in your heart, you must not be sad over Theo's death, I therefore want you to fill

343

your heart with joy, do not burden yourself with grief.'

'Oh, how silly of me!' she yelled. 'Forgive me, Father, of course I shouldn't be *sad*! I'm so sorry I forgot, I should be jumping for *joy*! I should be *singing* from the rooftops!' Erin, holding tight to the portrait, spread out her free arm as others stared at her outburst. Looking around at the bewildered strangers before her, Erin continued, 'My husband is *dead*! I should be full of *joy*!' Some threw her sympathetic looks whilst others dipped their heads. 'Joy, joy, joy!' Erin sang aloud as fresh tears sprang into her sunken eyes.

'Oh, Erin, what I mean is, it is okay to miss Theo but don't fill your heart with grief. Theo believed in the resurrection. He truly believed in life after death, you should therefore rejoice that he is now with Jesus Christ in his kingdom,' Father Fitzgerald said, holding out her bags for her to take. 'There is no point in staying here, it is only his earthly body that remains, his spirit will be with you and your little baby all the days of your life. Remember what I said to you before, you're being tested, Erin, and those that are put through such trials always come out the strongest in the end. Believe me, Erin, your weakness will one day be your strength. Erin, before you go, my parents asked that I give you this.' Father Fitzgerald unzipped the side of her luggage and placed a brown package inside before securing it again. 'It's Theo's share of the inheritance that he would have received. They want you to have it to help set up a life again for yourself and also to help you provide for the baby. They asked that I pass that message on to you before you go.'

'But I don't want to go,' Erin replied, allowing the tears to fall down her cheeks. 'I really, really don't want to return to Derry.' Her tone softened.

'You must. If things don't work out then I promise you, you can come back, but for now, you must go,' William said. 'You must do what Theo requested.'

'I don't want to.' Erin sniffed.

'You will be going on that ship if I have to carry you on myself!' William warned in his I'm-not-taking-no-for-an-answer tone.

Shaking her head with disgust, Erin glared at her brother. 'The greatest mistake I ever made was thinking you would actually be there for me when I needed you but I guess I was wrong.'

Feeling wounded, William replied, 'I'm only doing what is best for you, I love you, sis, but you have to return home.'

Taking her bags from Father Fitzgerald, Erin turned, with a face like a mannequin and narrowed her eyes at William before replying, 'Fine, but I'm telling you, William, I will *never* forgive you for making me do this!' she cast him an icy stare, so cold it could have frozen the Caribbean, before storming off towards the ship, leaving William to gaze after her, feeling the sting from her words and his heart shatter into a million pieces.

After weeks of travelling across the Atlantic, listening to

stories and endless singing, Erin was finally back home in Derry, back on Irish soil. There to meet her was her mother and father. Erin, feeling numb and confused, allowed them both to hold her tight as they wept bitterly. However, not one single tear fell from her own Spanish-blue eyes. How could she cry now? She had done nothing but weep on the journey, there were no tears left! The other passengers had tried to help her but it was of little use. She had placed an invisible guard around her and no one was to be allowed near.

'Oh, Erin, we're so, so sorry for your loss.' John Coyle kissed his daughter's cheek. 'We're going to be here for you, dear, we'll look after you, nothing will ever hurt you again, I promise you that.'

'Thank you.' Erin tried to sound cheerful but her parents knew at once there was a deep sadness in her pretty eyes. 'I feel as if I've been on that boat for years. What date is it?' Erin asked.

'It's February fourteenth,' Catherine replied.

'Aye, that's what I thought.' Erin sighed and licked her parched lips. Clutching Theo's scarf, Erin breathed in the familiar scent of the cologne he had always worn. How she was going to cope without him, she couldn't begin to imagine but she knew she didn't have much of a choice in the matter. One thing was certain, she was going to have to get through this tragedy somehow, if not for her own sake but for the sake of her precious unborn child.

'Today Theo and I should be celebrating our first Valentine's Day together! Today there will be no roses for me, instead my darling husband is packed away in his shiny casket in a six-foot hole in the ground! If that's not bad enough, I can't even place flowers at his graveside! Happy Valentine's Day! Not!'

Chapter 40

The pale, pearly sea looked as smooth as glass. The only sound audible were the gentle waves as they stroked the pebble shoreline. In the warmer months, the waters would be occupied with rowing boats and children paddling in the shallow water but today the weather was too cold for such activities. Across the bay, the outline of Dublin's busy port was visible through the early morning fog. The harbour was alive as usual with activity from the British goods being imported and the cattle boats leaving for England.

Patrick sat on a dry rock, his elbows resting on his knees and his hands clasped loosely. To his left a cluster of fishing boats floated above the shoreline, bobbling gently as the delicate waves knocked against them. Patrick, inhaling the salty air, observed as a group of fishermen emerged from one of the boats, their hearty laughs sailed through the air in the light breeze as they gathered their nets and spread them out, like huge spider webs, over some rocks to dry. To his right, Charlotte, sat next to him, the sea breeze tousling her silver-blonde hair. She brushed wisps of her hair from her face and watched a few hungry seagulls wheeling overhead in the dull sky in search for breakfast.

Picking up a shiny grey pebble, Patrick lobbed it into the sea and watched as it skimmed along the surface. His stomach did a quick lurch as he recalled the life-changing action he had made only days earlier, and one thing was for sure, there was no going back now. His life had changed forever.

'Can I come in?' Catherine, opening the door a fraction, popped her head in. 'Are you awake?' she whispered in the dimly lit room.

Erin, turning to face her nodded, 'Aye, come on in, I've been awake for a while.' The truth was she had tossed and turned most of the night and had barely slept at all.

'I've made you some dinner,' Catherine smiled. Pushing the door open with her hip she entered carrying a tray of food.

'Dinner?' Erin, feeling groggy and tired, asked, 'Why what time is it?' she sat upright.

'It's just after three, love,' Catherine replied, sitting down on the edge of the bed. 'I thought I would let you sleep, I'm sure you're still feeling tired after your journey.'

'I can't believe it's that time already,' Erin replied. Privately she couldn't imagine that she had spent half of the day lying facing the wall thinking of all the things that had happened since last year. Every scene and memory was implanted in her thoughts, none more so than the moment she learned Theo had passed away. Leonarda coming out into the corridor to break the news was perhaps the bitterest of all, her face full of anguish, there was no need for words. The look in her eyes said it all. Erin felt her world crumble beneath her feet. Right up until that very moment, she had truly believed that God would perform a miracle. Well after all, he did allow

349

the blind to see, the deaf to hear and he even gave life again to Lazarus. Therefore, she had thought if she prayed hard enough for Theo's life to be spared then God would be generous and answer it. My goodness she had prayed from the depths of her heart and soul but this was one miracle God was not going to permit. She couldn't understand why not. One thing was certain, if she could have saved him with her love alone, Theo would be in her arms right now.

'I've made you one of your favourite meals.' Catherine stifled a smile and sat the tray on Erin's lap.

Erin gazed at the plate of creamed potatoes, lamb chops, gravy, and fried onions, and to wash it all down, a glass of cool milk, such a typical Irish meal and although her mother was right, it was indeed one of her preferred dinners; she hadn't had this dish once whilst in America. Awash with emotion, Erin felt bitter tears fill in her eyes. She wanted to scream aloud that she didn't want her favourite dinner – she wanted her husband! She swallowed the lump in her throat and dismissed that idea, after all, it wasn't her loving mother's fault that her life had been dealt such a cruel blow, and besides, what good would shouting and yelling do? One thing was for sure, it wasn't going to change her miserable life.

'Thank you,' Erin replied, a mere whisper. She lifted the glass and took a swallow. The nice cold milk coated her dry mouth and slid delightfully down her throat. 'Goodness, I didn't realise how thirsty I was,' she said, before gulping down the remainder of the glass.

'I'll get you some more,' Catherine said, bouncing off

350

the bed and heading for the door.

'No it's okay, I'm fine honestly. Head you on, I'm sure you're busy, I'll be down shortly,' she lied, knowing fine well she had no intentions of leaving the room today or any day for that matter.

'Right, well if you need anything give me a shout, love.'

'Okay, thanks, Ma.'

Alone in the stillness of the room, Erin felt like the walls were about to cave in on her. Never had she imagined grief to feel this bad. Her stomach, tying itself in knots, released a loud growl, like an angry animal. Erin gazed at the plate of food with distaste. It looked as appealing as a plate of dead crickets. Her tummy roared again, alarming her that she not only needed to eat to keep herself alive but also for the little child growing within her womb.

Lifting the fork, she dug it into the creamed potatoes and whispered aloud, 'I'm only eating this for you, my precious child. I'm angry with God right now but I'm also thankful to Him for the gift of you, you are all I have left of your father.' A lonely tear escaped and trickled down her cheek. She ate the mouthful of food, feeling it go down like broken glass. 'I will love you so much, my innocent baby.' She forced some more into her mouth, with determination to eat the whole meal, regardless of how bitter her insides felt.

Minutes later she rested her head back on the pillows and looked with satisfaction at the empty plate. Closing her eyes, Theo's smiling face immediately flashed into her thoughts and Father Fitzgerald's words "You're being tested, Erin, and those that are put through such trials always come out the strongest in the end".

'Strongest in the end, eh?' she murmured aloud. 'Right now I feel like a helpless little bird that's just fallen out of the nest too early.' Glancing around the room a thought struck her, 'Maybe I did leave the nest too early. Well, regardless, what's happened has happened!' She sniffed as more tears welled up in her eyes. Looking up towards the ceiling, she continued, 'If you're listening to me up there, Theo, I wouldn't have changed meeting you for the world. I love you and I will love our baby so much.'

Wiping her eyes and directing her gaze towards the window, Erin pushed the tray away and climbed out of bed. Drawing back the curtains to let some light in, her attention was pulled to Patrick's house and her heart lurched somewhere in the pit of her stomach. The house stood there, curtains half open, no smoke from the chimney and looking as empty as she felt. She recalled how he was to get married in February and her heart sank a little deeper as she realised he would be married by now. 'I hope you're happy, Patrick, you deserve it,' she mumbled to herself.

The pavements were wet from the earlier April showers but the rain clouds had now moved on. Some children gathered in the middle of the road and appeared to be playing a game that Erin knew well. Erin was familiar with the kids, they all lived on her street and were all related to one another.

Opening the window a little and leaning out, Erin felt the cool Irish air brush against her skin.

The children, hiding their hands behind their backs, sang to their cousin at the top of the road, 'Caitlin, Caitlin, who's got the ball?' Taking turns to reveal their empty hands from behind their backs they continued, 'I haven't got it in my pocket, so Caitlin, Caitlin who's got the ball?'

Caitlin opened her eyes and called, 'You!' Caitlin pointed to the grubby toothless little Conor from next door. 'Is it you?' she asked with a grin.

'Ha, no chance of him catching it, he's too *wee!*' Andrew, his older cousin laughed and playfully ruffled his hair.

'Too right, Andy!' Ciaran, Conor's eldest brother, added. 'Wee Conor bear, wee Conor bear, he's too wee! He's too wee to catch the ball,' Ciaran sang.

'Ha, wee bear's not big enough!' his cousin Oran giggled back.

'If he'd have caught it we'd take it off him,' Callum, Conor's elder sibling, joined in and gave him a little nudge. 'Isn't that right, wee bear?'

'Get away!' Conor elbowed Callum in the ribs.

'Leave him alone, boys!' his cousin Caorise yelled at her annoying cousins. 'He's only a wain!'

'I'm not a *wain*! Look at them two!' Conor, clearly horrified, fired back and pointed to his youngest cousins, 'Keegan and Lennon are the wains, I'm a big boy! And don't forget the babies in the house, Elena and Preston! Don't ever call me a wain!'

Caitlin's brother Eoghan, the little redhead with the angel face, let out a shrieking laugh. 'Kick them in the butt, Conor!' he shouted.

'I'm going to kick them all and punch their lights out!' Conor shouted, his voice trembling as tears began filling his big, round eyes. 'And I'm going to tell my da, and my uncles Gerald and Dee, they'll sort ye all out! My mammy's brothers, uncle Sean and David, they'll help too, they're the best at kicking butts in Derry!'

'Ha, ha, your uncles Sean and David couldn't beat snow off a rope!' Diarmuid, Caorise's older brother, howled with laughter. 'They only *think* they're big boys!'

'Leave my da alone, he's a better fighter than your da!' Jodie, Sean's eldest child, felt protective of both her father and her little cousin Conor, fired back, 'Leave our Conor alone or I'm going to kick *all* your *butts*!' Pointing her finger at Andrew, she yelled, 'I'm going in now to tell your ma, you started it!'

'We're only winding him up,' Andrew teased. 'He's used to us joking with him, isn't that right, wee bear?'

'Aye, Andy's right, it's only a wee joke.' Oran shrugged. 'It's no big deal!'

'I'm going to tell *your* ma too.' Jodie narrowed her eyes at Oran. 'See how ye like that!'

'That's enough now! Leave my big brother alone!' Ava,

lifted her arms in the air and as she did so the ball fell from her grasp and rolled down the street.

The kids began giggling, their laughter echoing in the street below.

'Look, Caitlin, we did your job for you!' Andrew yelled up at Caitlin. 'Looks like little Ava had the ball!'

'Right wains, scone bread and pancakes are ready!' their granny Anne yelled from the doorway. 'Hurry up whilst they're nice and warm!' she chuckled.

The kids didn't have to be asked twice, Anne Quigley's scone bread is the nicest in Derry! They took to their heels and ran down the street.

Andrew running ahead shouted over his shoulder, 'First in gets the biggest bit!' he teased as the younger cousins scampered behind him.

Erin felt her heart warm, she loved the innocence of all these children, each of them with their own personalities and qualities. They may tease and wind one another up but blood is certainly thicker than water, they love each other unconditionally, and although they enjoyed teasing little Conor, if anything did happen to Wee Bear, they'd be the first to protect him.

Across the road, Suzy McGregor opened her front door and stepped out into the street followed closely by Frankie. My goodness, Erin couldn't believe it, was this really the same alcoholic that she'd lived beside all her life? Gone were the smelly, dirty clothes, the stubbled face and the glassy eyes.

Here he was looking fresh and... looking... looking... handsome! Never did she think she would see the day!

Frankie locked the front door and slipped his arm around Suzy's waist. Suzy smiled at him, her face portraying a woman in love. They looked so happy and perfect for one another. Erin at once felt so pleased for them both. If anyone deserved a bit of happiness in their lives, Suzy and Frankie did, she was so glad they'd fallen in love.

Suzy, catching a glimpse at the open window, felt her heart miss a beat at the sight of the familiar girl peering out. 'Hello, Erin.' She waved up and wondered what she was going to say next, welcome home would not be suitable considering the circumstances surrounding her return and besides she had been back now for over six weeks.

Erin nodded and smiled. 'Hello Suzy, hello Frankie.'

Frankie lifted his head in the direction of the window. 'Good afternoon, Erin,' he replied, leading Suzy across the street. They came to a halt under the window. 'We're both so sorry to hear your news.'

'Thank you,' Erin said. Determined not to cry in front of them, she managed to fight back her emotions.

'Erin, if you need anything at all please just ask, let us know and Suzy and I will help if we can.'

'That's very kind of you both and thank you for offering to allow me to stay at your home. My mother told me you had made that suggestion, it's very generous of you.'

'It's the least we could do. Suzy has it all shinning like

a new pin, and she's made you brand new curtains and bedding.'

'That's very thoughtful, Suzy.' Erin managed a smile.

'Erin, we'll understand if you want to stay with your parents for now,' Suzy said, 'You don't have to move into Frankie's old house if you're not up for it. We certainly don't want to push you into anything.'

'I appreciate that,' Erin replied. Secretly, she could never imagine herself living in Frankie's house or in any other home for that matter. 'I'll keep it in mind but at the minute I want to stay here.'

'That's okay,' Frankie said. 'You do what's best for you. You'll be in our prayers, Erin. God bless you. God will find a way where you think there is no way. He will set you back on track again. He will carry you through this difficult time in your life, believe me, He did it for me.'

Erin, feeling the tears prickle her eyes and her mouth twitch, just nodded.

'Take care, Erin, we'll leave you for now and remember we're only across the road if you need us,' Suzy, sensing Erin's pain, said, 'Come on now, Frankie, we'll leave Erin in peace, I'm sure she's tired.'

'See you soon, Erin.' Frankie smiled softly.

'Bye… and thanks.' Erin watched as the two newlyweds headed off down the street.

Looking up at the dull sky, Erin sighed, 'God will find a

way where you think there is no way,' she repeated Frankie's phrase. 'Well, if there is a God up there, not only to do you need to show me the way, you need to help me get through each day, for right now, the only direction I'm drawn to is heading back into that bed and staying there forever!'

Chapter 41

Spring soon crept into summer. Months passed, with each day similar to the day before, each trickling slowly by like a sluggish train chugging lazily to its destination. Erin remained confined to her quarters on most days. The safety of her bedroom allowed her to dream of days gone by in Theo's arms and permitted her to imagine scenarios of her life with Theo still here. Deep down, Erin knew only too well that this world, which she had concocted in her brain, was of little benefit. In her real life Theo was not here and never would be. Allowing her imagination to run away with itself was both unhealthy and useless, she knew that but still it was all she could do to try to remain sane.

Today upon waking, Erin decided to pull herself together, the baby was due any day now and it was time she started getting up and facing the world properly. Kicking back the blankets, she swung her legs out and got out of her bed. No sooner was she up when a dull ache came from out of the blue again across her lower back, she had experienced it earlier but had fallen back to sleep after it passed. Ignoring the pain, she got down on her knees at the foot of the bed, blessed herself and began reciting her morning prayers. Since Theo had taken ill, praying her morning and evening prayers had been abandoned but for some reason today she felt the urge to pray. Closing her eyes, she began to recite a decade of the rosary.

Father Lavery's regular visits since her return to Ireland had slowly helped her regain the faith that she was brought up with. Gradually, each day, she felt she was taking little baby steps towards God again. It wasn't easy, after all, she felt He was the reason for her pain and more importantly she truly believed that God could have let Theo live if He wanted to. It was her friendly priest's visit yesterday that finally hit home with her. Just as he was about to leave, Father Lavery gently explained that this life is short and for some reason or another Theo's early departure from this world was all part of God's plan that she should accept. He said that without acceptance she would never be able to move on with her life and enjoy the gift of the child that God had given her. Erin had at once known deep down that he was right, she had to be strong for her baby. She had to accept that what had happened had happened and nothing, or no one, was going to change that. In a strange way, she was beginning to get used to Theo not being about, and just as Father Fitzgerald had said, she did feel Theo with her, perhaps it was an idea she liked to imagine and a comforting idea that helped her get by.

She finished her prayers, blessed herself and carefully got back on her feet, not an easy task with a fully grown baby in her womb.

After getting washed and dressed, she made her way downstairs. As usual her mother was found up to her elbows in flour. Erin smiled at the picture before her, Catherine kneading away at the dough was singing aloud as she went about her task.

'Morning,' Erin announced, trying to sound as cheery as possible.

Catherine, looking over her shoulder, replied, 'Goodness, Erin, you scared me there, I was in a wee world of my own, pet. What are you doing up so early?'

'I've decided I need to try to get my life in order again, there's not much benefit sitting in that room day after day and it's not fair on our Mary, after all it is her bedroom too. I know she's been trying to tiptoe around me since I got back. She does her best not to disturb me, thinking that I'm asleep most of the time but I'm actually not, I waste so much time daydreaming.'

Abandoning the dough and wiping the excess flour off her hands on her apron, Catherine smiled, 'Oh, Erin, you don't know how happy I am to see you out of that room. Darling, it will do you the world of good,' she said. Turning to face her daughter she smiled and placed her arms around her, 'Come here, Erin.' She hugged her. 'I know it hasn't been easy for you but time is a healer and we have all noticed over the past few weeks you seem to be coming round to yourself again.'

The ache in the bottom of her back she experienced earlier quickly transformed into a sharp pain, a pain she had never experienced before. 'Oooh!' Erin released a little cry and stepped away from her mother's embrace.

'What's the matter?' Catherine asked.

'Oh, I've been feeling a dullness in my lower back, it woke me up in the middle of the night a few times, you don't think it's... ouch!'

Having been in labour enough times to know exactly

what it was, Catherine nodded. 'Aye, you could be experiencing early signs that the child is on the way. Perhaps you should go back to bed.'

'No, I'd rather not, anyway it's gone again. I'm up now so I may as well make the most of it. I was thinking I would love a run up to Austin's for a bit of shopping. I know you've got most of the bits and pieces in for the baby but it's been ages since I've been in a shop. Theo's parents insisted on giving me Theo's inheritance to get the necessary items for the baby and to help bring the child up but I haven't had a chance to spend it. It doesn't look like I'm going to be going too far today... ouch.' She gripped her stomach.

'Never worry, when the baby comes, it won't take too long to find a way to make a dent in it. You definitely won't be going shopping today, besides William has been sending regular donations, I managed to get everything you need.'

The very mention of William's name caused Erin's skin to crawl, she had been so nasty towards him before she departed. 'I need to apologise to William, I should have done it by now but I just wasn't feeling up to it. I'll write him a letter. I was so horrible towards him, I hope he forgives me.'

'Erin, you told me months ago how you spoke to him before you left. William will have already forgiven you. He's your brother and he thinks the world of you. Do not dwell on what you said. He has contacted me on many occasions to ask how you are. He will understand that you were going through a traumatic time and were not yourself. Darling, it's understandable.'

'Aye, I know you're right, but still, I should write him a letter. I'll do it soon, after all, sticks and stones can break your bones but poisonous words can wound the heart. I really should say sorry but that's the thing with words, once they come out of the mouth, they can't be taken back.' Erin sighed.

'Oh, Erin, don't worry yourself, as I said you were not acting like yourself. For goodness' sake, you had been through so much at the time, William will have understood. Are you sure you don't want to go back to bed? I can bring you up some breakfast.'

'No, I think I'll go out into the garden, get a bit of fresh air.'

'Okay, if you're feeling up to it, go you on out and I'll fix you up something to eat.' Catherine smiled.

'Just a glass of milk and a slice of bread and jam will do,' Erin replied as she headed out the back door.

Erin sat down on the wooden bench her father had proudly made when they were kids. In the summer months he would sit here after work, chilling out as he waited for his dinner. No doubt she would find him here later today after his hard day working.

Sandy, their faithful Labrador, lay at the bottom of the garden, hard at work watching the birds and butterflies swoop by.

'Hello boy!' Erin called to him.

No sooner had she the words out, his ears pricked to attention. Jumping to his feet, he scrambled towards her with enthusiasm. Yapping and tail swishing to and fro, he came bounding across the daisy-splashed lawn. Coming to a halt at Erin's feet, Sandy sat down and placed his muddy front paws on her knees.

'Have you missed me?' Erin asked, tickling him under his chin.

Sandy, enjoying every second of the attention, looked at Erin with his huge friendly eyes and barked at her with delight.

'You have, haven't you?' she said, tickling him a little more.

Today the golden butter-coloured sun was glowing in a cloudless duck-egg-blue sky, cascading its light down upon Ireland for a change. Catherine's beautiful arrangement of flowers had all turned to greet the morning rays. A few bumblebees buzzed about the rosebush at the end of the garden whilst a colourful butterfly twirled in and out of the primroses and another one danced right past Sandy's nose.

A sharp twinge once again shot through Erin, this time a little more intense than before and at once she felt her heart sink. No matter how hard she tried to put on a brave face, a piece of her heart had died with Theo, and the reality was, as much as she welcomed the new arrival, she longed for Theo to be holding her hand. Whatever way she looked at it, the birth would be bittersweet and she knew she had to prepare herself for that.

The pain passed just as quickly as it arrived. She sat back and allowed the sun's warm rays to bounce off her face.

Sandy hopped up on the bench and snuggled up beside her, content to have her by his side.

'Here you are, love.' Catherine handed her the breakfast.

'Thanks.' Erin took a sip of the cool milk.

'How are you now?' Catherine asked, looking concerned.

'I'm okay but I think you're right, the labour pains have started, I've just had another twinge.'

'Okay, love, you take it easy and give me a shout if you need me. I'll just be finishing off the bread. Once those pains become stronger we'll get you back to bed.' She smiled before making her way back to the kitchen.

Erin felt a nervous tingle in her stomach, as much as she longed to hold her baby in her arms, the thought of giving birth terrified her. She took another slow sip of her milk and broke off a piece of bread and jam.

Sandy, watching her every move with a look in his eye that desperately wanted a share of the delicious jam, licked his lips and waited in anticipation.

'Here, but don't tell the others.' She placed a piece of the bread in front of him. 'Remember you're not allowed sweet stuff.'

Sandy didn't have to be offered twice, he took the treat and gobbled it up in a flash.

A tickling feeling drew her attention to the little insect

that was now crawling along her arm. Her heart did a little flip at the sight of the beautiful red ladybird and at once the childhood memories came flooding back with Patrick immediately springing into her thoughts. As she watched the insect crawl slowly down towards her wrist, she couldn't help wonder what he was getting up to and how his married life was going, perhaps his new wife would also be pregnant. She hadn't seen him or heard from him since her return, no doubt his work and marriage were keeping him busy. The little ladybird made its way on down around her fingers. Smiling she allowed it to crawl on to her palm. Taking a deep breath, she sighed as she recalled many an adventure they had had as kids out searching for the pretty beetle. They had always been so perfect together. Part of her still missed their relationship but she still felt the pain of his rejection, regardless she hoped he was happy, he deserved it.

'You need to keep calm, Erin,' Catherine advised in a soothing voice. 'Try to control your breathing, you're doing great, love.'

'I can't! This is horrible!' Erin cried as the contractions shot through her. The ache she had experienced only hours earlier was nothing compared to these pains now. 'Ouch! Help! I can't take any more!' Erin yelled, her screams loud enough to be heard out on the street.

Mary stood behind her mother feeling useless. With something as trivial as a nosebleed enough to turn her queasy, she knew she better get out of the room as fast as she could. 'Ah... perhaps I should go and fetch Anne or Suzy or one of

366

the other neighbours, what do ye think, Ma?'

Catherine, knowing only too well what Mary was like, nodded. 'Aye, that might be a good idea.'

Mary didn't t need to be told twice, no sooner had her mother the words out, she made a quick exit. As she approached the top of the stairs, a loud bang sounded on the front door followed by another inpatient knock.

'I've heard you, I'm coming!' Mary shouted as she bounded down the stairs.

She opened the door with a flourish before another knock rattled. 'My goodness!' she said, her eyes widening as she came face-to-face with the unexpected guests. Her jaw dropped in disbelief. 'What the heck are you doing here?'

Chapter 42

'Looks like we've arrived just in time.' William stepped into the hallway past Mary. 'Come on, follow me,' he said over his shoulder.

Erin's screams intensified as they hurried up the stairs. William paused outside her room. 'Go you on in. I'll stay here, actually I'll head down and get a cup of tea. I'm sure it's not a place for a man right now.' He pushed the door open a fraction, 'Go on.'

Erin's eyes nearly popped out of her head at the sight of the visitor entering the room. 'LEONARDA! Am I hallucinating? What are you doing here? Ouch!'

Smiling, Leonarda made her way across the room. 'My dear, Erin, do you really think I would have let you go through this yourself? Cooking's not my only talent you know. I've helped deliver more babies than I can remember.' She chuckled and wriggled out of her cardigan.

'Oh, Leonarda, that's great but how did you get here? How did you find us?' Catherine asked.

'Ah, a bit of careful planning that's all it takes!' she beamed.

'Well it's so good to see you,' Catherine replied, moving away from the bed.

'And it's good to see you too, Catherine. I'm so glad we made it in time.'

'We?' Catherine asked.

'William and I, it was him that brought me here, who else?' Leonarda chuckled.

Catherine's face lit up at the mention of her son's name. 'William? William's here?' she asked, heading at once towards the door. 'I'll be back in a minute, love,' she called over her shoulder.

Leonarda, taking a seat at the edge of the bed, threw Erin a sunshine smile. 'Now let's see what stage you're at,' she said rolling up the sleeves of her blouse.

'Ahhhh… I'm at the stage I want this baby OUT!' Erin screeched. 'I can't take this pain anymore! Ahhhhh!'

'Right, Erin, with each contraction I want you to give a big push.'

Erin didn't have to wait too long, no sooner had Leonarda the words out when a mighty contraction ripped through her. 'Ahhhhhhh.' She pushed with all her strength.

'Good girl! That's it!' Leonarda encouraged.

'Ohhhh! Ahhhhh!' Erin gasped and clutched the bed as a great wave of pain gripped her again. 'I can't… I can't *do* this!' she cried.

'Yes you can, you're doing brilliant!'

Erin shook her head as perspiration trickled down the back of her neck, 'I *can't* Leonarda, I just *can't*!'

'Come on now, Erin, let's get this little baby out!' Leonarda replied in her usual cheerful manner.

369

Seconds later Erin felt the urge to push again like never before. Gathering herself and willing herself on, she closed her eyes tight, took a deep breath and, imaging she was holding Theo's hand, she gave a final powerful push.

'You're doing great!' Leonarda called to her as she witnessed the tiny head emerge. 'Now hold it a second and breathe slowly,' she advised, holding the child's head in her hands.

Erin did exactly as she was told.

'That's it, now give me a final gentle one.'

One last push and the sounds of a newborn's cries filled the room.

'Oh, Erin.' Leonarda, her face full of joy, cried, 'It's a little boy!' She expertly wiped his face with a towel and cut the cord. Taking him in her arms, like the most precious thing in the world, she placed him in the welcoming arms of his mother.

'Hello, my little one,' Erin whispered, her mouth brushing against his soft cheek. 'Look at you, my precious son, you're *perfect*!'

Leonarda gazed at them both, feeling as proud as ever for the young girl that had captured a piece of her heart. 'He certainly is.' Tears filled her eyes.

'He's so beautiful.' Erin gazed at him lovingly. Tears sprang into her own eyes as a mixture of both sadness and joy overwhelmed her. 'Theo would have been so proud,' she choked before a great sob erupted from her lungs.

'Yes, my dear. He would have been proud of you both.' Leonarda allowed her own tears to fall. Leaning forward she planted a kiss on Erin's cheek.

Downstairs, Catherine, overcome with the joy of holding her son in her arms, heard the little shrill of a baby's cries. 'No,' she looked at William and Mary. 'The baby couldn't have been born already!' She let go of her son and dived upstairs, William and Mary following close behind.

'My goodness, Erin!' Catherine cried. 'I'm sorry, I only popped out for a minute,' she said, making her way across the room to greet her first grandchild.

'You've a little grandson,' Erin, beamed, the bittersweet tears rolling down her cheeks.

'A boy! Oh, Erin, Congratulations!' Catherine, her attention fixed on the little pink-skinned infant wriggling in her daughter's arms, felt her heart was about to explode with joy. 'Oh, my darling, it was so quick, I'm sorry I left you.'

'Ma, stop apologising! It's okay.' Erin smiled, handing her son over to her mother to hold. 'William, it's good to see you.' Erin held out her arms. 'Come here, bro.'

William didn't need to be asked twice, he squeezed past Mary and his mother and embraced his sister.

'I'm sorry, I'm so sorry for everything I've said to you,' Erin sobbed.

'It's okay, there's no need to be sorry. I'm sorry I had to force you on the ship, but I guess it's a true saying, you have to be cruel to be kind.'

371

'It's fine, I realise that now.' Erin, overcome with grief, cried from the depths of her soul. She sobbed for her husband, her mended relationship with her brother and more importantly she sobbed for the little child that would never know the love of his father.

'Let it all out, Erin. A good cry is as helpful as a good laugh,' William said. Holding his sister, he felt his own tears roll down his cheeks and disappear into her hair.

Mary, feeling helpless, suggested, 'I'll make us all a nice cup of tea. I'll be back in a few minutes,' she said as she headed off downstairs.

Catherine and Leonarda helped wash the new arrival before dressing him and wrapping him in a beautiful knitted multi-coloured blanket, a gift from their neighbour Anne Quigley.

He appeared perfect. His raven-black hair all washed and fresh, his pudgy skin glowed with health, he was a picture to behold. It was difficult to tell who the child looked like but Catherine secretly admitted he resembled Erin when she was born. This child would more than likely look like the Coyles, she thought. She rocked him gently in her arms and in no time he had nodded off to sleep.

Erin dried her eyes and let go of William. 'Thank you for coming here. I'll never forget this act of kindness from you both.' She glanced from her brother to Leonarda.

'Not at all. It's the least we could do, and besides, I knew you wouldn't hold a grudge with me forever, I wanted to see you in person to straighten things out. I could have written but I had my mind made up from the very day you left, I decided I would return here and speak to you face-to-face.'

'Thank you, I'm so glad to see you both. How long are you staying for?' Erin asked.

'Two months. Mum had written to me and told me that Frankie McGregor had offered you his house for you to stay in and that you haven't taken him up on the offer. I contacted Frankie and Suzie and I arranged for Leonarda and I to stay there for a while. They were delighted to help and they promised to keep it hush-hush, we wanted to surprise you.'

'Oh, that's wonderful!' Erin's face filled with joy. 'How's everyone in New York doing?'

'They're all doing okay and all send their love. Ron asked me to tell you that he will always be grateful to you. He started working for the Fitzgeralds shortly after you left and not only does he tend the gardens but he keeps Theo's grave in order too.'

The reminder of Theo lying in a lonely grave gripped Erin's heart. She tried to push the thought out of her head and focus on the fact that his spirit was right beside her, this idea was her coping mechanism and she needed to stick by it. 'Tell Ron, I am very much grateful for that.' Erin swallowed to prevent the lump in her throat from mushrooming.

'I will do. Ron thinks the world of you, Erin. He prays for you daily and often says if it wasn't for your kind heart he would have still been on the streets.'

Mary, nudging the door open with her hip, beamed, 'I've made us a cup of tea.' She carried in a tray of cups and some freshly cut scone bread, smothered in blackberry jam, just as Erin liked it.

'I'm so hungry!' Erin eyed up the scone and lifted a piece and a warm cup of tea from the tray. 'Mmmm, this is delicious!'

'Erin.' Catherine looked up and whispered. 'Have you decided what you want to call him? Will you be calling him Theo after his father?'

Erin, recalling the conversation she'd had with Theo, shook her head and swallowed her food. 'No, we had discussed this and I suggested if we had a boy I would like to name the baby after him but Theo wanted the child to have his own name.'

Leonarda's face brightened, 'That sounds just like Theo,' she chuckled. 'So have you picked one?'

'I have indeed, I've just thought about it and it's perfect! Theo said as soon as the baby is born the name would come to me and he was right. I have therefore decided on something that will remind me of both Theo and my dear friend Leonarda here,' she said gazing lovingly at Leonarda.

'Oh?' Leonarda raised her eyebrows, 'What could that be?'

'It rhymes with Theo,' Erin glanced around the room at them all. 'And it's short for Leonarda. Everyone meet baby Leo!'

Chapter 43

'That looks good, if I may say so myself.' Erin stood back and observed the beautifully decorated Christmas cake with satisfaction.

'It does indeed, love.' John grinned, as he gently rocked baby Leo in his arms. 'Leonarda has turned you into a great cook. I have to admit we miss her and William being about, still, I suppose they had to return at some stage.'

'I'm not joking you, Da, if I had my way, I'd have kept them here forever. I'll be forever grateful to them both, they've helped me more than they will ever truly know.'

'I'll be forever grateful to William also. His regular donations mean I now no longer have to work in all conditions.'

Nodding and smiling Erin replied, 'I'll agree with you on that one. Do you know, Da, if they hadn't stayed for those couple of months after Leo was born, there's no doubt I'd have wallowed in grief and self-pity again. I'm sure I would have locked myself away to hide from the world but Leonarda would never have allowed that to happen. She has taught me how to appreciate everything around me and has helped me get by each day, all of you did but I have to admit, Leonarda's bubbly, positive attitude to life has helped lift my spirits.'

'You're right, love. Your mother and I would have no doubt allowed you to bury your head in the sand, we'd have done anything as long as you were happy.'

'Aye, so true. Da, let me tell you that everything I was told when Theo was passing away is gradually unfolding.'

'What do you mean?' John asked looking up at his daughter.

'Well, for instance, Father Fitzgerald told me life will get easier and that I'd feel Theo with me and I do. I actually do! Sometimes I imagine his arms around Leo and I and this makes me feel safe.' She shrugged. 'Maybe it's all in my head, I don't know, still it's a nice, comforting feeling. Don't get me wrong, I don't waste my time daydreaming of scenarios of him still in my life, like I had done for months after I returned here, I just allow myself to imagine him here, here at my side. Do you think I'm mad in the head, Da?'

'Not one bit! Erin, I can understand what you're saying. I remember the day I was told my father had dropped dead suddenly. At first, I didn't believe it for a second. I assumed that he was probably just not wakened up properly. In my mind, I told myself that as soon as I arrived I would sort everything out and my aul da would be okay again. I took to my heels, the blood pumping through me, and feeling as if my heart was going to explode as I raced towards his house. When I ran into his street, the neighbours had already gathered outside and they just shook their heads and threw me their sympathetic looks. It was only then that I knew that my father was in fact really dead. At once, my world caved in and it felt as if my heart had split in two. But the thing is, when I reached the house and witnessed my father's lifeless body lying on the kitchen floor, his lips blue, his body stiff and his face bruised from the collapse, I should have crumbled but I didn't, instead I felt as if my father had placed his arms around me, and I'm not joking you, Erin, I never felt a more peaceful feeling like it. I remember thinking I now have my own special angel in heaven looking after the family. So you see, love, I understand what you're saying when you explain that you can feel Theo with you. If you think about it, you were an important person in his life whilst he walked this earth, someone he loved dearly, of course he's not going to leave you. I believe the dead are with us in spirit.'

'I do too. So, you don't think I'm going mad, then?' Erin asked, wondering if perhaps she really was losing her marbles.

'Absolutely not! Speaking of the dead, I'll tell you what is mad, we're all dying to get into heaven but none of us wants to die!' John grinned. 'Wee Nellie McDowell told me that joke.'

'You've got that one right,' Erin replied. Her gaze fell upon Leo and she released a huge sigh. 'It's mad how much my life has changed since last Christmas Eve. Today I've spent my time baking a cake, to thank Suzy and Frankie for their kindness. This time last year I spent the day preparing Theo a nice dinner to announce the happy news that we were going to have a baby.' She reached out and allowed Leo to fold his little starfish hand around her finger. Gazing up at his mother, his deep blue eyes sparkling, his lips curled at the corners, he released a happy gurgle. 'He looks like me,' she whispered.

'He's your image, pet,' John agreed.

'Perhaps that's a good thing. I think if he looked like his father it might be too difficult.' Erin smiled down at her son and planted a loving kiss on his chubby cheeks.

'Aye, I agree.'

'I never thought I would say this, but time is an amazing healer. Life has got easier. Don't get me wrong, I miss Theo every day and I so badly long for him to be back in my life again but the ache in my heart has eased. I guess I'm starting to come to terms with everything that has happened.'

'That's good, love. I always knew you'd be okay. You're strong, you're a fighter. You have no idea how glad we were that you chose to come home, it's where you belong.'

'Chose?' Erin pulled a face. 'I wouldn't say I had much of a choice in the matter. I have to admit I put up such a huge fight. I certainly didn't leave easy but I'm glad I did come back. Theo was right, I suppose he knew what was best for me, especially as I couldn't even think straight let alone make such a decision. Do you know, Da, he actually told me to find love again, can you imagine that?'

'I can. That must have been very difficult for him but it proves how much he loved you, he wants you to be happy.'

'Well I don't think I could ever follow that bit of advice from him.' Erin shrugged.

'Why not? If the right man comes along, I'm sure Theo would want what was best for you. He certainly wouldn't want a young, beautiful girl like yourself going through life on your own.'

378

'Oh, Da, I'm not going to be on my own. Sure I have Leo and I have you lot and besides I won't be falling for another, it would seem like I was being unfaithful to Theo.'

'Nonsense, Erin, it's what Theo wanted. Actually, never mind about men for now, I might not be too happy,' John teased, 'I couldn't handle it if you left us and took this wee man away from us. Isn't that right, Leo?' John kissed Leo's chubby angelic cheeks. 'You have to stay here with your aul grandad! You're Granda's little boy!'

'There's no danger of that happening and one thing I can promise you, Da, I'll never be too far away for you. I certainly won't be looking to run back to America.'

'Listen to your mammy, Leo, do you think Granda' John would allow that, do you, wee cheeky face?' he planted more kisses on Leo's cheeks. 'Your Granda John loves you all too much!'

Leo, rubbing his tired eyes, began to whimper.

'Ah, don't cry, baby Leo,' John said softly. 'That's a nice wee babee, oh that's a nice wee babeeee.' John sang as he rocked Leo in his arms. 'La, la, la, la, la, la, that's a nice wee babeeee.'

'Right, Da, give me him over and I'll get him wrapped up.' Erin held out her arms. 'I'll take him over to see Suzy and Frankie and he'll stop crying once he's out in the air.'

'Put him in his pram, you can't carry him and the cake over, what if you dropped him?' John looked horrified.

Grinning, Erin replied, 'I'm hardly going to drop him,

379

Da, but if it keeps you happy, I'll push him in his pram.'

Leo stopped crying and let out an excited gurgle as Erin placed him in his pram. 'You know rightly you're going out, don't you, wee man?' she tickled under his chin and reached for his hand-knitted blanket.

'He does indeed.' John smiled with affection at the child that melted his heart.

'This is a treasured gift,' Erin said, as she tucked the blanket around the baby. 'There now, you're as sung as a bug in a rug!' She ran her hand over the beautiful knitted squares, all crafted with such detail in pastel colours of green, blue, pink, and lemon and bordered with a white trim. 'I have to say Anne Quigley knits the best blankets I've ever seen.'

'She does and she produces each blanket with so much love and attention,' John said. 'I don't think there's a wain in Derry that hasn't had a blanket knit by Anne. I've never seen anyone in my life that can knit so fast!' Lifting the cake with caution, he placed it in its box and with care sat it at the bottom of the pram.

'I'll not be long, Da, see you in a bit.'

'You'll be there all night if Suzy gets her hands on that wain. She adores him.' John laughed as he held open the front door for them.

Outside the frost was beginning to crystalize on the ground. Overhead gentle snowflakes tumbled lightly from the heavens and sifted through the cool air.

Erin pushed the pram across the street and knocked on

Suzy's door. The warmth of an open fire blazing and the welcoming aroma of homemade soup escaped as Frankie opened the door.

'Erin,' he said through a mouthful of bread. 'Come in, come in.' He bent down to lift the pram over the front step.

'I hope I'm not interrupting your dinner,' Erin said as she lifted Leo from his pram and followed Frankie into the living room.

Suzy's face brightened. 'Of course you're not. Would you like a wee bowl of soup?' she asked, lifting the baby gently from his mother's arms. 'Hello my little chicken,' she cooed.

'I'll get you a bowl.' Frankie beamed.

The smell of the soup was too tempting to turn down. 'Oh go on then, but only if you have enough,' Erin said, taking a seat next to Suzy.

'Of course, there's always plenty in the pot. Our Chris was to come home but he'd far rather stay in Dublin with his new fiancée.'

'Fiancée? My goodness, Suzy, I didn't know he'd got engaged,' Erin said, her face full of surprise.

'Aye, didn't I tell you? She's a lovely wee girl, suits him down to the ground, I'm sure they'll be perfect together.'

'That's great news, I'm pleased for him,' Erin replied. It was on the tip of her tongue to ask how Patrick was but she quickly changed her mind, surely he was cuddled up in the

381

arms of his new wife and as happy as he deserved to be.

'Hurry up, Frankie, with that soup,' Suzy teased. 'Erin's fading away in here waiting for it.'

'Give us a chance, woman!' Frankie called. 'Have a bit of patience!'

'It's great to see you both so happy.' Erin smiled. 'I can't believe the transformation in him, it's amazing,' she whispered.

'Oh, Erin, you have no idea how content I am. It never crossed my mind that I'd ever fall in love again. After my husband died I told myself I'd never meet another. I certainly had no intention of walking up the aisle again, but it just goes to show you, love can happen at any time.'

'I suppose that's true. I can understand how you felt after losing your husband, I feel like that now.'

'Of course you do, pet. The only advice I can give you, Erin, is that if the right man comes along, you'll know in your heart when that happens, don't let the past haunt your future. I've reared my boys, watched them grow from youngsters to big strapping adults and suddenly I found myself alone in this house. Nothing could have prepared me for those lonely nights but I told myself that was the way it was to be, that was until Frankie and I grew close. Now my time is filled with the company of a great man. If you're meant to fall in love again, then you will, and if not, then that's the way it is to be, but please, Erin, don't rule out happiness again. Look at me, here I am with the man I love, he brings me so much joy, a sense of happiness that I could never have imagined.'

'Ahhh you're going to bring a tear to my eye with all that sloppy talk.' Frankie, carrying a tray with a bowl of soup and some bread, edged the door open. 'Here you go, love, get some of this into ye. Just what the doc ordered to heat the bones up on a night like this.' Frankie grinned and sat the tray on her lap.

Erin, biting into the tasty bread, realised why she had called here in the first place, 'I nearly forgot.' She swallowed the bread. 'I've brought you a present.' Placing the tray on the ground, she jumped to her feet. 'I'll go get it.'

Back in the living room, Erin opened the box to reveal the carefully decorated cake she had spent hours preparing. The delightful chocolate cake, covered in a light dusting of icing sugar looked irresistible. 'It's just a wee gift to say thank you for your kindness towards William and Leonarda.' Erin handed Frankie the box.

'Thank you.' Frankie broke into a broad grin. 'That's very kind of ye. You've went and decorated it with berries and holly! I'll look forward to it later. A cup of tea and a slice of cake, now that *is* what the doc ordered!' He chuckled, holding the box closer for Suzy to view.

'Erin, you didn't have to do that. Thank you, love,' Suzy said as she gazed at her gift. 'Never mind later, we should have a slice now, you'll stay for a share, Erin, won't you?'

Erin, sitting back down and lifting the tray, replied. 'No thanks, I'll finish this and I'll head back. Leo will need to be fed soon and besides I want to go to the midnight Christmas vigil later.'

'No bother,' Suzy said, rocking Leo gently in her arms. 'He's going to sleep,' she whispered.

'I'll take mine on out to the kitchen and I'll do the dishes and let you women have a chat. Let me know if you change your mind, Erin, and I'll get you a cuppa,' he called over his shoulder.

'I'm grand, thanks, Frankie.'

'He's now fast asleep,' Suzy announced as she stroked his cheek gently.

'He's content in your arms, Suzy,' Erin said. Dipping the spoon into the bowl, she gazed at him with love in her eyes. 'You haven't lost your motherly skills.'

'I've certainly many years of experience.' Suzy grinned.

'Oh you can say that again.' Erin smiled. As she gazed at her content baby sleeping in Suzy's arms he reminded her of a little angel and at once Theo sprang into her thoughts. Oh, how much this child would miss out on his father's love. Her smile faded as a wave of sadness came over her.

Sensing her sorrow, Suzy's heart sank. 'Erin, I'm sure this time of the year isn't easy for you. Frankie and I have been thinking about you all week.' Suzy threw her a sympathetic look. 'If you need some time to yourself I can babysit for you, please let me know, I don't mind and I'd be so happy to help.'

'That's very kind of you, Suzy.' Erin dipped her bread in the soup and popped it into her mouth and tried to force the sad moment to pass. 'Thank you.'

'Not at all, it would be an honour to help.'

Leo opened his blue eyes and frowned.

'Hello, little angel.' Suzy smiled softly.

His lips curled up at the corners as he mirrored Suzy's expression. Lifting his little, chubby hand to his mouth, he began to suck, much to his dismay, no milk was forthcoming.

'He's hungry. I better go,' Erin said, finishing off the remainder of her soup.

No sooner had Erin the words out when Leo pulled his fist from his mouth and released a howling scream.

'Leave that tray at your feet. You see to this wee man and I'll sort that out,' Susy said, holding out the baby.

'Thanks,' Erin replied as she bundled him back in his pram. Thanks for the bite to eat, it was lovely. See you later, Frankie!' she yelled.

'Are you off? You're not staying for tea, then?' Frankie peeped his head in from the kitchen.

'No, some other time,' she said, rocking the pram gently. 'This boy's cries can be heard all over the Bogside when he starts.'

Leo managed to place his thumb in his mouth, and once back in the pram, he began to drift off again.

'No bother, see you soon.' Frankie waved.

'Bye.' Erin smiled as she headed towards the door.

'I enjoyed the wee chat, thanks for calling over,' Suzy said, holding open the front door. 'Oh look, it's snowing heavier now.'

Outside the pavements were covered in a white, glittery flurry.

'Aye, it was only coming down lightly when I first arrived.' Erin tucked Leo's blanket up close to his cheeks in a bid to block out the chilly air. 'I enjoyed our wee chat too, thanks, Suzy. I hope you and Frankie have a nice Christmas.'

'Thanks, Erin. I'll be thinking about you tomorrow, love. I'm sure your first Christmas without Theo won't be easy.'

Nodding, Erin replied, 'I'll be okay, I have this wee gift to keep me occupied and I know Theo will be looking down upon us both.' She managed to hold back her tears.

'He will indeed. Take care, love, and remember, call over anytime.'

'Will do, see you. Right, get you back into the warmth, all your heat is escaping. Get back in and get cosy.'

'You're right, see you, love.' Suzy closed the door.

Leo managed to kick the blanket off. He opened his eyes again and scrunched his nose as the snowflakes landed on his angelic face.

'Get those little hands back in,' Erin, whispered. She bent into the pram and tucked the blanket around him. 'That's better, we can't have Jack Frost biting those little fingers now can we?'

Behind her she heard a door open and close and the sound of footsteps crunch on the ground. Turning around expecting to see Suzy or Frankie she was taken by surprise.

The soft glow from the lamppost overhead reflected on his features. Recognising him at once, her heart stopped for a split second as their eyes locked.

He identified her too and his heart immediately leapt into his throat.

'Hi, Erin,' he said, his eyes fixed on hers.

Shaking in her shoes she managed to reply, 'Hello, Patrick.'

Chapter 44

Erin, her blood running through her veins at an alarming rate, drank in the sight of him and her heart twisted with emotions; all the old feelings stirred up inside her and whether she liked it or not, that attraction was still there. Feeling ashamed of herself for having such desires, after all he was now a married man, she swallowed hard and tried to control her breathing.

Little did she know the sight of her was having the same effect on him! Here she was in front of him, her glossy, raven-black hair falling loosely upon her shoulders and the moon reflecting in her incredible thickly lashed Spanish-blue eyes, beneath those defined, dark, shaped eyebrows. She looked as beautiful as always. Like many times before, he desperately wanted to take her in his arms and kiss her. 'It's good to see you,' he broke the silence between them. His breath, visible in the frosty air, came out in fast chilled puffs.

'You too,' she managed to reply. Part of her was pleased to see him and another part not so glad. Seeing him again in the flesh was tugging at her heart strings. At least when he was out of sight she could try to push him to the back of her mind, and she had done a great job of that, but here he was, right in front of her and moving closer.

Placing a gentle hand on her shoulder, he looked deep into her eyes. 'I'm sorry to hear you've had such a tough time.'

Hoping that he wouldn't feel the static and the zinging sensation his contact was creating, Erin nodded. 'Thanks.'

'I was actually on my way over to your house.'

'Oh, right,' she found herself replying.

'I just got back from Dublin today. I wanted to have a chat with you, you've been on my mind constantly. I had hoped to see you before now but I just couldn't get away from work, we've been so busy trying to meet deadlines.'

'Never worry, I can understand.'

Giving her shoulder a light squeeze, Patrick nodded. 'I also wanted to give you some space, some time to yourself. Please accept my condolences for the loss of your husband.'

'Thanks,' she whispered.

Looking over her shoulder he acknowledged the baby, 'I hear you've a new baby. Congratulations on the birth of your son, I can't begin to imagine how you must be feeling.'

'I have good days and bad days. It's bittersweet,' she admitted. 'Although, I'm slowly coming to terms with the whole thing.'

Leo released another whimper.

'I better get back home, he's hungry and when he wakens properly the whole street will hear him,' she joked.

'Sure. Can I meet you later? I was thinking maybe we could attend the midnight Christmas vigil, walk up together just like the old days.'

Secretly, Erin wanted to tell him it wasn't exactly like the old days, far from it, she was now a widow, a mother, and he was a married man. Still, she could manage to hide her true feelings for him and get on with being friends again. 'Aye, I don't see why not. I'll get Leo washed and fed and put him to bed. I'll meet you about eleven thirty?'

Smiling, he nodded, 'Perfect. I'll see you later.'

Just as she had done so two years previous, Erin buttoned up her coat, placed her scarf around her shoulders and stepped out into the snow-filled street. Like a flash from the past, there he was leaning against the very same lamppost across the road and looking so annoyingly handsome.

Forgive me, Father, for having this attraction to a married man, she prayed silently as she closed the distance between them.

His face brightened into a smile as she approached, 'Good to see you again,' Patrick said, offering his arm for her to link onto.

Thankful that he hadn't brought along his wife, Erin linked her arm in his and didn't bother to ask where his other half was, she assumed she didn't want to join them on this cold winter night.

In silence they walked together through the well-known streets of the Bogside. His familiar scent, together with the frosty air, took Erin right back to that night exactly two years ago. Back then nerves were jangling in the pit of her stomach as she prepared to tell him of her departure. Tonight that jittery feeling arose again. She couldn't help but note how natural it felt to be walking next to him but at the same time her stomach twisted as she recalled how he had rejected her. The subject would need to be brought up at some point, but not tonight, she thought, however that tingling sensation that she had experienced for so long in his presence was still there.

Erin gave herself a mental shake. Right, that's it, don't even think about it. He has the Dublin girl now. He's a married man for crying out loud! Get over him and let him go! He was clearly happy and if anyone deserved such contentment it was Patrick. Knowing that she needed to be pleased for him, emotionally she prepared herself to congratulate him on his marriage when the subject came up, even if she didn't feel it, she knew she had to put on a smile and pretend all the same.

'You're very quiet.' Patrick broke the silence.

'So are you,' she answered.

Taking her by surprise, Patrick stopped near an oak tree. The branches shivered in the cold, whispering December wind. Overhead, the huge bare limbs, weighed down by the snowfall, offered little shelter from the heavy snowflakes tumbling from the heavens.

'Why have you stopped?' Erin asked, the snow melting in their hair. 'We'll be late for mass,' she said as the chime of the church bells echoed in the distance.

'Never mind, we can go tomorrow,' he said. Stepping forward, he closed the space between them. 'We need to sort a few things out.'

Before she knew it, she was in his arms and his lips were only inches from hers. There was no denying the sparks between them; surely he felt the intensity too. Reading the signs, she held her breath and waited for the kiss. Feeling her head spin, she came to her senses and the word caught in her throat as she managed to say, 'Stop!' just before his lips met hers. As much as she wanted him, she didn't want him to be unfaithful to his wife. 'We can't,' she forced herself to say.

'What?' he asked, taken aback.

'I said we can't. What about your wife?' she asked, her voice trembling.

'Wife? You mean Charlotte?' Erin sensed the amusement in his voice.

'I'm not sure of her name but aye if that's what she's called. You should know better than me after all you *did* marry her!'

Patrick's lips curled into a smile. 'Don't you know I actually *didn't* marry her?'

'You *didn't*? But I thought you were engaged.'

'I was. Charlotte is a beautiful, fun, loving girl but I couldn't go through with it.'

'Why?' Erin asked in disbelief as the snow continued to fall like confetti on them both.

'Because I called the wedding off.'

'But…?'

Taking a deep breath, Patrick explained, 'I couldn't do it, I just simply couldn't marry her.'

'I don't understand, why not?' Erin was finding it hard

to take in this latest information.

Placing his arms round her waist, he drew her a fraction nearer. 'Don't you see, she isn't you?'

Erin felt her heart lurch into her throat. 'What?' Was she really hearing what he was saying? She breathed slowly and tried to make sense of it all. Despite the numbing air, a warmth was beginning to generate in the pit of her tummy.

'I'll admit, I liked Charlotte, I liked her a lot, but no matter how hard I tried I couldn't get you out of my mind. I had accepted that you were married but I realised I was jumping into marriage with her for the wrong reasons. I couldn't imagine spending the rest of my life with someone that I was only attracted to. Marriage is for life, and whilst I cared about her, I knew deep down I didn't love her. It's important that you know I didn't call the wedding off because of Theo's death. I didn't learn about his death until a few days after.'

'Patrick, surely she was brokenhearted, what did she say?'

'At first she was shell-shocked but when she realised how I felt she said she was grateful that I had spared us both many years of unhappiness. Her father hit the roof but Charlotte acted much more mature that he did, she soon sorted him out. Thankfully Charlotte is about to marry someone that really does love her. Would you believe it her and Chris have hit it off and they're now engaged!'

'Suzy was telling me Chris had a fiancée. My goodness

I would never have guessed he was engaged to your ex!'

Grinning, Patrick said, 'Aye what a web we have all woven.'

Erin nodded. 'Aye, you can say that again.'

His rejection still bothered her, part of her wasn't sure if she should feel hurt or angry for him not getting back to her and she wondered if he did receive the letter, or as Mary had suggested, it had gone elsewhere.

I called in to see Frankie and Suzy this morning. Your father was there helping Frankie cut some blocks in the back yard. We got a chance to have a little chat.'

'He didn't mention it,' Erin replied, wondering why her father hadn't said anything. Actually, come to think of it, neither Suzy nor Frankie said anything either.

'I told him that I was going to speak to you and he gave me his blessing. I asked them all not to mention it to you until I saw you myself. You see, Erin, the truth is, I couldn't marry Charlotte, or anyone else for that matter, because I could never love anyone like I love you.'

Before she got a chance to answer, his lips met hers, and her heart melted as fast as the snowflakes in her hair.

She was actually kissing him! After all the years of waiting for this moment and the countless nights dreaming of this event, an embrace that she had longed for, for as long as she could remember, was now happening for *real*! And it felt perfect! Some things were definitely worth waiting for. She found her arms reaching up and twining around his neck.

Tears of joy and sorrow rolled down her cheeks as he kissed her with so much love and passion.

Recalling Theo's words advising her to mend things with Patrick, she could feel more tears welling up. It meant a lot to her to know that Theo would be happy for them.

Sensing her warm tears, Patrick withdrew his lips and gently wiped her cheeks. 'I love you, Erin, and I know you love me also.'

'You do?' she sniffed, her tone playful. 'What makes you think that?'

Cupping her face in his hands, he said, 'Because I read it in the letter you sent me.'

'What?' she asked, stepping back. 'You read that letter and didn't get back to me, but why did you ignore it?' Erin fired back, feeling outraged.

'I only saw it today. Frankie gave it to me this morning. The postman had accidently got it mixed up with Frankie's post and he had forgotten about it. Suzy found it when she was clearing up his house for William to stay there. Do you seriously think if I had got that letter I would have done nothing about it? Erin, if I had saw it, I would have been on the first boat out to meet you, in fact I'd have swam across the Atlantic if I had to!'

Part of her couldn't believe her ears but it was all making sense now. 'Never mind, it was all meant to be, if things hadn't turned out the way they had, I wouldn't have married Theo and I wouldn't have my gorgeous son.'

395

'I agree.' He stroked her damp hair. 'Listen, Erin, I love you with all my heart.' Reaching inside his jacket pocket, he pulled out a box, shaped and painted like a ladybird. 'This is for you. This relationship of ours all began over a ladybird,' he whispered.

'On seeing the creatively designed little box, Erin beamed. 'It's pretty. I didn't get you a Christmas gift, sorry.'

'It's not a Christmas gift.' Patrick edged the lid up. 'It's a gift for life,' he said, opening the box fully. There sitting proudly amongst the satin folds was a beautiful diamond ring, the same ring he had thought she would never get the chance to wear.

Erin watched in shock as Patrick retrieved the band from its box and got down on one knee in the snow. 'Marry me, Erin!'

'What? I... I can't. I can't expect you to marry me and take on another man's child, it wouldn't be fair on you,' she said, her voice shaking, the tears now rolling down her cheeks at an alarming rate.

'That doesn't matter to me. I may not be Leo's father but he'll always be a son in my eyes. I will love him and bring him up like my own. You can both move into my house and we can be a family. We can have as many kids as you want. Please marry me, Erin.'

Erin felt like she was dreaming, was this really happening?

'I'm not getting up off this ground until you say yes, so

hurry up and give me an answer, my knees are getting soaked!'
he teased. 'But I'm warning you, don't cut off your nose to
spite your face. You know we'll be happy, give us a chance,
what have you got to lose?'

Chapter 45

'Another story, Daddy, one more pu-lease!'

'It's getting late, Leo, you need to close your eyes soon and get a big sleep.' Patrick kissed his little forehead and tucked the blanket around him. 'There, you're all cosy. Go to sleep now, son.'

'I want one more too!' Luke fired back his blanket.

'Tell us the story about the girl that goes to America!' Leo's face lit up. 'The one that comes back to Derry and marries her best friend!'

Patrick glanced over his shoulder at Erin and flashed her one of his usual heart-melting smiles. 'I think we have all heard that one more times than enough.'

Kicking the blankets aside and sitting up on the bed, Leo pulled his knees up and hugged them close to his chest. 'But it's my *favourite*!'

Erin, rocked her new-born daughter in her arms. 'Look, boys.' she whispered, 'Little Grace is fast asleep, Mammy and Daddy needs to get to bed too, so do as Daddy tells you and close those tired, little eyes.'

'But we're not *tired*!' Leo stuck his lower lip out and threw Patrick a puppy-dog look.

Patrick, unable to say no to the child he adored as much as his other two children, held out his hand. 'Okay, one last story then it's bedtime, other kids are normally tucked up fast asleep at this hour on Christmas Eve. C'mon, Luke.' He reached out and helped him out of bed too, and taking both children by the hand, he led them to the window.

Drawing back the curtains, he said, 'Look up at the sky, boys.'

The two children stared up at the inky night sky. A canopy of luminous stars lit up the ocean of blackness above their heads. The millions of twinkling stars were alive and a full moon shone brightly.

Erin, carrying little Grace, shadowed behind and she too followed their gaze.

'Well, up there, far beyond those stars, is heaven. Everyone in heaven is getting ready for baby Jesus to be born. Do you remember, Leo, how we told you about your father Theo being in heaven?' Patrick gazed into Leo's round, blue eyes.

'Of course I do,' Leo replied, 'I've got a special angel in heaven, an extra one than all the other boys and girls,' he said, his face full of joy. 'My father Theo went to heaven before I was born and I have you as my earthly daddy to look after me until we all meet again!' he said proudly.

Erin felt a boulder develop in her throat as she watched Leo release Patrick's hand and place both of his little arms around Patrick's waist.

'I love you, Daddy Patrick,' Leo purred like a little kitten.

'And I love you too, Leo. I love you both so much.' He

hugged the two boys closer to him.

'That's not fair, why do I only have one angel?' Luke asked with all the innocence of his three years.

'Actually, you have many angels up there in heaven looking down on us all. This is the room that your granny and grandad used to sleep in and I can tell you both of them will be smiling down upon you all. Your granddad Jim would have had some fun with you boys, just like he and I did when I was a little boy.' Patrick beamed. 'Now let's get back to our story.' Patrick continued, 'Up there in heaven is where everyone goes when they leave this earth but you have to be good to get in there,' he warned with a smile.

'We're always good,' Leo said.

'You are, but you have to go to bed when Mammy and Daddy tells you. Little five year olds and three year olds need their sleep so that they can grow up to be big and strong and have big muscles like me!' Patrick teased. 'You don't want to stay wee forever, do you?'

'No,' they both chirped together.

'So you want to be big and strong like me?'

Erin's face broke into a delighted smile as she watched both boys nod their innocent heads in agreement.

Rubbing his tired eyes and yawning, Luke replied, 'No, actually, Daddy, I'm going to grow up bigger than you.'

'Me too.' Leo, mirrored his brother's yawn. 'So what is heaven?' he asked, rubbing his eyes also.

'It's a place of joy and happiness, where everyone loves each other and there is no fighting or sadness.'

'What does it look like, Daddy?' Leo asked.

'It's a mystery, Leo, but in our bible it teaches us that heaven has many rooms and mansions. My father always described heaven as a place with no sun, moon or stars to light it up, as there is no need, for God's presence is enough to fill it with all the brightness you can imagine. He also advised me to think about the prettiest thing on this earth and then think that in heaven everything is much more prettier.'

'Like a lovely flower?' Leo said.

'Yes, I'd say heaven is much prettier that the most sweetest flower,' Patrick smiled.

'Pretty like my mammy!' Luke piped up.

Glancing over his shoulder, Patrick looked at Erin and instantly his heart swelled with love for her. 'Well, I'm not sure if there is anything prettier than your mammy, but yes, it's pretty like Mammy.' Turning his attention back to the sky above he went on, 'As I said, you have to be very good to get there. When we are down here we must all do our best for others, we must always treat others with love and kindness, even if they hurt you or say bad things, we must love them. If we do this, God promises us a reward and do you know what that reward is, boys?'

'What?' they both echoed.

'It's the crown of righteousness. Imagine having your very own crown!' Patrick's eyes widened.

'Like a king?' Leo asked, his eyes alive with surprise. 'Has my father Theo got a crown, do you think?'

'Well, I didn't know him, but going by what your mammy says about him, yes, I do think he will have a crown.'

'Whoa!' Leo gasped. 'A *real* crown!'

'I have no doubt your father Theo's crown is glittering with the finest jewels,' Erin said over Leo's shoulder.

'Look, Mammy, look at that star, far, far up there, maybe that's his crown twinkling!' Leo pointed to the inky sky as thick clouds moved closer.

'Tell you what, Leo, let's imagine that it is. Each night when you see that star twinkling, imagine your father Theo in heaven, wearing his crown with joy and looking down upon you,' Patrick whispered.

'That's a good idea, Daddy.' Leo yawned again. 'Oh, I'm so tired now.'

'Do you think you're ready for bed?' Patrick asked.

'Yes and I'm going to be extra good from now on. I'll help Mammy tidy up, then I'll get a crown just like father Theo!' Leo gazed into Patrick's eyes.

Patrick ruffled the little boy's thick, raven-black hair. 'You're already good, and you too, Luke.' He bent down and scooped the two boys in his arms and planted a loving kiss on both their cheeks. 'You're the best children anyone could ask for.' Moving aside he looked over his shoulder, 'Come closer, Erin.'

Erin, stepping nearer, placed her arm around Patrick's waist.

'And your mammy and little Grace are the best girls in the world!'

The heavy clouds now loomed overhead and blotted out the stars but the moon was still visible and it shone brightly, lighting up the ground below.

'Now everyone, look up to the moon.' Patrick indicated. 'Look at it, so far, far away,' he said as a soft flurry of fresh snow fell from the heavens, each flake swirling and dancing through the cool December air until it reached the ground below, falling like icing powder on the land and coating everything with a dazzling whiteness.

'It's really far, Daddy.' Leo blinked innocently. 'If I get a big, big ladder can we climb up to the moon?'

Patrick grinned. 'No one has ever been there yet, maybe one day someone will design a great invention to allow man to walk on it but I'm not so sure if a ladder will get you there.'

'I can't wait!' Leo beamed as he watched the silvery flakes tumble from the sky, glittering in the bright, luminous winter moon's light. 'Imagine walking on the moon.'

'Imagine that, Leo. I can't picture I'll walk on the moon,' Patrick said looking at each of them, 'It may be far, far away, and I haven't a ladder big enough, but I want you all to know, I love each of you *To The Moon And Back*!'

Lightning Source UK Ltd.
Milton Keynes UK
UKOW06f0046300716

279454UK00008B/239/P